The
Cure for Love
at
Christmas

De-ann Black

The Cure for Love at Christmas is the second book in The Cure for Love Romance series.

1. The Cure for Love
2. The Cure for Love at Christmas

Text copyright © 2023 by De-ann Black
Cover Design & Illustration © 2023 by De-ann Black

All rights reserved.
No part of this book may be used or reproduced in any manner whatsoever without the written consent of the author.

This is a work of fiction. Names, characters, places, and incidents are either products of the author's imagination or are used fictitiously. Any resemblance to actual persons, living or dead, businesses, companies, events, or locales is entirely coincidental.

Paperback edition published 2023

The Cure for Love at Christmas

ISBN: 9798863372082

Also by De-ann Black (Romance, Action/Thrillers & Children's books). See her Amazon Author page or website for further details about her books, screenplays, illustrations and artwork. www.De-annBlack.com

Action/Thrillers:
Knight in Miami.
Agency Agenda.
Love Him Forever.
Someone Worse.
Electric Shadows.
The Strife of Riley.
Shadows of Murder.

Romance:
Fairytale Christmas on the Island
The Cure for Love at Christmas
Vintage Dress Shop on the Island
Scottish Island Fairytale Castle
Scottish Loch Summer Romance
Scottish Island Knitting Bee
Sewing & Mending Cottage
Knitting Shop by the Sea
Colouring Book Cottage
Knitting Cottage
Oops! I'm the Paparazzi, Again
The Bitch-Proof Wedding
Embroidery Cottage
The Dressmaker's Cottage
The Sewing Shop
Heather Park
The Tea Shop by the Sea
The Bookshop by the Seaside
The Sewing Bee
The Quilting Bee
Snow Bells Wedding

Snow Bells Christmas
Summer Sewing Bee
The Chocolatier's Cottage
Christmas Cake Chateau
The Beemaster's Cottage
The Sewing Bee By The Sea
The Flower Hunter's Cottage
The Christmas Knitting Bee
The Sewing Bee & Afternoon Tea
Shed In The City
The Bakery By The Seaside
The Christmas Chocolatier
The Christmas Tea Shop & Bakery
The Bitch-Proof Suit

Colouring books:
Summer Nature. Flower Nature. Summer Garden. Spring Garden. Autumn Garden. Sea Dream. Festive Christmas. Christmas Garden. Flower Bee. Wild Garden. Flower Hunter. Stargazer Space. Christmas Theme. Faerie Garden Spring. Scottish Garden Seasons. Bee Garden.

Embroidery books:
Floral Garden Embroidery Patterns
Floral Spring Embroidery Patterns
Christmas & Winter Embroidery Patterns
Floral Nature Embroidery Designs
Scottish Garden Embroidery Designs

Contents

1 - Chaos in Cornwall	1
2 - A Merry Mumble	17
3 - Fashion in London	34
4 - Christmas Films Matinee	51
5 - Cosy Night at the Cottage	68
6 - Vintage Floral Designs	84
7 - Secret Recipe	103
8 - A Winter's Night	120
9 - Lunch at the Castle	136
10 - Makeshift Bride	154
11 - Midnight Mayhem	168
12 - Publicity Feature	185
13 - Picture Perfect	201
14 - Christmas Romance	217
15 - Mischief Maker	236
16 - Skating and Sledding	253
17 - Dress to Dazzle	272
18 - Snowy Night	288
19 - Dashing Through the Snow	297
20 - Festive Fun	315
21 - Love at Christmas	333
About De-ann Black	359

CHAPTER ONE

Chaos in Cornwall

'Christmas in New York? Oooh, how exciting,' exclaimed Mrs Lemon.

Daisy wasn't enthusiastic about her forthcoming trip, but lied politely. 'Yes, isn't it.'

Mrs Lemon, neat and trim, in her fifties, was known as a local busybody, a label she didn't deny. Her boucle coat was buttoned up against the winter's day and a hand knitted woolly hat perched on her head.

Daisy, a botanical illustrator, was an attractive young woman with a slender but shapely figure wrapped in a cosy cream coat with her grey cords tucked into her boots. Her blonde hair fell in silky waves around her shoulders, and her fair complexion bore a rosy blush from the brisk walk from her cottage to the shops in the small town's main street. She was a fairly new addition to the local community, having temporarily moved from her flat in London to a pretty holiday cottage in Cornwall in the summer. She'd extended her stay until it was now Christmastime, and was dating Jake Wolfe.

Daisy and Mrs Lemon were chatting in Jake Wolfe's health food shop in the lovely little town in Cornwall. As always, the shop smelled delicious, filled with the aroma of fresh baked bread, treacle scones, dark chocolate delicacies, dried fruits galore, jars of barley sugar and crystallised ginger, an array of herbs, baskets of fresh lemons, oranges, pears and apples, and various peppermint, vanilla and strawberry delights.

The shop was bright, quaint, situated in the main street, and well–stocked with products. Often it was overstocked, with everything from packets of herb tea and jars of locally produced strawberry, raspberry and bramble jam tussling for shelf space with the tasty wholemeal bread baked daily by Sharky the baker whose bakery shop was situated opposite.

A large Christmas cake, rich with raisins, sultanas and currents, and topped with glazed almonds and glacé cherries sat in Jake Wolfe's shop window display. Customers could order one, baked by Sharky using ingredients from Jake's shop, along with the speciality festive figgy pudding. Numerous names were already on the list and it was still a few weeks before Christmas. The scent of cinnamon and spices tempted Daisy to order one of each.

Shops in the main street already had their Christmas decorations up, and at four–thirty in the afternoon, the health food shop's token gesture of fairy lights draped across the front window highlighted the jars of herbs, sweets, wholemeal bread, the Christmas cake and a figgy pudding. Baubles and more lights were planned as soon as Jake had time to put them up. And decided whether he wanted a Christmas tree this year, or not.

Jake hardly had time to catch his breath these days organising everything for his trip to New York. A whirlwind tour to promote his latest book — a new book about his Cure For Love. A herbal cure for lovesickness that he'd been working on for years. Each time he'd gleaned a near perfect remedy, and then rejigged it to make it better, and now...well, his new book was the icing on top of the Christmas cake as far as he was concerned. The original recipe had been improved.

Mrs Lemon frowned. Sugaring the pill wasn't her style, and her comment cut right to the heart of the matter. 'You don't sound keen to go to New York for Christmas. What's wrong, Daisy?' The pom pom on her woolly hat wobbled as she stepped close to emphasise her point. 'Is it because Jake hasn't proposed to you yet?'

Daisy's beautiful green eyes widened. 'No! That's got nothing to do with it,' she lied. Sort of. A little bit.

Everyone in the tight–knit community had an opinion on why Jake hadn't asked Daisy to marry him, yet. A big emphasis on the *yet*. They were two busy people. Jake loved her, and she loved him. During the summer they'd had one of those tempestuous relationships where they first seemed to annoy each other, but then as romances do, they realised they were attracted to each other, and by the end of the summer they'd become a loving couple. A happy ending. Except...

Karen held up her ring finger, pausing from serving a customer in Jake's shop, to give Daisy the finger. A diamond and ruby ring sparkled at Daisy across the shelves of health foods, as if giving her a cocky wink. Karen, Mrs Lemon's daughter, was in her early twenties, a modern and attractive brunette. She wore her shop assistant's outfit and liked working for Jake, especially since she'd given up on her lust–

fuelled crush on him in favour of the fun–loving baker. Sharky adored Karen, and she'd recently decided to reciprocate the feeling. The diamond sparkler had sealed the deal, but she was genuinely happier than she'd ever been.

Daisy had lost count how many times Karen had held up that ring like a beacon of triumph, and perhaps it was, indicating that Sharky the baker had asked her to marry him. They'd fallen for each other after Daisy and Jake became close. The baker now made Jake look tardy in the romance stakes.

'We'd be getting married at Christmas,' Karen reminded Daisy, again, 'if it wasn't for Sharky having to bake loads of Christmas cakes and his figgy puddings.'

'A New Year wedding for you perhaps,' Daisy suggested lightly.

'Spring. I quite fancy walking down the aisle on a lovely spring day and having crocus, bluebells and daffodils in my bridal bouquet.'

Daisy smiled tightly. Karen had it all planned out. If she hadn't been Mrs Lemon's daughter, Daisy would've told her to stop saying the same things on a loop. But she liked Mrs Lemon, despite her acid tongue when it came to gossip, so she kept her comments to herself. New York was starting to look brighter. At least she wouldn't have to see Karen and her ring until mid January if she flew off with Jake to the Big Apple.

Jake's Uncle Woolley came clambering downstairs having been working in the shop's storeroom upstairs. Mrs Lemon had recently started dating Woolley after years of circling each other and some light flirtation and flagrant fallouts. Despite the gossip about what the pair of them got up to one rainy night, accidentally lit up in Mrs Lemon's cottage front window, though obscured by the net curtains, she insisted the intimacy of their dating that evening consisted of no more than sharing a pot of tea and a packet of gingernuts while Woolley adjusted her pelmet.

'I can't find the spare set of twinkle lights,' Woolley muttered through his bushy beard. 'I'm popping out to buy a set. I won't be long.'

Strong and fit, he was officially retired, but helped Jake out at the health food shop when business was busy. Lately, business had been thriving, as the publicity surrounding Jake's new book, *The Cure For Love*, a herbal cure for lovesickness, due to be published for Christmas, was creating quite a storm of interest.

As a freelance botanical illustrator, Daisy worked mainly for Franklin's publishing company in London. But Jake had wanted her to illustrate the herbs and floral elements in his book. Jake's agent and publisher had agreed to this. Daisy was now required to fly to New York, not only as Jake's girlfriend, but as the new book's illustrator. Jake's publisher had planned a whirlwind book tour extravaganza for him in New York to celebrate the launch of the title.

Daisy loved Christmas, and since moving from London to live in the Cornish town, while still working freelance for Franklin in London, she'd been looking forward to a cosy Christmas in Cornwall. Tucked up in the picturesque town, watching festive films with Jake, while drinking copious amounts of tea, eating gingerbread cookies, and snuggling on the sofa under a hand knitted blanket. And all while the blustery wind blew outside her cottage windows.

Franklin owned the holiday cottage, and had suggested Daisy take a summer break there to get over being broken hearted. Her weasel of a boyfriend, Sebastian, worked in the editorial department of Franklin's book publishing company in London. She'd dated him happily for a while, and he'd started hinting that he wanted to get married. This was true, just not to her.

Coming back to London from a business trip to Italy, Sebastian had become Franklin's potential son–in–law. While in Europe, he'd put a rock on Celeste's finger.

Celeste's father, Franklin, was almost as surprised as Daisy. Just not quite as horribly upset. Instead of becoming Sebastian's fiancée, like Daisy had anticipated, she'd become his ex–girlfriend and learned that Sebastian had been cheating on her with Celeste for months. Everyone at the publishing company in London knew about it except Daisy and Franklin, though he'd suspected a bit of skulduggery.

Daisy had been unaware that she was dating a two–timing rat until she'd walked into the publishing company and found Sebastian and Celeste celebrating their engagement surrounded by staff drinking a champagne toast to the happy couple.

A trip to Cornwall to relax in Franklin's lovely holiday cottage failed to make up the shortfall on that sledgehammer to her heart.

But all of that drama was in the recent past. Even the nasty bits had a benefit. If Sebastian hadn't been such a rat, she wouldn't have taken up Franklin's offer to run off to Cornwall to heal her wounds. And so she'd never have met Jake Wolfe.

Initially, Jake had wanted to ply Daisy with his cure for love when she went into his health food shop seeking solace, herb tea and strawberry jam. Being spotlighted by him the second she'd walked in, after he'd seen her reading the enticing sign in the shop's front window, he'd approached her with a heavy hand, causing ructions between them from the get go...

Jake had noticed the attractive blonde outside the window reading the sign. Being a small town it was easy to tell a newcomer. The gossip about Franklin offering Daisy his cottage had already reached Jake. He surmised this was her.

Daisy still remembered the words on the sign that started it all:

Broken hearted?
Feeling blue?
Come inside...
We have natural remedies for you.

She'd gone in and everything in her life changed when she met Jake Wolfe...

'Will you be home from New York for the New Year?' Mrs Lemon said to Daisy, breaking through her wayward thoughts.

'Eh, no, probably, but we're not sure, though Jake thinks it's not likely,' said Daisy.

'When is it you leave Cornwall?'

'A couple of weeks from now.'

'Well, I'm sure you'll have a very merry Christmas in New York.'

Daisy smiled. 'Thank you, Mrs. Lemon.'

'And don't trouble yourself over trivial matters. Jake is bound to propose soon.'

'We're in no hurry. We're both busy with our careers.'

'Yes, but still...we all expected you to be engaged by the end of the summer, or in the autumn, and now with the main street looking like a festive postcard, don't spoil your trip to New York thinking he's dragging his heels.'

With that colourfully painted thought now in her mind, Daisy smiled at Mrs Lemon and then left the shop. Whatever she'd popped in to buy, including parsley and herbs, wasn't urgent. She needed to get out into the cold December air, to clear her thoughts. So the last person she needed a call from was Jake.

'Where are you?' Jake demanded to know. 'Have you thought what clothes and other items to pack yet? I've packed some of mine, and hung the clothes I'm taking in one part of my wardrobe so they'll be ready to grab and go,' he told her.

'We don't leave for a couple of weeks,' she said. They planned to drive to London and fly from there to New York.

'Time flies though.' Jake sounded keyed up. All this talk of publicity, appearing on television and the radio, doing press interviews and that ilk in New York made him wish he'd wangled a better deal with the publisher regarding his involvement with the marketing of it. Now it felt like his time wasn't his own. It hadn't been for the past three months, popping back and forth from Cornwall to London for meetings with his agent and publisher had eaten up his time. He was at the mercy of the publicity machine that was churning more and more lucrative offers his way, while getting a stranglehold on his creativity. And time off. To be with Daisy. He'd hardly seen her some days.

Working in his health food shop during the day, then in his study at night mixing new concoctions for his herbal love cure, left precious little time for actual love. Maybe if he drank his own cure it would sort him out. He knew this was nonsense. It was a cure for lovesickness, unrequited love. Daisy loved him, and probably wanted to marry him, if he ever got the time to ask her properly. That had been his plan. Now all his plans were cast to the wind in a hurly–burly of book tours and publicity.

'We'll talk later,' he said urgently. 'I have to take this call from my publisher. It's their New York office phoning.'

And he was gone.

Daisy breathed in the crisp, wintry air and admired the twinkle lights in the shop windows. Everything sparkled with frost, making the main street look like one of those vintage Christmas cards sprinkled with glitter.

The town had a happy atmosphere, and the local residents enjoyed a lively version of a quiet life situated between the beautiful Cornish countryside and the sea.

Daisy had anticipated a relaxing time when she'd first moved into the holiday cottage during the summer, leaving her hectic life in London behind her to recoup from having her heart broken. But from the moment she'd arrived until now, the quietest times she'd had were her infrequent trips to London to meet Franklin to discuss her illustrations for his books.

Archie, her interfering neighbour had welcomed the task to keep an eye on her flat in London while she was away. The nosey parker in him accepted the keys with glee, promising not to rummage through her private things, a promise he'd kept, but he was happy to be in charge of making sure he jiggled her heating once a week as the temperatures dropped, ran the sink taps and binned her junk mail.

'It's fortunate you have me, a nitpicking fusspot as your neighbour,' Archie told her when she handed him the keys to her rented furnished flat. 'And I won't go rummaging in your drawers.'

Daisy smiled tightly. 'Lucky me.' There was precious little she owned there. A few items of forlorn clothing she couldn't have itemised if she'd tried. The clothes she actually wore and her artist's materials were now in the cottage in Cornwall. The only reason she didn't give up the flat lease was sheer fear of being left in the lurch again, having her world upended with another broken heart and nowhere to run back to. So she'd kept up the payments on the flat while living rent free, at Franklin's insistence, in the Cornish cottage.

She was due another trip up to London before flying off to New York, so there was that to shoehorn into her busy schedule. Relaxing was tentatively pencilled into her itinerary sometime in the New Year. Late January probably when they were back from New York. Her heart sank even though she kept throwing it a buoy. Oh to have a cosy Christmas in Cornwall... She sighed heavily, gazed over at Sharky's bakery shop and wondered if one of his chocolate cupcakes swirled with buttercream and sprinkles would brighten her up.

Temptation for one of those or maybe a Christmas scone baked with mincemeat was interrupted by Woolley scurrying along the street towards her.

Woolley trust a box of fairy lights under her nose. 'Do these look like a fair match for the ones in the shop window?'

Daisy looked at the image on the box showing red, green, yellow, pink and blue lights. 'A perfect match.'

Woolley beamed. 'Great...and eh, I was wondering if I could ask a favour...'

'What is it?'

He had a roll of wrapping paper tucked under his arm. 'I'm rubbish at wrapping presents. Would you give me a hand to parcel up the gift I've bought for Mrs Lemon's Christmas?'

'Yes, of course.'

'I'll pretend you're helping me unravel the lights,' he said in a conspiratorial whisper. 'I've got her pressie hidden upstairs in the storeroom.'

Realising he wanted her to help him now, she walked with him back into the health food shop.

Mrs Lemon was still in the shop chatting to Karen.

Woolley and Daisy swept by them. He held up the box of fairy lights. 'Daisy's just helping me to unravel these and then I'll put them up in the front window.'

And off they went, up the stairs to where he'd stashed the large box containing the secret gift for Mrs Lemon.

Woolley's eyes sparkled and he smiled through the fuzz on his face. 'I saw it on her online wish list. I know she's been wanting one for ages.'

'What have you bought her?' Daisy was eager to know.

'A new hoover with all the attachments,' he beamed at her. 'It's got brushes for getting into all her nooks and crannies.' He handed Daisy the wrapping paper, scissors, sticky tape and a ribbon bow. 'Here you go. I'll unravel the lights.'

Daisy unrolled the paper and wrapped the box, making a neat job of it.

'There you are.' She gestured to show him her handiwork.

'Thanks, Daisy. You've wrapped it lovely.'

He'd taken the fairy lights out of their box and partially unravelled them. He plugged them in to test that they worked. Then he shook his head and sighed.

'What is it?' said Daisy. The lights worked perfectly, giving a colourful glow to the storeroom.

'Can you keep a secret?' he whispered.

'Yes,' she whispered back.

'The hoover isn't the only gift I've bought for Mrs Lemon. I haven't told anyone, not even Jake, what I've bought for her as my back–up present.'

He scurried over to an old–fashioned roll top dresser and foraged around in one of the hidden drawers.

Daisy wondered what it was that he'd bought. And then he revealed the small, velvet jewellery box. A ring box. He opened it and a diamond engagement ring sparkled under the storeroom spotlights.

'An engagement ring!' Daisy said, taken aback.

'I wasn't sure what type she'd like. She'd went on about Karen's diamond and ruby ring, but I didn't want to get her the same type. I know she's not fond of emeralds, and I wasn't sure if she liked sapphires, so... You can't go wrong with diamonds.'

'No, definitely not. It's a beautiful ring.'

'Do you think she'll like it?'

'She'll love it.'

'I stole one of her rings so the jewellers could give me the right size. They recommended yellow gold rather than white gold, so that it'll match her wedding ring. They reckon from what I told them, she'd prefer a band of yellow gold.'

'Are you proposing to her on Christmas Day?'

'Yes. Roses, champagne, chocolates and a diamond ring. I'm pulling out all the stops so she'll accept my proposal. I don't see any point in waiting because she knows I love her and want to marry her. And if she says yes, I'd like to marry her in the New Year. Again, why wait. I love her and I think she likes me too.' And then he realised. 'I'm sorry, Daisy. I didn't mean to upset you. Jake's head is filled with work and his new book.'

'It's okay,' Daisy assured him.

'I should've buttoned my beard.'

'No, it's fine. And your secret is safe with me,' she whispered.

He smiled and then tucked the ring away again, just in time because Karen ventured upstairs.

'What are the pair of you up to?' Karen sounded suspicious.

Woolley held up the lights. 'Daisy is a dab hand at unravelling the fairy lights.'

'I could hear you whispering.' Karen studied them. 'And you look guilty, Woolley.'

'Indeed I am not,' he objected. 'We were sorting the lights.'

Karen eyed him carefully. 'Do you know that your beard curls up at the sides when you're telling porky pies.'

Woolley brushed his hand across his beard. 'It does not.'

'It does,' Karen insisted. 'My mother taught me what to look for when folk are fibbing. Jake for instance...when he's telling lies, he fiddles with his forelock.'

Daisy made a mental note of this.

'So keep that in mind when Jake's being cajoled into canoodling with women in New York,' Karen told Daisy.

Daisy frowned. 'What?'

'Jake is rich, handsome, successful, with a cure for lovesickness, another new book, owns a lovely big house up on the hill, and his own business. He's a prize catch. The women in New York will be after him. So a bit of advice...take your fancy lacy and silk undies with you in case of romantic emergencies.'

'Romantic emergencies?' Daisy shook her head. 'I don't own lingerie like that.' Hers were pretty and practical. Emphasis on the practical. Borderline plain.

'It's a tip I learned from my mother. She has some lovely lingerie for particular occasions.' Karen glanced at Woolley. 'Isn't that right?'

Looking flustered, he blurted out a reply. 'How would I know a thing like that! Your mother's knickers are a secret to me.'

Karen viewed him sceptically and then spoke to Daisy. 'His beard definitely curls up when he's telling fibs.'

Daisy had noticed his beard twitch, and was now inclined to check when Jake fiddled with his forelock. But she pretended not to take Karen up on her fancy knickers suggestions.

Karen shrugged. 'Don't say I didn't warn you. A man like Jake will be fair game in New York. And you'd better be on your A–game if you're hoping to have a ring like mine on your finger.'

With another flash of her sparkler, giving Daisy the finger yet again, Karen went back downstairs.

Woolley fussed with the fairy lights. 'I wouldn't wind myself up with what Karen says. Jake's not a man to have his head turned easily. And believe me, it's true. The macaroon girl from Devon tried again the other day. She waltzed into the shop and thrust her wares at Jake, tempting him with her festive macaroons. As it's Christmastime, he bought six boxes of them, but wasn't tempted by her. He insists he's never ever touched her macaroons.'

CHAPTER TWO

A Merry Mumble

The world draped itself heavily around Daisy's shoulders as she trudged out of the health food shop into the cold air. It was now teatime and the deep blue twilight arched over the shops, creating a beautiful backdrop for the large Christmas tree lit up at the far end of the cobbled square and the glow from the shop windows. Streetlamps were entwined with twinkle lights and she wished she could enjoy the sheer magic of walking in a real life picture postcard. If only she hadn't popped into Jake's shop for dried parsley, sea salt and other condiments to flavour the soup she planned to have for dinner.

A clutch of carol singers, dressed in vintage attire, carried lanterns and sang songs she'd long forgotten and yet knew the words. They were beckoning shoppers to join them in a chorus or two.

Daisy tried to deftly sidestep them, but got waylaid as she headed to the Christmas shop where Woolley had purchased the fairy lights. She needed a set for her decorations at the cottage. She'd sort of agreed with Jake that they'd forgo putting up real trees and extensive decorations as they'd be leaving soon, and coming back to these in mid January would look tawdry. But a string of colourful fairy lights wouldn't go amiss surely.

'Come and join us for an uplifting chorus,' one of the carol singers said to her, thrusting a lyric sheet into her hesitant hands. 'There's nothing like a sing–song to bolster your spirits and lift you out of the doldrums.'

Was it that obvious? Daisy sighed. Clearly it was. Unable to muster up a remark to refuse, she found herself looking at the words and starting to sing a few of them, quietly at first, a merry mumble.

But then as she saw the smiling faces of the carol singers, the cheery grins of people going by, and heard herself singing mainly in tune to a song she hadn't sung in years...she found herself smiling too.

'Go, Daisy!' Sharky shouted over to her from his bakery, smiling and clapping. Sharky was thirty, brawny, and had a cheery attitude.

She waved to him and continued singing, finally finishing on a high note after the third carol.

Handing back the song sheet, Daisy felt almost back to full strength again and wasn't inclined to mope about going to New York. Maybe it would be horribly good for her and Jake. A test of their resolve that they really were meant to be together. Her own private cure for love at Christmas. If they could weather the whirlwind storm of their trip to New York and emerge stronger than ever, it would show that their love wasn't just a summer fling.

One of the carol singers handed Daisy a leaflet. 'Are you coming to the Yuletide celebrations?'

Before Daisy could reply, another singer chipped–in. 'She's off to New York with Jake Wolfe.'

'Oh, sorry, that's right,' the first singer said. 'I hope you have a nice trip.'

'Thank you,' Daisy said, stuffing the leaflet in her bag anyway. Then she walked away to buy the fairy lights.

Picking up the same set Woolley had bought, as they were ideal for what she had in mind, she took them over to the counter and was served by one of the shop assistants.

'Are you putting up a Christmas tree?' the assistant commented as Daisy paid for the lights. 'I thought you and Jake were off to America.'

Taken aback by the comment she kept her answer brief. 'We are, but I'm putting up decorations in my cottage to enjoy before we leave.'

'Ah, well, good luck to you,' he said handing her the lights.

She left the shop carrying the lights in a bag and walked along the cobbles towards the large Christmas tree, drawn by the glow of it. Nearby, Christmas trees, fresh pines, spruce and firs of every size, were lined up for sale. People were picking one and adding their name to the delivery schedule. All the trees were being delivered locally the following day.

The scent of the pines reminded Daisy of Christmases past when there seemed to be time to put up a real tree and enjoy decorating it, wrapping gifts and looking forward to the whole festive season. Now, there was barely time to do anything other than plan for things ahead, while forgetting to have fun in the present.

One of the men selling the trees, Mr Greenie, approached Daisy with a cheery smile. 'They're lovely trees this year, aren't they.'

'They are, Mr Greenie. I love the scent of them.'

Mr Greenie was the town's handyman/gardener, electrician, fire chief and various other professions when needed. None of the jobs required his full–time attention so he wore different hats for each job when necessary. Helping sell and deliver the Christmas trees was his current task. He had a ready smile and cheerful nature.

'It's a pity you're flying off to New York and won't be able to have one in your cottage this year.'

Daisy looked at him, feeling his words spin around her, accurate and personal yet well–meaning.

'I would've put one up, but...' Daisy shrugged. It wouldn't last until she was home sometime in January. And what if they had to extend their stay until late January? No, a real tree wasn't practical.

As if reading her well, Mr Greenie gestured to a small selection of artificial trees tucked at the side of his stall. 'What about one of these trees? A sparkling silver or glowing gold. Or a realistic green one?'

'Yes, I'll have one of those,' she said deciding instantly that this would let her enjoy a tree. She'd planned to pin the lights up in her window, but a tree would be so much more festive. 'A sparkling silver one please.'

Light as a feather, he wrapped it up and handed it to her.

Armed with her little tree, lights and a load of determination, Daisy walked back along the main street and paused outside the pretty boutique selling ladies fashions and stylish winter woollies. She needed a cosy jumper like the pastel pink one on display, and warm socks. Her wardrobe was more suited to summer and autumn.

Emerging with the pink jumper and a pale blue one, several pairs of socks, and two sets of lace and silk lingerie in the boutique's bag, she headed back to her cottage as the night deepened. The air had a real wintry bite to it.

Daisy didn't mind. It added to the atmosphere, seeing the lights in other cottage windows as she walked along, and frost layering itself on the pavement.

Mrs Lemon hurried to catch up with her. 'I thought it was you. What have you got there? A Christmas tree?'

'Yes.' Daisy explained about the tree and the lights as they walked along. Their cottages were diagonally opposite each other, and Mrs Lemon kept an eye on Franklin's cottage when it was unoccupied.

'Good on you. Celebrate Christmas here before you go.' Mrs Lemon was carrying a bag of groceries and eyed Daisy's purchases. 'I hear you were carol singing and buying saucy undies.' She glanced at the boutique bag.

Daisy went to deny the knicker buying, but then decided it wasn't worth her breath. 'They're not saucy, just fancy lace and silk. And I'll probably never wear them. They were an impulse buy.'

'I'll tell Karen you took her advice, in case of a romantic emergency of course, that's not likely as Jake thinks the world of you. I'm sure you'll have a lovely time in New York.'

Daisy's deep breath filtered out into the cold night air. 'Yes, it's just that...I wish we could've had our first Christmas together here in Cornwall, not on the other side of the world. I've always been a homebody at heart.'

Mrs Lemon stopped and glanced over at Daisy's cottage. 'But your home is in London,' she reminded Daisy.

The truth jarred Daisy.

'You're living here temporarily in Franklin's holiday cottage,' Mrs Lemon added. 'And from what you've told me, you rented your flat in London fully furnished. Do you have many things to call your own?'

'No, I suppose not.' Daisy's voice was filled with realisation. Apart from the clothes and artwork supplies she'd brought with her from London, there was precious little else that she owned.

'But you've done well for yourself,' Mrs Lemon then bolstered her, seeing the faraway look in Daisy's eyes. 'You've built a great career for yourself in London, illustrating beautiful books for Franklin's company, and found a flat to rent. Without any help from anyone. I know you're on your own without any family. Working and living in London, and then taking a wild chance on coming here, you don't sound like a homebody to me. Especially as you don't actually have a permanent home of your own.'

'You're right,' Daisy said thoughtfully. 'I really don't have a home.'

'You will if Jake proposes. You'll live with him in his big house up on the hill.' Mrs Lemon glanced round and gazed up at the mansion high on the hill, on its own, overlooking Daisy's cottage and the town.

Daisy's heart ached seeing the lights glow in the window of Jake's study. So near and yet so far.

'I don't mean to distress you,' Mrs Lemon insisted. 'I want the best for you and Jake. So don't let anyone in New York look down on you. They're bound to think you're from Cornwall too. But you're a city girl. A successful and determined young lady from London with a career she built from her own talent and hard work. They don't know what's coming for them if they misjudge you. And I think it's a given that they will, so use it to your advantage, and come back even stronger than when you left here.'

Daisy's eyes looked away from the mansion and she nodded firmly at Mrs Lemon. 'Thank you. I will.'

Heading into their respective cottages with a friendly wave to each other, Daisy set about putting up the tree in the window of the cottage's front lounge.

Rummaging through the hall cupboard, she found a box of Christmas baubles and a spare set of fairy lights that she put to use.

By the time she was finished, padding about in a pair of her new cosy socks, the lounge glowed like she'd hoped it would and it started to feel a bit like Christmas.

Franklin's cottage had a well kept front garden with a small lawn. Roses and other florals added to the traditional quality of the cottage during the summer, and gradually blended into a burnished autumn, and now on frosty evenings, winter jasmine, clematis, pansies and Christmas roses brightened the garden.

Inside it was comfortably furnished in shades of cream. The front lounge had a traditional log fireplace that glowed along with the Christmas tree in the window.

The kitchen was light and airy with a view of the back garden and everything from the cooker to the sturdy table and chairs had a modern vintage vibe.

As she stood admiring her tree, and sipping a mug of tea, a loud knock on the front door startled her.

She peered out the window and saw Jake standing outside. And he wasn't smiling.

His classic winter jacket suited his tall, broad shouldered stature. His hands were thrust into the pockets and the collar was turned up against the cold night.

Jake dressed well and she'd yet to see him do casual unless it was stylish. Suits, shirts, waistcoats and ties were his usual attire, something she liked about him. Undoing his tie, unbuttoning the top buttons of his shirt and maybe taking off his waistcoat was his idea of relaxing. He matched the traditional decor of his house, especially his study with its dark wood, vintage oak desk and chair and old–fashioned ambiance.

The only quirky and disruptive element in his study was a cuckoo clock with an attitude of its own that tended to chime when it felt like it. A slight disruption to Jake's well–organised chaos as he created his herbal potions. A ratio Daisy thought matched her own. He'd never dated anyone like her. A city girl. One who'd arrived in his world with a broken heart and an attitude determined not to take some remedy to mend it. That they'd fallen in love with each other, such opposites, was one of life's wonderful surprises.

Jake saw her peeking out the window and brushed the wayward strands of silky dark hair back from his brow. The troubled expression on his face didn't lessen his handsomeness. He had a sexy smile but tended to ration it, more inclined to have a curious and serious attitude to things.

All of these traits, Daisy loved. It's what made Jake Wolfe the man she believed was for her.

Putting her tea down, she opened the door and expected him to step inside the hall, but he didn't.

'I won't come in. I've a ton of work to tackle this evening. But I saw the Christmas tree all lit up in your window.' The disapproval in his tone was evident.

'Is there something wrong with me putting up a tree?' she said outright.

'Yes, and no. I couldn't tell from a distance that it was artificial. I've decided not to put a tree up this year as it'll be a waste of time and someone will have to clear it up while we're away.'

'I'd have put up a real tree if we'd been celebrating Christmas here. But it would wither and be such a mess to tidy up when we got back. We could be away for a while. You still don't know. And I didn't want to foist the task on to Mrs Lemon.'

'Franklin pays her to attend to the cottage.'

'Yes, but I'm living here now and for however long.' She shrugged. 'Though obviously, I don't have a home of my own.'

'You have a flat in London.'

'That I haven't lived in for months. And it barely has anything belonging to me.'

His aquamarine blue eyes looked right at her. 'What has Mrs Lemon been saying?'

'Nothing that wasn't true.'

'You seem upset.'

'And you seem to disapprove of my tree.'

'It's very nice, very sparkly, very you.'

A silence settled between them.

'I have to get back to my work, Daisy. I'm sorry if I've sounded sharp. There are so many things I have to do, to organise, to get ready to tackle New York.'

She felt the weight of the pressure on his shoulders. 'I know. I understand.'

He nodded, relieved somewhat. 'I'll see you tomorrow sometime.'

'Yes.'

He started to walk away and then spun around, came back and kissed her, pulling her close for a moment, and then strode away back up the hill to get on with his work.

Halfway up the hill he started chiding himself. He should've told Daisy that he loved her. She knew he did. He'd told her, but probably not often enough. Something he wanted to rectify when he had the time.

Forcing himself not to look back down at the cottage where the only woman he'd ever truly loved could be watching him fading into the night, he trudged on up the hill. Waving to each other from a distance always made him feel sad, and they'd been doing a lot of that recently. Something else needing rectified.

Peering out the window through the Christmas tree lights, Daisy watched Jake walk up the hill until his shadow disappeared into the darkness.

The weight of his workload cast the shadow of an uneasy figure. She wished she could help lighten his load, but only Jake could do Jake's work. When she'd previously tried to assist him in his study, he'd burned more time explaining to her what he was doing than actually doing it. Be a help not a hindrance was her motto now. Letting Jake work without interruption was her best bet. A lot of the time he lived in his own thoughts of creating herbal potions and there wasn't room for her when he was being inventive.

Daisy got on with her work too. After a light dinner of soup without parsley and herbs, but still tasty with bread baked by Sharky, she settled down to work on the floral illustrations Franklin had asked her to create for one of his new books.

She'd just settled down, drawn a bluebell and a pansy, when her phone rang. It was Franklin.

'Are you busy tomorrow?' Franklin said to her.

'Not particularly, why?'

'Could you pop up to London for our scheduled editorial meeting rather than later in the week? I know it's short notice, but I've a special commission I'd like to discuss with you. I'm publishing a book on vintage flowers and floral designs used in vintage fabric. I'd like you to illustrate it. The deadline is pretty tight, and I know you're off to New York, but I thought you could make a start on it now and finish it when you get back. Maybe even sketch a few while you're away.'

'I'll come up to London tomorrow morning,' she promised, suddenly feeling like this was the perfect escape from her current pressure cooker situation. A trip to London was just the ticket.

'Thank you, Daisy. See you tomorrow.'

Daisy relaxed back on the sofa, admiring her tree, and then messaged her trip news to Jake.

Franklin phoned. I'm popping up to London for a meeting tomorrow morning re illustrating a new vintage floral book. I should be home, as usual, late tomorrow night.

Jake's reply arrived a short while later.

Safe trip. See you when I see you.

She was sure he wasn't being flippant, but his response did him no favours. It only served to bolster her resolve to mine her own diamonds while the world swirled around her. And she scolded herself for taking advice from Karen of all people! Deary me, she thought, wishing she hadn't succumbed to buying fancy knickers.

Jake sat at his desk in his study having dinner, a tasty pasta and salad he'd rustled up. Mrs Lemon often cooked for him when he was busy, as did Woolley, or he'd order something from Sharky's bakery. But as his schedule was recently so erratic, he'd taken to making his own meals, although his culinary skills left a lot to be desired.

He read his notes while he ate, skimming over the lists of herbs he'd tried for various concoctions, remembering this particular selection of essences and memorising them so he could recall them when he did the interviews.

His study was full of books, files, jars and various paraphernalia. In Jake's world it was normal to have jars of potions with labels such as — jealousy, paranoia and spite.

From his window he could see Daisy's Christmas tree glowing in the night, and felt his heart ache, wanting to be with her. And yet he knew he had so many tasks piling up that needed his attention.

Woolley came in, as he often did, dropping by for a chat and a cup of tea.

Jake ate the dinner he'd made while his desk was piled with stacks of files and information about his books and herbal remedies.

'The publisher's New York office phoned me,' said Jake. 'They told me I'll need information on all the herbs and other ingredients that I've used in past and current blends of the remedy to discuss in interviews. They want me to email the details so they can start including them in the publicity releases.'

'It's a lot of work. Did they say it's necessary?'

'Yes, I tried to wriggle out of it, but they said that the pre–sales of the book have been great, even better than they'd anticipated. Apparently, I'll have to discuss all the ins and outs of what I've been up to these past few years. I don't keep records of everything. You know what I'm like.'

'Spur of the moment, sparks of genius, taking the main notes but not wasting time on logging everything.'

'Exactly. But they want everything. If I'm asked and don't have a ready reply it'll make me look incompetent.'

Woolley shook his head. 'It seemed like a wonderful opportunity earlier in the year when your publisher in London said they were pushing the book forward for a Christmas release. But now...' He shook his head again. 'I've barely had a chance to talk to you this week. And I know that Daisy must be feeling the same.'

'I think I upset her. She's put up a Christmas tree in the cottage and I more or less shot it down in flames. I was wound up with work, then I saw it in her window and assumed she'd put up a real tree that we'd sort of agreed would be a waste of time this year. I've been trying to get her to pack her things and get ready for the trip, but I think she's upset about us leaving Cornwall.'

'She'd been looking forward to a small town, cosy Christmas.'

Jake couldn't finish his dinner and sat back in his chair. 'I know. So had I. But this whole publicity circus is like a double–edged sword. I want the book to be a success and it's looking promising. But it comes at a cost, and that is time to do the things we'd planned for, hoped for. I've barely seen Daisy. And when I have, I've acted like I'm putting the publicity ahead of everything, especially her.'

'Nothing is worth that, Jake.'

'I know that too.'

'Do you want me to talk to her in the morning? Pop in with breakfast rolls and help explain the situation,' Woolley offered.

'She's off to an editorial meeting with Franklin in London tomorrow.'

Woolley didn't like the way things were heading. 'You'll have to be careful, Jake. You don't want to cure Daisy of loving you by letting her slip through your fingers. Busy or not. You need to do something to assure her that you love her.'

'Daisy knows I love her. I've told her that.'

Woolley was hinting that Jake should propose, but he didn't want to force him. Jake's mind was in such a whirl the suggestion didn't even register with him.

'There's a Christmas party at the castle tomorrow night.' Woolley put a leaflet down on the desk. 'I came in to drop this off. I thought you could take Daisy, have a night out.'

Jake read the leaflet. 'Roman Penhaligan's castle? A Christmas party with a banquet buffet and dancing.'

'It'll be a fine night. From what I hear the castle's all done up for Christmas. And according to Mrs Lemon, Roman's on–off relationship with his girlfriend, Daphne from London, is currently off. So he's spending a lot of time at the castle these days. Daphne doesn't like castles apparently and prefers a modern life in London.'

'Roman rather liked Daisy, didn't he?' The hint of jealousy was barely disguised.

'He did, but he knows you two are a couple now, so there's no chance of him trying to cut–in on you to woo Daisy with his impressive castle, wealth, handsome looks and cheery company.'

Jake wasn't assured in the least.

'I'm taking Mrs Lemon to the party. Sharky is taking Karen. A lot of local folk are going. We've all been invited. Roman has a party like this every year. You went to one of them. Didn't you dance with the macaroon girl from Devon?'

'No, I'm sure I didn't.'

'Well, you could dance with Daisy.'

'Yes, she's usually back from London around nine in the evening. I assume the party will be in full swing by then, but it'll continue until midnight at least. I'll surprise her as soon as she gets home. Whisk her off to the castle.'

Woolley smiled. 'That would be very romantic.'

Agreeing on this plan, Woolley went to head out and then paused to comment. 'And remember, you don't leave for New York for a couple of weeks. You're out of sync with the time scale. There's plenty of time to enjoy a night out with Daisy.' Giving a cheery wave, he left.

Jake glanced again out the window at Daisy's cottage. A night out was just what they needed. Woolley was right about the time. He'd probably packed his things too early. And he needed to make more time for romance with Daisy.

As he gazed out the window at her cottage, the cuckoo clock on the wall juddered into life, and out popped the little wooden bird at twenty–four minutes past the hour, chipping–in its tuppence worth.

'Cuckoo!' it spluttered.

Jake could've sworn that it gave him a steely–eyed glare.

And then the mechanism that he kept meaning to oil, creaked and rattled, and the cuckoo disappeared back inside the old–fashioned clock with a defiant click of the little doors.

CHAPTER THREE

Fashion in London

Daisy worked on her botanical illustrations late into the night, sitting by the fireside, enjoying the cosy warmth of the log fire. She'd never lived anywhere that had a real fire, and welcomed the colder evenings so she could light it and relax in the cottage.

She sat with her sketch pad, watercolour pencils and pens, and her laptop. And a mug of tea.

Franklin had emailed details of the new vintage book he wanted her to illustrate. She confirmed she'd received it, that she'd be at the meeting in the morning, and intended to then whiz around the fashion shops in London.

After studying the type of floral artwork he was interested in, she sketched a few flowers including tea roses, lily of the valley, lavender, lilac, pansies and viola.

The theme of the book required lots of floral illustrations, something she excelled at and enjoyed working on. The brief he'd sent interested her as she loved vintage style designs and artwork. Botanical art was her forte and many of the flowers he was looking for, such as violets, iris, lilies and daisies were already stashed in her portfolio. But she loved inking flowers. It was relaxing.

After drawing several flowers using a fine ink pen on artist's quality paper, she packed the sample up ready for the morning along with the other illustrations she'd been working on. With everything packed in her portfolio and bag, she got ready for bed.

Before going through to the bedroom, she turned the Christmas tree lights off, and peered out the window for a moment. The lights were still on in Jake's study. What a couple of night owls they were, she thought, and then headed through to her bed.

Snuggling under the covers that included a beautiful handmade quilt, she thought about Jake and tried not to fret about their current situation. She did miss him, but this was a busy time for both of them, and once things settled down, they'd have time to be together like they had during the summer and autumn.

Jake had written a few other herbal theme books, but his latest book was starting to gain a lot of interest. He'd told her weeks ago that he'd be busy with the book launch in December, but he thought it would only be in London. The New York aspect had taken him by surprise, but the opportunity was too great to be missed.

Manhattan would look wonderful at Christmastime, she told herself. She'd never been to New York, but she'd seen films and photographs where all the stores were lit up and the city was iced white with snow. It always looked magical.

With thoughts of Jake still running through her mind, she drifted off to sleep with her phone set with an early morning alarm.

Jake glanced out the window of his study and his heart reacted seeing that the Christmas tree no longer glowed in the window of Daisy's cottage. She'd probably been working on illustrations to take with her to London to show Franklin.

He checked the time and sighed. She'd be tucked up in bed. He wished he'd called her to say goodnight, even though this was something he rarely did. But he was missing her, more than ever. With a pile of files on his desk that he'd still to pour through for information about his herbal mixes, he concentrated on the task in hand, preparing to work for a bit longer before going to bed. He kept data about his work on his computer, but had always tended to scribble details in notebooks and sheets of paper that were then filed away in a cabinet or his desk drawers. A mix of old–fashioned and modern methods worked well for him. But it was time consuming when he had to piece the information together into a format suitable for the book interviews in New York. And it didn't help that delving into the past made his mind drift to those times, and it was giving him ideas for new herbal variations that he was then jotting down on a fresh notepad

Finally easing off the tension from his shoulders, he switched off his desk lamp and headed upstairs to his bedroom.

The view from his bedroom window looked down on Daisy's cottage and the other cottages nearby, with the lights of the small town in the near distance. He could see the large Christmas tree in the town's square sparkling in the night.

Further along the coast was Roman Penhaligan's castle and he saw the dark outline of the turrets against the inky sky. He was looking forward to the party and surprising Daisy when she got back from London, whisking her off for a night of dining and dancing.

Striped down to his pyjama bottoms, he again eased his muscles from the long hours working in his study.

He was lean and fit, with long muscles honed from hard work, physical work at the health food shop loading new stock, and tending to the herbs and flowers he grew in his garden. And a busy lifestyle. There was Woolley's boat too that he used to go sailing off the Cornish coast, particularly to search for the elusive blue sea flower that he added as part of his cure for love remedy. He'd taken Daisy with him during the summer, and smiled when he recalled how she enjoyed sailing. They'd gone swimming in the sea too, making the most of the hot summer sunshine. Now with everything frosted, the heat of the recent past seemed like a lifetime ago. But he loved the winter, always had, and so too did Daisy from what she'd told him. And she definitely loved Christmas. He hadn't had time to think what to buy her as a gift, but maybe he'd see something wonderful in New York.

Forcing himself to clear his thoughts, he fell asleep through sheer tiredness after the busy day and didn't stir until the morning.

Daisy had forgotten how dark winter mornings were as she got ready to leave for London very early. It was more like the depths of the night as she checked she had everything she needed to take with her for her meeting with Franklin. Her portfolio of artwork.

Check. A bag with her art materials, watercolour pencils, sketch pad, ink pens and spare sheets of white paper to scribble on. Yes, she had those too. Her voluminous shoulder bag with her laptop and other odds and ends. All accounted for.

She wore her new pale blue jumper with a pair of dark blue stretch velvet trousers tucked into her comfy boots. The jumper felt soft and snug and she loved the ice blue colour.

A light layer of frost iced the car windows. She cleared that and then put her cream coat on the back seat along with her scarf and gloves. A woolly hat kept her hair tidy as she popped back and forth from her car to the cottage. The pale blue hat was a fair match for her jumper and it had a couple of subtle sparkly snowflakes in the design.

No lights shone from any of the nearby windows, and the crisp silence made her want to keep quiet as she locked the cottage secure and got into the car. Everyone was sensibly tucked up in bed, including Jake. There was no glow from the windows of his house. Glancing around, there was the feeling that she was the only one up and about except...

Sharky drove by in his bakery van, pulled over and jumped out to chat to her for a moment.

He wore his clean and tidy baker's whites, including a hat that barely contained his thick brown hair, and a jovial smile that matched his nature.

'Heading to London?' He didn't look surprised to see her, knowing her well enough to surmise she was on her way to visit her publisher.

'A publishing meeting with Franklin.'

'Be careful you're not ensnared by that snake Sebastian,' he warned her.

'Franklin makes sure my meetings with him are a Sebastian and Celeste free zone,' she assured him.

'Good man.'

Then he hurried to the back of the van, opened the doors, reached inside and grabbed a bag filled with fresh baked buns. He handed them to her. 'Here you go. These are my new recipe sticky cinnamon buns with extra spice this Christmas. Franklin used to enjoy them.'

She accepted them gladly. 'Thank you, Franklin will love these. And so will I.'

'Okay, I won't hold you up.' He got into his van and spoke to her via the open window. 'Safe trip and have fun in the city.'

'I'm planning a whirlwind shopping spree to buy new clothes to get ready for New York.'

'Ah, but is New York ready for you?'

She frowned.

'You're a trouble magnet, Daisy.'

She straightened her woolly hat, brushed stray strands of hair away from her face and denied his accusation with a smile. 'No, I'm not.'

Sharky shook his head. 'You fidget when you fib.' He started up the van. 'Remember to keep your eyes peeled for sneaky snakes,' he called to her as he drove off with a cheery wave out the window.

She heeded the warning and got into her car, put the buns in the back seat, and glanced over at the pretty cottage.

Putting the key in the ignition and turning on the engine, she pulled away from the cottage, feeling the tug on her heartstrings as she did so. Leaving Cornwall for the drive to London was becoming a little bit harder lately.

Motorways and main roads made it an easy and pleasant enough drive. Setting off early helped her avoid the morning traffic and she usually arrived in London in time for morning elevenses with Franklin in his office.

Fuelled up on a breakfast of cereal with creamy milk and a cup of tea, she watched the Cornish coast disappear into the distance as she drove towards the city.

Jake ate breakfast at the kitchen table, a bowl of muesli topped with berry fruits. He'd been up early, but when he'd looked out his bedroom window he noticed Daisy's car had gone.

They had an easy agreement that he wouldn't phone when she was dealing with her work in London. The drive itself took a few hours, creating a tight schedule that was workable if she didn't have any social interruptions.

He finished his cereal and carried his cup of tea through to the study. The leaflet advertising the party at the castle was still on his desk. He checked the details. Guests were requested to arrive around seven–thirty in the evening. A buffet was provided along with a band playing live music throughout the evening until late. He pictured picking Daisy up when she got back from London and driving her to the party.

Taking a sip of tea, he began tackling the day's work while looking forward to his night out with Daisy.

London had a familiar feel to it as Daisy arrived, a sense of excitement that the city evoked in her.

She loved shopping in London and some of her favourite fashion stores were within easy reach of Franklin's publishing company.

Armed with her portfolio and lots of ideas for the vintage book, she headed into the company, through reception and along to Franklin's office that was the perfect blend of old money and new wealth. Antique furniture accommodated cutting edge technology. Popular book covers, published by his company, adorned the walls in vintage walnut and modern silver metallic frames. Two trophies were perched on a Victorian writing desk.

The door was open in welcoming. He sat behind his desk and smiled as she walked in, delighted to see her. A view of London watched his back while he faced incoming visitors head on.

Franklin was tall, dashing, fit and fifties. From his attire, he still had a penchant for immaculate light grey suits, white shirts and bright patterned bow ties, his only allowance of bold colour.

Daisy sat down opposite him at his large antique desk and opened her portfolio. 'I studied your email with the brief for the vintage book and sketched a few ideas down last night.'

Franklin smiled. 'I almost didn't send it. I knew you'd start work on it, probably well into the late evening.'

Daisy shrugged. 'I love vintage designs, especially florals, and from the information you gave me, I started to picture how some of the designs would work in the book.'

She showed him the illustrations.

'These are excellent, just what I had in mind. There's demand for beautiful vintage pieces and as the editorial includes features on classic embroidery designs on clothing and framed as artwork, several of your floral illustrations will be adapted and added as embroidery patterns.'

Daisy brightened. 'That's a lovely idea. I'll keep that in mind when I'm drawing them.'

'Do that. Several flowers would be perfect.'

'The bluebells would work well I think.' Daisy showed him the inked bluebells.

Franklin agreed. 'These pansy prints are lovely too, along with the violets and old–fashioned roses.'

'And this is the finished artwork for the other book. All done.' She put a folder of floral artwork, inked illustrations and watercolours on his desk.

While he poured over her portfolio, Daisy gazed out at the view of the city, the historic architecture that the artist in her loved and admired, her favourite park nearby, the shops with their windows festooned with sparkle for the festive season and the streets themselves adorned with Christmas lights and decorations. The busy thoroughfares teemed with people all looking like they were going somewhere important.

Franklin admired and approved the designs. 'Fantastic.'

The meeting went well, and as they chatted over tea and Sharky's cinnamon buns, discussing the agreement of the new deadline, the time flew in and they were done just before lunchtime. Sometimes, when Franklin's schedule allowed, they'd head out for lunch, but this hadn't been agreed during her current visit as he was extra busy with publishing business.

'I'll keep these illustrations,' he said, picking up her designs for the vintage book, along with the finished artwork for the current book.

Daisy opened her bag and handed him a small present and a card. 'I know we said we wouldn't do Christmas gifts this year but...'

He looked delighted as he opened it. 'This is exquisite.' The glass paperweight depicted the beauty of the sea, swirling blues and greens with a little book in the frothy waves.

'The local craft shop makes these and I liked that this one has a tiny book in the glass.'

Franklin sat the paperweight on his desk and admired it. 'I love it. Thank you, Daisy.'

He opened his desk drawer. 'I have a little something for you too. Perhaps not as personal as yours, but I thought under the circumstances a practical present was better.' He handed her a Christmas card. 'You mentioned you planned to go shopping when you were here, so...'

She opened the Christmas card and found three substantial gift vouchers inside. Each one was for a different fashion outlet.

Daisy's eyes lit up. 'This is perfect.' It really was. 'And far too generous.'

'As are you with your time and the trouble you go to when working on the illustrations. Your talent and effort is truly appreciated.'

She gave him a hug and he hugged her back. If anyone had felt like a fatherly figure in her life, it was Franklin.

'Any special plans for Christmas?' she said.

'I'm working up until Christmas Eve and then taking three and a half days off.'

'The half day really matters,' she joked.

'It does in this hectic business. Anyway, I've gleaned tickets to three shows I've been wanting to see, so I'm looking forward to nights out at the theatres. I'll peruse the art galleries too at my leisure and enjoy any glasses of mulled wine along the way.'

'That sounds quite enticing.'

His tone lowered. 'You're not looking forward to New York, are you?'

'Is it that obvious?'

He smiled knowingly. 'A bit.'

She sighed. 'I'd been so looking forward to a small town Christmas. Now it'll be a celebration again in the city. Albeit another city. But I shouldn't complain. Others would love a trip to New York at this time of year.'

'Not if they had their heart set on something completely different.'

She felt the warmth of his understanding wash over her, like a salve that made her feel she wasn't so terribly ungrateful.

Franklin walked her out. 'We'll have lunch when you get back from New York,' he promised.

She nodded and smiled. 'I'm going to hit the fashion shops now. Then pop in and check on my flat before driving back down to Cornwall.'

'Safe travels, Daisy. And have a merry Christmas.'

'You too.' She gave him a hug and kiss on the cheek, and then headed to the nearest shopping mall.

Popular Christmas songs from yesteryear played throughout the mall and the stores, and she enjoyed being part of it all.

In a whirlwind of efficient and eclectic excitement, she emerged with two new cocktail dresses, very sparkly, totally impractical, but ideal for the Christmas party season. She'd intended buying one, but couldn't decide on whether to opt for the scintillating silver or the gorgeous gold, so she indulged in the two, especially as they were great bargains. The fashion shops had bargain rails with lots of enticing designs, making the most of Franklin's gift vouchers, with plenty of balance left on each of the cards for a later date.

From cocktail dresses, she swung to the other end of the scale and bought a new pair of burgundy stretch velvet trousers, a deep emerald pair and a few tops to mix and match to create various outfits. Added to her current wardrobe, she figured she'd have everything she needed for every meeting, interview and party in

Manhattan. All within a reasonable budget. Franklin's vouchers were the perfect gift.

Dumping the shopping bags in her car, she wanted a peek at her favourite park where she used to sketch a lot of her floral artwork.

Walking into the park she breathed in the cold December air and admired the trees, grass and flower beds that were sparkling with frost in the pale, winter sunlight. It was rather sad to see most of the flowers gone, with only a few hardy florals holding strong, but standing in the heart of the London park, she felt the past catch up with her, filling her thoughts with memories of all the days she'd sat there sketching.

'Hello, Daisy,' a man's familiar voice said over her shoulder.

She spun around and gazed up at Sebastian's handsome face, and gasped. 'Sebastian! What are you doing here?'

'I heard you were at a meeting with Franklin. I tactfully made myself busy. But I wanted to talk to you before you headed back to Cornwall.'

'How did you know where to find me?' She searched his face, wondering how he knew where she'd be.

He stepped closer and gazed down at her. 'I always know where to find you.'

Sebastian was as devilishly handsome as ever. He was tall, lean, elegant, with well–cut light brown hair and cold blue eyes. Aged thirty, he looked like a successful young businessman. His dark grey suit, worn with a black coat, screamed money and taste. No wonder she'd fallen hard for Sebastian. Her heart reacted seeing him again, but not in a loving way, just wary.

He attempted chit–chat. 'I've been promoted, much to Celeste's chagrin.'

'Franklin promoted you over his own daughter?' She found this hard to believe.

'Yes. I was surprised, but Franklin said he needed a ruthless and capable editorial director like me to navigate the tricky waters of the current industry.'

'He's no doubt got the top person for the job.'

'I bet that hurt to acknowledge.'

'You'll never know.' She started to walk away.

'Are you free for a late lunch?' His breath filtered into the cold air, and she noticed that his car was parked illegally nearby.

She paused. 'No, I only popped into the park for a peek.'

'Nostalgia.' His voice sounded so assured, and her heart thundered just being near him. He always had a knack for disconcerting her.

'I'm heading to my flat now, to check on it, and then driving back to Cornwall.'

Sebastian glanced up at the suddenly darkening sky. Grey clouds scudded across the sky, shading out the sunlight, bringing a cold breeze with them.

She shivered but didn't show it.

'It looks like it's going to rain any minute,' he said. 'Let me give you a lift to your flat.'

'No thank you.'

His firm lips curved into an enticing smile. 'You'll get soaked to the skin.'

Her words were precise in her rebuttal. 'I have my car. But if hailstones the size of golf balls were raining down, I'd still prefer to walk rather than take a lift from you, Sebastian.'

He. Didn't. Flinch. His smile remained. 'Still not forgiven me, then.'

For cheating on her with Celeste when she'd trusted him and loved him? For breaking her heart? For all the lies and deceit? No, forgiveness was off the table.

Icing him with a defiant stare, she turned and walked away across the park, feeling his eyes boring into her back.

'You're heading the wrong way,' he shouted to her. 'Your flat is that direction.' He thumbed behind him.

Spinning on the heels of her boots, she stomped back towards him heading in the right direction. She hated that he disconcerted her so much, but marched on.

'Mr Wolfe is well–named,' Sebastian said to her as she went by.

Daisy didn't falter.

'I hear that he's not the marrying kind.'

She came to a defiant stop and turned to face him. 'What have you heard?'

'That Sharky has put a ring on Karen's finger, but Jake hasn't even hinted about getting engaged to you.'

His comment cut deep. She hoped he didn't see the hurt in her eyes.

'Jake won't marry you, Daisy.' His tone was so assured.

She resented that there was something in his voice that made her tilt towards doubting Jake's intentions. She was more than a summer romance that had lasted into the winter. Wasn't she?

Out of barbed comments, she walked away from him.

'I made a mistake with Celeste. Can you ever find it in your heart to forgive me?'

She paused and glanced round. 'The last time I was in this park with you, I trusted everything you said. You told me you were going to the book convention in Italy, but failed to mention that it included Celeste. Then you asked her to marry you, and you and came back to London as Franklin's potential son–in–law.'

'I know. I made mistake, but I'm sorry. I told you that before.'

'Sorry doesn't cut it. In this park I asked you if there was anything else I could do for you while you were in Italy. And you had the temerity to tell me — *yes, love me forever.*' She shook her head in dismay. 'But all the time you knew you intended asking Celeste to marry you.'

'It wasn't planned. Not the way you're suggesting. It was a spur of the moment proposal. Summer in Europe — the romance of it swept me away. But we didn't last. The engagement was a mistake. I've had nothing to do with Celeste for months.'

Daisy shrugged wearily, feeling the weight of the day and its topic press down on her. She'd heard all his excuses before. 'That changes nothing, Sebastian. I don't love you now, and I never will again.'

She walked on.

'I know you're angry, but circumstances change,' he called to her. 'We could be happy together. We could get engaged at Christmas.'

Daisy kept walking, feeling the tears burn like acid. There had been a time when such a proposal would've made her so happy. But that time was long gone.

Disappearing into the crowd that didn't notice how upset she was, she walked to where her car was parked. She sat composing herself for a few moments and then drove the short distance to her flat and hurried inside as the rain started to pour.

Shaking a few droplets from the shoulders of her coat, she approached her front door and fished out her keys.

But she didn't need them. The door was unlocked.

CHAPTER FOUR

Christmas Films Matinee

Archie's little paper party hat was secured at a jaunty angle with a piece of thin elastic. He balanced a tray of glasses that tinkled as he pulled his front door shut and stepped towards Daisy's flat. He was so focussed on the tray that he didn't notice her standing there until he'd almost bumped into her.

'Daisy!' His tone was three octaves too high, and his pale complexion burst with a bright blast of guilty colour that he'd been caught red–handed. Whatever he was up to made her realise she'd arrived at an opportune time to see what he was up to in her flat.

Archie, thirties, was taller than her with a wiry frame. His jumper had a snowflake pattern and she had the distinct impression that he was in the mood to party.

He gasped. 'What are you doing here?'

'I live here.' Obviously not at the moment, but it was her flat.

'You weren't supposed to be here until a few days from now.' The glasses rattled almost as much as Archie's equilibrium.

'Franklin rescheduled the meeting.'

'Oh.'

Daisy smiled tightly, and was about to ask Archie what he was up to when the sound of cheerful voices sounded from the stairway and several boisterous partygoers arrived in a bundle of excited chatter.

Seeing Archie and Daisy didn't deter them. Instead, it fuelled their delight as if they were being welcomed, and Daisy was swept inside her flat by the group hugs and bustling chatter.

Apart from seeing the well–dressed and happy strangers making themselves at home, the first thing Daisy noticed about her flat was that it was tidy. Very clean. Someone had kept it spick and span. That person was Archie. Being a fusspot had its advantages.

The second thing she noticed were the trays of bite size snacks set on two tables like a festive buffet.

Archie put the tray of glasses down.

One of the couples, a man and woman of similar age to Archie, busied themselves in the kitchen making tea and hot chocolate.

Meanwhile, others, including Archie's new girlfriend, set up the television, making sure the two couches and comfy chairs were arranged to view it.

Archie steeled himself as he approached Daisy. 'I can explain.'

'I don't think you need to. You've been using my flat to hold parties rather than messing up your flat.'

He blinked and swallowed hard. She'd nailed it in one.

Daisy stepped aside as one of the guests made coffee using a coffee maker set up on one of the snack tables. She frowned at Archie. 'I have an espresso machine?'

'No, that's mine. I'm letting you borrow it.'

'That's very kind of you, Archie.' Her sarcasm was lost on him.

He smiled, thinking maybe she wasn't too mad at him.

'The films start in five minutes,' one of the women announced, causing everyone to put a spurt on, making tea, coffee and hot chocolate, grabbing a snack and then sitting down to watch whatever was the nub of them being there.

'Two classic Christmas films are about to start. A double feature,' Archie said to Daisy, sounding excited. 'You still have your subscription to that movie channel—'

Daisy cut–in. 'I'm still paying for that?' She hadn't realised.

Archie's eyes were filled with gratitude. 'I thought you'd kept it as a bonus for me. You know I love that channel and I don't have it. I assumed it was a sort of perk for me doing the hoovering.'

'You hoover my flat?'

'The dust bunnies don't jump into the bin by themselves, Daisy.' The snippy tone of the Archie she knew sounded clear.

'Come on you two, the first film is about to start,' one of the men beckoned them urgently.

'This is Daisy by the way,' Archie announced hurriedly.

A rousing cheer went up and several smiling faces caused her to smile back at them.

Feeling like she was in a wind tunnel not of her own making, yet in her own flat, made Daisy hesitate, so Archie helpfully sat her down on the couch, grabbed two mugs of hot chocolate, handed one to her while someone else gave her a plate with a cheese vol–au–vent and crisps.

Sandwiched between Archie and a complete stranger, Daisy planned her escape as the lights were dimmed and the film began. Everyone knew the theme song and sang it as a prelude to what was in store for her.

And yet...the hot chocolate smelled delicious, perfect for a rainy December afternoon when the daylight was barely stronger than a wishy–washy grey. Inside the flat felt cosy, and although these were strangers, they were Archie's friends, now hers by proxy, and she really did love this film. It was one of her all–time favourites. One that set the mood for the festive season.

Maybe she'd just watch a bit of it. The beginning was always great. Drink her hot chocolate and...she bit into the cheese pastry and...oh yes, she'd linger for a little while and then make a big bid for freedom.

Halfway through the film she was joining in the singing at appropriate times, accepting a chocolate from the box that was passed around, and found herself laughing and cheering at the good parts. And it was sort of all good.

When the film finished there was a scurry of people dashing through to the kitchen to make more tea and hot chocolate, the coffee machine was switched on and more cheesy snacks were handed around along with a box of luxury Christmas biscuits someone had brought with them. Daisy had a piece of chocolate–dipped shortbread.

Archie grabbed everyone's pizza order and then phoned in advance so that it would arrive just as the second film finished.

Everyone called their selection over to Archie. He noted it down.

'What type of pizza do you want, Daisy?' Archie said to her.

'Eh, cheese and tomato,' she heard herself blurt out as he signalled her to hurry up.

'Ice cream?' he added.

'Chocolate chip,' Daisy replied.

Archie relayed the order over the phone moments before they dimmed the lights again and settled down to another dose of Christmas entertainment — and tasty treats.

Daisy glanced out the window. It was late afternoon and a dark, rainy twilight made being indoors feel safe and cosy.

Another round of singing was required for the theme song of the second film, and Daisy sang as loud as everyone else this time.

Jake took delivery of stock for his health food shop, helping to unload it from the delivery van and carried the boxes through the shop and upstairs to the storeroom.

Organising the stock for the festive season, dealing with the accounts and running the overall business for the shop, and the other shops he owned that were run by managers and staff, made the day go in quickly.

The extra lights in the front window and baubles gave a Christmassy glow to the shop and he'd heard customers commenting on how festive it looked.

Woolley was helping Jake with the delivery, and Sharky popped in with a tray of cinnamon buns.

'I'll put these down over here near the treacle scones and the bread.' Sharky noticed that the bakery shelf was understocked.

'The bakery items have been selling well today,' Jake told him. 'And thanks for the top up of buns.'

'I saw Daisy this morning before the crack of dawn,' Sharky revealed to Jake. 'She was off to London for a meeting with Franklin.'

'Yes, she should be home around nine. I'm taking her to the party at the castle.'

'Karen and I are going.' Sharky motioned towards Woolley. 'And this rascal is accompanying Mrs Lemon.'

'She's getting her hair done,' Woolley told them. 'From what I hear, it's going to be a grand night.'

'Does Daisy know you're taking her to the party?' Sharky said to Jake.

'No, I plan to surprise her when she gets back from London. Whisk her off to the castle. She doesn't know a thing about it.'

'I like surprises like that,' Karen piped up while serving a customer.

'I'll keep that in mind,' Sharky told her. 'But now I'd better get back to work.' He smiled and headed out.

Jake followed him to pick up the last box from the delivery van.

They spoke for a moment outside.

'Have you got anything planned for Daisy's Christmas gifts?' said Sharky. 'Will you take them with you to New York, or give them to her before you leave?'

Jake looked rattled. He hadn't thought about this. 'I haven't done my Christmas shopping yet.'

'What do you plan to buy her?'

Jake's blank expression answered that question.

'Any ideas what you'd like to get for her?' Sharky kept fishing, surprised that Jake didn't seem to have a clue.

'I don't know what she'd like,' Jake confessed.

Sharky wasn't impressed. 'I've got my presents for Karen sorted out and wrapped. It's the first Christmas I've had a girlfriend to buy gifts for. A fiancée,' he corrected himself. 'And I've bought something for Mrs Lemon. Two ladies in my life now.' He sounded happy.

Jake's guts twisted while Sharky confided what he'd bought. 'I've got a bracelet for Karen. With her initials on it. So if you see her wearing it in the shop, please notice.'

'Noted.'

'I decided to buy her a few smaller gifts so she has lots of presents to open on Christmas Day.' He thumbed over at the fashion shop. 'They sell lovely woollen hats so I bought a pale pink hat with a scarf to match. Karen loves pink and yellow. And Woolley was thinking of buying Mrs Lemon a sewing basket, but I told him I'd buy that for her. I couldn't decide between the blue and the yellow, so knowing that

Karen would want one when she saw what I'd bought for Mrs Lemon, I bought both. I've wrapped the yellow one up for Karen.'

'You've certainly got all your Christmas shopping sorted out.'

'You should do the same. Buy things Daisy definitely likes.'

Jake looked unsure.

Sharky threw a few suggestions at him. 'This morning she had a woolly hat on. Buy her a new one with a scarf to match. The shop has a nice selection. Daisy loves pale blue.'

'She does.' It was more of a statement than assuredness.

'Daisy's not one for necklaces, but I've noticed she wears a couple of brooches — a strawberry one and cherries, and she likes bracelets.'

'That's right, she does.'

Sharky tactfully didn't mention an engagement ring. 'Think of the things she's interested in. That's what I do. I'm interested in Karen. So I'm interested in what interests her. If you know what I mean.'

Jake did. It meant he'd fallen short on that scale.

'Daisy loves her art, so...' Sharky prompted him.

Jake couldn't think what he'd buy an artist, and his mind was already swatting him for not being attentive enough.

'So buy her stuff from the craft shop,' said Sharky. 'A new small set of travel paints. She likes to paint outdoors. Or an easel. She doesn't have one but she mentioned to me weeks ago that she wanted a folding one to take outdoors for painting.' Sharky was in full swing picking gifts for Daisy. 'And...a large bag, fashionable. You know how she often carries those shoulder bags packed with her artwork. Buy her a new one. The shop might have one. Or buy it when you get to New York if you're giving her gifts when you get there.'

'All great advice, thank you.'

Sharky lowered his voice. 'Karen's peering out the window. She knows we're talking secret stuff.' Sharky hurried away. 'Think about what I've said.'

'I will,' Jake called after him.

Jake stood for a moment holding the lightweight box of wheat puffs and marshmallows, and carried them inside and upstairs to the storeroom.

Woolley tucked a couple of boxes on a shelf and stacked others. 'That was a handy delivery. We're going to be well–stocked through Christmas.'

Jake added his box to the shelf. 'We are.'

'You sound deflated. What was Sharky saying to you?'

'He was being helpful.' Jake sounded disappointed in himself.

'Sharky has his moments.'

'He has.' Jake checked the time. 'Daisy should be driving back from London. I'm popping out for a few minutes. There's something I want to buy for her.'

'Got your Christmas shopping organised then?'

'Just starting.'

The cold air blew through Jake's shirt as he walked towards the fashion shop. And he looked at the Christmas lights and decorations all around him, as if seeing them properly for the first time this year. He'd been wearing his busy blinkers and needed to widen his view.

The fashion shop had a great selection of clothes and accessories on display in the window. He stood there and tried to decide what to buy for her. This wouldn't be her main gift, but he liked Sharky's ideas of lots of presents, though he didn't know whether they'd open them before they left Cornwall or after they got back. He couldn't take them with him to New York. It's wasn't practical. But buying gifts in Manhattan would be easy enough. Wouldn't it?

He checked the time again. Yes, Daisy would be driving back to Cornwall right now, he thought, and hurried into the shop.

Daisy's slice of pizza was dripping with cheese and she was laughing, trying to bite into it without causing a mess, and dancing to the lively music in her flat.

The pizza and ice cream had arrived in time for the second film finishing, and now the party was in full fun mode.

Archie had brought a selection of festive tunes and played them while they all tucked into their food, and all while gearing up and jiving to the songs from Christmases past that put everyone in party mood.

Daisy laughed at Archie as they boogied. 'This is fun!'

By the time the pizza and ice cream had been consumed, they all danced a conga around the flat.

Daisy couldn't remember the last time she'd let her hair down and had so much fun.

Jake emerged from the shop with a bag full of fashionable items he hoped Daisy would like. The shop assistants advised him on a few of them and seemed familiar with Daisy's style and colour preference. Something he needed to learn, when he had more time.

He put the bags in the boot of his car that was parked nearby and then went back into the health food shop to get on with his work.

Daisy checked the time. 'I'd better start heading back to Cornwall,' she said to Archie as the party happily continued. She'd stuck to tea, hot chocolate and soft drinks, even though he was now offering her a cocktail.

'You're not staying the night?'

'No, I'm driving back to the cottage. But I've had fun.'

Archie looked pensive. 'I thought you'd have moved in with Jake Wolfe by now.'

'I don't want to do that yet. The cottage belongs to Franklin, but I still feel like it's sort of my own place at the moment.'

'You need a firm commitment from Jake.'

'Yes.'

'Still affected by the things Sebastian did to you?'

Daisy sighed heavily. 'I met him today.'

'At the publishers?'

'The park.'

'Did he upset you again?'

'He said that Jake isn't the marrying kind and won't marry me,' she confided.

'Sebastian is so manipulative.'

'And he said that we could get married at Christmas.'

Archie was taken aback. 'You and Sebastian?'

'Yes.'

One of the party guests came sauntering over to join them. 'Hey, Daisy. If you ever decide to give up this flat, please give me first dibs.' The woman smiled hopefully.

'Daisy will tell me and I'll tell you,' said Archie.

The woman danced happily away to join the others while Archie and Daisy continued to chat.

'Do you think you'll ever come back to live here in London?' he said.

'I don't plan to, but I'll hold on to it for a little bit longer.' She checked the time again. 'I really better get going.'

'Merry Christmas, Daisy. Enjoy your trip to New York,' said Archie.

'Merry Christmas to you too, Archie. I'll see you sometime in the New Year.'

Daisy put her coat on, picked up her bag and headed towards the door.

Archie and the others hugged her and waved her off.

Daisy hurried out into the cold night. The rain had stopped but the roads were wet and reflected the Christmas lights of the city as she drove through the streets heading for the motorway and the long drive to Cornwall. The last time she'd driven through the night like this was the evening she'd run off from London for a break in Franklin's cottage. There was a feeling in the night as if everything had sort of come full circle. Nothing was settled in her life even though summer had turned to autumn and now it was winter.

She put Christmas songs on and sang along to a few as she drove away from the city. The roads were fairly quiet as she headed down to Cornwall, wondering if she should stop to call Jake and tell him she'd be back really late. But then she decided to keep driving. He was probably busy working in his study anyway and she didn't want to disturb him.

Woolley phoned Jake. 'Are you coming to the party?' The sounds of lively music and merriment sounded in the background.

Jake looked out the window of his study at Daisy's cottage. No lights were on. 'Daisy's not back yet from London.'

'Running late?'

'Yes. Maybe her meeting with Franklin trailed on into the late afternoon and perhaps she had dinner in London. I don't know.'

'You haven't phoned her?'

'No, we don't usually do that. I give her the freedom to do whatever she needs for her work in London. Then she drives home.'

'I think you should give her a call. Mrs Lemon and I are having a great time at the castle with Karen and Sharky.'

'Daisy is bound to be back soon. Then we'll join you.'

'Okay. See you later.'

Jake finished the call, gazed down at the darkened cottage, and then settled to work at his desk again. He didn't want to call her when she was driving.

He'd made huge progress with researching the data he needed, so Daisy being a bit late was fine. The party was on until after midnight, and even if they only turned up at the tail end of it, they'd still have a nice time.'

The castle sat on the coast overlooking the beautiful Cornish sea. Lights glowed from the windows and turrets as the party continued into the night.

The driveway leading up to the castle was bordered by immaculately cut lawns, trees and bushes, and the massive front doors were open in welcoming to guests. A wide staircase lead to the upper floors and added a sense of drama to the entrance and reception.

Roman Penhaligan had inherited the castle, and with its grand main hall for functions it had become popular for weddings and other celebratory events. He was around the same age and height as Jake Wolfe. A gorgeous looking man with blond hair and grey eyes. He wore a grey dinner suit, white shirt and silk cravat, and had an elegant manner.

The main hall was set with long tables along the sides. Other tables were situated around the edges of the dance floor. White linen, silverware and chandeliers added to the grandeur. The huge fireplace was lit, and everything sparkled with fairy lights and Christmas decorations.

Woolley sat at a table with Mrs Lemon, Karen and Sharky.

'It's getting late,' said Woolley. 'I don't think Jake's going to turn up for the party.'

'Maybe Daisy isn't back yet from London,' Sharky suggested.

Woolley nodded. 'Probably. I don't want to phone Jake again in case he's either busy with his work or with Daisy.'

'If he was going to be here, he'd have arrived by now,' said Mrs Lemon.

Roman Penhaligan smiled as he approached their table. 'Enjoying your evening?'

'We're having a great time,' Woolley confirmed, as did the others.

'I expected Jake Wolfe would be here,' Roman commented. 'But I've heard he's getting ready to head to New York for the launch of his new book.'

'He is,' said Woolley. 'But he did intend coming to the party, but we think Daisy got held up in London with a meeting with Franklin.'

'Ah, well, maybe another time.' Roman walked away to talk to other guests.

Sharky excused himself. 'I want a quick word with Roman about his, eh, cake order. I'll be back in a jiffy.'

Karen sipped her glass of wine and smiled happily as Sharky went to talk to Roman.

A cheerful Christmas song started playing. Woolley stood up and offered his hand to Mrs Lemon. 'Would you like to dance?'

She smiled as she accompanied him on to the dance floor and waltzed around the room.

Sharky finished his chat with Roman and then went back over to Karen, taking her hand and leading her on to the dance floor too.

A huge Christmas tree stood in the corner of the main hall, lit with fairy lights and decorated with baubles. The whole room was beautifully decorated and the lights dimmed as couples took to the floor for a romantic last dance having enjoyed the party night at the castle.

Jake nodded awake, realising he'd fallen asleep at this desk. His first instinct was to glance out the study window. The cottage was in darkness.

He checked the time. The party would be finishing by now.

And still no sign of Daisy.

Worried, he went to phone her, but at that moment he saw her car pull up outside the cottage. Relieved, he clicked the phone off, threw his jacket on and hurried down the hill to see her.

The Christmas tree in the window suddenly lit up as he was halfway down, giving him a sense of relief. She must be okay if she'd turned the fairy lights on. The meeting must've run quite late. That was all.

Daisy eased her shoulders from the long drive and put the kettle on for a cup of tea.

She'd noticed the lights were on in Jake's study, indicating he was working late. Often she'd just go to bed and talk to him in the morning rather than disturb his workflow. He hadn't called her, so she had to assume things were okay, and it was so late now. It would be better to talk to him in the morning.

The knock on the front door startled her. She peered out and saw Jake standing there, and her heart lifted at the thought that he'd come down to see her when she'd got back.

She opened the door and beamed a smile at him.

'I wanted to see you were okay,' he said, pulling her close, clearly pleased to see her.

'Sorry, I didn't leave London until late. I was at my flat. Archie had thrown at party.'

'At your flat?' He sounded surprised.

The kettle clicked off. 'I'm making tea. Do you want a cuppa?'

This time Jake came in and followed her through to the kitchen while she made the tea and explained about Archie.

'A double–bill of Christmas films?' Jake could understand the temptation.

'That was in the afternoon. Then he ordered pizza and ice cream for everyone, including his new girlfriend. They seem to be getting along nicely. The party continued into the evening. I eventually left them all to it, but it made me rather late.'

They took their tea through to the lounge and sat by the glow of the Christmas tree. She sat on one of the comfy chairs and he took his jacket off and sat on the sofa.

Daisy cupped her mug of tea. 'What have you been up to?'

CHAPTER FIVE

Cosy Night at the Cottage

'A Christmas party at the castle!' Daisy exclaimed. 'If I'd known, I would've come back in time for that.' She could've enjoyed the matinees at her flat with Archie and the others and then left London to drive to Cornwall to go to the castle's Christmas party. A night out dancing with Jake would've been great and she imagined the castle all done up for Christmas. She could've worn one of the new dresses she'd bought too.

Jake's intense blue eyes looked at her. 'I wanted to surprise you.' He sometimes thought he wasn't dynamic enough when it came to dating. Surprising Daisy seemed like a good idea at the time. Now he wished he could rewind the day and tell her what he'd planned. 'You're usually back around nine. I didn't expect you to be partying at your flat.' It was a statement, not an accusation.

'Neither did I. I've never had a party in my flat.' When she'd moved in, she hadn't considered having a party. She'd been busy working on her illustrations when she'd arrived there, and setting up her drawing desk and an area where she could get on with her artwork had taken priority. 'I only popped in to check on it, thinking it would be cold and dull. Empty of energy, full of thoughts of the past.'

Jake looked deep into his cup. 'I should've told you. I just pictured surprising you, whisking you off to the party. I know you've got a couple of glitzy dresses you could've worn. When you first arrived in Cornwall you said you'd thrown the contents of your wardrobe into your car and that your dresses were sort of snazzy, suitable for the London party scene, rather than a night having a business dinner with me at my house.'

She smiled at the memory. 'Cocktail dresses.' When he'd invited her to his house for dinner to discuss business, she realised she'd nothing suitable to wear. She hadn't wanted to go casually dressed, and then not wanting to be late, she'd thrown on one of her gorgeous sequin cocktail dresses. A midnight blue. Less vibrant than the red sequin dress she owned. Or the gold or silver. Looking back, she definitely had a thing for sparkly dresses. And having bought another two earlier in the day, she still did.

Jake nodded and smiled too, remembering Daisy turning up for dinner in a dress that looked like a midnight sky scattered with stars. 'That blue sequin cocktail dress is burned happily into my memory forever.'

'It was totally inappropriate.'

'Much to my delight.'

Daisy laughed.

'And the red sequin one you wore to the party at my house was a dazzler,' he added. 'You looked gorgeous. You took my breath away. I've heard people say that, but you really did. Then I acted like a complete fool because I was so thrown by your beauty.'

She blushed at the bombardment of compliments. 'That dress had more sparkle than my Christmas tree.' She glanced at the tree aglow in the window.

'No competition. I was dazzled. I still am.' He paused and looked at her. 'I know I haven't expressed this properly recently, but it doesn't mean that I don't love you as much as ever.'

Her heart melted hearing him say this. 'I understand, Jake. I feel the same. It's like I can see Christmas coming at us at speed. It's all around us. Everyone is gearing up for the festivities, doing their gift shopping, wrapping presents and putting them under the Christmas trees.' She paused. 'And here we are burning through the days and nights, getting ready to leave for New York.' She shook her head. 'I think that's why I hid for a few hours in my flat in London with Archie and a bunch of strangers, who are now new friends. A pocket of strange normality in our crazy circumstances.'

'I'm glad you did, despite missing the party at the castle.' He'd heard how happy she was telling him what had happened in London.

She tipped her hand against her brow. 'I'm up to here in hot chocolate, pizza, ice cream and cheese vol–au–vents.'

He laughed. 'I could've done with share of that. I've barely eaten anything all day. I assumed I'd have plenty to eat at the castle. You know what Roman's banquets are like.'

She did. 'I still remember the one we went to in the summer.' The banquet had been lavish.

'Woolley was there tonight with Mrs Lemon. Sharky told me he was taking Karen.'

'I'm sure we'll hear all about the party tomorrow.'

'Woolley phoned me from the castle to check if I was turning up, but I told him you weren't back from London.' He shrugged his broad shoulders. 'I kept looking for your Christmas tree lights to come on while I worked in my study. Then I fell asleep at my desk.'

The thought that he'd been watching for her coming home warmed her heart. 'You must be exhausted.'

'No more than you. You're the one that drove to London and back. How did the meeting with Franklin go?'

'It went well. He wants me to work on a new vintage floral book. It'll highlight floral designs in fashion and home decor. I'm really interested in the fashion aspect of it, delving into the various styles that were popular in the past — and fabrics for clothing and home furnishings. Special events too, like weddings, so I'll illustrate bouquets and garlands as well as fashion.'

'That sounds fascinating.'

'I'm quite excited about it.'

'When will you start work on the designs?'

'I already have. I gave him some illustrations I sketched last night and he likes them, so I'll work on the book before we leave for New York and take a sketch pad with me to illustrate while we're away,' she explained. 'We were finished the meeting before lunch, and he liked the glass paper weight I gave him for Christmas.'

Jake frowned.

'You were busy when I tried to show it to you. I bought it from the local craft shop.' She explained the details, including Franklin giving her shopping vouchers.

'I'm surprised you're home yet. From what you've told me, when you go clothes shopping in London sometimes you're not seen for days.'

She swiped at him playfully. 'That's not true. Well, maybe a bit. Sort of, okay. But I was a total whirlwind when I hit the shopping mall today.'

'Then straight to your flat where you succumbed to Archie's movie matinee.'

Daisy looked guilty. 'Not quite.'

'What do you mean?'

'I eh...I went to the park first. The one where I used to love drawing flowers. It's near Franklin's company. I wanted to look at it before checking in on my flat.'

'And...?'

She took a deep breath. 'I met Sebastian.' Even the mention of his name sounded wrong in the cosiness of the cottage. Nothing about her ex–boyfriend belonged where her life was now.

And yet...she needed to tell Jake that she'd spoken to her ex. He might find out through the local gossip. Sebastian would mention to Franklin that he'd met her, and Franklin would tell Mrs Lemon when she wangled the latest news from him during one of their regular phone calls. Although Mrs Lemon didn't need to keep an eye on the cottage while Daisy was living there, their long established habit of updating each other had continued. Franklin still paid Mrs Lemon for things he needed done in Cornwall, and news was passed back and forth.

'Sebastian was in the park?' Jake questioned, hating the stab of jealousy that invariable shot through his heart at the mention of the twister's name.

'Yes. Sebastian always knows where to find me.' It was a horrible truth in a complicated world.

Jake didn't doubt it. The rat had driven down to Cornwall in the summertime and had the audacity to try and win Daisy back. That scenario hadn't worked out well for his rival, but that didn't make it any less annoying.

'What did he want? Did he upset you?'

Daisy carefully selected the latter question to answer. Telling him that Sebastian suggested they could get married at Christmas wasn't something she could wrap prettily. No, that remark had to stay tucked in her back pocket, possibly forever. And she definitely didn't want it to jar Jake into action, forcing him to ask her to get engaged. Sebastian had upturned so much of her life. She was determined not to let him ruin any chance of a genuine proposal from Jake. When he was ready.

'He didn't upset me,' she began, 'but seeing him there...it rattled me. The park was frosted and looked so lovely. I just wanted a few minutes to...I don't know. Sebastian suggested it was *nostalgia*.'

'Nostalgia?' Jake's heart jarred. 'You're not having second thoughts about leaving London to live here in Cornwall?'

'No, not at all. I love living here. The cottage is perfect. Cornwall is beautiful and although I've been a city dweller all my life, I think at heart I'm more of a small coastal town type. That's why I suppose I sound ungrateful about our trip to New York. It's a city, and I would've preferred Christmas here, just you and me, and the friends I've made here.'

She put her cup down on the table and looked uneasy.

'What else did Sebastian say?' He steeled himself for her reply. Nothing Sebastian ever said was trustworthy. He was a prize manipulator.

Don't tell him about the accusations. It was none of Sebastian's business about Jake not being the marrying kind. She didn't believe this anyway. Sebastian had always been adept at dropping niggling doubts into her mind.

Jake waited on a reply.

She shuffled the cards of truth and played a mild hand. 'He said that Franklin had promoted him over Celeste.'

'Franklin promoted Sebastian instead of his daughter?' He sounded surprised and then rethought this. 'Mind you, I wouldn't trust my business affairs to Celeste. Sebastian's a twister, but he seems to be good at his job.'

'I think that's what it came down to.'

Jake was inclined to accept this.

She took a deep breath. 'Anyway, let's not get upset about Sebastian. I left the park, refused to take a lift from him, and would have even if I didn't have my own car.'

He noticed the shopping bags from London where she'd left them. 'You seem to have quite a haul of fashion shopping.'

'The shops had lots of festive bargains. I do enjoy shopping in the city.' She looked thoughtful. 'We've never actually had a day out together in London. You've had meetings with your publisher and agent, and I've met up with Franklin. But we've never been there together.'

He realised this was true. 'That's something else we need to rectify when we get back from New York.'

And there it was, the block again on everything until the New Year.

She sighed wearily and nodded. 'Christmas will be over by then. It would've been nice to enjoy London during the festive season.'

'We could schedule a day soon, before we leave,' he suggested, though neither of them thought this was practical.

She planned to make a start on the drawings for the vintage book. He had work to do.

He clasped her hand and pulled her over to sit on the sofa beside him. A cosy blanket was on the back of the sofa and he wrapped it around them.

Daisy snuggled into him and gazed at the lights on the Christmas tree.

His strong arms wrapped around her, more comforting than the blanket.

Leaning her head on his shoulder she relaxed and enjoyed the glow of the tree.

The fairy lights illuminated part of the garden outside the window. 'The garden seems magical covered in frost.' She had a mind to sketch and paint it.

'I love how my garden looks in winter. It's like something out of a frosted fantasy. I'm guilty of opening the kitchen door and letting the frosty air in, either in the quiet of the late night or early in the morning when everything is crisp and cold.'

'Perfect for snuggling.' Daisy leaned against him.

'A blustery walk along the shore in winter feels wonderful too.'

'We should do that.' They'd enjoyed days down the shore in the summer. The coast was beautiful with a long sweeping bay. The views along the coastline were lovely during the summertime and she pictured they'd look quite dramatic in winter. She wanted to experience all the seasons here with Jake.

He squeezed her tight, reassuring her that they would. 'The sea is inviting in the summer, but there's something about the coast during the winter that's so invigorating.'

'Say we'll go for brisk walks together along the coast, even if it's raining.'

He smiled at her, and then kissed her. 'I promise. And if it's pouring, you can wrap up in the rainwear that's hanging in the hall cupboard. Including the Wellington boots.'

She nodded firmly. 'Snug as a bug.'

He held her close and for a moment they both relaxed and gazed at the Christmas tree.

The colourful lights cast a warm glow in the lounge, reflecting on the white walls and making the cottage feel like home. Daisy loved staying there during the summer and the autumn, but this was the homeliest she'd ever felt it. Maybe it was because it was Christmastime, or that Jake was there with her. And for a moment she sensed this is what their life would be like if they became a permanent couple. Evenings together after working throughout the day, having dinner together and then snuggling up on the sofa. But of course, the cottage wouldn't be their home. Jake's house would be where they'd live. And she loved his house, so either way, she'd be happy just being with Jake and having cosy times together like this.

'This is the most relaxed I've felt in weeks,' he said, feeling the tensions of the day fade.

Daisy agreed. 'It's been a whirlwind of a time. Summer doesn't seem long ago. Autumn was a blur of activity and now suddenly it's December, and you're busier than ever.'

'And you've a new vintage floral book that Franklin wants you to work on.'

'Yes. I've lots of flowers to illustrate for it. I thought I'd start with roses, violets, lavender and pansies. Some of the artwork will be adapted to make embroidery patterns that will be included in the book.'

'I found photos I took a few years ago of the flowers in my garden. You can use them for reference if you want. I have the flowers you mentioned and loads of others from different seasons. Everything from snowdrops and primroses to sunflowers and Christmas roses. I could email them to you.'

'That would be great.'

Jake's garden was old–fashioned, natural but not untamed, with flowers, herbs and greenery and a view of the glistening sea in the distance from its location on the top of the hill. The original style, landscaped many years ago, was unchanged. A stone path led to a small swimming pool that was more or less hidden in a niche, surrounded by greenery in the warmer months, and a stark beauty in winter. Holly, ivy and evergreens created shades of green against the frosted plants and neutral tones. Daisy loved the garden at Jake's house, never having owned a garden in London. A patch of wildflowers provided wonderful contrast to the cultivated flora, and she'd painted both spectrums sitting in his garden during the summertime.

'Are you hungry?' she said, realising he probably was. 'If you've had very little to eat all day, do you want me to make you tea and toast?'

'That sounds tasty. But let's sit here for a little longer.'

She was happy to do this, but as he leaned close to kiss her, his phone rang interrupting the moment.

He checked the caller and sighed. 'I have to take this. It's New York.'

Daisy frowned. 'Phoning so late at night?'

'I told them I worked late most nights, and not to bother about the time difference. To call if they needed to talk to me.'

Daisy got up and went through to the kitchen while Jake spoke to the publisher.

She filled the kettle for tea and switched the grill on to make toast.

The kitchen always felt cosy and she liked the vintage styling of it mixed with the new cooker and other electrical appliances. But the overall look of the kitchen was old–fashioned.

She put slices of bread under the grill and set up the cups for the tea.

Jake's voice filtered through to the kitchen...

'Yes, I got the list of questions you emailed earlier. I'll make sure I have succinct answers to all of them,' Jake assured Valerie. He'd been dealing with two or three staff in the publisher's New York office, including Valerie. She dealt with the publicity and marketing side of Jake's book. Valerie was in her early thirties and had several years experience working for the company on non–fiction titles. They'd spoken numerous times on the phone and seemed to have developed an easy rapport.

Efficient and forthright, Valerie had plenty of contacts in the media to secure interviews for Jake to promote his book.

Jake was still talking to Valerie as Daisy carried through a tray with tea and hot buttered wholemeal toast.

She put it down on the table.

Jake reached for a slice while it was still hot and took a bite while listening to Valerie telling him what she wanted him to do on one of the forthcoming phone interviews. He'd agreed to chat to a magazine about his book, and she'd arranged for the features editor of the magazine to phone Jake the following afternoon.

'We'll make the magazine's deadline for their next issue if you do the interview tomorrow,' Valerie told Jake in her classy New York accent. 'I've given them a press release so they're up to speed on what you're doing, and they're keen to feature your new book in their magazine. They have photos of you and the book cover and inside spreads of a couple of the pages. But they're looking for quotes from you and answers to the relevant questions. It's all on the list.'

Jake sipped his tea to wash down the mouthful of toast. 'I'll have the answers prepared.'

'Great. I'll call ten minutes before they do to go over the relevant details,' said Valerie.

The call finished with Jake saying he was looking forward to the interview.

He put his phone away in his pocket and took another bite of toast.

'Thanks for making this,' he mumbled.

Daisy had decided to forgo the toast as she was still topped up on everything she'd eaten at the flat. But she sipped her tea and chatted to Jake about the interview.

'What type of questions have they lined up for you?'

He reached into his jacket pocket. He'd put his jacket on the back of the sofa. A folded sheet of paper was printed with the questions. He handed it to Daisy.

She read the questions.

'Test me,' Jake said to her, helping himself to another slice of toast.

'Okay. What are the ingredients in your cure for love potion?'

'They're a secret. Like any special recipe, the ingredients are a well kept secret. I use a blend of herbal essences to create the mixture. It includes a special ingredient, a very rare sea plant that's found off the Cornish coast. I dive for it myself. Sometimes I find it, sometimes not.'

'Is it true that you have bottles of mixtures in your study that include jealousy and spite?'

Jake smiled. 'I do. The remedy is created to deal with the emotions involved when someone is heartbroken. To help ease those emotions, make them less intense so you can start to feel better.'

'Can the cure be used to make someone fall in love?'

'No. It doesn't make anyone fall in love. It's a cure for lovesickness. Unrequited love.'

'Who was the last person you tested it on?'

Jake gazed right at Daisy as he replied. 'A broken hearted young woman walked into my health food shop in the summer. She'd seen the notice in the front window that I offered natural remedies for a broken heart. But she was very independent and had been hurt by her two–timing boyfriend, and didn't want me interfering with her emotions. At first. Later, she drank the remedy, a few sips.'

'Did it work?'

'Yes, it made her feel better, but it's not a remedy for treachery. I've improved it even more since then.'

Daisy put the paper down and asked her own question teasingly. 'What happened to the woman?'

Jake pulled her close. 'I fell in love with her.' He kissed her gently and then with passion.

His kisses warmed her heart. She sighed as she gazed deep into his eyes. 'And she fell in love with him.'

He gently brushed a stray strand of her blonde hair back from her face. 'So I'd like to think that I was her true cure for love.'

'I believe he was,' she murmured.

Jake wrapped the blanket around them and they snuggled on the sofa for a few moments before continuing with the interview list.

Daisy picked up the paper and read the last few questions. 'You're a herbalist. Will your remedy ever be produced and made available in your shops?'

'Hopefully one day, but for the moment it's still a work in progress, though it does seem to work quite well for some people. The book explains the work I've done to create and perfect the recipe.'

Daisy folded the paper and tucked it back in his jacket pocket. 'I think you'll do great with the interview.'

'Will you be there when they phone? They might want to speak to you, ask about your illustrations. Would you be able to give them reasonable answers?'

'I think so.' She sat up. 'But test me. Ask me some questions.'

Jake plucked the questions out of thin air, surmising what she could be asked during any interviews. He was aware that he would be the main focus, but there was every chance she'd be involved.

'What type of illustrations did you design for the book?'

'Floral watercolours and ink illustrations. Flowers, plants and herbs that Jake uses for his remedy.'

'Watercolours? Are you a watercolour artist?'

'I'm a botanical illustrator and work in watercolours, acrylics and pen and ink,' she said.

Jake nodded approvingly. 'You're better at this than me, Daisy.'

'That's not true. You're the herbal expert.'

'The book looks wonderful due to your lovely artwork. The watercolours are gorgeous and they're featured on the cover of the book.'

Daisy blushed. 'I worked closely with you to make sure the artwork matched the high level of your editorial.'

Jake looked deep into her eyes. 'You wouldn't ever take the cure for love now, would you?'

'No. If I was unfortunately broken hearted again, I'd try Woolley's method. The one he said he used when Mrs Lemon fell out with him.'

Jake was genuinely interested. 'What's his remedy?'

'An old–fashioned cure — whisky and a pork pie.'

Jake laughed.

CHAPTER SIX

Vintage Floral Designs

Jake woke up after two in the morning realising he'd fallen asleep on the sofa. Daisy was tucked into him with her head on his chest and snoozing contentedly wrapped in his arms with the blanket around them.

He bit his lip. Should he wake her? As tempting as it was to stay where they were, he nudged her gently.

'Daisy,' he said softly. 'Wake up.'

She jolted awake, staring like a startled rabbit, wondering for a moment where she was and then realised she'd nuzzled into Jake and fallen sound asleep.

'What time is it?' she said, glancing out the window at the darkness, but recalling how it had looked like that early in the morning when she'd set off for London. It could be late bedtime or early breakfast. She'd no idea.

'After two.' He tried not to sound abrupt as she'd obviously been startled out of her slumber.

'In the morning?' She needed clarification. And a cup of tea. The need for a cuppa confused her. It felt more like breakfast time in the heart of December when the daylight was sandwiched between dark mornings and early twilights.

'Yes, we fell asleep. I wasn't sure whether to wake you or not. You looked so comfy.'

Daisy eased the crick in her neck and kept her snippy comment to disagree with him to herself.

She unravelled herself from the blanket, and Jake, and stood up.

He stood up too, towering over her as she tried to decide whether to invite him to stay or cast him out into the cold night.

Jake took the decision out of her hands. 'I'd better be going and let you get to bed for some proper sleep.'

Daisy didn't argue. This seemed like the optimum decision. Though in hindsight she might kick herself for missing the chance to have Jake sleepover at the cottage.

She'd stayed a few times at his house, but they'd both agreed they'd rather not move in with each other. Not yet. And then all the work, their hectic schedules, especially Jake's new book, had taken over and time had marched on until here they were, snoozing on the sofa. Unintentionally. Both exhausted from the events of the day.

Jake put his jacket on and walked through to the hall.

Daisy followed him. His broad shoulders always seemed to fill the narrow hallway and at six feet, he almost had to dip his head to step out from the front door into the icy cold night.

The air blew in, turning the warmth of the cottage chilly in moments.

Daisy hugged her arms around herself and shivered.

'Close the door. Keep the heat in. Stay warm. I'll see you in the morning.' He kissed her quickly and then hurried away.

Daisy didn't do as he'd suggested. Arms folded across her chest for futile warmth, she watched him walk away.

He must've sensed her watching him, because he turned and waved before heading up the hill.

She waved back, and then as his shadowy figure merged with the night, she went inside and closed the door to an evening she'd never forget. An evening that started with partying at her flat in London, and ended in the cottage in Cornwall with Jake. Somewhere in the middle, she'd missed the chance to party at the castle, but the disappointment of that had worn off. A few hours cosy time with Jake outshone any party.

As she tidied away the tea and toast dishes and carried them through to the kitchen, a message came through on her phone from Jake.

Have elevenses with me in the morning. I'll show you the flower photos before I email them to you.

I'll bring scones. And jam.

I have bramble jam. Maybe even strawberry. But bring the scones. And yourself.

See you in the morning.

She clicked the phone off and then got ready for bed.

Climbing in and snuggling under the covers, she rewound the exciting events of the day. She got to the encounter in the park with Sebastian before she fell asleep.

Dreaming about Sebastian set Daisy's nerves on edge the next morning.

She blamed the thoughts she'd had before drifting off to sleep. Never think about Sebastian when you're in bed and intending to have a good night's sleep, because you won't. You'll dream about him and all the things he didn't do, and almost managed, and the things the twister did as well.

Confusing herself, she got tidied up, put on her new pink jumper, jeans, boots and her cosy red coat and headed out to the main street to buy scones.

The cobbled streets shone with frost in the bright morning light, and she breathed in the fresh air, feeling it reviving her senses which had felt a bit scattered from a night dreaming about Sebastian. Like all her dreams, it had seemed so real.

In the cold light of day she could still feel Sebastian's arms around her, trying to persuade her to forgive him. He'd tried to put an engagement ring on her finger and in the dream they'd become engaged at Christmas.

This wasn't a dream she told herself as she headed for Sharky's bakery shop. This was a nightmare. Engaged to Sebastian? Never, ever. No way.

There was a queue at the bakery, with customers buying up fresh bread, rolls, scones and cakes.

She waited. Still mulling over the dream. The ring had sparkled exaggeratedly with diamonds. Three diamonds in a row. All big and sparkling and expensive.

But she knew what Sebastian could do with his ring. The two–timing traitor couldn't buy his way back into her heart even with all those glittering carats.

The frown on her brow and vehement expression was evident as Sharky said to her, 'What can I get for you this morning? Something to take away whatever is irking you?'

Daisy jarred out of her deep thoughts and looked over the counter at Sharky's smiling face.

'Sorry. A rough night.'

'I heard you and Jake had a pyjama party for two.'

'We did not,' she refuted strongly. 'Who said that? Mrs Lemon?'

Sharky pressed his lips together.

'We fell asleep on the sofa rehearsing for his interview today with a magazine from New York. They're interviewing him over the phone this afternoon.'

'Some of that is true. Some is not. But okay, what can I tempt you with? Fresh baked bread? Cream cake? Sticky buns?'

'Scones.'

'Fruit, buttermilk, cheesy or Christmas recipe?'

'What's in the Christmas recipe?'

'Imagine fruit scones, only with a hint of mincemeat — more raisins, sultanas, spices. Christmassy.' He gestured to them on a tray in the display.

'Those look tasty. I'll have two of those and two buttermilk scones.'

Sharky bagged the scones. 'Jake likes my treacle scones too. I'll pop a couple in for good measure for your elevenses.'

Daisy looked at him.

'What?' Sharky shrugged and tried to look innocent, but he'd heard the tittle–tattle about Daisy and Jake.

If she hadn't been so jarred by dreaming about her ex–boyfriend, maybe she'd have been snippy about her private life being gossip fodder. Instead, she smiled tightly and paid for the scones.

'Did you enjoy the party at the castle last night?' she said to Sharky as he handed her the bag of scones.

'We had a great time. Sorry you missed it, but Woolley said you'd been held up with work in London.'

'Yes.' She didn't elaborate. No doubt the nitty–gritty details of her trip to London would circulate around the town. It would save her explaining.

'Thanks for the extra treacle scones,' she said. He hadn't charged her for them.

'Enjoy.'

Daisy left the bakery shop and stood for a moment in the main street, taking in the pretty decorations that sparkled in the winter sunlight. Shop windows had their trees lit up with twinkle lights, and the atmosphere was cheery and Christmassy.

Woolley came out of the health food shop and hurried over to Daisy.

He always dressed in tweeds and twills, and as he made a speedy beeline for her, she wondered if there was something wrong.

'Ring alert!' Woolley told her. 'Are you going into the health food shop?'

'Not especially. Should I?'

'No. I saw you from the window. I thought that you often pop into the health food shop after buying stuff from the bakery,' Woolley explained.

'Does the ring alert have anything to do with Karen?'

'Yes, she's had her ring buffed up. Apparently the ruby and diamonds sparkle brighter than the sunlight now.'

'Thanks for the heads up.'

'Personally, I don't see any difference. But she's flashing it at customers and you know how she loves to let you admire her ring.'

Daisy laughed, feeling the tension in her face ease. The first real smile of the day.

'Wait until Mrs Lemon parades her sparkler.' Daisy kept her voice down. 'Karen is going to have some tough competition.'

'If she says yes to my proposal.' Woolley sounded unsure.

'She will. No way she'll resist you and that dazzling diamond ring.'

Her comment bolstered Woolley's confidence. 'I was thinking of giving it to her before Christmas.'

Daisy giggled.

'The ring,' Woolley clarified, trying not to laugh. 'It's burning a hole in my pocket trying to keep it to myself. Do you think I should ask her now or wait until Christmas Day?'

'Tricky one. Your plan for roses, champagne, chocolates and a proposal on Christmas morning sounded so romantic. But...maybe you could both enjoy being engaged now while you're looking forward to Christmas Day.'

'That's what I've been thinking. After Christmas things go a bit quiet, or as quiet as it gets around here, which isn't much.'

'Well then...?'

'I could still do the flowers, champagne and chocolates this evening, couldn't I?'

'Yes. Were you planning to see Mrs Lemon this evening?'

'We get together most nights. She was lining up a night watching two full episodes of a telly series we both like. Karen will be round at Sharky's house as usual. He cooks dinner for them most nights. We have dinner by ourselves.'

'It sounds like an ideal evening, just the two of you.'

Woolley looked determined. 'I'm doing it. Thanks for the encouragement, Daisy. Enjoy your scones with Jake.' And off he scurried along to the grocery shop to buy the champagne and chocolates.

'I heard you were in London,' a man's voice said over Daisy's shoulder as she waved to Woolley.

She looked round and there was Roman Penhaligan. His blond hair shone like burnished gold in the wintry sunlight. He wore a classy suit and equally classy winter jacket. Subtle money, but wealth nonetheless.

'Yes, I didn't know about your party or I'd have made an effort to be back for it. I was in London dealing with my publisher.'

'Still working for Franklin?'

'Yes. I'm about to start a new book. Vintage floral designs.'

His attractive grey eyes sparked with interest. 'I'd buy that. The vintage florals at the castle, on the furnishings, carpets, curtains and bed covers are my favourites. You're welcome to drop by if you need to see any authentic patterns.'

'I might pop along for a snoop around.'

'Make sure it's lunchtime. We'll have lunch and catch up on what we've both been doing lately. I hear you're off to New York for Christmas.'

'I am. With Jake, to promote his new book.'

'The Cure For Love.'

'Yes.'

'I'd definitely take the remedy, if I needed it.'

Daisy tactfully didn't mention Roman's ex–girlfriend, Daphne. Apparently, the love of his life.

'I could've done with it when Daphne and I split up for the last time fairly recently. But I seem to have gotten over her easier than the first time. Practise I suppose.'

'Maturity and knowing that she's not the one for you.'

'No, she's not.'

'Daphne didn't like castles.'

'A bit of a major stumbling block.' He smiled wryly.

'Just a bit, considering you own and live in one of the most beautiful castles I've seen.'

'Thank you, Daisy.'

'But I believe that Daphne preferred London.'

'She did. Is it a wrench for you to live in a small, coastal town having been a Londoner yourself?'

'Not at all. The complete opposite. I don't miss the city. I think I've found my perfect niche, here in Cornwall.'

'With Jake Wolfe.'

'Yes.'

There was a hesitation in him, and she sensed he wanted to comment, as others had, on her relationship status with Jake, but politely kept his remarks to himself.

Daisy filled the awkward pause. 'Is business at the castle going well?'

'It is, especially the wedding events that I've been developing. The castle's function facilities for weddings are almost fully booked until the spring.'

'That's excellent. I've heard that couples are coming from far and wide to hold their wedding receptions at your castle.'

'They are. And a few local couples too. One was booked last night during the party.'

'A local couple? Is it a secret?'

'Top secret. The gentleman in question isn't sure if his bride–to–be would like this. I'm sure the gossip will circulate fairly soon. No secrets for long in our world.'

'Too true.'

'Well, I won't keep you standing here in the cold any longer, Daisy. But remember, drop by for lunch and I'll let you see the vintage designs at the castle.'

'I'll do that.'

Giving her a polite nod, Roman walked away to get on with his business.

Daisy headed away from the main street and started to walk up the hill to Jake's house. The wind whipped up from the sea the higher up she ventured, but she welcomed it, hoping it would blow the last remnants of her dreams of Sebastian away.

Jake's house stood on its own, and allowed him to get on with his work without constant interruption to his studies. The main visitors were Woolley and Mrs Lemon, and now Daisy herself.

Not one Christmas decoration or hint of festive sparkle adorned the house, but as always, she admired the traditional structure of it perched high on the hill with a garden surrounding it. Jake's fortress.

His study overlooked the main view of the town and coastline, and she saw a light shining inside, his desk lamp, indicating that Jake was hard at work, as usual.

Thoughts of Sebastian were mixed with her encounter with Roman Penhaligan. Roman definitely had loved Daphne, but there had been moments earlier in the summertime when he'd hinted heavily that he could've turned his attentions to Daisy, if she'd been interested.

Daisy thought Roman was a fine looking man, and she actually liked him, as a friend, but that spark of attraction hadn't ignited and so friends they had remained, and would continue to do so. Maybe one day Daphne would decide she did like castles after all, or Roman would find someone else to love who appreciated living in a magnificent castle.

But Daisy did wonder about the local couple Roman hinted at. Had Woolley made tentative enquires about hiring the castle? Woolley had mentioned about not wanting to wait, if Mrs Lemon accepted his proposal, and would marry her in the New Year. Had Woolley made a wedding booking pending Mrs Lemon's response to his proposal?

Daisy was still pondering this as she knocked on the front door and then walked into the house knowing she was expected.

'It's me,' she called through to Jake's study. 'I've brought scones. I'll take them through to the kitchen.'

'Great,' Jake called back to her.

In the kitchen, Daisy shrugged her coat off, hung it on the back of a chair, and then filled the kettle for tea and set up plates for the scones.

Jake came wandering through, smartly dressed as always, and sexy handsome.

He leaned on the kitchen doorway and watched her prepare the scones. He thought the pink jumper she was wearing was new, but as he wasn't sure he didn't want to remark and get it wrong.

'You look lovely,' he told her.

She smiled over at him. 'New jumper. I bought the blue one I wore yesterday and this pink one from the local fashion shop.'

'Very nice. Pink suits you, as did the blue.'

'Have you been working hard?' She sensed tiredness and tension in him, even though he was clean shaven and well dressed in his light blue shirt, silk tie, waistcoat and dark trousers, both part of a suit. Ever the businessman, even in the relaxed atmosphere of his own home.

'I've been trying to read through my notes from the past couple of years to find nuggets of interest for the interview.'

'Find any?'

'One or two, though I don't know how to summarise their inclusion in the remedy without giving away my secret processes.'

'Can I help? Act as a sounding board?'

'Yes, but we'll have our elevenses first.'

'Okay.' Daisy popped the teabags in the ceramic teapot ready to make the tea when the water boiled.

Jake's kitchen was bigger than the one in her cottage, but the old–fashioned quality of the styling mixed with modern appliances was similar. A sturdy wooden table and chairs sat in the middle of the kitchen. They'd had many a meal there, just the two of them. Jake wasn't a whiz in the kitchen. And that was putting it nicely. He was a master at mixing potions, but a bit of a walking disaster in his own kitchen.

Daisy didn't mind taking charge of the culinary tasks when she visited him, and she still smiled at his failed attempt to impress her with his cooking not long after they'd first met. Sharky had supplied the food via the kitchen window at the back of the house. But she'd found it funny, endearing, and was flattered that Jake had tried so hard to impress her.

Now it was almost taken as stat that she'd take charge in his kitchen, though he was always willing to help.

Mrs Lemon was Jake's part–time housekeeper, and he tried to keep a tidy house himself whenever he could. She often dropped off some home cooking for him too — soups, stews, things he could heat and eat easily.

'Did you see Woolley today?' he said.

'Yes, in the main street this morning. Why?'

'Did he seem a bit...hyper and distracted to you?'

'No,' she lied, almost letting slip about the engagement.

Jake took her at her word. 'He phoned about ten minutes ago.'

'What did he want?' She wondered if Woolley had hinted about the proposal.

'I have no idea. He waffled about everything and nothing. But he sounded happy, if hyper.'

'The excitement of the Christmas season kicking in,' she suggested.

Jake walked over to the table. 'Probably.'

Daisy brushed aside further discussion about Woolley and showed him the selection of scones. 'I bought a selection of scones, including treacle scones. Sharky said you like them.'

'I do. And his new Christmas scones, whatever is in them.'

'Extra raisins, sultanas, citrus peel and spices.' She put one of those on his plate too.

'They look tasty. I'll make the tea.'

'I'll get the jam.' She opened the cupboard and lifted out a jar of bramble jam.

Jake circled back to his conversation with his uncle. 'Woolley's up to something.' Jake poured the tea.

'Christmas shopping secrets.'

'Yes, maybe he's bought me something and wants to keep it a secret,' he surmised.

Near enough, she thought to herself, spreading bramble jam on two Christmas scones and on an extra treacle scone for Jake. She kept the other scones in the bag, wrapping it tight to keep them fresh for later.

They sat down at the kitchen table to enjoy their tea and scones. The scent of the spicy Christmas scones filled the air as did the sweet–tangy aroma of the bramble jam.

Daisy steered the conversation away from the topic of Woolley. 'Franklin emailed more ideas for the vintage book including specific flowers he wants me to include.'

'I'll show you the photos of the flowers from my garden after we've had our tea.'

'I brought my sketch pad.' Just in case. It was in her bag along with pencils and pens. She rarely went anywhere without a pad to scribble ideas and designs on.

Jake nodded, biting into one of the scones and mumbling that it was delicious.

Daisy tucked into her scone too.

They finished eating and took their tea through to the study. Jake had his computer on his desk and his laptop set up on a table showing the flower photos.

He gestured to the laptop. 'I thought you could have a scroll through these and see if there's any that are of use to you.'

Daisy looked at the pictures. 'These are great.' She took her sketch pad out of her bag and sat down at the table. 'But first, can I help you summarise your answers for the interview.'

Jake had a pile of notes on his desk. He rummaged through them and read out details of the various herbs he'd used to create his remedy.

Daisy listened to everything he said.

'I don't want to give away my secret ingredients or the proportion of the items I use,' he explained.

'Tell them that you use lots of different herbs and essences to make your remedy,' she suggested. 'Name one or two, and then let the interviewer move on to the next question.'

Jake asked Daisy's opinion on what herbs sounded interesting and other ideas for the interview. She found that her numerous editorial meetings with Franklin, discussing topics of interest for the books she'd worked on over the past few years, came in handy when advising Jake.

Finally, he shuffled his notes, put the most relevant ones to the top of the pile ready to reference, and tidied the others away, making his desk look less overwhelming.

'Thanks for your help, Daisy.'

She smiled at him and then studied the flower photos. There were plenty she envisaged using for her illustrations. 'Your garden looks lovely in all seasons. I don't know which one I prefer.'

'I'd like to add more spring flowers and extend the herb garden area.' He came over to point to a few of the photos to indicate what he had in mind. 'I plan to broaden the range of herbs from the edge of the apple tree and along to the pond. And I'm thinking of having a summerhouse over there, near the rose trees and lavender hedging. What do you think?'

'A summerhouse would be wonderful.'

'Maybe it could double as an art studio for you.'

Daisy blinked. 'A studio for me? In your garden?'

'Yes.' He looked at her to gauge her reaction.

'I love that idea. Painting in the garden would be perfect.' She pictured sitting in the summerhouse during mild spring days when the crocus, daffodils and bluebells were flowering in the garden. And then enjoying the warmth of the summer days and long, lingering hot twilights. It would be cosy in autumn and winter too. Yes, she felt excited at the prospect of the summerhouse.

'I'll make plans to have it built when we get back from New York.'

'I'd like that.' There was an assurance to his plans that appealed to her. Building a future together.

Settling down, they each got on with their work, while commenting on things of interest, especially the flowers Daisy was sketching.

Jake leaned over and admired her artwork. 'Those forget–me–nots you've drawn look beautiful.'

Her pencil sketches were the first part of her design process. Once she was happy with a pencil drawing, she'd ink it on to fine art paper ready to be scanned into her computer and sent to Franklin.

'I love forget–me–not flowers in pen and ink illustrations, but I'll paint these in watercolour too,' she said. 'The blue tones are always gorgeous and such a classic for vintage designs.'

Jake agreed. 'What about tea roses. I took loads of pictures of those, and the old–fashioned rose bushes.'

Daisy scrolled to the pictures of the roses and sighed. 'Oh yes, I'm definitely including these. Look at the deep pink petals on that flower, and there's a perfect red rose, so romantic.' The colours ranged from rich creams to burgundy.

'The scent of the roses was wonderful,' he recalled. 'We'll make sure we have those near the summerhouse. Woolley is great at planning and building garden sheds and things like that, so we'll get his advice.'

This brought the topic back round to Woolley.

Jake frowned. 'I still think Woolley is up to something. Maybe I should phone him.'

'No,' Daisy was quick to quash that idea. 'He's probably busy doing whatever it is he's doing. Let him call you. Besides, your editor is due to call soon from New York.'

'That's true. I should focus on that for now.'

Daisy smiled, hoping that the interview went well for Jake, and that Woolley's proposal plan would be a success and not a fiasco. She'd become accustomed to the latter since moving to the small town where mayhem was a daily occurrence.

Jake's phone rang. 'It's Valerie phoning from New York,' he said quickly to Daisy before taking the call.

'I know it's short notice, Jake,' Valerie began in a confident tone, 'but is there any way you could do this interview like a live video chat? The magazine threw this idea at me a few minutes ago, and I agree with them — it would make the interview more personal if they could see you. And maybe you could show them some of the things you use to make your remedy, like those bottles of potions I saw in the photos you sent of your study.'

Jake glanced at Daisy.

Daisy was nodding.

'Yes, I could set that up.' He was sure he could. He'd done live chats in the past when talking about his health food business.

'That would be amazing,' Valerie enthused. 'I'll call them right now and tell them you're doing it.'

And then Valerie was gone, leaving Jake and Daisy to get ready for the interview.

CHAPTER SEVEN

Secret Recipe

Jake fiddled with his forelock.

The interview started well, and they viewed each other on screen as they chatted. But it quickly veered from discussing his work as a herbalist to a personal note. Very personal.

'As an attractive and eligible man, you must've broken a few of hearts in your time,' the interviewer said. The woman, a New York magazine feature writer in her early thirties, seemed keen to get down to the nitty–gritty details of Jake's effect on women. Her manner was pleasant but probing.

The question threw Jake for a loop. He'd been prepared for the odd outlandish question, after all, he was talking about a cure for love. But the personal note caught him off–guard, and if Mrs Lemon's theory that Jake fiddled with his forelock when he was telling fibs was right, it was about to be put to the test.

'I don't consider myself to be the heartbreaker type,' he replied, fudging the truth.

The feature writer clearly anticipated Jake's response, and parried with a countermove. 'Well, while researching people's initial reaction to advance copies of your book, that includes a picture of you on the back cover, your good looks have been a topic of conversation. Don't you think it's relevant that the man who has possibly come up with a cure for lovesickness is a heartbreaker himself? There's a touch of irony in that, don't you think?'

'No, it hasn't crossed my mind,' Jake told her. He glanced at Daisy for her reaction. Jake wasn't great at discussing his feelings with her, never mind sharing personal information for the feature.

But Valerie had told Jake that Daisy wouldn't be part of the magazine interview. Daisy sat on the sidelines of the study out of view of the camera while Jake was the focus of the chat.

Valerie intervened, having made herself part of the interview prior to it starting. She'd told Jake that she would only comment briefly, but as she dealt with the publicity and marketing in New York, it would be a good idea for her to chip–in remarks about Jake and the book.

'I think Jake is far too modest.' Valerie's tone was light and she smiled out from the screen. She was sophisticated, very attractive, with dark chestnut hair, sleek and stylish, and ice blue eyes.

Daisy was there to bolster Jake and that's what she aimed to do. She furtively pointed to Jake's herbal essences, encouraging him to body swerve the personal remarks and bring the conversation back round to the remedy.

Jake picked up on Daisy's cue.

'All the essences I use in the remedy are carefully measured for their emotional effectiveness,' Jake explained, pasting a confident expression on his flustered face. He reached up and selected two of the bottles from a shelf and held them up for them to see on screen. 'Jealousy is a key ingredient.' He showed a close–up of the old–fashioned essence bottle with the handwritten label — *jealousy*.

The interviewer took the bait and followed through with a question. 'Is jealousy something that is part of the potion?'

'It's a strong emotion, and from my studies I've realised that it plays a key role in lovesickness,' said Jake.

The interviewer looked right at him. 'Would you say you're the jealous type?'

More fiddling with his forelock followed that question. 'No, not especially,' he lied. Even the thought of Sebastian made him feel as if his blood turned green with envy. Daisy wasn't dating Sebastian now, but secretly, Jake was a bit jealous of how close they'd been. So close that Sebastian had broken her heart into pieces when he'd ditched her in favour of Celeste.

Jake blinked out of his thoughts, realising that further comments from him were required. But he didn't know what to say.

Valerie stepped in again. 'Perhaps before we finish, we could hear what first motivated Jake to search for a cure for love.'

Jake's heart sank. He knew this was relevant, but tried to sidestep highlighting it. He summarised his motivation. 'My father was a herbalist, and I had an interest in his work from an early age.' He took a steadying breath. 'When I was a young boy, my mother ran off and never came back. My father was heart broken and never got over her leaving. He spent the rest of his life searching for a cure for love. I then carried on his work. I've been working on an improved version of the remedy, and this is what I talk about in my book.'

'What is in the actual remedy that makes it special?' the interviewer said to him, having another run at him to glean the recipe's ingredients.

'Various herbal essences, matched to emotions such as jealousy, paranoia and spite. The actual remedy is a secret recipe,' he said.

'One final question,' the interviewer concluded. 'As a single man, would you take the cure for love if you ever needed it?'

For the third time, Daisy saw Jake fiddle with his forelock, brushing an anxious hand through his silky dark hair that had a tendency to fall sexily over his brow.

His guts twisted. Since meeting Daisy, and now dating her, he didn't consider himself single. Though he supposed others would. He wasn't married to Daisy, and he hadn't even proposed to her.

'I have a girlfriend,' he heard himself explain.

'How long have you been dating?' Valerie said, suddenly taking charge of this part of the interview.

'Since the summertime,' he said. This seemed like a fairly long time to him, though others might view it as lightweight.

'If you needed to, would you take your cure for love?' the interviewer said to him.

'I hope I never need to,' he replied.

Daisy remained quiet on the sidelines as the interview came to a conclusion.

The interviewer spoke straight to camera, as if this was a clip that would be used on the magazine's online updates about the forthcoming interview. 'This is author, Jake Wolfe, discussing his new book, The Cure For Love.' Thanking Jake, they finished their chat, leaving Valerie to talk to Jake for a moment before the whole scenario finished.

'That was great, Jake,' Valerie bolstered him. 'You're a natural at this.'

Jake didn't believe this for a moment, but he smiled politely. 'I hope this will help with the promotion of the book.'

'Oh it will,' Valerie assured him. 'I'll keep you posted about this and any other interviews.' Without further discussion Valerie ended the call with a promise to chat to Jake soon.

Jake tugged at his tie, feeling the need to ease the knot, relieved the interview was done with.

'That was a disaster, wasn't it?' he said to Daisy.

'No, you handled yourself well under tricky conditions.' This was mainly true.

'The interview veered so far off topic. I didn't expect them to focus on me and my private life.' He didn't want to bring up the subject of being single. That was a rabbit hole he'd no intention of venturing down at the moment.

'Different publications will have their own readership. They'll know what their readers are interested in.'

Before Jake and Daisy could discuss whether the interview was a total disaster, Karen phoned from the health food shop. Jake could hear people chattering happily and the shop sounded hectic in the background as Karen manned the till and served customers.

'A delivery of split peas, lentils, broth mix, herbs and spices has arrived at the shop,' Karen told him. 'Woolley's not here. Sharky says he's seen him gallivanting up and down the main street buying stuff. He was supposed to be here to cover while you were doing your interview. But he's been away secret shopping. I don't know what he's bought.'

'I knew Woolley was up to something,' Jake muttered.

'Sorry, what?' said Karen.

'Nothing. I'm on my way.'

'Do you want me to sign for the delivery?' Karen offered.

'Yes, but leave it where it is and attend to the customers. I'll carry the boxes upstairs.'

'Okay.' Karen clicked off and continued to serve the customers.

Jake threw his jacket on. 'Woolley's gone AWOL. I have to go and deal with a delivery. Karen is holding the fort on her own.'

'Can I help?' Daisy offered.

'Could you email the flower photos to yourself and turn the laptop off,' said Jake. 'I can handle the shop work. Woolley is bound to turn up later to help me stock the shelves.' He grabbed some notes he'd scribbled down to remind him of things he needed to do and stuffed them in his jacket pocket. 'Customers have been buying lots of items for their festive home baking. We were almost out of crystallised ginger, raisins and glacé cherries yesterday.'

'If you change your mind, call me and I'll come and help,' Daisy told him.

'Thanks, but you need to get on with your work too.' Jake grabbed his car keys and hurried away.

Daisy watched him drive off. A stab of guilt shot through her, but she'd promised Woolley she'd keep his secret.

Emailing the photos to herself, she switched Jake's laptop off, tidied up his desk without disturbing his notes, and then headed out.

The air was bitingly cold but it helped to clear her head. She shrugged her bag up on to her shoulder and walked down the hill, admiring the view. Cold sea air and clouds hung low over the coast creating a wintry effect that was quite ethereal. She stopped to snap a picture of it with her phone. The image was a perfect depiction of December on the Cornish coast, something she intended painting.

Putting her phone in her coat pocket, she continued on down to the cottage, rewinding the interview in her mind as the sea air whipped up from the shore.

The fresh, salty tang of the sea made her want to take a walk along the coast, and so she dug out her pink woolly hat from her bag, pulled it on and then ventured towards the shore.

The closer she walked along the shore road, taking the rough coastal route along the grassland that bordered it, the stronger the wind became. In the summer, this part of the coast was a favourite of hers. She loved setting up her watercolours and sitting in the sunshine painting. One of her paintings now hung in Roman's castle. He'd seen her painting it and insisted on earmarking it for himself. Now framed and part of the castle's art collection, it showed the coastline with the castle perched high above all it surveyed. The turrets had been tricky to paint, but she'd managed them, and Roman loved it.

She often painted in all seasons in the park in London, though not when it was raining unless she was sheltering in a part of the park that had a canopy to shield her from the downpour. But blustery days in the London park, although a challenge when trying to keep her paper from blowing away, had such an energy to them that she believed transferred to the artwork. True or not, she did some of her top work on colder days rather than at the height of summer.

This made her view the coast with a clear perspective. A scattering of wildflowers and rugged blooms made her decide to sketch them in all their cold, winter beauty. Her sketch pad was in her bag.

She sat on a flat marker stone on the grassy headlands and perched her sketch pad on her lap. Then using watercolour pencils she sketched the hardy flowers against the view of the rough sea, with all those shades of silvery greys and the white froth along the tips of the waves that washed on to the sand.

Steeped in the blustery beauty, she forgot about New York and became lost in sketching the Cornwall coast.

'I need a fancy cake,' Woolley said, bustling into Sharky's bakery laden with two bags of shopping. He'd popped in while there were no other customers in the shop.

Sharky eyed the bags but made no comment. 'A fancy cake, eh? Do you need it iced to last until Christmas?'

'No, it's for tonight.' Woolley spoke in a confiding tone.

'Something special you're planning for this evening?'

'Maybe.'

'Okay, so what type of cake do you want? Chocolate? Fruit cake? A fresh cream sponge?'

'Something...*romantic*.'

'Ah,' Sharky said knowingly and reached into one of his display cabinets and brought out a white iced cake decorated with fondant roses. 'I always keep something like this on hand.'

Woolley looked delighted. 'That's perfect. I'll take it.'

Sharky put it in a white cardboard cake box and sat it on the counter. 'Anything else you need for your special night?'

'I'll have a couple of your sticky buns.'

Sharky frowned. 'Mrs Lemon was in earlier. She said the two of you were having a night in watching the television. She bought your favourite sticky buns.'

Woolley's heart melted. 'She did?'

Sharky nodded and smiled.

'She really is the woman for me.'

Sharky leaned across the counter. 'Are you popping the question tonight?'

'Yes. It's a secret. I'm hoping to surprise her. The only thing I haven't been able to get is fresh flowers. The grocery shop was sold out. And I pruned my garden last weekend, cut it back for the winter, so I've nothing left to pick. No winter greenery, nothing.'

'I haven't gotten around to trimming my garden yet. I'm busy during the day with the bakery, and Karen keeps me occupied in the evenings. Not that I'm complaining. So help yourself to any flowers that are left in my garden. It's a bit of a jungle. You're bound to find something to make into a bouquet or whatever.'

'Thanks, that would be great. I'll do that. I'd planned to have roses—'

Before Woolley could explain, he glanced furtively out the window seeing Jake drive up and park outside the health food shop. He jumped back out of view, causing Jake to look across, suspicious.

Jake came striding over.

Sharky saw the panic on Woolley's face. 'Hurry up through the back of the shop. The kitchen leads on to the old narrow street.'

Woolley grabbed the cake box, went to pay for the cake, but Sharky hustled him away.

'Settle up with me later,' Sharky told him.

'Cheers,' Woolley said and scurried away moments before Jake walked in.

Sharky smiled. 'What can I get for you?'

'Was that Woolley I saw?'

'Woolley? No, it was Mr Greenie. He was wearing his window cleaning hat today. He left by the back entrance. Why?'

'Woolley is supposed to be helping look after the shop, but he's scarpered, off doing his Christmas shopping.'

'Nothing wrong with that. Woolley's surely entitled to enjoy his retirement. He works hard for you most days.'

Jake blinked. 'Yes, you're right. He's always reliable, but he should be able to do what he wants as well.'

Sharky picked up a paper bag. 'So, can I tempt you with a sticky bun?'

'Eh, no, thanks. I'm fine. But I enjoyed your scones.'

Sharky smiled. 'Glad to hear it.'

Customers came in and Jake smiled and hurried out and across to his health food shop.

'The delivery driver left the boxes of items over there, near the stairs,' Karen told him as he walked in.

'Thank you, Karen.' Jake lifted a few of the boxes and carried them upstairs to the storeroom. Then he restocked the shelves with other products from the delivery.

'Have you heard from Woolley?' Karen said to Jake.

'No, I think he's been doing his Christmas shopping.'

Karen shook her head in disapproval. 'I think he's doing something secretive. I heard him whispering to Daisy when they were upstairs in the storeroom supposedly unravelling the fairy lights.'

'Woolley hasn't told me anything,' said Jake.

'No, he wouldn't. You're rubbish at keeping secrets.' Karen's bluntness made Jake balk, but it was a truth he couldn't dispute.

'It's not intentional,' Jake said in his defence. 'I'm just not the devious type.'

A customer came in and Karen served them, thankfully saving Jake from further remarks from her.

Daisy tucked her sketch pad into her bag as the daylight faded to a winter's twilight.

The sea rocket flowers, and several other hardy flowers were just what she needed for the vintage designs that would be part of the winter season section of the new book.

Walking back along the shore, the darkening sky created a Christmassy feeling, and the brisk sea air blew across the bay. Cottages and houses were dotted around the coast, and she could see Christmas trees lit up in the windows.

Windblown but invigorated, she arrived back at her cottage. Taking her coat and hat off, she hung them up in the hall and went through to the lounge to switch her tree lights on.

The day was almost done, and she lit the fire, adding extra logs and kindling.

The fire crackled in the hearth and cast a cosy glow to the lounge as she sat on the sofa looking at her artwork. The sea rocket was particularly suitable for the designs she had in mind. She'd drawn with the watercolour pencils dry. This gave subtle tones to the flowers and added a sort of faded look to the designs that was ideal for the theme of the new book. She dipped a fine tipped brush into water and dabbed it on parts of the flowers to create a lovely watercolour effect. When the artwork was completely dry, she scanned the flowers into her laptop and studied them on the screen. Any stray marks or splodges were easily cleaned up digitally, but for the most part, she kept this to a minimum so that the art retained its lovely hand painted quality.

Sketching other flowers, she saw the lights were now on in Jake's house. His shop would be closed for the day. Across the road she noticed that the Christmas tree in Mrs Lemon's cottage was aglow, and wondered if Woolley would stick to his plan to ask her to marry him that evening.

She was thinking about this when she saw Woolley walking towards Mrs Lemon's cottage carrying a shopping bag and a bunch of flowers. They didn't look like roses, as he'd planned. The bouquet had a rustic quality as if the flowers had been freshly picked from the garden, using whatever winter florals were in bloom.

Woolley looked spruced up, and unless she was mistaken, keyed up too as he headed towards Mrs Lemon's cottage and knocked on the front door.

Daisy was compelled to watch as the door opened and she saw Mrs Lemon lit up in the glow from the hallway. Then Woolley disappeared inside and the cottage door shut.

Daisy hoped Mrs Lemon accepted Woolley's proposal, and as she continued to work on her illustrations, she glanced every now and then wondering what was happening.

She was about to make a cup of tea and put more logs on the fire when Woolley came bursting out of the cottage, arms raised in triumph, gave a resounding cheer, and then disappeared back inside.

Daisy smiled to herself at the happy outcome.

Daisy sat by the fire having a mug of lentil broth and wholemeal bread when Jake phoned her.

'Woolley called to tell me he's proposed to Mrs Lemon — and she's accepted.'

'I'm so happy for them.'

'He said he'd shown you the diamond ring but asked you to keep his plans secret.'

'Yes, I wanted to tell you, but I promised Woolley I wouldn't.'

'It's fine. I'm not great at keeping secrets.'

'Did he say when they're getting married?'

'Late spring or the summer. After Karen and Sharky tie the knot. Woolley suggested the New Year, but Mrs Lemon doesn't want to steal Karen's thunder. And apparently she's happy to enjoy a longer engagement.'

'I'm pleased she said yes. I think they're well suited.'

'They'll make a happy couple.' Jake paused, and then said brightly, 'So, what have you been up to?'

'I went for a walk along the shore and sketched some flowers. Now I'm working on the designs and having a cuppa and soup.'

'Well, I'll let you enjoy that. I just wanted to tell you the news about Woolley and Mrs Lemon.'

'The local gossipmongers will have plenty to chatter about in the morning,' she said.

Bidding each other goodnight, they finished the call.

Daisy ate her soup and relaxed by the fire.

Jake dealt with the accounts for the health food shop, and tied up other aspects of his business. Once that was done, he continued with the work from earlier.

Mulling over the interview with the magazine, he wondered if he should suggest to Valerie that he could do all the interviews like this — and forgo the need to go to New York.

He phoned her with this idea and was politely but firmly told no. There was no wriggling out of his contract to promote his book personally in New York.

It had been a wild idea and he wasn't entirely surprised that he'd been knocked back, but at least he'd tried. Christmas in Manhattan was still on the cards.

Sighing wearily, he sat in his study and delved into his archives for the notes he'd made for specific ingredients that were part of his remedy.

'Ah, yes,' he muttered to himself, seeing an essence he'd noted.

Reaching up to one of the shelves that was filled with bottles of potions, he lifted one down and read the label. *Wild Abandon. Use sparingly.*

Mrs Lemon blew out the little candle on the cake Woolley had brought her.

'Did you make a wish?' he said.

'Yes, but I can't tell you or it'll not come true.' She smiled happily, and kept admiring the diamond ring on her hand. She still couldn't believe it. Woolley's proposal had come out of the blue. Karen was at Sharky's house, and she'd phoned her daughter to tell her the news. Karen was delighted for her mother.

Woolley already had his wish come true. Mrs Lemon had accepted his proposal.

'We'll need to have an engagement party before Christmas,' said Mrs Lemon, cutting two generous slices of cake and handing one to her new fiancé. 'Nothing outrageous, just a get together here with a few friends. The cottage is looking lovely with my Christmas tree up and the decorations.'

Fairy lights were draped around the fireplace, and the tree sat in the front window all aglow.

Sitting together by the fire, they ate their cake and planned the engagement party.

'If we do it soon, Jake and Daisy will still be here,' said Woolley. 'I'd like them to be part of the celebration.'

'We could have it a couple of nights from now,' Mrs Lemon suggested.

'Yes,' he said. 'We'll order plenty of cakes and pies from Sharky.'

'I could bake some too.' Though she pictured that Sharky would want to supply everything they needed.

After making their plans, they settled down to watch two episodes of their favourite television series.

Daisy was pleased with the progress she'd made with the vintage artwork, and tidied it away as the clock struck midnight. She'd a tendency to work far too late into the night.

The fire had almost burned itself out in the hearth, and as she flicked the Christmas tree lights off, only the amber glow from the embers illuminated the room.

Glancing out the window, she saw that the lights were still on in Mrs Lemon's cottage. And Jake's study was lit up.

Heading through to the bedroom, she got ready for bed and tucked herself under the covers.

She felt the tiredness kick in as she thought about the magazine interview...and walking along the windswept shore...and Woolley and Mrs Lemon's engagement...and reminded herself that she didn't want to think about Sebastian. She didn't want to dream about him again.

CHAPTER EIGHT

A Winter's Night

'Turn the ring around on your finger three times and make a wish,' Mrs Lemon told one of the customers queuing in the health food shop. The woman was a long–time acquaintance and had been congratulating Mrs Lemon on her engagement.

Karen stood behind the counter serving customers, smiling, clearly delighted that her mother now had a diamond sparkler too.

Daisy had run out of muesli for breakfast and had popped down to buy a box of the cereal. She'd welcomed the brisk walk and cold fresh air, hoping it would clear her thoughts from dreaming again about Sebastian. Her own fault she mentally scolded herself for even thinking about him as she fell asleep. She'd woken up in the morning feeling as tired as when she went to sleep. In the dream she'd been running away from Sebastian after they'd danced the night away at a grand ball. He'd been trying to give her an engagement ring. Obviously, her head was filled with Woolley and Mrs Lemon's engagement, and somehow their scenario got mixed up in her own disturbed thoughts about her ex–boyfriend. Another night of dreaming about Sebastian and him trying to encourage her to become engaged to him set her nerves on edge.

'*I always know where you are, Daisy,*' he'd called to her in the dream. '*I'm the only man who really knows you and understands you.*'

For some reason, this comment disconcerted her more than anything. Sebastian didn't know her. If he had, he'd realise that pursuing her was futile. She was finished with him.

She shook away the uncomfortable thoughts and picked up a box of muesli with extra fruit and nuts in the mix, and took it over to where the chatter and excitement emanated as local acquaintances wished Mrs Lemon well on her engagement.

'Morning, Daisy,' Mrs Lemon said, beaming with delight. Despite being up late the previous night she looked perkier than ever, while Daisy had dimmed by comparison. 'Would you like to make a wish on my ring?'

Daisy accepted the offer and put the ring on, turned it three times and then wished she could stop dreaming about Sebastian... No! She instantly changed her mind. She wasn't going to waste a wish on Sebastian, whether it would come true or not. She'd wasted too much time and effort on him already. Rethinking what she really wanted to wish for, she then handed the ring back to Mrs Lemon.

'Thank you,' said Daisy. 'It's a beautiful ring.'

Mrs Lemon slipped it on her finger and held her hand out, admiring the diamonds scintillate under the shop lights. 'It's perfect. Woolley knows what I like. It's wonderful having a man who really knows and understands me.'

Daisy agreed, but the words jarred her senses back to her dream with Sebastian.

The excited chatter swirled around Daisy as others congratulated Mrs Lemon and admired her ring.

Daisy stepped forward and put her box of muesli on the counter.

Karen picked it up and beeped it through the checkout.

Daisy paid for it while Karen eyed her carefully.

'Late night?'

'No later than usual, but...bad dreams,' Daisy told her, confiding more than she'd intended.

'Dreaming about Sebastian?' Karen hit the bullseye, causing Dairy to jolt and confirm her assumption.

Daisy blinked and frowned. How did Karen know?

Without needing prompted, Karen explained. 'Whenever I've been backstabbed by an ex–boyfriend, I still dream about him for months. It's one of those horrible backlashes of romance, for me anyway, and I suspect for you. Especially as you dated Sebastian for quite a while. I dated him one and a half times, and without going into the details, I was gutted when he didn't want me. I hated dreaming about him. But Sebastian is a hard man to forget, despite that we both think he's a shrewd fox. That's part of his allure.'

Daisy felt as if she'd been emotionally plastered to the wall by Karen's fairly accurate insight. Karen! Of all people.

'Don't look so surprised, Daisy. We were both taken in by Sebastian. Fortunately, my entanglements with him were short and bittersweet.'

Daisy was reminded that he'd two–timed her for months on end while he diddled around with Celeste.

'But now you're settled with Jake,' said Karen. 'Though seeing Sebastian in London recently is bound to have rattled you.'

Mrs Lemon and the other customers had become quiet, listening to the one-sided conversation, and exchanged knowing glances at each other as they agreed with Karen.

'I'll have a packet of lemon drops,' Mrs Lemon said, breaking through the awkward atmosphere.

Karen served her mother as Daisy stepped aside.

'I'm having an engagement party at my cottage tomorrow night,' Mrs Lemon said to Daisy. 'I hope you'll come along and celebrate with us. Woolley is inviting Jake.'

'Yes, I'll be there.' Daisy forced a smile, and then left the shop and stepped out into the cold morning. The sounds of the busy main street, filled with the usual hustle and bustle of the morning getting its act together, seemed to circle around her, far away in the distance, while Daisy felt detached from everyone.

Walking back to the cottage, she breathed in the icy air and blinked back to reality. She was done with Sebastian. But Karen was right.

Her boots crunched on the icy surface of the cobbles as she trudged on, wondering if it was her recent encounter with Sebastian in London that had thrown her senses back to thoughts of her past with him. Probably that, and her reluctance to have Christmas in New York. She didn't love Sebastian any longer. But perhaps she didn't feel as settled as she'd hoped with Jake.

A call jarred her as she walked along, and her heart twisted when she saw that the caller was Jake.

'Woolley has invited us to the engagement party at Mrs Lemon's cottage. I said we'd be there.'

'Yes, I met Mrs Lemon at the health food shop. I said I'd be at the party too.'

'Any thoughts on what we should buy them as an engagement present?'

'None at the moment, but I'll put my mind to it.'

'Great. You'll have a far better idea what to buy them than me.'

A call came through for him from his agent in London.

'My agent's phoning. I have to go.'

And he was gone again.

Daisy continued walking on to her cottage to get on with her day.

Her morning consisted of breakfast, and then inking some of her sketches to finished artwork level, scanning them into her laptop and forwarding them to Franklin.

He replied with a large thumbs up.

Bolstered that Franklin approved of her designs, Daisy kept going, working through lunch, grabbing a salad and cheese sandwich and a cup of tea, and then using the photos of flowers from Jake's garden to add to her collection of floral illustrations.

Steeped in her work, she'd let the cottage become a bit cold as the day darkened in the afternoon.

Easing the tension in her shoulders from all the drawing, she lit the fire and made a cup of tea.

Ideas for engagement gifts had been on her mind while she'd been working, and she'd narrowed it down to a couple of presents. She messaged her suggestions to Jake rather than interrupt his work, or hers, with a phone call.

Jake replied a short time later.

Great suggestions.

She'd included links to where they could buy the gifts, including one of the local shops.

I like the four champagne flutes engraved with their names, and a bottle of champagne. I can buy this locally, he told her.

Remember wrapping paper and a card too, she reminded him.

I'm at my shop. I could buy these this afternoon.
Do that.
Okay. Speak later.

Daisy put her phone aside, sat by the fire sipping her tea, then picked up her sketch pad to get on with her drawings. And she decided to make a personal gift for Woolley and Mrs Lemon.

While working on her illustrations in the afternoon, she sketched Woolley and Mrs Lemon's names, using floral art to create the lettering. She added the date of their engagement to the design. Then she inked the lettering on to artist quality paper ready for framing. The flowers in the design included pansies, lavender, roses, thistles, forget–me–nots and lily of the valley. She planned to give them the artwork at their engagement party.

Woolley unpacked a box of deliveries upstairs in the storeroom while Jake wrestled with his thoughts.

Jake was happy that Woolley had proposed to Mrs Lemon, but he hadn't anticipated that his uncle would get engaged before him. Jake's plan to ask Daisy to marry him kept being pushed aside in favour of work. A gnawing doubt was playing on his mind. Did he have his priorities wrong? Or was his relationship with Daisy so strong that he didn't need to rush the proposal when life was so hectic? In an ideal world, he'd wait until the publicity for the book was finished, and then propose in a romantic and timely manner.

'Are you okay, Jake?' said Woolley. 'You're very quiet.'

'Yes, fine, just a lot on my mind.' Jake put aside the box of festive chocolate specialities he was checking that had been delivered. 'I need to pop out to the shops. I'll be back in about half an hour.'

'I won't be gallivanting off today,' Woolley assured him.

'Okay, but phone if you need me or if another delivery arrives.'

Jake shrugged his warm jacket on and hurried downstairs.

'We're running out of baking ingredients for the gingerbread houses,' Karen called to Jake as he went by. 'Especially the chocolate buttons for the roofs. And ginger and cinnamon.'

'Tell Woolley. There are plenty upstairs.' Jake continued out into the cold, late afternoon. All the shop windows were lit up, and the large Christmas tree in the town square glowed brightly against the dark grey sky. The topmost star shone like a beacon.

Jake hurried along to the craft shop to buy the glasses and champagne. The engraving was done on the premises by the owner, a skilled craftsman. Jake asked for Woolley and Mrs Lemon's names to be engraved along with the date of their engagement.

He left the craft shop and was due to go back and collect the finished glasses in an hour, along with the wrapping paper and card he'd bought.

Working again in the health food shop, Jake continued to deal with the stock and the accounts. Everything needed to be in order for when he went away to New York.

Daisy checked the time. The craft shop would be closing soon. Throwing on her warm, red coat and woolly hat, she left the cosiness of the cottage and walked briskly to the main street.

Arriving at the shop, she knew exactly what she wanted — a glass picture frame. She'd seen the glass frames in the window and thought it would suit the style of the illustrative floral lettering.

Happy with her purchase, she headed out into the main street.

The health food shop looked busy as she walked past and continued on her way back to the cottage. The front garden was already covered with frost, and her fingers felt the cold as she turned the key in the lock and went inside.

She put the glass frame down safely in the lounge, added logs to the fire, loving the scent of them as they sparked into life, and then went through to the kitchen to prepare a tasty but easy dinner.

Searching through the freezer she dug out a vegetable pie topped with mashed potatoes and popped it in the oven.

While the pie heated, Daisy put the illustration in the frame. She hoped they'd like a memento of their engagement date and names entwined with flowers.

Before wrapping it in the paper she'd bought, she snapped a photo of it and sent it to Jake with a message.

I've inked a personal item for Woolley and Mrs Lemon. What do you think?

Jake replied. *That looks so classy. I like the glass frame. A nice elegant touch.*

I'm glad you like it.

I bought the fluted glasses and champagne. Wrapping paper at the ready. He took a photo of the glasses and champagne. They came in a gift box.

Daisy viewed the image. *Perfect.*

Pick you up at the cottage tomorrow night. The party starts at seven.

See you then.

The timer pinged in the kitchen and she went through to take her pie out of the oven. It smelled delicious, and as she served it up on a plate she realised she was quite hungry. The heat from the oven had made the kitchen feel cosy, so she sat at the kitchen table to eat her dinner.

Sometimes it hit her how far she was from London, and how her life in the city seemed like a part of her past she was never going to go back to. She enjoyed living in the cottage, especially on winter night's like this when it felt warm and cosy.

After finishing her meal, she took her tea and a hot mince pie through to the lounge and sat beside the fire watching the flames flicker. The rich aroma of the spicy fruit filling reminded her of Christmases past. Now here she was in the present, snuggled up in the cottage.

She doubted she'd see Jake before the party the following night as Valerie had lined up another two interviews for him with other magazines. Daisy wasn't required to be part of the interviews. Starting to feel that she was surplus to requirements for the book's publicity, she decided not to let it rile her. She had enough work to be getting on with.

Setting up her artwork, she tackled the designs for the tea roses while watching a cheery Christmas movie — a romance with lots of snow, sparkles and a happy ever after.

Bright winter sunlight shone in the kitchen window as Daisy ate her breakfast the following morning. Up early to make the most of the day, she intended hunkering down and getting on with her artwork.

Cupping a hot mug of tea, she opened the back door and blinked against the sunlight streaming across the garden. The air was bitter cold, but she wore her pink jumper and welcomed the freshness, breathing in the scent of the sea air wafting up from the shore and blending with the countryside. A perfect mix to start the day.

Closing the door, she then spent the morning drawing flowers, all sorts of flowers, trying out different designs to see which ones looked suitable for the vintage theme. Having time work on the illustrations without interruption was a sheer luxury, and she managed to ink a few flowers to finished artwork level ready to be emailed to Franklin for his approval.

Lunch was a tin of leek and potato soup and wholemeal bread, followed by an afternoon of more sketching and illustrating.

As the daylight dimmed in the late afternoon, she packed her artwork away and started to get ready for the party. Mrs Lemon would have plenty of tasty treats for her guests, so Daisy skipped dinner and just had a cup of tea.

Styling her hair smooth and silky, she fixed her makeup and got dressed into her party outfit. She wore a pair of black, slim–fitting trousers and an aquamarine blue sequin top. It was a camisole design so she shrugged on a cardigan for warmth. As Mrs Lemon's cottage was only across the road, she didn't bother with a coat or jacket.

She'd just picked up her bag when there was a knock on the door.

Jake had arrived.

She went through to let him in, and judging by the look of approval on his face she'd chosen the right outfit.

'You look lovely,' he told her, stepping inside the doorway. He put the gift he'd brought with him on the hall table along with the card.

He'd worn a warm jacket to walk down from his house, and was wearing one of his dark suits with a white shirt and tie. Those silky strands of hair fell across his brow, tempting her to brush them back with her fingers as he pulled her close to him and kissed her.

'Come on you two!' Sharky shouted to them as he drove by in his bakery van. 'Stop canoodling and come and join the party.'

Daisy and Jake laughed.

'We'll be right over,' Jake called to him. Then he handed Daisy the card. 'I've said it's from both of us, but I thought you should sign it personally.'

She grabbed a pen from the table and signed her name next to Jake's.

He put the card in the envelope, picked up the gift and got ready to leave.

Daisy lifted up her present too, and walked with Jake over to Mrs Lemon's cottage. The front door was open and the windows were lit up. Christmas music filtered out into the cold air and Daisy squeezed Jake's arm as she looked forward to a night out at the party.

A few guests were already there, and Daisy and Jake were given a warm welcome by Mrs Lemon and Woolley.

Mrs Lemon looked lovely in a navy blue dress that had chiffon sleeves and sparkling dark blue details on the neckline.

Karen wore a pink dress that suited her slim figure and Sharky wore a smart suit, shirt and tie. Everyone had made an effort.

A buffet table was set up in the lounge, piled with sandwiches, savoury treats, cakes and scones, and guests were told to help themselves.

Sharky had contributed plenty of cake and other items from his bakery, including an engagement cake, an iced fruit cake, that had the happy couple's names written in fondant icing.

Daisy admired Mrs Lemon's Christmas tree that sat in the front window. It was a real tree she'd bought from Mr Greenie's selection, and she'd decorated it with a set of colourful fairy lights, little lanterns she'd had for years, and baubles that ranged from yesteryear to some she'd bought recently.

The front windows of the cottage were trimmed with fairy lights, and put Daisy in the notion of doing the same with her windows if she'd been staying there for Christmas.

Outdoor lights shone in the garden, draped around a cherry tree and wound through the hedging that bordered the property. It looked really pretty and festive.

'Congratulations,' said Jake, handing Woolley and Mrs Lemon the gift and card.

Mrs Lemon's reaction showed that the champagne and glasses were very much appreciated.

'Look,' she said, showing other guests. 'Our names are on the champagne glasses and the date of our engagement.'

Daisy then handed them her gift.

Mrs Lemon's face lit up when she saw the framed artwork. 'Oh, I love this!' She hurried over to where she had a Christmas ornament hanging on the wall, took it down, and replaced it with the glass framed artwork. She stood back and admired it. 'Thank you, Daisy. You've got such a talent for art. I really do love this.'

Woolley was as delighted as Mrs Lemon and he went up to take a close look at their names created from various flowers.

'There are roses, pansies and one of my favourites — lily of the valley,' Mrs Lemon told Woolley. 'I'm definitely having those flowers in my bridal bouquet.'

Daisy smiled, pleased to see that they liked their gift, even more than she'd anticipated. It seemed as if it would be hung for a while in the lounge for all to see.

The engagement cake was cut after a toast and a welcoming few words from Woolley.

'I'm glad you've all come along to share in our celebration,' Woolley announced. 'So eat up and drink up. And let's get the dancing started.'

A space in the middle of the lounge had been cleared so that the guests could dance the night away.

Jake danced with Mrs Lemon, Karen and others, while Daisy was partnered with Woolley, Roman Penhaligan, Mr Greenie and finally Sharky.

'I love the artwork in the glass frame,' Sharky said to Daisy. Then he lowered his voice. 'Could I commission you to do one like this with Karen's name and mine? I'd like to surprise her.'

'I'd be happy to draw one for the two of you. You don't have to commission me,' she whispered to him.

'Thanks, Daisy. I'll pay you in cakes and sticky buns.'

Daisy laughed, and then Sharky whirled her around to the lively Christmas music.

Jake finally cut in, smiling at them. 'What are you two whispering about.'

'It's a secret,' said Daisy. 'But I'm being plied with cakes and sticky buns. I got the best part of the deal.'

Jake smiled and then started to dance with Daisy.

'I can't tell you what Sharky wants me to do because you're no good at keeping a secret,' she said as Jake tried to wangle it out of her.

'That's true,' he agreed. 'It's never intentional. I always seem to let it slip out. I need to practice being more devious.'

'Maybe you've got a potion for that,' she suggested jokingly.

'Perhaps I should make one. Mix up facets of your character — secret squirrel with a dash of talented troublemaker.'

She laughed. 'Is that how you sum up my character?'

'Nooo, you're far more complex than that. I'd need to add mischief maker and heartbreaker.'

'Heartbreaker?'

Jake pulled her close. 'You are to me.'

'Anyone for eggnog?' Mrs Lemon carried through a tray of glasses filled with the mixture. 'It's my special recipe.'

'Save me from Mrs Lemon's eggnog,' Jake whispered anxiously to Daisy.

But Mrs Lemon made a beeline for him, brandishing the tray. 'Here you go, Jake. I know how much you like my eggnog.' She lowered her voice. 'And I've tweaked the recipe, rather like you and your cure for love remedy. I've improved it. This version has an added kick to celebrate my engagement.'

Daisy saw the whites of Jake's eyes override the blue as he geared up to take a sip.

Mrs Lemon stood there holding the tray of glasses watching him, smiling happily.

CHAPTER NINE

Lunch at the Castle

'This eggnog is delicious.' Jake downed his second glass and happily accepted a refill from Mrs Lemon. 'What's in it?'

'Extra...*everything*.' She gave him a knowing wink.

'Brandy, whisky, rum, sherry?' he suggested.

'It's a potent brew,' she confided, and then wandered off to offer it to other guests.

Sharky backed away slowly. 'I'm driving my van home tonight, and I have an early start in the morning.' He pasted a grin on his face and felt relieved when she nodded her understanding and targeted Roman Penhaligan.

Not knowing the treat he was in for, Roman accepted the glass, lifted it in a cheers and took a sip. 'Oh, very...eh, strong, but rather sweet and tasty.'

Moving on, Mrs Lemon served it to other guests.

Woolley swiped a glass and grinned at her.

Mr Greenie had taken charge of the music, using his DJ skills to liven things up. He was on his second glass of the festive brew.

Daisy held her glass of eggnog, barely touched. The aroma itself was strong enough to indicate its potency, but looking around, there were plenty of party revellers eager to drink it.

'Are you going to drink that?' Jake said, causing Daisy to blink out of her thoughts.

'No, I'm not one for eggnog.' It was the first excuse she could think of. Envisioning herself dancing on the table in view of the neighbours made her decide to err on the side of caution. She wasn't much of a drinker.

Jake helpfully took her almost full glass out of her hand and lifted it in a cheers.

'Maybe you should go easy on the eggnog,' Daisy suggested, seeing a rosy flush across his cheeks.

'You're probably right, as always, Daisy. Ever the practical one of the two of us.'

Mr Greenie changed up the music and the party atmosphere notched up a few gears as more eggnog and champagne were consumed along with nibbles from the buffet.

Daisy ate a flaky pastry and then was pulled into the lively dancing before she'd had a chance to finish it.

'Come on, Daisy,' Jake encouraged her. 'Let's party!'

Seeing a whole new and possibly delightful side to Jake, she joined in, and as the laughter and merriment whirled around her, she let go of her hesitancy and gave in to the joy of the party revelry. But not the eggnog.

As the party dancing continued, it culminated in a conga, led by Woolley.

Daisy hadn't danced a conga in years, and now she'd notched up two in one week.

Mr Greenie turned up the music and the guests threw themselves into the dancing. A conga around the lounge was fun, but then Jake decided to lead them outside into the cold night.

The women, wearing their party dresses, heels and outfits not ideal for dancing outside in freezing weather, dropped out of the line, leaving Jake, Woolley, Roman, Sharky, Mr Greenie and other men to form a short but energetic conga outside into the front garden.

Daisy, Mrs Lemon, Karen and other ladies stood at the front door clapping and cheering the men on.

Jake started singing as he led the others happily astray.

'Jake, no,' Daisy called to him. 'You'll disturb the neighbours.'

The man at the tail end of the line grinned and called back to Daisy. 'I don't mind.'

Realising that he was one of the neighbours, as were several of the men giving it large, attempting to limbo under a gate railing, Daisy gave in and committed the scene to memory. The night Jake went wild. If only his agent and publishers could see him now. Jake was packed and ready for New York, but were they ready for him?

Mrs Lemon and Karen compared their engagement rings in the nightglow and giggled.

'Both of us engaged!' Mrs Lemon exclaimed.

Karen squeezed her mother's arm and smiled. 'Isn't it great!'

Daisy was momentarily distracted by their cheeriness and didn't notice that Jake had whipped his shirt and waistcoat off. Somehow, he'd managed to keep his tie on, and was standing bare–chested in the garden.

'No, Jake, don't! You'll do yourself a mischief!' Daisy shouted to him as he was about to attempt to limbo under a particularly low rod that was entwined with climbing roses.

'I can do it, Daisy. Watch me.' The determination in his tone vetoed any further attempt to save him from his shiver inducing shimmy.

'Jake's very flexible isn't he,' Karen mused as they watched him bend like a banana and clear the rose thorns by a whisker.

Jumping upright, Jake punched the air in triumph. 'Yeah! Any takers?'

Mrs Lemon warned Woolley not to even think about it, and as Mr Greenie was occupied filming the antics with his phone, the next challenger was Sharky. He was well up for it, even without being bolstered by eggnog.

'I think Sharky can do it,' Karen whispered excitedly to her mother and Daisy. 'Unless last night's antics were too much for him.'

'We don't need the details of what you and Sharky got up to,' said Mrs Lemon, sensing Karen was gearing up to paint a vivid picture.

Sharky kept his shirt on and began to shimmy on the frosty lawn, easing himself under the rod. Having a bit more bulk on his torso, he couldn't quite make it and fell backwards.

Ever helpful, Jake grabbed him by the ankles, trailed him out from under it and with the assistance of

Woolley, they stood Sharky upright and dusted him down.

'You nearly did it.' Jake clapped him on the back.

'It's my new trousers,' said Sharky. 'I'm not used to tight–fitting trousers. I've always got my baggy baker's ones on.'

Agreeing that this was the reason for Sharky's failure, another challenger stepped forward — Roman Penhaligan.

As Karen wrapped herself around Sharky, congratulating him on his attempt, Roman lined up to tackle the task.

'What do you think?' Mrs Lemon whispered to Daisy. 'Roman is a fit looking man.'

Daisy needed to calculate the odds based on his inebriation. 'How much eggnog did he have?'

'Two glasses too many to stop him making a fool of himself in my front garden tonight.'

Daisy swithered. 'It'll be close, but my money is still on Jake winning.'

Roman took his shirt off. He hadn't worn a tie, just an expensive shirt that he hung from a tree branch. Flexing his lean muscles that were a fair match for Jake's build, he shook his legs to limber up and then went for it.

The onlookers cheered him on.

Bending for all he was worth, Roman would've made it if his chest hairs hadn't snagged on a rose thorn. With a yelp and a tug, Roman slumped down and was out of the game.

Jake jumped up and raised his arms in triumph, but was the first to bound over and offer Roman a hand up.

'That was rotten luck,' Jake commiserated with him.

'Another time, Jake. Maybe we can make this a Christmas limbo tradition.'

'Absolutely,' Jake agreed.

Mrs Lemon spoke up. 'Right, everyone inside and get a heat at the fire, and something to eat.'

Everyone went back inside and continued to party into the night.

There were a few takers to finish off the dregs of the eggnog.

'I think you've had enough to drink,' Daisy told Jake calmly. He'd put his shirt and waistcoat back on, but his tie was squinty and his hair was ruffled.

'I feel quite elated but sozzled,' he confessed. 'Drinking on an empty stomach isn't a great idea. I didn't stop for lunch and skipped dinner because I thought I'd have plenty to eat here. And I have.'

'And plenty to drink.'

He twirled her around in his arms as they danced. 'It's been another one of those days.'

'We seem to be having a lot of those recently.' She looked thoughtful. 'Did the interviews go well today?'

Jake's expression answered that question.

'What went wrong?'

'What went right is easier to explain.'

'So, explain.'

Jake stopped dancing as he confided in her. 'According to Valerie, she's now had other publications eager to take her up on her offer to interview me about the new book. Their questions are quite prying about my private life. I wriggle out of answering most of them, but it's pretty obvious that I'm side–stepping details about me being single, eligible as they like to say.'

'They're bound to wonder.'

'Yes, but...'

'You told me Valerie said that the first interview you did the other day was right on target.'

'That's true.'

'Well then, just keep doing what you're doing. Valerie seems happy with your interviews.'

Jake nodded. 'You're right. I'm just a little keyed up about everything.'

'Come and have something to eat at the buffet.' Daisy led him over and encouraged him to have a couple of the savoury puff pastries with tomato and mixed pepper salad. She helped herself to the sandwiches. And Mrs Lemon organised tea and hot chocolate for everyone.

Daisy wasn't sure of the exact time the party finished, but it was before the dawn, so she knew she'd have a few hours sleep before getting up to start another day. Roman had invited her to have lunch at the castle and she'd agreed to drop by.

Jake had another interview to do that Valerie had lined up for him, so Daisy planned to have lunch at the castle and take her sketch pad with her to make notes on the vintage designs.

The last she saw of Jake, he was being piled into Sharky's van, along with Roman, Mr Greenie and a couple of other guests, all having succumbed to Mrs Lemon's hospitality.

Waving to Sharky, knowing he was dropping them off safely at their respective houses and the castle, Daisy bid Mrs Lemon and Woolley goodnight, then walked across to her cottage and got ready for bed.

It had been a great party, and Mr Greenie promised to give her a copy of the festive fiasco he'd filmed. Something to look forward to she thought, flopping into bed, exhausted from dancing, partying and having a night filled with fun.

She didn't have to stop herself from thinking about Sebastian because he wasn't in her thoughts. The only things on her mind were the antics at the party, picturing Jake's somewhat inebriated performance in Mrs Lemon's garden.

And then she wondered what to pack for her trip to New York. Jake had been right. The time had flown in. Not long now until they were on their way. A rush of excitement charged through her, clashing with a longing to stay in Cornwall.

Jake told her at the party that he'd tried to wriggle out of going, hoping to do the interviews by phone or via live chats, but his suggestion had been knocked back. At least he'd tried.

Tugging up the covers to stay cosy, she peered out the window at the cold night. The air was so clear that she could see hundreds of stars twinkling in the dark sky, and fell asleep thinking that she was living in a star–sprinkled Christmas scene.

Jake phoned Daisy the next morning as she got ready to leave for her lunch meeting at the castle.

'My agent in London has arranged a phone interview for me tomorrow afternoon. He says it's a press interview. The journalist wants to talk to you too. He's interested in discussing your illustrations for the book. Would you be able to come up to the house tomorrow?'

'Yes, I'll be there.' She was beginning to think that no one would want to talk to the illustrator of Jake's book, so she was pleasantly surprised to be included in the interview.

'They know I asked you to illustrate my book. And they sort of know that you came to Cornwall to get over a broken heart.'

'Did you tell them?'

'No, I haven't spoken to the journalist yet, but he's my agent's regular London–based contact for publicity features like this. They're on friendly terms and my agent told him that we met when you left London to get over being jilted by Sebastian.'

'It sounds as if they know quite a bit.'

'I'd like your illustrations acknowledged in the press. I'm sure you can handle the personal questions far better than me.'

'Is there anything you don't want me to tell them?'

'No, keep it straightforward and as near the truth without revealing everything about our relationship.'

'Should I tell them we're dating?'

'Yes. That's not a secret. But they'll probably bring up about you being broken hearted over Sebastian, running off from London to stay in

Franklin's holiday cottage here in Cornwall, and that you saw the sign in my shop window and walked in to see what the remedy was.'

'And you wanted to test the latest version of your cure for love on me.'

'But you didn't want me messing with your emotions. You'd had enough of that from Sebastian.'

Daisy sighed. 'This sounds like it could be more about us and less about your book.'

'My agent assures me it'll be a balanced interview.'

'Okay, I'll do it.'

'I'll see you tomorrow afternoon, around two.'

'Yes.'

'Are you still having lunch at the castle?'

'I am. I'll be leaving soon to drive there in time for a tour of the castle followed by lunch.'

'I thought he'd given you a tour in the summertime.'

'He did, but this time he wants to show me the original vintage designs on the furnishings and decor. The last time it was a tour of the turrets, the main hall, the sweeping staircase, that sort of thing. I didn't study the fabrics on the furnishings or the decor designs. It could be useful for the book, especially as the patterns are from an authentic castle.'

'Ah, right.' Now he understood.

Jake sounded rather the worse for wear from the party.

'Have you recovered from last night?' she said.

'I woke up feeling like I'd been limbo dancing outside on a freezing cold night,' he joked with her.

'I'm pretending I didn't make a complete fool of myself. That it was just a dream.'

'I won't show you the video Mr Greenie sent me this morning then,' she said chirpily.

Jake perked up. 'You've seen it?'

'Twice. It's...very entertaining.' She stifled a giggle.

'Woolley dropped by for breakfast. He wants a copy. He says it's to keep as fond memories of the engagement party, but I'm sure it's because he wants to re–watch me acting like a fool.'

'I'll send it to him right now.' She had Woolley's number on her phone. She pressed send.

'What was the worst bit? I sort of remember shimmying across the lawn half naked.'

'There are no worst bits. It's all highly entertaining.'

'You're relishing this, aren't you?'

Daisy laughed. 'Sorry. I particularly liked that you kept your tie on.'

Jake laughed too. 'You should've stopped me.'

'There was no stopping you, Jake. You were well up for the challenge.'

'Mrs Lemon's eggnog has a lot to answer for.'

'Keep telling yourself that.'

On that light–hearted note, they ended the call.

Daisy put her cream wool coat on over her white jumper and cords, checked that she had her sketch pad and pencils in her bag, and headed outside to drive to the castle. She was looking forward to the tour and a view of the archives.

It was a blustery day and the sea rolled in with white–crested waves washing on to the shore as she drove along the coast road.

The castle looked beautiful against the vast grey sky as she ventured through the open gates and along the driveway leading up to the main doors.

She'd visited the castle in the summer, but hadn't been back since then. The dramatic structure with its turrets and surrounding gardens filled her with excitement.

The gardens had looked lovely with colourful flowerbeds and immaculate lawns in the summertime, but they now bore a stark beauty that somehow suited the winter season in a timeless manner.

She stepped out of her car and stood for a few moments gazing up at the grandeur of the castle. It was so impressive.

Sweeping stray strands of her hair back from her face, she took a picture of it.

The salty scent of the sea blew up from the coast and mingled with the country air. She imagined that this is how it would've looked and felt over a hundred years ago. The main telltale that it was the present and not the past were the cars parked outside the castle, though Roman Penhaligan's classic car, a vintage model that he used regularly, was the perfect accessory for the setting.

Roman had seen her car drive up. He stood at the massive front doors, smiling to welcome her and waved her inside.

'It's a blustery day, Daisy. Come in and get a heat by the fire.'

He wore a stylish suit, shirt and silk cravat, and led her through reception to the main hall where a fire burned in the huge fireplace. Tables set with white linen circled the dance floor. No one was there. Guests were having lunch in the smaller dining room.

'An anniversary dinner dance is scheduled for this evening,' he said, leading her over to a table set for two near the fire and the large Christmas tree. The tree sparkled with fairy lights and baubles.

'I love your Christmas tree,' Daisy told him.

'It's gorgeous, isn't it. I do enjoy the festive season.'

She walked over for a closer look. The scent of the fresh pine mingled with the logs burning on the fire.

'Can I offer you a cup of tea to heat you up before I give you the tour?' Roman offered.

'That would be lovely.'

Tea was served by Roman's personal butler, a man in his early sixties, named George Butler.

Pushing a silver tea trolley, he set their tea down along with a cake stand filled with frosted fairy cakes, petit fours and slices of Christmas cake.

Daisy took a sip of her tea and succumbed to a fairy cake that was swirled with buttercream icing sprinkled with sugar crystals.

Roman opted for a slice of Christmas cake with his tea.

'I'm not entirely sure what you need for your book, but I've jotted down a rough itinerary of things that might interest you.' Roman handed her a list of items.

Daisy scanned them and nodded at each one. 'These are great. Will you have time to show me all of them?'

'Yes, I've cleared my schedule for the whole afternoon. We'll start with the large sitting room. The decor there is different from the smaller sitting room on the first floor. Then we'll stop for lunch, and continue with the remainder of the castle and finish with a look through the archives of the library.'

'I appreciate you doing this,' she said. 'Franklin thinks it'll really help with the book's content, and he's offered to credit you in the publication, if you want.'

'Oh, yes, that would be wonderful.'

'I won't use any of the designs in their exact form,' she explained. 'It's only to let me see the type of patterns that were used in bygone times. My illustrations will be original, but give a feeling of the designs. And I'm interested to see the brocade fabrics and the crewelwork embroidery and tapestry work.'

'I think you'll like the brocade fabrics. They're an exquisite example of opulence from an era when the texture of the fabric was particularly rich. Silk threads were woven through some of the fabric on the curtains and other drapery. We keep those in a private collection. They're not used by guests, but we have kept the feel of the past in any new bedding we use. Many of the curtains are the original pieces though, as are some of the wall coverings and wall hangings.'

'I can't wait to have a look at everything.' Daisy drank her tea and finished eating her cake.

Roman stood up. 'Shall we?'

Nodding to him, she left her coat on her chair, shouldered her bag and followed him as he led the way through to the large sitting room that had a view of the gardens at the rear of the castle.

Rose prints dominated the room, and the windows let in plenty of daylight, showing the designs to full effect. The sofas and armchairs were upholstered with a mix of large and small rose prints of various hues on white and beige backgrounds. The deepest tones of roses were in pinks and burgundy with a few shades of blue. The lighter colours had a faded quality with pastel pink, eau–de–nil and sky blue.

'This is a lovely sitting room,' Daisy said, taking photos of the rose designs, and making notes in her sketch pad about the aspects she wanted to highlight. 'These look like they range from the 1930s to the 1950s.'

'They do. The castle is over a hundred years old and includes lots of antique furniture and ornaments. But when I inherited the castle it had been redecorated at least twice, so there's an eclectic mix of vintage decor.'

From the large sitting room, he led her up the wide, sweeping staircase to the first floor's small sitting room. The rose prints were present but didn't dominate. A wide range of floral prints were on everything from the sofas and chair upholstery, cushions, curtains and table linen. There were pansies, bluebells, violets, lavender, daisies, peonies and numerous other flowers depicted, some bold, others pastel or faded, and included ditsy prints along with larger designs.

The view from the windows overlooked the coast.

'This is what I call the cosy sitting room. I have private accommodation on the first floor of the castle, and this is my little hideaway when I want to think or relax and enjoy the view.'

Daisy wandered over to one of the windows and peered out. The silvery sea glistened under the light grey sky and she felt herself relax just looking at it.

'You're fortunate to live in a castle like this.'

'I consider myself extremely lucky. And I'm thoroughly enjoying building up the wedding and function side of the castle's facilities. As you know, my financial business dealings are what keeps the castle solvent. But now there's a notable profit from the weddings and party events, and it's nice to have plenty of guests bringing life to the castle.'

'It's a beautiful setting for weddings.'

'I like that it's becoming popular for local couples to have their receptions here too, and not just those from further afield. I vary the wedding packages so that it's reasonably affordable while keeping it exclusive. A bit special.'

'You seem to have achieved the right balance. I've had a look at your website and it's brimming with photos of weddings you've held here and you're booked well in advance.'

'Spring and summer weddings were our most popular at first, but now autumn and winter weddings are catching up in popularity. Showing photos on the website is one of the main ways I market the castle.'

'I enjoyed scrolling through the pictures. The catering is top class too, and I notice you offer to supply the wedding cakes.'

'Sharky is my main cake supplier. I rely on him. His sugar craft is excellent.'

'His Christmas cakes are very popular. Even I've ordered one. And his figgy pudding. I'll need to eat them before I go to New York.'

'Not long now until you leave.'

A trill of excitement shot through her. 'I'm starting to plan what to pack.'

'I've been to New York a few times. Once at Christmastime a few years ago. It was wonderful in December. I'm sure you'll love it. Manhattan looks magical when it's snowing.'

Daisy nodded, and then made notes of the designs in the room. 'I love this fabric on the sofas.'

'It's tapestry fabric, woven to create intricate patterns,' he explained. 'Ideal for upholstery.' Then he pointed to the mahogany and walnut table tops. 'Floral marquetry was used to create these.'

Daisy took pictures of the marquetry. 'This is incredible craftsmanship.'

'The bureau has marquetry too.'

She went over for a closer look and ran her fingers over the satin smooth polished rosewood surface. And then she continued making notes while Roman extolled the benefits of castle living.

Moving on, he gave her a tour of the other rooms, including bedrooms where new quilts made from old–fashioned designs covered the beds.

'The quilts are stitched locally,' he said. 'I have a couple myself. The quilters source quality cotton with flower prints that have a vintage vibe.'

'I've seen quilts like this in the local craft shop.'

'That's where I buy them from. This room is one of the bridal suites, and the quilt includes lily of the valley and orange blossom fabric, and a wedding ring design.'

'Mrs Lemon would love it.' She made a mental note to consider a quilt like this as a wedding gift.

Roman continued to show her the other two bridal suites.

'Your knowledge of the fabrics and designs is impressive,' she told him.

'I enjoy the background information about everything we put into the castle for guests. My financial business is all number crunching. So it's fun to balance that with creative work.'

She agreed, and added notes about the quilts on her sketch pad.

He checked the time. 'Shall we head downstairs for lunch?'

Daisy put her sketch pad in her bag. 'Yes.'

He led the way down to reception and through to the main hall. 'We have a delicious festive lunch menu. Roast potatoes, parsnips and carrots, mustard and chestnuts...' Roman rattled off the selection.

'It sounds tempting.'

Rubbing his hands together, delighted that she was happy to sample the menu, they sat at their table near the roaring log fire and chatted while dining in style beside the huge Christmas tree.

CHAPTER TEN

Makeshift Bride

Daisy could've happily spent the remainder of the afternoon browsing the books in the castle library and enjoying the relaxing atmosphere. The books ranged from bygone times to modern classics and included non–fiction titles about the surrounding area from the coast to the countryside.

After the delicious lunch, Roman gave Daisy a tour of the other rooms in the castle, culminating in looking at the designs in the private library. They had it all to themselves. Books lined one wall, and comfy armchairs were arranged to create a convivial haven of tranquillity. Situated on the ground floor at the rear of the building, the windows offered a view of the gardens and trees beyond the edges of the estate.

Daisy sank down into one of the brocade upholstered chairs and flicked through a book filled with pictures of the Cornish coast from yesteryear.

Roman gestured to one of the wall tapestries and Daisy saw examples of the crewelwork embroidery, stitched from fine wool thread, framed beside floral drapery.

'It's so quiet,' Daisy said, feeling the need to keep her voice down to a calm whisper.

Barely a second elapsed before loud knocking sounded from a room next door to the library.

Daisy jolted from the stark interruption and stood up. 'I spoke too soon.'

Roman listened for a moment to the intrusive hammering, and then it dawned on him. 'That'll be Mr Greenie. He's here today working on the wedding arch. We plan to use it for couples wishing to be photographed standing under it, rather like the little figures you find on top of wedding cakes.'

Daisy frowned, unsure what this could be.

'Come on, I'll show you.'

Daisy put the book back on the shelf and followed Roman next door to the large storeroom where Mr Greenie was putting the finishing touches to the arch he'd constructed. It looked like the garden arches that were erected outside in the castle grounds for wedding ceremonies, but this one was made to be folded away and kept specifically for indoor shots of couples after they were married.

The white painted wooden arch had a detachable base that resembled the top of a white iced wedding cake and could be conveniently stored until needed.

'I've almost finished it.' Armed with a hammer, Mr Greenie stepped aside to show Roman and Daisy his handiwork.

'Excellent work, Mr Greenie,' Roman told him, heading over for a closer look.

'It's lovely.' Daisy admired the white silk flowers, mainly roses, that were wound around the arch.

Mr Greenie grinned cheerily. 'I brought a few props with me from the fancy dress party you held here.' He put his hammer down and rummaged through a large bag containing four items — a groom's top hat and dark grey tailcoat, a long, white bridal veil attached to a sparkling hair band, and a bride's bouquet made from silk flowers and trimmed with ribbons.

'Props?' Roman said to him.

'Yes, I was going to ask your butler and the castle's receptionist to wear them and stand underneath the arch so that I can gauge the ideal height and width of it.' Mr Greenie handed the items to Roman and Daisy. 'But as you're both here, perhaps you could pop these on and stand on the base so I can measure the arch.'

Roman had no qualms about doing this, and seemed quite up for a bit of fun as he shrugged the tailcoat on and added the top hat.

'How do I look?' Roman said to Daisy.

'Very smart.'

He stepped under the arch and felt the distance from the top of his hat to the tip of the arch. 'You'll probably need to heighten this a smidgen.'

Mr Greenie agreed. 'You're quite tall, and I thought the hat would account for someone well over six feet, but the tip of it is brushing against the roses. I can easily adjust it.'

Daisy was encouraged to put the long, chiffon veil on and stand beside Roman under the arch. Roman, as tall as Jake, towered above her.

Mr Greenie handed her the bouquet. 'For effect.'

While Mr Greenie got his phone ready to take a few pictures of them, Roman thanked Daisy for helping them.

'A lot of couples love having their photos taken under one of the wedding arches,' Roman explained. 'But when the weather is inclement, especially in the winter months, I thought I'd offer this as part of their special day. I plan to have it set up in the main hall when needed or in another part of the castle. We've previously used the garden arches, but this would be handier.'

Mr Greenie held up his phone. 'Let me take some photos to see how the proportion of the arch looks in an actual picture.' He clicked a few shots and then said, 'Smile, Daisy, and link your arm through Roman's. That's it.'

'I hope you're okay with this,' Roman said, sensing her slight hesitation.

'Yes,' she lied. She was sort of okay with this. It helped Mr Greenie see how a newly wed couple would look under the arch. And yet...standing there beside Roman, dressed as a makeshift bride, felt a bit odd. She'd never worn a bridal veil before, not even for dressing up when she was little. She'd worn fancy dress outfits as a fairy with sparkly wings and a fairytale princess with a glittering tiara. But this was her first time as a bride, and the man standing next to her was Roman Penhaligan, not Jake.

Mr Greenie bounded over and showed them the pictures. 'You look like a lovely couple, but I definitely need to adjust the height of the arch, though the width is perfect.' He put his phone away and lifted up his hammer. 'I'll have it sorted in a jiffy.'

Daisy unlinked herself from Roman's arm, stepped aside from the arch, put the bouquet down and took the veil off.

She put them back in the bag and shook her hair, and herself, trying to shrug off the feeling of being a pretend bride.

Leaving Mr Greenie to get on with his work, Roman walked Daisy through to the main hall to pick up her coat and then escorted her outside to her car.

'Thank you for the tour, and for lunch. Those were the tastiest roast potatoes and parsnips I've had in ages,' she said.

'And thank you for the impromptu help as a makeshift bride.' Roman sounded grateful, and there was no awkwardness on his part.

He'd wanted to say that it was ideal practice for when she married Jake, but the lack of an engagement ring on her finger made him keep his remark to himself. There was no hint of Jake proposing to Daisy. Personally, Roman would've asked her by now if he'd been Jake, but as he didn't know their private circumstances, it was none of his business.

Daisy got into her car and waved as she drove off. A pang of sadness shot through her. This was the last time she'd be at the castle this Christmastime. Parties galore were lined up for the festive season, but she'd miss out on them. New York beckoned. In the back of her mind she wished that somehow the publicity would be rescheduled until after Christmas, but futile wishes like that never came true and only caused her to feel downhearted.

Telling herself to brighten up, she drove away from the castle and along the coastal road. The sea looked particularly wild and wonderful. She pulled the car over and stepped out, breathing in the strong and invigorating scent of the sea, letting it blow through her hair and clear away the cobwebs of doubt about Jake's intentions.

The day had darkened to teatime as Daisy sat sketching illustrations in her cottage. She'd been so steeped in her artwork, her mind whirring with ideas after her trip to the castle, that she hadn't noticed that it was now five o'clock.

There was a cosiness to being snuggled up in the lounge by the fire doing one of the things she loved best — artwork. Seeing her ideas come to life on the paper had boosted her enthusiasm to continue illustrating until the day was nearly done. The illustrations included a lily of the valley spray, sunflowers, gardenia and cornflowers.

Floral lettering for Karen and Sharky was finished too and ready for framing. The lettering included pansies, daisies and forget–me–nots, and she'd added tiny cupcakes as a nod to Sharky's baking.

She phoned Sharky at his shop. 'I've finished the lettering for you.'

'I'll pick it up from you on my way home. I should be there in about half an hour. I can't wait to see it.'

'See you soon.' After the call, Daisy put the lettering safely in a folder and continued to work on her illustrations.

A short while later Sharky's van pulled up outside the cottage.

Daisy welcomed him in and led him through to the lounge.

She opened the folder to show him the lettering, hoping he liked it.

The look on Sharky's face confirmed that he did. 'You've added cupcakes! That's great. And the flowers are beautiful. Karen will love it.'

Daisy went to close the folder but Sharky had other plans.

'I bought one of the glass frames from the craft shop.' He had it with him in a bag. 'The shop said that this is the same size as the one you used for Mrs Lemon and Woolley's lettering.'

'Yes, it is.'

'I don't suppose you'd frame it for me.'

'I'd be happy to.'

Sharky watched as Daisy expertly trimmed the artwork to size and popped it in the glass frame. 'There you are.' She handed it to him.

He held it up and admired it. 'Thank you so much, Daisy. I'm heading over to Mrs Lemon's cottage to pick up Karen and take her to my house for dinner. This will be a wonderful surprise for her.' He started to head out, but paused at the front door, and sighed heavily.

'Something wrong?'

'Local gossip.' He held up his phone to show her a picture. 'Woolley sent this to me after you'd phoned.'

Daisy blinked as she saw a picture of her standing with Roman Penhaligan under the wedding arch. 'Where did Woolley get this?'

'Mr Greenie sent it to Woolley. I think he meant well, but now there's gossip about you and Roman rehearsing for your wedding.'

'That's nonsense. Mr Greenie asked me to put the veil on and hold the bouquet so he could gauge the arch he was making.' She explained the details.

Sharky shrugged. 'I believe you, but...some folk seem to have the wrong end of the stick. And with Jake not proposing to you yet, there's gossip that Penhaligan's stepped in and plans to marry you instead. At the castle at Christmastime.'

Daisy's heart jolted. 'But that's not true.'

Sharky gave her a despondent look.

She studied the picture and realised that Mr Greenie had added their names along the edge of the white base they were standing on, and embellished it with hearts. Her white, slim–fitting jumper with its long sleeves blended with the veil.

'This looks bad. If Jake sees this...' She shook her head in dismay.

'Jake's bound to see it. Woolley will show him. The picture is doing the rounds.'

'Thanks for the heads up. I'll tell Jake before anyone else does. He'll understand once I explain.'

Sharky smiled tightly. 'Good luck. Let me know if you need me to back you up.'

Daisy nodded, and then watched Sharky walk down the garden path, get into his van and drive over to Mrs Lemon's cottage. She could only imagine the two extremes of him presenting Karen with the floral lettering and then discussing Daisy's dilemma.

Closing the door, she went through to the kitchen to make a cup of tea and phone Jake. She'd just filled the kettle when Jake sent her a message.

Nice wedding picture of you and Roman Penhaligan.

I can explain.

No need. Woolley explained.

She sensed that Jake wasn't happy, and she didn't blame him, but he was keeping a lid on being upset.

I trust the tour of his castle went well.

It did. The vintage designs were beautiful. I've been sketching ideas for the new book since I got back to the cottage.

I'll let you get on with your artwork. Are you still coming up to the house tomorrow afternoon for the interview?

Yes, I'll be there before two.

Okay, Daisy. See you then.

And that was that.

The kettle clicked off and Daisy made a cup of tea feeling totally deflated.

Instead of staring despondently into her tea, she headed out into the cold night. She didn't even bother putting a jacket on, and trudged over to Mrs Lemon's cottage and knocked on the front door.

Mrs Lemon looked surprised to see Daisy standing on her doorstep.

Daisy's tone was dour and desperate. 'Do you have any of that eggnog left?'

'No, but I can recommend my special hot chocolate. It's my own recipe.'

Mrs Lemon gestured for Daisy to come in and led her through to the toasty lounge. She was on her own. 'Sit yourself down and get a heat by the fire.'

Daisy sat down while Mrs Lemon rustled around in the kitchen making a mug of hot chocolate for Daisy, and one for herself.

A lot of mixing sounds wafted through from the kitchen, along with the rich aroma of chocolate.

As Daisy sat by the fire, her thoughts drifted to Jake, wondering what he was thinking...

Jake tried and failed to stop studying the picture of Daisy smiling out from his phone. Seeing her as a bride wrenched at his heart and threw his plans for a night working at his desk, that was piled with paperwork, into turmoil. He couldn't concentrate on any of the herbs or potions he'd planned to work on that evening.

He slumped back in his chair and gazed despondently at her beautiful face framed by a wedding veil. Daisy suited being a bride, and as this was only an impromptu fancy dress outfit, he could only imagine how wonderful she'd look if she was dressed as a bride for real.

Woolley had reassured him that Mr Greenie had helpfully enhanced the photo, but still...Daisy looked beautiful, and he felt like his heart had been ripped to the core seeing her standing there with the happily grinning castle owner.

Sighing wearily, he glanced down at her cottage from his study. Her Christmas tree was lit up in the window. She'd be in there busily working on her illustrations for the book. He wanted to run down that hill and wrap her in his arms and ask her to marry him. But this would taint their special moment. And all because she'd helpfully stood as a fake bride under a wedding arch with a fake groom. No, this wasn't the memory he wanted for them when he proposed.

Putting his phone aside, he concentrated on his work, being as diligent as Daisy was, no doubt working hard on her illustrations in her cottage...

Mrs Lemon carried two mugs of her special hot chocolate through to the lounge. The whipped cream topping was dusted with chocolate sprinkles.

'Sharky picked Karen up so she's at his house having dinner, and Woolley won't be here until later. We're free to chat.' She handed Daisy a mug of hot chocolate.

Daisy took a sip. 'Strong stuff. Is there brandy or sherry in this?'

'Yes.' Mrs Lemon sipped her drink and sat at the fireside too.

Daisy drank another couple of mouthfuls and sighed. 'Have you heard the gossip about Roman and me?'

'I have. Quite a few people have been taken aback thinking you've given your affections to Roman because Jake wouldn't propose.'

Daisy went to explain, but Mrs Lemon held up her hand. 'I understand that you were just helping Roman and Mr Greenie, but surely you can see why people are gossiping.'

Daisy nodded, and then the potent effect of the drink kicked in causing Daisy to reveal a few secrets she'd kept to herself.

'Sebastian wants to marry you at Christmas?' This news made Mrs Lemon jolt. 'The cheek of him. He's the cause of you being here. He's the one that made you broken–hearted. Just because it didn't work out for him with Celeste, it doesn't mean he can waltz back into your life and expect you to forgive him — and marry him!'

Sitting by the fireside, Daisy told her she'd been dreaming about Sebastian.

'A diamond engagement ring from Sebastian!' Mrs Lemon exclaimed. 'I know it was only a dream, but sometimes dreams can be uncannily accurate. Sebastian is a confidant scoundrel and I wouldn't put it past him to drive down here from London and propose to you. He could've bought you a ring. Three diamonds in a row. All big and sparkling and expensive. That sounds like his style. All flash and fancy extravagance.'

'I haven't told Jake what Sebastian said to me in the park. I didn't lie. I just didn't elaborate about everything that was said.'

Mrs Lemon understood. 'It's a tricky situation. Karen says Jake is very keyed up at the moment with this book launch and publicity.'

'He is. And we're both doing an interview tomorrow afternoon. His agent has arranged for a journalist he knows to phone from London to talk to us. I've been told that some of the questions could involve me being broken–hearted over Sebastian and running off from London to Franklin's cottage.'

'So you'll be talking about Sebastian whether you want to or not.'

Daisy had almost finished her hot chocolate, feeling the potent effects of it. 'Yes, the interviewer wants to write about how I first met Jake when I walked into his shop. Jake's agent knows the story and he's told the journalist, so I'll be talking about that.'

'And now you're the topic of local gossip with that picture of you and Roman.' Mrs Lemon pursed her lips. 'Bad timing.'

'Stinking, rotten, bad.' Daisy's words dripped with verbal poison.

'Are there any other secrets that could crop up that you've been hiding from Jake?'

'None that I can think of.' Though she wasn't thinking entirely straight due to the potency of the drink. She mentally rewound anything else she'd deliberately omitted from telling Jake.

'Think, Daisy. Is there something else that Sebastian did or said recently in London?'

'No, but—' Daisy hesitated.

Mrs Lemon sat forward. 'What?'

'Sebastian said he'd heard that Jake wasn't the marrying kind. And he cast up about Sharky putting a ring on Karen's finger.'

Mrs Lemon gasped. 'That's none of his business.'

'I know, but Sebastian obviously keeps tabs on what goes on down here.'

'He doesn't get any information from me,' Mrs Lemon insisted, and then she paused. 'But I do tell Franklin the local news, so he's probably the one telling Sebastian.'

'Did you tell Franklin that Jake wasn't the marrying kind and wouldn't marry me?'

'No, I've never said that, but Franklin is of the opinion that Jake is a bit of a lone wolf.'

'That's maybe where that comment came from,' Daisy surmised.

'What else did Sebastian say?'

'He said he'd made a mistake getting involved with Celeste. He hoped that I could find it in my heart to forgive him. But I don't want to get back together with Sebastian. The dreams aren't real. They're just fanciful thoughts. Sebastian used to say to me — *love me forever*. But I don't love him now.'

'Did Sebastian mention about him and Celeste?'

'Yes, but he said he hasn't had anything to do with Celeste in months.'

'Do you believe him?'

'I do, and even Franklin says that Celeste has nothing to do with Sebastian now. They both work in the publishing company, but Franklin keeps them apart, working on different books and editorial business.'

'It sounds to me like Sebastian is trying to stir things up between you and Jake, something he's good at. You'll need to be careful not to let him get to you. And don't make any other silly mistakes with Roman.'

Daisy agreed. 'Sebastian said that he knows I'm angry with him, but that circumstances change. As I walked away from him in the park he insisted we could be happy together. And could get engaged at Christmas.'

CHAPTER ELEVEN

Midnight Mayhem

Jake sat at his desk trying to work, but he kept thinking about Daisy.

With a sigh, he finally put his notes down and stood up. He checked the time. It was late in the evening, but not that late. The lights from Daisy's Christmas tree shone like a beacon of hope that she was still working and hadn't gone to bed.

As he grabbed his jacket, the mechanism in the cuckoo clock on the study wall creaked and the little doors opened at four minutes past the hour.

In no mood to be distracted by an out of sync clock, Jake cast it a disgruntled glare.

Reining in his tiny wooden beak, the bird sank back into the clock and the doors closed without a single cuckoo sound being uttered.

Jake glared at it again and then shrugged his jacket on, zipped it up to the collar for warmth and headed out into the cold night.

Determined to talk to Daisy, if only for a few minutes, Jake strode down the hill, feeling the icy air against his skin. A wintry wind blew up from the shore, sweeping his hair back from his furrowed brow and helped clear his thoughts as he approached Daisy's cottage.

He wouldn't bring up the subject of her posing as a bride with Penhaligan. No, he'd focus on telling her...what? That he missed her? Wished they weren't going to New York at Christmastime? Wanted to enjoy a cosy Christmas with her in Cornwall?

Before he could decide, he was walking up the garden path to her front door. The glow from the Christmas tree was the only light that he could see inside the cottage. Perhaps she'd gone to bed and left the fairy lights on by mistake? Or she'd fallen asleep on the sofa like they'd both done recently.

He knocked on the door and waited, pulling up the collar of his jacket against the biting wind. His breath filtered out into the air as he stood and waited, but there was no response from Daisy.

Stepping aside, he peered in the lounge window, cupping his hands on the glass, shading the glow from the Christmas lights so that he could see if she'd fallen asleep on the sofa.

But there was no sign of her.

He knocked again, louder this time with a firmness that sounded in the quiet night. Glancing around, there was no one out and about at this time of night, only him, though there were two cottages that still had their lights on, including Mrs Lemon cottage. Her Christmas lights shone in her front window and the garden lights were on, but apart from that, he looked like the unreasonable person visiting Daisy's cottage at this late hour.

With a resigned sigh he turned and started to walk away, but then he thought...perhaps she was in the kitchen.

Trying not to look like he was creeping around the cottage, he sank into the shadows and sneaked round to the back garden.

Everything was quiet, making the frosted grass and crisp winter foliage sound clear beneath his feet as he trudged over it.

The kitchen, bathroom and bedroom lights were off. The cottage was in total darkness. She must be tucked up in bed and had forgotten to turn the Christmas tree lights off.

Cold blue moonlight streamed across the garden illuminating him, so he stepped into the shadows and was about to walk away when his phone rang.

'Yes,' he whispered, taking the call from Valerie.

'Hi, Jake. I wanted to go over an idea for the publicity with you. I have your schedule here for when you arrive in New York. It's pretty packed, but I'd like to fit in an invitation to a large dinner party the night you arrive. Lots of media will be there. It's a newsy event. Perfect to announce your arrival in Manhattan.'

Keeping to the shadows so as not to attract attention, Jake walked back round to the front of the cottage while he listened to Valerie.

He noted that Daisy's car was parked outside so she hadn't gone gallivanting anywhere like...he didn't know. Hopefully not to the castle for a rendezvous with Roman.

Pushing thoughts like this aside, he concentrated on confirming with Valerie that he'd attend the dinner event with Daisy.

'Dress to impress, Jake. That's the look we're going for. And Daisy will need to wear a suitable evening dress. Homespun is fine, but not homemade, if you get my drift.'

He did. But he'd no qualms about Daisy dressing to impress. Those sparkly cocktail dresses she had would out–dazzle most of them.

Walking up the hill to his house, he continued the call, unaware that Daisy had emerged from Mrs Lemon's cottage two mugs of potent hot chocolate and a cream–filled brandy snap the happier.

Waving to Mrs Lemon, Daisy ran across to her cottage, feeling the cold air chill her in moments. She'd been so cosy by the fire.

Hurrying inside, she flicked the Christmas tree lights off and headed straight through to the bedroom to put on her comfy pyjamas and get some sleep.

Jake was at the top of the hill when he finished the call with Valerie.

Glancing back down at Daisy's cottage, he noticed the fairy lights were now off.

He paused and wondered. Had she woken up and realised she'd left the lights on? It crossed his mind to head back down if she was awake now, but then decided otherwise. He didn't want to look like a frantic fool knocking on her door at this time of night.

Reluctantly, he continued on into his house, planning to work in his study for a while longer before going to bed.

Daisy was about to snuggle under the covers when Mrs Lemon phoned her.

'Woolley's just arrived and says he saw Jake at your cottage. He must've been looking for you.'

'Thanks for letting me know. I'll give him a call.'

Jumping out of bed, Daisy hurried through to the lounge and peered out the window. The lights were on in Jake's study.

She phoned him.

'Jake, is everything okay? Mrs Lemon says that Woolley saw you at the cottage.'

'Yes, I popped down to see you. I didn't mean to wake you.'

'I wasn't asleep. I was at Mrs Lemon's cottage. We were chatting and having hot chocolate.'

'Her special hot chocolate?'

'Maybe.'

Jake smiled.

'Is everything okay?' she said.

He told her about the call from Valerie rather than admit he'd been longing to see her because of the gossip about Roman.

'A dinner party?'

'Yes, a dress to impress event with lots of media there. Valerie thinks it would be a great way to introduce us. The venue is near our hotel. But we'll be thrown in at the deep end as soon as we arrive in New York.'

She heard the hesitation in his voice, wondering if she was okay with that.

'I guess I'll need a glitzy cocktail dress,' she said, confirming she was willing to go along for the ride.

'You'll outshine them all.'

'The red sequin sparkler it is then.' Her tone was light, but her heart felt the weight of this whole trip looming ahead of them. Now there wouldn't even be time to breathe after their flight. It would be a mad dash to their hotel, throw on their gladrags and then head to the dinner party.

'We can do this.'

The rich tone of his voice resonated through her, reminding her of the manly strength she felt from Jake that made her heart ache to be with him.

'It's late. You should get some sleep,' he said, bringing the call to a close.

'Goodnight, Jake.'

'Goodnight, Daisy.'

She looked up the hill, seeing the light in his study continue to burn brightly in the dark. Standing gazing out the window for a moment, she shivered, partly from the cold night, but mainly from the thought that they'd be leaving the cosiness of Cornwall soon.

Hugging her arms around herself for warmth and comfort, she padded back through to bed.

Moonlight streamed in the window, cutting across the bedroom in a wintry glow so bright she couldn't see the stars in the sky. No stars to wish on, hoping that they wouldn't have to leave.

Pulling up the covers against the icy glow, she felt the tiredness of the day, and the effects of the special hot chocolate, help her drift off to sleep.

Jake spent the next morning working in his health food shop and redressing the balance of the rumours that he'd been replaced by Roman in Daisy's affections. He didn't know which one was more tiring — working in the storeroom, running up and down the stairs and stocking the shelves with produce, or fending off the gossip. Probably the latter as it felt personally draining.

One of Mrs Lemon's neighbours was in the shop buying dried apricots and wholemeal bread and trying to wangle information out of Karen. The neighbour had seen Jake sneaking around Daisy's cottage the previous night and wanted to know what he was up to.

Karen rang their items through the checkout and bagged them as she refuted their suggestion that Jake was snooping.

'Jake wasn't sneaking around Daisy's cottage,' Karen told them firmly. 'He was popping by to chat to his girlfriend, not knowing that she was visiting my mum.'

'Oh, right.' The neighbour accepted Karen's explanation, took their shopping and left without another word.

Woolley walked in as the customer left and headed upstairs to where Jake was checking the accounts and organising the stock.

'What were you doing sneaking around Daisy's cottage last night?' Woolley came right out and asked him.

'I wasn't sneaking, I was trying not to wake her. I wanted to talk to her, but I thought she was asleep. I didn't know that she was at Mrs Lemon's cottage.'

'Is everything okay between the two of you? Daisy had two full mugs of hot chocolate.'

'Yes, fine. It's just the gossip about her being Roman's potential bride. Nothing important.' Jake didn't try to hide the sarcastic tone in his reply.

'Jake!' Karen called up to him. 'Roman Penhaligan is here to talk to you.'

'Send him up.' Jake let out a heavy sigh and gave Woolley a resigned look.

'Do you want me to skedaddle?' Woolley offered.

'No, this shouldn't take long.'

Roman popped his head up into the storeroom, cautious of Jake's reaction, but Jake motioned for him to come up, putting Roman at ease.

'I suppose you've heard the silly gossip about Daisy and me,' Roman began.

'I have, as has half the town. But I've put them straight, so the rumours that you're replacing me and marrying Daisy at your castle at Christmas should fade by the end of the day. Some other ridiculous gossip will take precedence.'

'Right, well, I just wanted to make sure there were no ructions in our relationship, Jake.'

'None. Though I'd prefer it if you didn't encourage my girlfriend to dress up as a bride on your wedding cake arch prop in future.'

'Consider it a one–off faux pas,' Roman assured him. Then he brought two tickets out of his jacket pocket and handed them to Jake. 'These are complimentary tickets to the castle's Christmas Eve Ball. I grabbed these on my way out, and then I realised you and Daisy won't be here. But perhaps you'd like to give them away to a couple of your customers. Karen and Sharky already have their tickets to the ball. As do Mrs Lemon and Woolley.'

Jake accepted the tickets and tucked them in one of the roll top dresser drawers for safe keeping. 'Thanks, I'll do that.'

'I won't keep you from your work any longer.' Roman headed down the stairs.

Jake followed and walked with him to the front entrance of the shop.

Roman paused outside. 'You'll be off to New York any day now, so have a great Christmas.'

'Yes, we're leaving on Friday. We're driving to London to catch the flight to New York.' Jake extended his hand. 'Merry Christmas to you.'

Roman smiled, pleased that they'd settled any awkwardness. 'Still on for a festive limbo next Christmas?'

'Absolutely.'

They shook hands, letting passers–by see that everything was fine between them. The equivalent of tipping water on the flames of the gossip.

Roman headed over to Sharky's bakery while Jake went back upstairs to get on with his work. He hoped to get as much done as possible before it was time to go home to prepare for the interview.

While working away, he heard the voices of the local carol singers wafting up from the street below.

Woolley had gone downstairs to refill the shelves.

Jake went over and peered out the window, looking down on the happy gathering as they meandered along the main street. For a moment he saw how festive the hub of the town was, festooned with fairy lights and with the huge Christmas tree aglow in the cobbled square. He realised he'd been so steeped in work and travel preparations that he hadn't taken time to enjoy the atmosphere of it all.

A wave of sadness swept through him. The festive fair, a Christmas market with lots of local stalls and fun attractions, was advertised on posters. It was being held this weekend, starting on Friday, the day Daisy and him left for their trip. Something else they'd miss out on. Daisy would've enjoyed it, and although many people didn't realise, he really loved Christmas and all the local traditions that made happy memories each year.

Last year he'd been asked to switch the tree lights on, something he did with glee. This year should've been extra special now that he was dating Daisy. But that plan had been scuppered months ago when he agreed to promote the book in New York. He hadn't thought things through at the time and was just so enamoured with Daisy, and that the publishers were pushing for a Christmas release of his new book.

With a heavy heart, he turned away from the window and got on with his work, throwing himself into racking and stacking boxes of products in the storeroom and tidying everything up in preparation for leaving.

Sharky carefully packed the three–tier wedding cake in white cardboard boxes and sat them on the bakery counter.

Roman lifted one of the boxes and then went to balance the next one on top.

'No, I wouldn't do that.' Sharky vetoed that plan. 'Bring your car over and park it outside and lift each one separately. The icing on these took me ages, so don't mess it up.'

Roman nodded firmly. 'I'll get the car.'

The cake had been ordered for a wedding at the castle the following day, and although Sharky usually delivered the cakes to the castle himself, Roman had offered to pick it up when he'd popped in to buy a bag of the sticky buns he liked so much.

Sharky wrapped the cake's accessories up in a bag and put it on the counter too.

Roman returned and picked up the first box and the bag.

Sharky carried the second box out to the car, placing it gently in the boot, while Roman brought out the third box.

'This is quite heavy,' Roman remarked, wedging the boxes safely so they wouldn't move during the drive to the castle.

'The fruit cake is packed with raisins, currents and sultanas, and the icing comprises of two layers with extra rose swirls around the edges,' Sharky explained.

'Excellent work. I'll settle the bill with you as soon as I get back to the castle.'

'Drive carefully. And if your chefs aren't sure how to assemble it, phone me.'

Roman closed the boot of the car. 'Will you be having a cake like this for your wedding?'

'Karen wants four tiers, with spring flowers iced around it, and white satin ribbons, so I'll be making that for us. All rich fruit cake, treacle, orange zest, apricot jam and marzipan with layers of white icing and fondant pansies, roses and spring flowers.'

'Sounds like a masterpiece.'

Sharky smiled. 'I hope your couple enjoy their wedding cake.'

'I'm sure they will.'

Sharky tapped the roof of the car and went to wave when Roman spoke to him out the driver's window.

'Between you and me, do you think Jake intends to propose to Daisy when they're in New York? Is that why he's not asked her to marry him yet?'

Sharky leaned down and spoke in a confiding tone. 'I don't think so. But none of us really know. Woolley thought that his engagement to Mrs Lemon would spur Jake on, but if anything, it's made Jake more focussed on the book promotion and less on his romance with Daisy.'

'That's surely not a good move on Jake's part.'

Sharky shrugged. 'When it comes to romance, Jake's pretty clueless. Look at the pickle he's gotten himself into with Daisy. Neither of them are looking forward to going to New York. But for many folk, they'd love a trip to Manhattan at Christmastime.'

'I can understand though that it's their first Christmas as a couple and they'd like to spend in here in Cornwall.'

Sharky agreed. 'But I think the whole fiasco has put a strain on their relationship.' He leaned closer so no one overheard him. 'Woolley says that Jake recently asked his publishers in New York if he could postpone the trip until the New Year, but it was a firm no.'

Roman nodded thoughtfully. 'I hope things work out for them.'

'So do I.'

Giving an acknowledging wave to each other, Roman drove off with the wedding cake and Sharky went back into his bakery shop.

Jingle bells sounded from an old–fashioned van as it drove along the main street. It was part of the festive fair and picking up items contributed by local businesses to be sold at the Christmas market. The driver, Mr Greenie, rang the bells and smiled at people as they waved to him on his way to the town's square. Everything was being stored nearby in preparation for the event, and Mr Greenie was in charge of the extra electrical work required to string a mesh of fairy lights above the area where the stalls were due to be put up.

Jake looked out the storeroom window at the van, recognising it from all the past years it had been used as part of the local traditions. Mr Greenie kept it in his garage and liked tinkering with the engine and polishing the paintwork. Often it was used at other events including the summer fair and autumn harvest party.

Jake checked the time. 'I'd better get going.'

'I hope the interview goes well for you,' Woolley told him, continuing to work in the storeroom.

Jake put his jacket on and headed downstairs. The shop was busy and Karen didn't even notice him leave as she served customers, taking orders for the Christmas cakes and figgy puddings.

The air was crisp with pale sunlight forcing through the grey clouds. A rainstorm was fighting for victory against the sunshine. Jake's money was on the bright side winning as he got into his car and drove home.

'The designs from the castle are wonderful,' Franklin told Daisy. He'd phoned to encourage her with the illustration ideas she had for the book after she'd emailed him samples.

'I'll push on with the illustrations,' she said, pleased he'd confirmed her suggestions. Then she told him, 'I'm due to be interviewed by a London–based journalist, a regular contact of Jake's agent. He wants to talk to me about what happened with Sebastian. It'll be brought up about you offering me your holiday cottage as a hideout escape. Is it okay with you if I mention this?'

'Yes, it's not a secret. Everyone in the company knows the scandalous details of what Sebastian did. Celeste helped perpetrate the gossip, so she won't be upset about it. And I'm fine with the press knowing you ran off to my cottage in Cornwall.'

Daisy was relieved. 'The story will receive a bit of press coverage.'

'Mention my book publishing company by all means,' Franklin confirmed.

'Can I mention about the new vintage book I'm working on? It's bound to be brought up.'

'Yes, any publicity for this is ideal. The title is already on the new list of forthcoming books on the company website, so it's not under wraps.'

'Great, it could be handy publicity and it's easier if I can tell them what I'm working on.'

'Let me know if the journalist needs a quote from me. Give him my number.'

'Thanks, Franklin.' She saw the time was wearing on. 'I have to dash now. I'll let you know how the interview goes.'

'Do that.'

After the call, Daisy put her coat on, grabbed her bag with a few notes she'd made that she'd probably never need or use, and hurried out. It was almost twenty to two and she'd told Jake she'd be there early, so she put a spurt on as she walked up the hill.

The air had a real bite to it, and the blustery wind whipped through her hair as she walked higher up the hill.

Arriving tousled but on time, Daisy shrugged her coat off as she hurried into Jake's study.

He'd set up his desk with a chair for her opposite him. 'I'll put my phone on speaker and place it on the desk between us so we can both chat to the journalist.'

'Franklin says I can mention whatever I want, so that'll make it easier to talk about what happened with Sebastian, if they bring that up.'

'They'll definitely bring it up.' Jake sounded totally sure.

Daisy frowned at him as she sat down.

'My agent called half an hour ago. He says that the journalist phoned him this morning to talk about the details of how we first met. The story is going to be slanted to emphasise how we met in the health food shop, tied in with my cure for love remedy.'

She dug out her notes from her bag and riffled through them. 'I've made notes, but I'm inclined to think that I won't be able to concentrate on them and talk to the journalist.'

'Use them for reference if you get stuck, but I don't think you will. You're the most self-assured woman I've ever known.'

Daisy blinked at the compliment. 'You think so?'

Jake paused and looked right at her. 'I always have, from the first moment you walked into my shop. I cringe thinking how arrogant I was to assume you'd be willing to try my cure for love.'

Daisy smiled at the memory. She'd refused to take his remedy.

'You were having none of it,' Jake confirmed, causing her to smile at him. 'What are you smiling at?'

'Just you, being you.' She gazed at him. He looked so handsome in his white shirt, navy blue tie and waistcoat, all broad shoulders and lean torso. It was only a phone interview, but as always, Jake was dressed to impress. He always impressed her, and she loved him all the more for it.

With time to spare, they were about to discuss the topics of the interview when they were interrupted.

A rusty rattle sounded from the cuckoo clock, causing Jake to panic and check the time. Then he relaxed, realising the little bird had got it wrong again. Or had he?

On the first cuckoo sound, that chimed an alert in the quietude of the study, the phone rang early, causing Daisy and Jake to jump and look startled.

Jake accepted the call.

Daisy took a deep breath, sensing trouble.

And the cuckoo clock doors closed quickly again, two cuckoo calls short of a full chime.

CHAPTER TWELVE

Publicity Feature

'Your agent gave me a copy of the book's press release so I have all the details of the book's contents and your background, Jake.' The journalist took charge of the interview and the tone of his voice indicated his interest in doing the interview.

'Great.' Jake was relieved he wouldn't have to go over the details as everything they really needed was in the press release.

Daisy nodded at Jake. So far so good.

Jake's eyes viewed her across the desk with a steady look. They could do this.

The journalist continued to lead the interview. 'I have the photographs that accompanied the press release, but I'd like some fresh ones. Pics that will be exclusive to my interview.'

'What type of photos?' Jake sounded wary. The pictures were one of the strongest pieces of information in the press pack he'd thought. They showed the cover of the book, contents, samples, and there were pictures of him sitting at his desk supposedly working on his cure for love remedy. He was outside in his garden too, picking herbs on a sunny day. What was missing?

'I need pics of you and Daisy. One of the two of you standing outside your health food shop.'

Jake's interest dipped at the thought of the journalist pushing the romance aspect, then lifted at the prospect of his shop being featured. He glanced at Daisy. She stared at him wide–eyed, clearly surprised that they'd be pictured as a couple in the press.

Neither of them expected this angle.

Daisy had rehearsed her answers to awkward questions in her mind while she'd been doing her illustrations, but she hadn't anticipated there would be photos. She was of the same opinion as Jake. The photos from the press release were more than enough for any interviewer. But she nodded firmly at Jake. They could do this too.

'Okay,' Jake confirmed. 'It's winter, so the photos will look like they were taken at a different time to the others.'

'Exactly. I want them to be current, so show some Christmas lights and festive decorations. I'm sure you have your shop window done up this time of year.'

'I do. It's looking great — fairy lights, Christmas cake, figgy pudding—'

'Excellent. Do you have a local photographer to take the pics, or should I send someone down?'

'We have someone. Mr Greenie takes first class photos. He'll be glad to help.'

'At short notice? I'd like the pics emailed to me later today.'

'Yes, I'll sort that out and get them to you,' Jake assured him, while feeling unsure.

Daisy shrugged, concerned they could pull this off, but Jake mouthed to her: *Phone Mr Greenie now*! He pointed to his notebook that had all the local numbers.

Daisy quickly tapped the number into her phone and ran off to the doorway of the study to make the furtive and frantic phone call out of earshot of the journalist.

'I'm aiming for a tight deadline,' the journalist continued to explain to Jake. 'I've blocked in the story, highlighting what I know about you and Daisy meeting in your health food shop in the summer, and all I really need is to go over specific details regarding your relationship — how the man who'd made a cure for love fell in love with a broken–hearted woman from London. It's a great story. I've run the idea by one of the main publications I supply stories to and they love it. They'll run it asap, if I can get the copy to them in time. I can. All I need are the pics to go with it.'

'Do Daisy and I get to approve the editorial before it goes to press?' Jake doubted it, but needed to ask.

'I'm afraid not. But this isn't a hit piece. Talk to your agent. He'll assure you that this isn't what I'm aiming to do. This is something that readers will enjoy at this time of year. Romance, broken hearts mended, happy ending. If the two of you end up getting married I'll do a follow up. But as that's way off in the future, let's keep it to your current situation. Dating broken–hearted Daisy and falling in love.'

Daisy hurried back and sat down. She gave Jake the thumbs up. Mr Greenie was set to help them.

Jake looked relieved.

'Can I speak to Daisy?' The journalist sounded eager to pry some private comments from her.

Her heart triggered, and she took a deep breath.

'She's right here.'

'Daisy, can I ask you why you ran off from London in the middle of the night and drove all the way to Cornwall when you'd just been horribly jilted by your boyfriend Sebastian?'

Jake gulped. Hearing it put so raw reminded him of what had happened. And his inappropriate behaviour when he'd first met her.

Daisy had a ready reply. 'I'd just found out that Sebastian was engaged to Celeste. Franklin offered me the use of his holiday cottage in Cornwall. Celeste is his daughter. I work as a freelance botanical illustrator for Franklin's book publishing company in London. He's always been very kind to me. He thought that taking a break in Cornwall would let me get away from the whole situation, to give me time to decide what I wanted to do.'

'And you decided to stay in Cornwall. You're still living in the cottage.'

'Yes. I'd never been to Cornwall before and I like it here.'

'Now you're obviously dating Jake. Am I right in saying you first met him shortly after you arrived in Cornwall when you went into his health food shop looking for his cure for love?'

'That's correct. But I didn't know it was a cure for love. A remedy for those feeling broken–hearted and feeling blue was advertised in the shop window, so I was curious...'

'And very broken–hearted?'

'I was. I'd arrived at the cottage at the crack of dawn and later that day I went down to the shops in the main street and saw the sign in the health food shop window.'

'Jake offered you his cure for love, but you refused it. Why?'

'I was upset with the break–up. I didn't know Jake was well–known for his remedies.'

Jake piped–up. 'My approach to Daisy in the shop was too blunt. I'd heard that she'd arrived in the town. Local gossip. I guessed that she was the woman everyone was talking about. We knew Franklin had given her the use of his holiday cottage. It was easy to spot a newcomer to the town when she walked in.'

'So you knew she was Daisy, but she'd no idea about you or your remedy?'

'None,' Jake confirmed. 'But she soon found out, and still didn't want to test the remedy. I'd been working on improving it and wanted to test the potency on someone in the throes of being broken–hearted.'

'Daisy, looking back, do you regret refusing to test Jake's cure for love when you first arrived in Cornwall?'

'No.'

'Why not?'

Daisy sighed. 'Because things worked out well eventually. I'll never know if I'd have decided to leave Cornwall if I'd felt better about Sebastian. Staying longer let me get to know Jake.'

'And fall in love with him?' the journalist prompted.

'Yes, so I couldn't have wished for a happier ending.'

'Jake, would you take your own cure for love if you ever needed it? If, for example, Daisy decided to pick up her life in London again?'

A coil of tension knotted in the pit of Jake's stomach at the thought of this. He sidestepped the question. 'Daisy still works for Franklin, and makes regular business trips up to London. She's currently working on a new book for his company and was in London a few days ago. She's kept the lease on her flat there.'

This triggered the journalist's suspicions. 'Are you making sure you have a route back to your life in the city, Daisy? If you ever need it. If you decide to forgive Sebastian and get back together with your first love.'

These suggestions ignited Daisy's defences. 'Not at all. And I have no intention of ever renewing my relationship with Sebastian.' The latter was true. But the first part of her reply was a grey area. Did she really still need her flat in London? Was it a safety net in case things didn't work out for her and Jake. Was it? In her heart the answer was no, but in truth she didn't like admitting, the net was a slight assurance. Something she wouldn't need if Jake ever asked her to marry him.

'One last question on this, Daisy. If Jake repeated what Sebastian did to you, and broke your heart, would you take the cure for love?'

'No.' The swiftness of her reply made Jake blink, and the journalist got the message. 'No, I certainly would not. My heart belongs to me. My feelings are my own to deal with without any interference from anyone.'

'Well, thank you for chatting about this. Is there anything you'd like to add?'

Daisy remembered Franklin's offer. 'Franklin says you're welcome to contact him if you need to speak to him or get a quote.'

'That would be great. Do you have his number?'

'Yes.' Daisy rattled it off.

The interview came to an end with Jake promising to send the photos outside the shop and email them to the journalist.

Daisy felt drained.

Jake stood up and glanced out the window. 'Let's get the photos taken while there's still daylight. Can you phone Mr Greenie?'

Daisy put her coat on and headed out to Jake's car while she made the call.

'Mr Greenie will be there in five minutes. He's working in the town square,' Daisy said, getting into the car.

On the drive down to the shop Jake assured her she'd done well with the interview.

'I feel totally wrung out.' She sounded overwrought. 'I'm not sure we should've agreed to this interview.'

'It'll be fine. My agent has assured me.'

'Okay.' Daisy took a calming breath, brushed her hair and refreshed her lipstick for the photos.

Mr Greenie was waiting outside the health food shop as they drove up. He had his phone ready to take the photos.

Jake wore his shirt, tie and waistcoat and hadn't bothered to put on his jacket. Daisy took her coat off and left it in the car along with her bag. She wore her pale blue jumper and grey cords and stood beside Jake.

'Stand nearer the door so I can capture the front window of the shop,' Mr Greenie told them.

They moved over and stood together. The fairy lights in the window were lit and the Christmas cake and other items on display looked festive.

'Smile, try to look cheery,' Mr Greenie encouraged them.

Woolley and Karen popped out to see what was going on.

'We need photos for the press interview,' Jake summarised.

'Oh, right.' Woolley hurried back into the shop, taking Karen with him.

Mr Greenie gestured to Jake and Daisy. 'Now stand further out so I can include the view of the main street. I don't know if your journalist wants this, but it's better to have extra just in case.'

Jake and Daisy agreed, and as they did this, Jake put his arm around her shoulder and pulled her close. 'Take one for us, Mr Greenie.'

Daisy smiled and leaned into Jake, feeling better, happier.

'I'll send these photos to you now, Jake,' said Mr Greenie. 'I hope they will be of use for your feature.'

'Thanks for helping at short notice,' Jake told him. 'Come on into the shop and I'll pay you before you go.'

Mr Greenie waved Jake's offer aside. 'Not at all. I'm pleased to have helped. And I'll be thrilled if any of the photos make it into the papers or magazines.' With a cheery wave, he headed away.

Jake and Daisy went into the shop. Karen was serving customers and Woolley stood anticipating hearing about the interview.

'The interview went okay, I think,' Jake said hesitantly. 'It was quite a personal one about Daisy and me, how she walked into the shop, the remedy, that sort of thing.'

'When does it come out?' Karen called over to them.

'Soon,' Jake replied. 'It was a London journalist, a press interview, so he wanted fresh photos of us outside the shop.'

'The shop's looking lovely,' said Karen.

Jake agreed, though the tension in him still kept him wound up. 'It is. He wanted a festive photo, so I'm going upstairs to select what we need and email them off to him.'

Leaving Karen and Woolley downstairs, Jake and Daisy went up to the storeroom where Jake looked at several of the pictures, forgetting that the last one was of them cuddling close.

'I'm going to let him select what he wants,' said Jake, sending them in bulk to the journalist.

Daisy let Jake get on with that while she wandered around the storeroom. She was still reeling from the interview, the intensity of the questions. All the preparation she'd done hadn't armed her well enough to handle the interview the way she'd planned. But it was done now. She had to rely on Jake's agent assuring them it would be a balanced feature, though she couldn't help feeling anxious.

Wandering over to the window she peered down at the busy street. It was bustling with people getting ready for Christmas. Rolls of wrapping paper peeped out from shopping bags that were loaded with items, no doubt including gifts they'd bought ready to be parcelled up and tucked under their Christmas trees.

Glancing over her shoulder to where Woolley had stashed Mrs Lemon's hoover, she noticed it was gone. He'd taken it home and hidden it there ready for Christmas morning.

She looked out the window again as Jake answered business emails after sending the photos, and saw Sharky's bakery all lit up and filled with cakes galore. The bakery was busy, and she remembered she had the Christmas cake and figgy pudding to eat before they left for New York.

'I'll drive you back to the cottage,' said Jake. 'I have to deal with quite a lot of business.' He sounded tense, in work mode.

'No, I'd prefer to walk, get some fresh air.' And shrug off the effects of the interview. She smiled and walked over to him, gave him a kiss and went downstairs.

Woolley and Karen were busy in the shop with customers. Daisy headed outside unnoticed. Jake hadn't locked the car, so she picked up her coat and bag and started to walk along the cobbled street to the cottage.

The light had faded to a festive twilight, and she gazed up at the stars starting to twinkle in the vast wintry blue sky above her. No blustery wind, just a cold stillness. The scent of the countryside mingled with the coast. If it had been bottled as perfume, the top notes had a zing of the fresh salty sea air, offset with the deeper fragrance of the fields, grassland and distant hills that coddled the coast so well.

As she walked up the path to the cottage a call came through from Franklin.

'The journalist phoned me,' he began, sounding excited.

Daisy unlocked the door and went inside the cottage.

'He wanted to confirm details of the interview, and asked me about the book you're working on now. I told him it has a vintage floral design theme, and I mentioned Roman Penhaligan's castle, which he seemed keen to hear about too. And he wanted a couple of floral illustrations of your recent work, so I emailed them to him.'

'That's wonderful.'

'It could be excellent publicity all round.'

She heard one of the printing staff call to him.

'I have to dash, Daisy. I'm looking forward to reading the feature when it comes out.'

Daisy hung her coat up in the hallway and then wandered through to the kitchen and filled the kettle for tea. She breathed deeply. What a day!

While the kettle boiled, she put the Christmas tree lights on and lit the fire. The scent of the fire always made her feel at home, even though it was temporary.

As she went back through to the kitchen to make the tea, a calendar on the hall wall reminded her that it was almost time to pack her bags and leave.

Pouring the tea, the fluttering of her heart made her realise she was even more keyed up about leaving than she'd anticipated.

Sharky's Christmas cake sat in a box on a shelf tempting her to cut into it. Giving in to temptation, she sliced through the white icing and cut a wedge of the rich fruit cake.

Sitting by the fire in the lounge, she drank her tea and ate the cake which was one of the most delicious she'd ever tasted. Sharky had a real talent for baking. No wonder his bakery business was thriving.

If his figgy pudding was half as tasty as the cake, she was in for another treat.

She'd wondered recently whether or not to invite Jake to the cottage for dinner one evening before they left Cornwall. But she decided not to put that pressure on him. He would've tried to make time for this, resulting in adding to his hectic schedule. Instead, she tried to imagine all the wonderful eateries in New York where they could have dinner together.

The dinner party when they arrived didn't count as it was a large event. The dinners she had in mind were where they had a table for two with a view of the lights of New York. Something special. Just the two of them.

An unexpected rainstorm swept along the Cornish coast soaking everything in its path, including Jake as he ran from his car into his house after finishing work at his shop.

Shaking the rain from his hair, he brushed it back and went into his study. His shirt and waistcoat were speckled with droplets, but he shook them off and sat down to make notes of last minute things he needed to do in preparation for the trip abroad. He dug out a set of keys to give to Woolley so he could keep an eye on the house while he was away.

His agent had called him while he was at the shop informing him that there was a high chance of the feature appearing in the following day's press or the next day at the latest. Everything was happening so fast, so he made notes to keep things in check.

Remember to phone Daisy, he wrote on his notepad, and then scored it out and called her.

'My agent spoke with the journalist. The feature could be in one of the papers tomorrow or the following day.'

'So soon?'

'Seems like it, but at least we'd be able to read it before we leave for New York. I'm keen to see the feature.'

'I am too.'

'What are you up to?'

She'd set up her watercolours and was working on a painting, a Christmas gift for Jake. Months ago, he'd mentioned that he'd love a painting of his house with the garden in full bloom to hang in his study. She'd kept this in mind and had been working on it recently. It was almost finished, except for an extra special touch she planned to add — a little figure, a watercolour impression of a man working in the garden — Jake. Using photos taken during the summer, a few of them included Jake, and she'd tried to capture him in the garden with the house in the background in light washes of watercolour with splashes of bright hues depicting the flowers and a gorgeous pale cobalt sky.

Before she could reply, Jake filled in the answer for her. 'Artwork?'

He meant her illustrations, but this enabled her to reply, 'Yes,' without hinting that she was creating a painting for him. The watercolour paper was A3 size, so when it was framed with a stylish light cream mounting board around the edges, it would be a fair size and suitable she thought for his study wall near his desk. She'd bought the frame and board weeks ago and planned to frame it herself, something she was quite adept at doing.

Like Woolley, she had a back–up gift — a new, vintage style satchel briefcase. Jake liked traditional items and although he had a bag like this, it was invariably stuffed full of paperwork, his notebooks, folders and all sorts of bits and pieces. A second bag would surely be handy, and she had it hidden in the hall cupboard, wrapped and ready to give to him for Christmas. Though whether to give him the presents before they left for New York or when they came back in the New Year was something she was still mulling over. Perhaps the briefcase beforehand and keep the painting for when they came back home.

'I'll let you push on with your work then, and I'll do the same,' he said.

'Hopefully the feature is in the paper tomorrow. Do you know what pictures the journalist ended up using?'

'No idea, but apparently he was pleased with the new photos, so...'

'We'll just have to wait and see what's published.'

'Yes.'

'Okay, goodnight, Jake.'

'I'll see you tomorrow.'

Daisy clicked her phone off and looked out at the rain lashing down outside the window. The wind had picked up and was sweeping the rain along the street. But she felt cosy in the cottage, working on finishing Jake's painting, listening to the sound of the rain hitting off the windows and the fire crackling with warmth.

The night wore on, and amid stopping to have tea and hot buttered toast, she finished and framed the painting. Sitting it up on a chest of drawers in the lounge, she sipped her tea and judged her handiwork. Seeing the house, and the lovely flowers, and the figure of Jake working in his garden, made her view his world with longing. What a great life there was to be enjoyed here. The promise of a summerhouse that she could use as an art studio filled her heart with hope. Once the trip was over, and the publicity for Jake's book was done with, there would be more time to relax and have fun together.

With this bolstering thought, she started to tidy away her paints and brushes, hid the painting in the hall cupboard just in case Jake dropped by and saw it, and got ready for bed.

The rain had eased to a gentle pitter–patter on the bedroom window, soothing her to sleep. But her mind kept rewinding the interview, the questions that jarred her senses, especially when the journalist mentioned Sebastian.

No! She scolded herself. Don't dwell on thoughts of him before going to sleep. So instead she gazed at the rain on the window. Again, there were no stars to be seen in the sky through the overcast night. No chance to wish for the trip to be scheduled for the New Year.

Jake worked late, sitting at his desk, making progress as he ticked off the tasks on his list.

But one task remained unsolved — *what else to buy Daisy for Christmas.*

He'd wrapped and hidden the small gifts he'd bought her recently from the fashion shop. A woolly hat and scarf set, a large bag that looked both practical and stylish, a watercolour paint travel kit, new paint brushes and other items from the craft shop including an easel and a folding stool they'd recommended.

But what else? He didn't know. Perhaps he'd find something extra special to buy in New York.

Needing to get some sleep, he turned the lights off in the study and went through to bed.

Gazing out at the rainy night, he thought about Daisy, hoping the press feature turned out well, and wishing that their whirlwind trip to New York would be postponed until after Christmas.

CHAPTER THIRTEEN

Picture Perfect

Daisy went to the grocery shop to buy fresh milk the next morning. The shop was filled with chatter. Customers were talking animatedly to the grocer about something that had happened. She couldn't see over the shelves displaying tinned products and fresh fruit and vegetables to tell what the topic of the morning's gossip was.

'There she is!' the grocer said, noticing Daisy standing there holding the milk and wondering what the fuss was.

Daisy smiled tightly, and then blinked when the grocer held up one of the daily newspapers.

'You and Jake are in the paper. And so are some of the shops in the main street. Including mine,' the grocer enthused.

Daisy rushed up to the counter, put the milk down and grasped the paper he held out to her.

'Your story is near the entertainment news,' the grocer told her.

Daisy flipped the pages at speed and stopped when she saw the main photograph. There she was, standing next to Jake outside his health food shop. It was the one where he had his arm around her shoulder and they were smiling happily. The picture that was supposed to be a personal one for them.

The other pictures included the front cover of Jake's book, one of him sitting at his desk in his study working on his remedies, and one of Daisy's floral illustrations.

Heart racing, Daisy skim–read the feature.

The cure for love is brewing in a small town...

Loveless Londoner finds the remedy for romance...

Daisy's duplicitous boyfriend Sebastian's shock engagement to London publishing company boss' daughter Celeste...

Running off at night from London to find solace in Franklin's holiday cottage in Cornwall...

Small, friendly community...

Health food shop owner Jake Wolfe offers broken–hearted artist Daisy his cure for lovesickness...

Daisy refuses to take the cure for love, but falls for the remedy's creator Jake...

Was Jake Wolfe Daisy's true cure for love...?

Jake's new book published at Christmas...

The book's botanical artwork illustrated by Daisy...

Plans for the remedy to be available from Jake's shop sometime in the future...

Meanwhile, love finds its own way to mend a broken heart...

With her mind in an excited whirl, she paid for the milk and two copies of the newspaper.

The grocer was still delighted that his shop was included in the main picture. 'In all the years I've had my shop it's never been pictured in the paper.'

Daisy smiled, pleased that he was happy, but then dashed across to the health food shop to show Jake the news.

Sharky waved from the bakery and called out to her. 'My bakery is in the paper.' He held up a copy of it, grinning.

Daisy waved at him and then ran into Jake's shop armed with the two copies of the paper. Jake was stacking fresh lemons and oranges in the fruit baskets display.

'We're in the paper!' Daisy thrust a copy at him.

Hearing this, Karen ran over to take a look as Jake flicked through the pages until he saw the feature.

'They've used the personal photo of us,' said Daisy. 'And some of the local shops are pictured — the grocers, craft shop, Sharky's bakery, the fashion shop...'

Jake's eyes scanned the feature, taking in the lead photo, noticing how nice his health food shop looked, along with the other shops. A close–up of Daisy and him smiling together was inset in a circle within the main photo.

'I'm running across to buy a copy,' said Karen, hurrying out.

'Buy several. I'll pay for them,' Jake shouted after her.

Karen gave an acknowledging wave and ran over to the grocers.

'What do you think?' Daisy looked at Jake, eager for his initial opinion of the feature.

'It's wonderful...isn't it?' He was both sure and unsure. 'I need time to read it properly, to take it all in. What do you think?'

'I didn't expect it to be so prominent. We've got a whole page to ourselves. The shop owners are delighted they're included. The town's huge Christmas tree in the square looks gorgeous.'

'It makes the main street look like it's a hive of activity.'

Daisy's phone rang. 'It's Franklin,' she said, taking the call.

'The feature is in the paper,' he announced.

'Jake and I are reading it right now.'

'My phone's been ringing with people calling to tell me that I'm mentioned in the feature.'

'Does Celeste know?' Daisy said tentatively.

'She does, and the only thing she's snippy about is that her picture wasn't included. Sebastian knows too, but he's making light of it. It'll take more than a few scathing comments to dent his confidence. You know what Sebastian is like.'

She did.

'I love that they included one of your floral illustrations, and they've mentioned you're working on the new vintage book,' Franklin told her.

'Where does it say that?'

'Near the bottom of the page.'

Daisy read the relevant part. 'So it does.'

'Roman Penhaligan's castle gets a mention too,' Franklin added.

'I'll make sure to tell him.'

'Well done, Daisy. It's a brilliant feature all round,' Franklin enthused as they ended the call.

Karen arrived back armed with a number of copies of the paper, tucked them under the counter and then started to read one herself.

A couple of customers came in and as the excited chatter started, Jake took Daisy upstairs to the storeroom where they could read the paper in private.

His agent called while they were pouring over the feature.

'It's a winning editorial, Jake. Great publicity.'

'Tell your journalist friend thank you,' said Jake.

'I already have. He phoned me late last night to tell me the feature made the deadline. I didn't want to phone and wake you, or get your hopes up in case it didn't make the morning's news.'

'Everyone here is excited, including the local businesses.'

'That's a bonus, isn't it. That picture of you and Daisy is wonderful. Great photographer.'

'Mr Greenie can turn his hand to most things.'

'Calls are coming through from other papers,' his agent explained. 'The feature is being syndicated to several publications.'

Jake thanked his agent again before clicking his phone off and reading the feature again, especially the parts that highlighted Daisy and him falling in love.

The sound of Woolley's boots thundering up the stairs signalled that the news had ignited the local gossip.

Woolley had a copy of the paper rolled up like a winner's baton as he grinned through his bushy beard. 'Mrs Lemon told me your story is in the news. And Mr Greenie is thrilled they used the picture he took.'

Daisy noticed he'd been credited in the feature at the edge of the main picture. *Photo by Mr Greenie.*

Daisy smiled, but her heart was still beating wildly with all the excitement, which continued with a phone call from Roman Penhaligan.

'I didn't expect my castle to get a mention in your feature,' Roman said to Daisy. 'My butler saw the paper this morning and the staff are pleased that the castle is included. I've had a few calls from people that read the feature and they're interested in booking the castle for their weddings.'

'That's wonderful,' Daisy told him.

'In fact, I think that's another call now. Must dash. Thanks again, Daisy.'

With Jake in the midst of a hectic morning at the shop, Daisy took a copy of the paper and left him to get on with his business.

'We'll talk later,' Jake called to her as she headed downstairs, giving him a wave.

Downstairs in the shop Karen, Mrs Lemon and a few customers chatted about the feature.

Mrs Lemon had a copy of the paper and was extolling the benefits of it. She smiled when she saw Daisy.

'It's so exciting, isn't it,' Mrs Lemon said to Daisy. 'A feature in the newspaper. What a great photo of you and Jake — and if you look carefully at the window of the health food shop behind you and Jake, you can see my Karen and Woolley peering out watching you getting your picture taken.'

'I hadn't noticed that,' Daisy told her.

Mrs Lemon thrust the picture into Daisy's view. 'See, there they are.'

'Oh, yes,' Daisy confirmed, pleased that they'd been captured in the photo.

Karen piped–up. 'And Sharky's standing at the front door of his shop looking over at you and Jake.'

Daisy studied the paper and saw that Sharky was in full view standing outside his bakery, unaware that he'd been captured in the frame. 'So he is!'

Karen sounded pleased. 'Sharky looks very fit in his baker's whites.'

'He does,' said Daisy.

'I think he's naturally photogenic,' Mrs Lemon surmised.

Karen was eager to agree. 'Yes, Sharky's definitely photogenic. I've never seen a bad photo of him ever.'

With this cheery chatter set to continue, Daisy smiled, saying she was going back to the cottage to have a late breakfast. And breathe.

'You'll be leaving for New York soon,' said Mrs Lemon.

Daisy paused. 'Yes, a few days before it's time to go. We're leaving mid morning, but I'll be up early to shower and wash my hair so that it's tidy for the fancy party we have to attend the night we arrive.'

'A party, right after you've flown to New York?' Mrs Lemon needed clarification.

'Yes, we've been invited to attend. Jake says we'll take a taxi from the airport direct to our hotel, quickly get changed into our gladrags, and then grab a taxi to the function.'

'Won't you be exhausted?' Karen commented.

Daisy shrugged. 'We've agreed to do it. We can flake out after the party.'

'I hope you're wearing something gorgeous,' Karen told her.

'A red sequin cocktail dress. Festive and flashy. In a decent way. Sparkles. I've a pair of shoes that look like I'm walking on glitter heels. They work with all my cocktail dresses and despite being killer heels, they're okay for partying in.' They were her go–to shoes when she used to go out socialising in London with Sebastian. She'd yet to wear them since meeting Jake.

Karen gave Daisy the thumbs up. 'Sparkle to the max. That's what I would do in your circumstances.'

'Yes,' said Mrs Lemon. 'Don't be a shirking violet.'

They laughed.

'*Shrinking* violet,' Mrs Lemon corrected herself with a grin.

'Maybe the first suggestion is closer to how I feel,' Daisy admitted.

'Nervous?' Mrs Lemon said to her.

'Yes. I wish we were on our way back, but...' Daisy pressed her lips together and said no more.

'Remember,' Mrs Lemon reminded Daisy. 'We want updates, pictures, and newsy gossip from you daily.'

'Will do,' Daisy promised.

'We'll probably enjoy your trip to New York better than you do,' Karen quipped.

Daisy didn't argue. 'I'll see you both before I leave.' Smiling, she headed out, hearing Mrs Lemon planning to have the newspaper feature framed to put up in her cottage.

The next few days were a whirlwind of furore and fuss, packing and checking that she had everything she needed for the trip. Jake's frequent phone calls and messages kept swirling around her, creating a vortex of emotional drama and excitement. Yes, excitement.

She'd decided to embrace the hurly–burly of getting ready to take Manhattan by storm. Even if it only ended up being a light drizzle. She was all set to go.

They'd agreed to exchange Christmas presents when they came home, and this took the pressure off, wondering if, when and how to give Jake the briefcase and the painting.

'Something to look forward to,' he'd suggested, and she was relieved to go along with that plan.

Jake's other plans were multi–layered. Not wanting to thwart anything, she let him take notes and make a timetable that accounted for delays and disaster. She didn't ask him to elaborate on the latter. He seemed to know what he was doing, and as he'd been to New York before a few times, she figured experience was more important than her interference.

If he'd said he had satellite links to wherever to keep them on track, she was prepared to let him plot that course. Go Jake.

So, they were ready. They were. All she had to do now was get a decent night's sleep. An early night to stock up on those zzz's so she could tackle the time zones challenge with aplomb.

'Don't even think about jetlag,' Jake had advised her.

She didn't. It hadn't initially occurred to her so she tucked it out of the way, and went to bed early having set three alarms. Just in case.

On the morning they were leaving, Daisy was ready to go ten minutes before Jake was due to arrive to pick her up.

Her bags were in the hall, her coat hung there too, everything was sorted except her thoughts. Those were in total disarray. She sat at the front window beside the Christmas tree. The fairy lights were on. She'd intended packing it away the previous night, but then decided to leave the tree up.

Whether it was nerves or excitement or a mix of both, she'd skipped breakfast and only had a cup of tea. Jake had said they could stop for something to eat on their way to London or at the airport.

Mrs Lemon was due to keep an eye on the cottage, like she did for Franklin, but Daisy had cleared out the fridge and tidied everything up anyway.

Sitting gazing out the window, she saw Jake drive down the hill, park outside and hurry towards the cottage.

Daisy turned the Christmas tree lights off and ran through to the hall and opened the door.

'You're early.'

His hair was still damp as if he'd recently jumped out of the shower, but he was well–dressed as always. 'It's snowing in London,' he announced, picking up her bags and heading out to the car. 'We'd better get going. There could be traffic delays.'

Daisy grabbed her coat and hurried out, locking the front door behind her.

'Snow? I thought the forecast was light rain,' she said getting into the passenger seat while Jake put the bags in the boot, slammed it shut and then jumped into the driver's side.

'Flurries of snow, an unexpected change in the weather,' he summarised. 'We'll still be on time. I scheduled in extra travelling time in case of delays.'

He started up the engine and drove off, taking them through the main street.

Daisy peered out the window as Jake slowed down so they had a chance to give a last minute wave to anyone they knew. The goodbyes had been exchanged en masse the previous day, but he took this route, wanting to drive by the health food shop to maybe wave to Woolley or others.

'There's Mrs Lemon chatting to someone outside the grocers,' said Daisy, sitting up ready to wave. But Mrs Lemon was so engrossed in her conversation that she didn't see them.

'I don't want to beep the horn to parade ourselves,' said Jake.

Daisy agreed.

In the moments it took to drive the length of the main street, they saw Karen working in the health food shop, serving customers while Woolley appeared to be adjusting the fairy lights in the window display. Karen and Woolley were too busy to notice Jake's car drive slowly by.

'There's Roman heading into Sharky's bakery,' Daisy told Jake. Through the bakery window they saw Sharky busy in his shop. Again, no one noticed Jake and Daisy.

By now they'd reached the large Christmas tree at the square. The festive fair had started. The Christmas market was busy with lots of local stalls set up and fun attractions.

Stalls were selling hot chocolate with marshmallows, and there were artisan specialities and lots of local crafts.

And there was Mr Greenie getting into the post office van to deliver the mail, unaware that Daisy was waving at him.

No one saw them.

Daisy glanced at Jake, looking as disappointed as he felt.

'Never mind.' He forced a tight smile. 'I should've taken the other route. I just though it would be nice to...' his words trailed off and he wrung his hands on the steering wheel.

The road ahead showed no signs of snow, but as they left Cornwall behind, snowflakes started to flutter across the windscreen, and the nearer they drove to London, the heavier the snowfall.

The traffic slowed down at one section of the motorway.

'Don't worry. We have plenty of time to get to the airport,' Jake assured her. 'We won't be driving into the centre of London anyway. We're just heading straight to the airport, so relax and enjoy the snowscene.'

Daisy did enjoy seeing the countryside change from pale winter green to white as they continued on their journey.

'Did you have breakfast?' he said.

'No, just a cup of tea.' She hoped he hadn't heard her tummy rumble. It wasn't through hunger, just enough butterflies that made her feel she could fly to New York on her own steam.

'Same here. I thought we could make a pit stop for something to eat on the way, but with the snow slowing things down, it would be better to wait until we get to the airport.'

The traffic slowed down again as the snow became heavier.

'Are you sure we're going to make it to the airport on time?' she said.

'Yes, so relax. As I said, I scheduled extra time for delays.'

Daisy decided to relax back in her seat and stop fretting about catching the plane. Would it be so awful if they missed the flight and had to reschedule their trip until after Christmas? Shame on her for even thinking thoughts about the benefits of their trip being scuppered.

Jake had no qualms now about the trip. They'd make the flight with time to spare. The drive from Cornwall took a few hours, but they didn't fly out until the late afternoon.

They were two hours into their drive when Woolley phoned them from the health food shop. Daisy took the call on Jake's phone, putting it on speaker.

'I saw the news. It's snowing in London.' Woolley sounded worried. 'Will you make your flight time?'

Jake spoke up. 'We will. We're heading straight to the airport.'

Woolley chatted for a few minutes to them. 'The shop's deliveries arrived on time and I've stocked the shelves as usual. The shop has been extra busy this morning with the Christmas market being on. Folk are gearing up for Christmas, and there's still so much interest in your new book because of the newspaper story.'

'Did you get the letters from Santa that arrived last night?' said Jake.

Woolley wondered if he was hearing right. 'Letters from Santa?'

'Yes, one for you and one for Karen,' Jake told him. 'They're under the front counter.'

Woolley hurried over and found the two white envelopes. His said: *To Woolley. To be opened before Christmas*. Woolley opened his and smiled broadly.

'A Christmas bonus for you and for Karen,' Jake explained. 'For all your hard work and help.'

'You didn't have to do that, Jake. It's far too generous.'

'I want you to have it. Buy something nice for you and Mrs Lemon.'

Karen overheard and opened her envelope and gasped. 'Thank you, Jake!' she called out.

'No, thank you for all your hard work, Karen.'

The conversation finished with Woolley telling Jake what he had planned for that evening at Mrs Lemon's cottage. 'She's making one of her delicious casseroles with mashed potatoes. I love that. Then we're snuggling up together to watch a new film we've been looking forward to.'

Jake glanced at Daisy, feeling a pang of longing, wishing they had a night like that ahead.

Daisy wished the same for her and Jake, but didn't say anything. There was no point. They would soon be soaring across the sea to New York.

'Okay,' Woolley said finally. 'Safe flight and take care the two of you.'

'Thanks, Woolley,' Daisy said to him before the call ended.

Woolley put his phone in his pocket. Karen and Mrs Lemon were eager to know if the snow had changed Jake and Daisy's plans.

'Jake says they'll still make their flight on time,' Woolley told them. 'Jake is excellent at organising things like this, so he'll have accounted for delays with the traffic.'

'I'm going to pop along to Daisy's cottage to check that any milk and other fresh food has been cleared out of the fridge and the cupboards,' said Mrs Lemon. 'Daisy said she'd do it, but her mind has been in a whirl since the newspaper feature and then getting ready to leave for New York, so I'll double check the cottage — then I'll start preparing the casserole for our cosy night in.'

Woolley waved her off, and then attended to the shop, while Karen tucked her bonus envelope in her pocket.

'Do you think Jake and Daisy's flight could be cancelled because of the snow?' Karen said to Woolley.

'Nah! The next time we speak to them, they'll be partying in Manhattan.'

A short time later, Sharky came running over to the health food shop carrying a tray with a large apple strudel. Made from pastry filled with apples, raisins and a hint of spices, it was drizzled with white icing.

He hurried in and thrust it under Karen's nose. 'This is my new festive apple strudel. Bigger than before. My festive strudel is longer than ever this year. There's at least an extra two portions.'

Karen didn't doubt it. The strudel stretched across the length of the tray. The spicy apple and pastry aroma made her want a slice. She went to touch the icing.

Sharky pulled it out of temptation's way. 'Ah, no. It's for our dinner at my house. I'm so excited with how well it's risen. It's long enough now that I can pleat it across the top. I thought I'd give you a big one tonight.'

Woolley snickered through his beard.

'I heard that,' Sharky scolded him jokingly.

'I'm looking forward to it,' Karen said, smiling lovingly at Sharky.

'And the apple strudel,' Woolley muttered under his fuzz as Sharky ran off back to his bakery taking the delicious pastry with him.

Karen swiped playfully at Woolley. 'Cheeky rascal!' And then got on with her work.

CHAPTER FOURTEEN

Christmas Romance

Daisy gazed out the window of the plane as it taxied along the runway. Jake had given her the window seat and sat beside her.

'Here we go.' He gave her hand a reassuring squeeze as the plane took off, soaring into the late afternoon sky.

London became a distant view of lights and traffic as they left the city behind and headed into the grey winter yonder.

The snow had eased and created no delays, but sleet was forecast for later, so they'd made their flight on time.

'Remind me again how our time schedule works,' she said.

'The flight is over seven hours. London is five hours ahead of New York, so when we arrive it'll only be after six o'clock in the evening,' he explained.

'It's like travelling back in time.'

'If only we could. I'd do a few things differently. Including how bluntly I approached you the first time you walked into my shop,' he said wistfully. 'Wouldn't you?'

'I don't know. I kind of like where we are right now.' She smiled. 'Not flying over the Atlantic, but just us, as we are now. You and me.'

Jake smiled back at her and nodded. If he'd done things differently maybe Daisy wouldn't be here with him now. Perhaps she would've gone home to London.

Daisy settled into her seat, feeling calm for the first time in days now that they were on their way.

'Would you like to watch an in–flight film?' Jake offered her, pulling up a selection that they could view from their seats. As they'd already eaten at the airport, they'd told cabin staff they didn't require any meals.

Daisy brightened, keen to do this. 'What would you like to see?'

'Nothing with snakes.'

'No snakes, noted,' she said and then added her own veto. 'No sharks for me.'

Neither of them wanted to force the other into a choice they wouldn't have made.

Jake had paused at a shark adventure movie, but willingly scrolled on.

'We have a screen each. We could watch different things,' he offered.

'No, let's watch something together.'

Jake looked thoughtful. 'Pretend I'd fallen asleep. What would you have watched on your own?'

'The Christmas romance.' No hesitation. It was festive, fun and romantic.

'Let's watch that then.' He hit the play button.

'No, you don't have to do that. I know that action and adventures are more your taste. Not romance.'

'I can be romantic,' he said, settling down to enjoy the movie she'd picked.

'I know you can but—'

'This looks Christmassy,' he cut–in. 'Besides, there will be plenty of action and adventure when we arrive in New York.'

Daisy thought about the media party they were due to attend. 'And sharks.'

'There's bound to be a few of those. This is a competitive business. But don't let anyone make you feel like your botanical illustrations for the book aren't important to its success.'

Daisy nodded, and then they relaxed back to watch the movie.

Neither of them knew if they'd fallen asleep first, but Daisy blinked awake to see the lights of New York glittering like hundreds of diamonds as they flew over the snow–covered city.

She nudged Jake awake. 'We're here.'

Jake took a moment to rattle his brain into gear. 'Where?'

'New York.'

He checked the time. 'Already?'

'We've fallen asleep and snoozed right through the flight. But on the upside, we should be perky enough for the party and the long night ahead.'

'Perky? Yes.' Or was he feeling edgy? He'd planned to relax during the flight, not fall asleep. His plan had gone awry and they hadn't even arrived.

A taxi drove them from the airport to their upmarket hotel in Manhattan, where another part of Jake's plan was altered. Instead of the double room that Valerie agreed she'd book, they had two single rooms.

'I tried, but it's the holidays,' Valerie said when Jake called her for an explanation. 'At least the rooms are almost next to each other.'

With no time to argue or complain, Jake got changed into his suit, shirt and tie for the party.

Daisy did the same in her room two doors down. Casting her travel clothes aside, she threw on her red sequin cocktail dress, stepped into her glitter heels, ran a brush through her silky blonde hair, freshened her makeup and gulped down a glass of the complimentary iced tea that the hotel had provided. A glass jug was filled with the amber liquid and sat on a serving tray on the table along with artisan nibbles.

Mmm, the iced tea tasted really good. Very refreshing. Since the cup of tea at breakfast, and the light snack and tea they'd had at the airport before boarding the plane, she'd barely had anything more than a sip of water. Being dehydrated wouldn't help with jet lag, which she was definitely not thinking about at all.

Refilling her glass with a second helping of the iced tea, she grabbed her coat and evening bag and, glass in hand, hurried along the plush hallway to Jake's room.

She knocked on the door. 'Jake, it's me.'

He opened it, and they both laughed when they saw that they each had a glass of iced tea in their hands.

'Come in. I'm almost ready.'

Daisy stepped into the stylish hotel room, the same as hers, with a view of the city. Everything glittered just like she'd seen in the movies.

'I see you've tried the tea,' he said, drinking down a second glass.

'There's something about it that's so...refreshing. Maybe it's the water here. I haven't drank much iced tea so it's difficult to know if this is a special concoction or just really strong tea.' She drank it down.

Jake noticed there was a welcome message beside the almost empty jug on the table. He picked it up and read it, skipping over the usual welcome to the hotel message and then staring when he saw what they'd been drinking. 'Oh, no!'

'What's wrong?' said Daisy. 'Is there something wrong with the tea?'

'Yes and no.'

'What do you mean?'

'It's Long Island iced tea.'

Daisy was starting to feel the effects of the strong, alcohol content mixed with the tea. 'Oh. No wonder it seems so...special.' She put her empty glass down.

Jake fought to find an upside to the situation. 'It's important to stay well hydrated to help with jet lag.'

Daisy nodded firmly and then giggled. 'Which I'm not supposed to think about.'

Jake put his jacket on and wondered if the lovely rosy glow on Daisy's cheeks was from the blusher she'd applied.

'Come on. We'll grab a taxi downstairs.' He led her out of the room.

They jumped into a taxi outside the hotel. It had been snowing earlier and everything was dusted with snow and frost, creating a magical feeling to the city at night.

Daisy sat in the back of the taxi and gazed out the window at Manhattan. 'It looks just like I've seen in movies. I can hardly believe we're here.'

Jake felt the effects of the two glasses of iced tea, gulped down in quick succession. For the remainder of the evening he'd drink soft beverages. Flashes of the recent limbo fiasco flickered through his mind. He didn't want a repeat of that this evening.

'Oh look at the gorgeous Christmas decorations in the streets and the shop windows,' Daisy enthused. 'They look fantastic.' She hiccupped.

'Are you feeling okay?' Jake asked tentatively.

'I feel great.'

The assurance and high tone of her reply concerned him. Daisy wasn't one for drinking at all. Neither was he, but he was sure he could handle being slightly inebriated better than her. He planned to keep a close eye on her. They could make a brief appearance at the party and then head back to their hotel to sleep off the effects of the potent cocktails.

The taxi pulled up outside the upmarket hotel where the party was being held.

Jake escorted her inside, helped her off with her coat and led her into the large function room where the party was in full flow. The opulent surroundings included chandeliers and a decor that was as stylish as the guests milling around. The party was busy.

Everyone was dressed to impress.

'Do I look all right?' Daisy whispered to Jake.

'You look beautiful. Dazzling.' He meant every word. She looked great in her red sequin dress.

'They're here,' Valerie said to one of her main assistants, Wes. He was a good looking man in his thirties with light brown hair and worked in book marketing.

'I see Jake,' Wes said, recognising him from the promo interviews and photo on the jacket of the book. 'Where's Daisy?'

'Red sequin dress.' Valerie told him.

Wes did a double–take. 'That's Daisy? But she's—'

Valerie glared at him.

'She's very...sparkly, for someone from a small, quaint town. She looks more like she belongs in the city,' he observed.

'Well, she doesn't, but she illustrated the book so she'll be part of the publicity rounds. But not all of them. The interviews tomorrow are Jake only.'

'Why is she twirling like that?' He watched Daisy attempt what looked like a pirouette near the large Christmas tree.

Valerie didn't have a reply. But she loved that dress. And the glitter heels.

'Keep an eye on Daisy during the next couple of days,' Valerie told Wes. 'I'm going to be busy with Jake, but I don't want her wandering off and causing trouble. She's not used to the big city.'

Cole, a journalist acquaintance of Valerie's sidled up to them. 'Who is the gorgeous blonde firecracker with Jake Wolfe? And why is she attempting to spin on those heels she's wearing?'

'That's Daisy,' said Valerie.

The journalist looked surprised. 'The book's illustrator?'

'Yes.'

Cole, tall and sexy handsome with blond hair and wearing a stylish suit, sipped his glass of bourbon and gazed over at the firecracker.

'Hold my bag.' Daisy shoved her evening bag that matched her shoes into Jake's reluctant grasp. 'Did I ever tell you that I wanted to be a ballerina when I was little. I took ballet classes for a year. Twirls were my speciality. Watch, I'll show you. It's all in the head turn, keeping an eye on one thing and then...spinning.'

Daisy somehow managed a perfect spin, causing several guests to stare.

'I can do it even faster. Watch me, Jake.'

He grabbed her around the waist before she could pirouette into the Christmas tree. Pulling her close, he smiled, making it look like they were having fun.

Valerie and Wes approached them.

'Jake, it's wonderful to meet you for real, though I feel as though we've met when we connected online.' Valerie extended her hand. She wore a black cocktail–length dress and her dark chestnut hair was clipped up in a chignon.

Jake shook hands with Valerie and Wes. He went to introduce Daisy.

'Hi, Daisy,' said Valerie. 'I'm so pleased you could both make it. Come, I'll introduce you to everyone who is anyone you need to know.'

Linking her arm through Jake's, she led the way over to a group of media executives and magazine journalists.

Wes escorted Daisy.

She hiccupped as she was introduced to one of the journalists, Monica, who was due to interview them. Monica was attractive with dark blonde hair. Glasses of champagne were proffered to the group by attentive staff.

Daisy went to reach for a glass, but Jake clasped her hand and squeezed it.

'We're tea total this evening,' Jake said to them.

Daisy giggled and hiccupped. 'Totally tipsy on tea.'

'I'm excited to read your book, Jake,' Monica said to him.

'Monica will be interviewing you tomorrow morning at the publicity event I've arranged at your hotel,' Valerie told him.

Jake's blank expression showed it was the first he'd heard of this happening.

'I emailed a copy of your schedule to you this morning,' Valerie explained. 'I guess you haven't had a chance to check your mail.'

'We fell asleep on the plane and missed the entire flight,' Daisy announced to Valerie and anyone in their circle listening.

Cole smiled at Daisy. He was all well–cut blond hair and chiselled features with an educated mien. 'Plenty of energy then for partying?'

'Tons.' Daisy wafted a carefree hand in the air. 'I'm looking forward to having fun this evening.'

Cole's sexy smile lit up his face. 'I'm sure you will, Daisy.'

The way Cole said her name, so smooth and assured, made her lean back on her heels and appraise him. 'You remind me of a friend of mine. Roman Penhaligan owns a magnificent castle in Cornwall in Jake's town.' She nodded, agreeing with her assessment. 'He's smooth and wears classy suits, just like you.'

Daisy almost tipped too far back on her heels, and Cole reached out and grasped her, steadying her.

'Whoa, there!' He smiled down at her, almost as tall as Jake. 'I think the tiredness from travelling is kicking in.'

'Nope. I'm fine. Still perky. Very perky. Blame the wobble on the tea. I had two full glasses of iced tea in quick succession on an empty stomach. Strong stuff.'

Cole tilted his head at a quizzical angle. 'Tea? I thought you British folk thrived on it.'

Daisy gave him a knowing wink. 'Special tea.' She took a deep breath. 'But it's kicked me into party mode.' She threw her arms wide, gesturing around her. 'When does this party get going? Isn't anyone dancing?'

Cole held out his hand to Daisy. 'May I have this dance?'

'You may.' She lathered on the politeness.

While Valerie and Monica engrossed Jake in conversation, Cole led Daisy on to the empty dance floor and started to waltz her around.

'Tell me all about this castle in Cornwall,' said Cole.

'They do weddings. Wonderful bridal packages with all the trimmings, including fantastic wedding cakes baked by Sharky. He's the local baker, another friend of mine.'

'You sound like a real friendly young lady.'

'Oh, I am.'

He looked at the dazzle from the sequins on her dress. 'You look like the spark this party needs to get started.'

Daisy smiled and started dancing with more flourish. Not embarrassingly, but enough to gain attention.

Jake was still talking to Valerie and Monica, when he became distracted by Daisy and Cole whirling around the dance floor.

'Excuse me,' Jake said to them.

Marching over to Daisy and the man bedazzled by her, Jake cut–in. 'My turn to dance with my girlfriend I think.'

'Oh, so you two are a thing.' Cole wagged his finger between them.

'If a thing means she's the love of my life, then yes,' Jake told him, giving him a bold stare.

Cole didn't balk. Confidence showed from every angle of his handsome face. Fierce green eyes blatantly noted that there was no engagement ring on Daisy's finger.

Jake caught the look.

Nothing was said, but everything was insinuated.

'Do something before a fight erupts,' Valerie hissed at Wes.

Stepping into the fray, Wes clapped his hands to gain everyone's attention.

'As you know, we're all here to party, but this evening we're pleased to announce the arrival of Jake Wolfe whose new book, The Cure For Love, comes out this Christmas. So please welcome, Jake Wolfe.'

The guests applauded and Jake smiled and raised his hand in acknowledgement.

'Enjoy your evening,' Wes concluded, effectively breaking the tension between Jake and Cole.

The guests smiled, and the interruption became part of the fun of the event.

Jake took Daisy in hold and waltzed around the floor with her.

'Swing me around like you did during the summer in your garden,' she encouraged him. 'We had fun then.'

'We did have fun, didn't we,' he recalled.

Daisy smiled up at him.

Under other circumstances, Jake wouldn't have made a show of them, especially as they almost had the dance floor to themselves. But under the influence of the unintentional cocktails, Jake lifted Daisy up as if she was a feather and twirled her around.

Mrs Lemon switched the television off. 'That was a great night's viewing.'

Woolley stretched and sat up where he'd been relaxing on the sofa watching Christmas movies. After the casserole and mashed potatoes they'd had for dinner, they'd snuggled up as planned for a cosy night in her cottage.

'Do you want a cup of tea before you head home?' Mrs Lemon offered.

'Nah, I'm fine. It's late. I'll be on my way.' He stood up and gave her a hug and a loving kiss in front of the fire.

She walked him to the door, but as he stepped outside, he noticed a message had come through for him on his phone. He paused to read it.

'It's a message from Jake. They've arrived in New York and are on their way to the party.'

'I hope they're having a nice time. They'll be tuckered out after the long flight,' said Mrs Lemon, shivering in the cold air after being so cosy by the fire.

Woolley agreed. 'Jake told me they just need to put in an appearance. Show face, mingle and then fade into the background so they can head back to their hotel to get some sleep.'

'Wheeeee!' Daisy smiled and giggled as Jake danced around with her.

Monica tried to fathom where she'd estimated things all wrong. 'I thought these two Brits would be subdued and demure, a bit posh, standoffish, not a couple of party animals with Christmas bells on.'

'Jake's just full of surprises,' said Valerie.

Lost in the moment, it was only when Jake noticed several people watching them, including Valerie, Wes and Monica, that he paused and put Daisy down.

'You go and chat to Valerie and the people that she wants you to meet,' Daisy told him, stepping back and regaining her balance.

'Are you sure?' Jake frowned at her, reluctant to circulate separately.

'Go on, I'll get something to eat at the buffet,' Daisy assured him. 'Food and a soft drink, maybe even a coffee, should help water down the effects of the iced tea.'

'I'll join you for something to eat later,' he assured her.

'Fine, now go and chat to the journalists. I'll be okay. The buffet looks delicious. You're here for the publicity. This is wall–to–wall journalists and media people. Maybe go with the flow this evening. Do what you excel at, talk about your cure for love.'

Leaving her on her own, Jake walked back over to talk to Valerie and the others.

Daisy headed for the buffet, having her eye on the selection of salads and classic pasta dishes. The range of cheeses and other savoury dishes were tempting too, and the festive desserts. Sampling a mini meringue filled with fresh fruit and cream, Daisy then went to pour herself a cup of strong, black coffee.

'Allow me,' a man said behind her.

She glanced round, surprised to see Cole standing there.

He lifted a cup and filled it for her.

'Thank you,' said Daisy.

He poured a second cup for himself. 'Tell me more about this castle owner friend of yours.' His keen green eyes viewed her with interest edged with scepticism. 'Is it a real castle or just a fancy mansion?'

'It's a real castle, situated near the coast with a view of the sea. The estate stretches into the surrounding countryside. It has turrets and everything.'

'The real deal, huh?'

'Yes, Roman owns it.' Daisy took her phone from her bag, scrolled through it and held up the image of her standing with him on the cake. 'This is him.' If the coffee hadn't been so hot, she'd have drank it down and perhaps have sobered up slightly. And maybe she wouldn't have been so willing to show a news journalist the picture.

Cole was taken aback. 'Are you married to this guy?'

Daisy panicked. 'No, it's not what you think. I was helping Roman with his wedding promotion stuff.'

Cole wasn't convinced. 'It kinda looks like you're having your wedding photo taken on top of a cake.'

'That's a prop, for couples to stand under the arch after the ceremony.' She heard herself sound flustered and not convincing.

Cole leaned close. 'It's okay. You can confide in me. Are you and Jake pretending to be together for the sake of the book's publicity? Did you break up because you married the castle owner guy?'

'Nothing like that.' Daisy shook her head and pointed to the picture. 'Look, it's not even a real wedding dress.'

'You're wearing a bridal veil and he's wearing a tailcoat and top hat.' He tried to get her to confide in him.

'They're fancy dress outfits.'

'Okay, Daisy, if you say so.'

'I do.'

'Something wrong?' Wes said, intervening.

'I thought that Daisy was married to the wealthy castle owner in Cornwall,' Cole told him.

Wes glanced at the picture on Daisy's phone. 'Is that your wedding photo?'

She put her phone in her bag. 'No, it's like this party, all fake and nonsense.' She stomped off, taking her coffee and heading out to the balcony.

Standing in the freezing cold soon sharpened her senses, along with the coffee. The view of New York distracted her wayward thoughts, and for a moment she gazed out at the city, something she'd only seen in movies.

It was breathtaking. Beautiful, covered in snow and sparkling with lights, so alive and exciting.

'I'm sorry if I upset you,' Cole said, joining her.

Daisy shrugged off his apology and kept gazing out at the snow–covered city.

Cole took his jacket off and draped it around her shoulders. 'It's freezing out here.'

'Manhattan looks just like I've seen in films.'

'First time in New York?'

'Yes, and probably the last. I seem to keep messing things up for Jake. First the iced tea, then the wild dancing, and now I've shown you a private picture that makes it look like I'm married to Roman Penhaligan.'

Cole tried to soothe the situation. 'Not bad considering you only arrived in New York this evening.'

'Trouble follows me around,' she told him.

'You're a trouble magnet?' He sounded as if he doubted this.

Daisy gestured to him standing there. 'You followed me out here. And I reckon you're trouble. Big trouble.'

Cole laughed. 'I can be, but I'm not out to reveal any of your deep, dark secrets, Daisy.'

'You're a news hound. Isn't that in your blood?'

'Sometimes, but I have my moments when I drop my guard.'

She glanced at him sceptically.

'Like now,' he said. 'I just wanted to know about your friend and the castle.'

Daisy's expression showed she didn't believe him.

'Now which one of us won't believe the other?' he countered.

She sighed heavily and breathed in the cold air. It felt so different to the winters in London, or the blustery days recently in Cornwall. The air had a different quality and energy to it.

'Why are you interested in finding out about Roman and his castle?' Daisy challenged him to explain.

'You mentioned that he offers weddings. I have friends who are looking for a special venue for their wedding next spring. They want somewhere incredible.'

'The castle is beautiful.' She accessed the website on her phone and showed him.

'It looks great.' Cole noted the name and details.

'I'm working on illustrations for a new book and I was at the castle recently to view the vintage designs on the decor.'

'A new book with Jake?'

'No, its for another publisher I work for in London.' She explained the details.

'Is this a secret or can I mention it when I'm covering Jake's book? I'd like to highlight your artwork.'

'It's not a secret. A journalist in London did an interview with Jake and me, and he included it in the feature.'

Cole absorbed the details and then noticed she was shivering from the cold 'You should come inside before you freeze.'

Taking another breath of air, Daisy gave Cole his jacket and went back inside to join the party. Noticing that Jake was still chatting to others, she headed over to the buffet.

Cole searched the web for the feature. The interview had been syndicated and was readily available online. He read it on his phone and studied the photos, wondering if there was an angle he'd like to cover.

Wes approached Cole. 'Valerie has organised interviews at Jake's hotel tomorrow. Did you get her message? Will you be attending? Monica and several other journalists will be there.'

'Yeah, I'll drop by,' Cole confirmed. 'Is Daisy going to be there? I'd like to interview her too.'

'No, it's just Jake tomorrow.'

Cole held up his phone. 'Have you seen this feature?'

Wes shook his head. 'Where did you find it?'

'Daisy mentioned it.' He lowered his voice. 'Between that wedding photo with the castle guy, and this press interview, I think there's a lot more to Daisy than I first thought.'

CHAPTER FIFTEEN

Mischief Maker

'What's the deal with you and Jake Wolfe?' Monica sidled over to stand beside Daisy at the buffet.

Daisy was helping herself to the sweet potatoes and mini pastries. She paused and glanced at her.

'I'm Monica by the way. I'll be interviewing Jake tomorrow.'

'There's no big deal. I illustrated his new book.' Daisy kept her reply on a business level, wondering how much Monica knew.

'But you're dating him.'

'I am.' Keep it short and sweet, Daisy told herself. The coffee and fresh air had helped ease the effects of the iced tea, but waves of underlying mischief kept washing over her.

Monica looked at Daisy. 'Come on, there's more to you two guys than that.'

Daisy fudged the issue. 'I'm not sure what else would be relevant to the book.'

Monica's voice took on a confiding tone. 'Are you secretly married to the guy who owns the castle? Wes says he saw the wedding picture.'

'No. That was a promotional photo to help Roman. Nothing more. I've never been married.'

Monica pounced on this comment. 'Any plans to?'

'Nothing planned.'

'Jake hasn't popped the question then?'

Daisy forced a smile. 'No.' She tried not to sound perturbed about this.

Monica picked up on Daisy's attitude anyway. 'And that bothers you?'

'Not at all,' Daisy lied, suddenly having no appetite for the buffet food.

Monica wouldn't let it go. 'Jake's a real handsome guy. I mean he's...gorgeous.'

'He's a looker, yes.' Daisy tried to sound perky. 'And really talented at what he does.'

'I'm sure he is.' Monica found herself being boxed in with Daisy's replies. She circled back round to talking about the castle. 'Being from a quaint little town, it must be nice living by the coast where there's a castle and everything.'

'I've enjoyed it so far. It's such a change from the city.'

Monica frowned. 'The city?'

'I'm not from the quaint little town in Cornwall. I've only lived there since the summer.'

Daisy saw Monica's expression change. 'Where are you from?'

'I'm from London, Monica.' Daisy held her gaze strong and steady.

'Okay,' Monica said, forcing a smile while she recalibrated her tactics to wangle information out of Daisy. 'Enjoy the buffet. I'm sure we'll talk some more on the publicity circuit.'

Wes pulled Jake aside. 'I saw Daisy's bridal picture,' Wes confided. 'Is everything between you and Daisy on the up and up?'

'Where did you see that?'

'Daisy was showing Cole. I saw enough to glimpse that she was standing under a wedding arch. The guy was dressed as a groom.'

A short time later, Jake came over to join Daisy for something to eat. 'I'm hoping we can escape soon, head back to the hotel and get some sleep.'

'I can recommend the sweet potatoes, green salad and mini pastries,' said Daisy, keeping the conversation she'd had with Monica to herself. Jarring Jake into proposing to her to calm the rumours was the last thing she wanted.

Jake took her recommendation and stood next to her, while having a breather from the pressure of mingling with the media guests.

Daisy saw the tension in his shoulders and he kept glancing around, making sure no one was overhearing their conversation.

'Are you okay?'

He kept his voice down. 'Wes and some others wondered if you were married to Roman.'

'Oh, I eh...I showed Cole the picture and Wes saw it. I wish I hadn't.'

'I told them what happened, that it wasn't what they thought.'

'Thanks, Jake.'

He smiled at her and put his food down. 'Do you want to dance with me?'

'I'd love to.'

Jake led Daisy on to the busy dance floor. He took her in hold and danced around the room to the lively music.

After a few dances, Jake said to her, 'Let's get out of here and head back to the hotel.'

Saying their goodnights to Valerie and others, they made their way to the front entrance. The traffic was busy, but Jake managed to hail a cab. They jumped in the back and Jake asked the driver to take them around the block, circle the park and take a slight detour to admire the Christmas lights.

Daisy gazed out the window at the snow–covered city and pointed excitedly at the Christmas trees and sparkling lights. The department store windows had gorgeous displays and everywhere she looked there were beautiful decorations for the holiday season.

'It's magical,' Daisy enthused.

Jake smiled, enjoying the festive displays and Daisy's reaction.

Finally, the taxi circled around and dropped them off at the front entrance of their hotel.

They hurried inside out of the cold and headed to their rooms.

Jake walked Daisy to her room. She opened the door, turned the soft lighting on and bid him goodnight with a loving kiss.

'Sleep tight,' she murmured.

'You too. I'll see you in the morning. Call if you need me.'

He went to leave but she said, 'What's the plan for tomorrow?'

'We'll have breakfast early, then Valerie has lined up interviews for me at the hotel with various journalists. They'll all receive press releases detailing the new book, but each of them will have ten minutes to chat to me individually.'

'That sounds...hectic.'

'Valerie says it's a bit intense, but it's a great way to do a whole load of interviews efficiently. It allows each journalist to use the press release information and add their own angle, depending on what they want to ask me.'

Daisy nodded. 'It makes sense.'

'She says she didn't include you in this round of interviews, but you're welcome to join me, or hang around the hotel.'

'I think I'll head to the shops, wander around and see the lights and explore the city.'

'Are you sure? I don't want you to think that I'm forcing you to go shopping.' There was a smile in his voice.

Daisy laughed. 'There is no such thing. Window shopping in New York is going to be incredible. And of course I intend to buy secret Christmas gifts too.'

'Secrets, huh?'

'Top secret.'

Jake smiled at her. 'Okay then, I'll see you at breakfast.' He walked away to his room and she closed the door and got ready for bed.

Her travelling clothes were scattered where she'd thrown them in her hurry to get ready for the party. She tidied them away and hung her cocktail dress in the wardrobe.

Wearing her snuggly pyjamas, she stood for a few minutes gazing out the window. The view from her hotel room was mesmerising — the lights of the city all aglow and everything iced white. Flakes of snow started fluttering down, adding to the atmosphere. She could've stood there for an hour just admiring the view, but she felt the tiredness wash over her and climbed into bed.

Jake was ready for bed in his room. The lights were off and he wore only the bottom half of his silk pyjamas. He padded across the soft carpet in his bare feet to the window and took a few moments to admire the view of snow falling gently over New York. Then he went to bed and fell sound asleep, not stirring until the morning.

Daisy and Jake ate breakfast downstairs in the hotel restaurant. His hair was still slightly damp from the shower and he wore a classy suit, while Daisy was dressed warm and casual in jeans and a white jumper.

They both had cereal and toast, and shared a pot of tea.

Daisy lifted the teapot and topped up their cups. 'You'll handle the interviews fine.'

'I imagine I'll be answering the same kind of questions on repeat.'

'At least you'll know the answers.'

He smiled across the table at her.

The sound of Valerie and Wes talking near the entrance to the restaurant signalled it was time for Jake to go.

'Don't cause any trouble,' he told Daisy.

'Trouble? Me?' She jokingly pretended she didn't know what he was talking about.

He grinned. 'Have fun secret shopping.'

'I will,' she assured him.

Jake headed away and joined Valerie and Wes.

'Where's Daisy going?' Valerie said, seeing Daisy putting her coat on to leave the hotel.

'Shopping, exploring New York.'

Valerie frowned. 'I thought she'd hang around her hotel room.'

'I can call her back if she's needed for the interviews,' Jake offered. 'But I thought you said she wasn't included in them today.'

'That's right, I just...' Valerie smiled tightly. 'Everything's fine. Let's get you set up for the interviews. I've hired a room for the day.'

As Jake walked ahead, Valerie took a moment to whisper to Wes. 'Keep an eye on Daisy. She's not used to the city.'

Wes gave Valerie an assuring nod.

Daisy buttoned up her warm red coat and stepped outside the hotel. She tilted her head back and gazed up at the snowflakes fluttering down from the pale wintry sky. Digging her pink woolly hat from her coat pocket, she put it on, along with a pair of woollen mittens.

Feeling excited, she shrugged her bag up on to her shoulder and headed for the large stores and shopping malls, eager to explore the city.

The snow became heavier as she walked along, taking photos with her phone and checking to see that they weren't a blur of snowflake close–ups.

Thankfully, the pictures captured the array of store window displays and decorations.

Remembering that she'd promised to keep Mrs Lemon up to date with her trip, she sent several pictures to her along with a message.

Shopping in New York. The stores look wonderful — and it's snowing!

Aware that Cornwall was five hours ahead, she estimated that it would be an ideal time to send the pics. Mrs Lemon would no doubt share them with Karen, Sharky, Woolley and others back home.

Distracted by the fabulous fashions on sale in one of the stores, she went inside and succumbed to trying on several items of clothing, including a shimmering pink cocktail dress that was definitely going home with her. And she bought two glittery evening bags, one gold, one pink, gifts for Mrs Lemon and Karen. She'd intended taking them something back from New York and these were perfect.

She'd just stepped back out into the snowy day when a message popped up from Mrs Lemon.

Wow! Look at you in New York! It looks wonderful. Are you and Jake enjoying yourselves?

We are. We went to the media party last night.

Did you dazzle them?

My dress did. I wore the red sequin cocktail dress.

It sounds perfect. Woolley and I were wondering if you made it to the party when you'd just arrived in New York.

We did. It was hectic, but we slept all the way over on the plane, so we had enough energy to dance and enjoy the buffet. We unintentionally drank too much

Long Island iced tea before we went to the party, and turned up a bit tipsy.

Oh, dear. How much trouble did you cause?

Enough.

Karen and Woolley are laughing. They're reading this with me. I'm in the health food shop. Karen's waving hello, and Woolley's asking if Jake's there with you?

Jake's doing press interviews this morning at the hotel. I'm exploring the city. It's like walking through one of the snowscenes I've seen in films, like a Christmas movie.

I know you're a city girl, but don't wander too far from your hotel.

I won't. I'll keep you posted.

Yes, please do. We're all going to a party at the castle this evening. It's part of the local festivities.

Daisy felt the disappointment of missing out on all the festive parties that Roman was holding at the castle, and other local events. But she kept her disappointment to herself and replied.

Enjoy the castle party. Wear something dazzling. It worked for me.

I'll do that. Ah, Woolley's nodding.

Send me pics of your night at the castle.

I will, Daisy. Take care.

You too.

Daisy put her phone in her pocket and sighed, torn between missing the fun back home, and the people, and enjoying the trip of a lifetime. A coffee shop nearby enticed her to go in and have a mid–morning cup of tea. Sitting at the window, she watched the people go by, and planned to head to the park after she'd finished her tea and the iced doughnut she'd succumbed to.

'Long Island iced tea. That's tasty but potent stuff,' said Sharky, catching up on the news when he came into the health food shop carrying a tray of wholemeal scones and mincemeat tarts.

Woolley laughed. 'It would put a spring in their steps on the dance floor.'

Karen spoke up. 'Can we have iced tea cocktails at the party tonight?'

Sharky put the tray of scones and tarts down. 'I'll ask Roman. I've a cake delivery to make to the castle today.'

'Ask me what?' Roman said, walking in and hearing the tail end of the conversation.

'Daisy and Jake have been drinking Long Island iced tea cocktails in New York,' Sharky explained. 'Could we have these at the party this evening?'

'Yes, I'll make sure they're on the cocktail menu.' Roman was happy to oblige.

'Daisy has sent us pictures from New York.' Mrs Lemon showed them to Roman.

'She seems to be having a fine time. And eh...she's been talking about my castle to the press over there,' he revealed.

'Really?' Mrs Lemon sounded keen to hear more.

'Yes, I received a call from a journalist, Cole, on my way into town,' Roman told them. 'He said that Daisy told him I offer weddings at the castle and he asked me to send details so he can recommend the venue to his friends. They're getting married in the spring.'

Sharky glanced at Roman.

'But there are plenty of dates available for spring weddings, so I'm sure I'll be able to accommodate Cole's friends.' Roman's tone was aimed to assure Sharky, while not making Karen suspicious. Sharky had secretly booked a wedding date at the castle in springtime as a surprise Christmas gift for Karen. No one knew about this except Sharky and Roman. Sharky hadn't even confided in Mrs Lemon in case she blurted it out. The booking was expensive but Sharky wanted their wedding to be extra special, and he knew that Karen loved the castle.

'As I'm in town, can I pick up the cakes for tonight's party?' Roman said to Sharky.

'Yes, come over to the bakery and I'll load them into your car,' said Sharky. 'It'll save me a delivery trip, and give me more time to get myself all suave and spruced up for the party.'

'We're all looking forward to it,' Woolley told Roman.

Valerie ushered in the next journalist scheduled to chat for a few minutes to Jake, and then stepped out of the room to phone Wes.

'Are you keeping an eye on Daisy? Don't let her get lost in the city.'

'She's wearing a bright red coat and pink hat and gloves. I can see her from half a block away,' Wes joked with her.

'I'm serious.'

'Relax. I'm looking out for her. I think she's heading back to the hotel now. No, wait, she's going into the park. I'll call you back.' Wes clicked the phone off and hurried to catch up with her. Red coat or not, there were so many places in the park that he could lose sight of her.

'No, it's a cure for lovesickness, unrequited love,' Jake said for the umpteenth time to yet another journalist, but he kept his tone pleasant. It was a reasonable question, even though it was explained in the press release.

Happy with the information, the journalist left and Monica was next in line to chat to Jake. She began with the usual questions and then hit him with...

'If I had a crush on a guy and I wanted him to fall in love with me, could I use your remedy? Would that work?'

'It wouldn't work, no. It's a cure for love. Not a remedy for romance,' Jake told her.

Monica flicked her silky blonde hair in mild disappointment and then continued. 'So, your remedy is just to soothe a broken heart. Is that what it is?'

'Yes, that's right. A remedy for lovesickness. A blend of herbs and so forth. It's a secret recipe and I'm still perfecting the blend, but the current remedy is quite effective. The details are in the press release.'

'I skimmed it. But I prefer to write my features from talking directly to you. It keeps my features fresh. Anyway, as you're apparently dating Daisy, your book illustrator, would you say that you'd be able to mend her broken heart if you guys split up?'

Jake felt jarred to the core. 'I, eh...in theory, I suppose so, though we're not splitting up. But Daisy wouldn't take the cure.'

Monica leaned back in her chair and looked at him in disbelief. 'Daisy is dating the guy that created a cure for lovesickness, but she wouldn't take the remedy? Why not?'

Jake shrugged off giving an explanation. 'You'd need to ask Daisy about that.'

Monica scribbled a few notes. 'I'll do that. Where is she?'

'Shopping, in the city.'

'Ah, yes, Daisy is a city girl from London.'

'She's from London, yes.'

'Living in a little town now?'

'Daisy has moved to Cornwall.'

'Wasn't she just staying temporarily in the holiday cottage? I'm sure I read that in the feature.'

Jake didn't respond.

'Cole mentioned to me this morning in passing that there was a press feature about you and Daisy. I read it online. Nice pic of the two of you outside your health food shop.' Monica tapped her pen on her notepad and looked thoughtful. 'But you have to wonder if a small town will be enough for a career woman like Daisy. Or if she'll go back to her city life in London — and Sebastian.'

Jake jolted. 'Sebastian has nothing to do with my book.'

'But isn't he the reason Daisy went to Cornwall, to get away from London where she'd been jilted by her boyfriend, Sebastian?'

'Yes, but—'

'People are interested in your book, your cure for love, but they want to know about you Jake. The man who created the love cure. Have you ever been broken–hearted? You hired Daisy when she was broken–hearted to illustrate your book.'

'I've been fortunate in never having had my heart badly broken when it comes to romance.'

Monica noted this.

Valerie intervened. She looked at Monica and tapped her hand on her wrist.

Monica stood up, stuffed her notes in her bag and smiled at Jake. 'One last question. Would you take the cure for love if you were broken–hearted?'

'Yes, I would,' Jake told her.

Monica smiled again and let Valerie escort her out while the next journalist sat down to interview Jake.

Cole took out his journalist's voice recorder and sat it on the table. He began with an ice–breaking comment. 'I like the look of your new book. From the press release notes, it looks great, especially the illustrations.'

'Thanks. Daisy is an excellent botanical artist.'

'Yeah, she was telling me at the party last night that she's working on a new book of vintage designs.'

'She is, for another publisher that she works for freelance.'

'Franklin's publishing company in London.' He shrugged casually. 'I've been doing my research. I saw a recent feature about you, your new book, and your background story with Daisy. I like the angle of that.

A cure for lovesickness brings the two of you together and mends Daisy's broken heart.'

Jake smiled tightly, wishing the interviews were done.

'Oh, and I spoke to Roman Penhaligan earlier this morning,' Cole revealed.

Jake couldn't hide his surprise. 'You spoke to Roman?'

'Yeah, I called him at the castle. Daisy told me he hires it out for weddings and he's sending me details to give to friends that are getting married in the spring. They want a special venue.'

'It's a beautiful castle.'

Cole nodded. 'You live in a lovely part of the country. I saw the pictures of your house and garden. Is that where you grow your herbs for your remedies?'

'Yes, it's a well–established garden and has all the herbs I use. Daisy was able to sketch them first–hand. It made a difference having the book's illustrator collaborate with me on the artwork. I wasn't able to do that with my previous books. That's why the botanical illustrations in this new book are perfect.'

'Daisy's artwork on the book's cover is so classy. I love the look of it. Vintage yet modern.'

'She certainly worked hard to hit the right balance.'

'Valerie says that pre–sales of the book are shooting up. The topic is creating quite a buzz. But I think the look of the book, the artwork, adds to the whole feel of it.'

'Daisy designed the cover art too. My publisher loved it.'

Cole glanced around. 'Where is Daisy? Is she here? I'd like to get a couple of quotes from her.'

'She's out shopping in the city.'

Cole looked out the window behind Jake. 'I hope she likes the snow. It's snowing pretty heavy.'

Jake looked round and saw the snow falling outside the window, blurring the view of the city.

'I'm sure she can handle it. London gets plenty of snow days like this, doesn't it?' said Cole.

Jake nodded vaguely, but still felt concerned.

Cole turned the recording off and stood up. 'Good luck with the book.'

'Thanks.'

As Cole left, Jake quickly phoned Daisy.

'It's snowing, Jake!' she squealed excitedly before he could say anything.

'Where are you? Are you okay?'

'I'm in the park. It's like a winter wonderland. They have an outdoor ice rink. I'm tying on my hire skates as we speak.'

'You're going skating! Can you skate?' What if she fell and hurt herself. A mild panic shot through him, but he didn't want to sound like a worry wart.

'I used to skate every winter in London. Indoor rink and outdoors sometimes. My skill level is somewhere between wobbly and winning.'

'Is that good or awful?'

'Average. Don't worry. I won't take a tumble.'

The next journalist seated themselves down and got ready to chat to Jake.

'I have to go,' Jake told her. 'The interviews are hectic.'

Daisy's tone was playful. 'I'll think of you while I'm skating around the rink.'

Jake smiled to himself. 'Mischief maker.'

Daisy put her phone in her pocket and then saw a familiar figure walking over to her.

'Wes, what are you doing here?'

'Just enjoying the snow. Out for a walk while Valerie handles the interviews at the hotel.' And tailing you, a whirlwind of shopping activity and now skating.

'Want to join me?'

'No, I'll cheer you on from the sidelines.'

Daisy shrugged. 'You don't know how much fun you're missing.'

Watching daring Daisy skate around the rink made him reconsider. 'Don't go away,' he shouted to her. 'I'm going to hire skates and join you.'

Daisy smiled and put her hands up, arms outstretched at her sides, feeling the whole atmosphere of the snowy day's magic sprinkle around her.

CHAPTER SIXTEEN

Skating and Sledding

Daisy sat down at the side of the ice rink and took her skates off, having exhausted herself, and Wes, whizzing round and playfully challenging each other.

Wes flopped down beside her. 'I concede. You edged in front of me on the last lap.'

'Let's call it a draw. I encouraged you to try those spins. You nailed at least two.'

'You think?'

'Yes, I was impressed.'

Wes perked up. 'I love skating in the park in winter.'

'Are you from New York?'

'Born and raised. I know all the best eateries, coffee shops and stores that sell bargain fashions.'

'Bargain fashion shops?'

'Vintage clothes shops. You can pick up a real bargain. Designer pieces. Classic couture.'

'I'm up for some bargain hunting. But first, I'd like to try...' Daisy pointed over to where people were sledding down a snowy slope.

'Sledding? I thought you were exhausted, or maybe that's just me.'

'I've got my second wind.'

'I lost my second wind trying to overtake you on the ice. That was before I lost my third wind attempting those spins.'

Daisy stood up. 'Come on, it looks like fun.'

'It is. I love sledding.'

'I've never tried it.'

Realising Daisy wasn't going to leave the park without sliding down the slopes, Wes gave in.

Handing in their skates, she left her bags in the locker and they walked over to the sledding area.

Standing at the top of the slope, one sled each, Daisy viewed the downhill run with slight trepidation. 'This looks tricky. What do I have to do?'

'There's nothing to it. Just sit on the sled, hold on tight and enjoy the ride. I'll be right beside you.'

Daisy pulled her woolly hat down over her ears, sat on the sled, gripped tight and...with a helping push from Wes, she was off, whizzing down the slope, feeling the cold air blow around her, squealing and laughing all the way to the bottom.

Wes was seconds behind her, having jumped into his sled.

'That felt exhilarating!' Daisy shouted to him.

'Are you up for another run?' he challenged her.

'Oh, yes.'

Trailing their sleds back up to the top of the slope, they set off again...and then again...

Wes gasped and lay on his back at the bottom of the last run. 'I'm officially exhausted.'

'Are you sure you don't want to have one more run?' she teased him.

He hit the snowy ground with the palm of his hand. 'I'm tapping out. You win.'

Daisy held her hand out and pretended she needed to help him up. Wes played along. Their laughter sealed an easy new friendship between them.

'I need coffee — and a croissant,' he said.

'Lead the way. You know all the best coffee shops.'

With Wes helping her carry her shopping bags, they left the park and walked the short distance to a coffee shop where they sat down at a window seat.

'You have to try the croissants,' he said, showing her the menu, but not needing it himself. He knew exactly what he wanted to order.

'I'll have what you're having, but tea for me,' Daisy shrugged her coat off and relaxed back.

Wes was happy to order double of his favourite treat.

Coffee, tea and croissants were served up to them.

Daisy breathed in the appetising aroma of the pastry. 'This looks delicious.'

'It tastes twice as good as it looks.'

She lifted it up and bit into the light layers of pastry filled with rich chocolate. 'Mmm,' she mumbled, crumbs tumbling around her.

'Dig in.' Wes took a bite of his croissant not even trying to control the crumbs. 'You are a bad influence on me by the way,' he muttered through a mouthful of chocolate and pastry.

Daisy tilted her head to one side. 'How so?'

'Valerie sent me to keep an eye on you, to make sure you didn't get lost in the city. I'm supposed to be working.'

'You are, sort of. You kept an eye on me while I was skating, sledding and now...well, I won't tell if you don't.'

'Coffee breaks are allowed,' he joked.

'What about vintage clothes shopping?'

Wes grinned across the table at her. 'There's this great shop not far from here. We could take that route back to the hotel.'

'A working excursion.'

'Exactly.'

They laughed and continued to enjoy their croissants.

'I wish I'd known about Jake Wolfe's cure for love a year ago,' Wes confided, putting his napkin down and sitting back in his seat.

'You had a broken heart?'

'Shattered.'

'Sounds awful.'

'I had a bad break–up with my girlfriend. I thought she was the love of my life. She thought I was the putz of her life. Turned out she was right. She was only dating me to make her ex–boyfriend jealous.'

'Oooh! Nasty.'

'Her ex had been cheating on her, but she forgave him, again, and now they're married.'

'I'm sorry.'

'It's fine. Really, I'm okay now. But at the time I felt like someone had ripped my heart out and thrown it to the wolves.' He pointed to the crumbs on his plate. 'I couldn't even eat a croissant for months. Croissants were our thing.'

'What did you do to mend your broken heart?' Daisy was curious to know.

'Time healed it.' He shrugged. 'Nothing fancier than that. One day I got up went to work and things felt okay again. Later, I came in here and had two croissants all to myself. I don't love her any longer. Sure, I've got the scars, but that's the risk we all take when falling in love.'

'You ever bump into your ex in the city?'

'A few times. She's fake sweet. I really don't have feelings for her now, but she thinks I do. That kind of bothers me. I'm not dating anyone at the moment, but I'm ready to find real love one day. Like you and Jake.'

'I wouldn't have met him if I hadn't been broken–hearted.' She told him about everything that had happened between her and Sebastian.

'Cheating ex's! Never get back with that guy,' Wes advised.

'I won't.'

Wes paid the bill, and then they headed out into the snow and he led her to the vintage clothes shop.

Daisy admired the dresses in the window. 'I love these designs.'

'Come on, let's browse.' He held the door open and they went inside.

The shop was fairly small but they'd made the most of every nook and cranny of shelf and rail space.

Wes held up a silk tie. 'This is mine now.' He went to take it over to the counter to buy it when he stopped and darted behind a rail of clothes.

Daisy wondered what was wrong, but then she noticed an attractive woman, around the same age as herself, hunting him down.

'Wes, I thought it was you.' The woman's fake friendly voice cut icily through the warmth of the shop.

He smiled tightly, pretending he'd been rummaging through the pre–loved jackets.

Daisy was behind the woman and mouthed to Wes. *Is that her?*

Wes gave a subtle nod, confirming that she was his ex–girlfriend. This was one of her favourite shops too.

Daisy grabbed a woolly hat from a bundle on sale, stepped forward as if she hadn't noticed the woman as anything other than a random shopper, and beamed a smile at Wes.

'You have to let me buy this for you, Wes.' Daisy pulled the hat on his head and adjusted it, fussing with the pom pom. 'There. It suits you.'

'Thank you, sweetie,' he said, playing along.

Daisy smiled lovingly at him. 'You'll need it for when we go ice skating and sledding in the park again. But we'll have coffee and our favourite croissants first. My treat.'

The woman stepped away as if she'd been swatted, and eyed the beautiful young woman who was making a fuss of Wes.

'Nice seeing you,' Wes called after his ex as she made a miffed exit.

Daisy went to pull his woolly hat off and put it back in the pile.

'No, I'm keeping this. But I'm buying it.' Then he whispered. 'Thanks, Daisy.'

She smiled at him, and started to browse through the rails of dresses, tops and accessories. The patterns on the fabrics interested her as did the clothes themselves, and she bought several items that were real bargains including a floral patterned silk scarf, a long sleeve wiggle dress suitable for day or evening wear, costume jewellery and hair accessories, timeless pieces from bygone eras. The jewellery was mainly brooches — vintage marcasite florals including a daisy spray, entwined roses, a sprig of lily of the valley, and a bouquet tied with a silver metallic bow, plus a sparkling snowflake in diamante, and an aurora borealis star. The hair accessories were clips and barrettes. The cost was minimal for the quality and Daisy couldn't believe her luck in finding them, but the shop was bursting with bargains.

The day had darkened when they emerged from the vintage shop and headed back to the hotel.

Snow fell gently from the late afternoon sky and all the shop windows dazzled with Christmas lights. They walked along while Wes gave her a running commentary on the city.

A message came through on his phone. He checked it and sighed.

'Valerie is threatening to send out a search party if we don't show face back at the hotel.'

'I guess we should head back. Jake will be finishing up the interviews by now.'

They chatted all the way to the hotel and were still chatting and laughing when they walked along the corridor that led to where Jake and Valerie were waving off the last of the journalists.

Daisy and Wes' bubbling chatter filtered through the air.

Jake recognised Daisy's giggling, but he was surprised to hear Wes so cheerful.

Daisy paused when she saw Jake looking bemused at them. 'Jake! Wes showed me a great vintage clothes shop.' She held up one bag. Wes had insisted on carrying the others.

Before Jake could respond, Valerie spoke up. 'You went shopping, with Wes?' Valerie sounded incredulous.

'Yes, I wanted to find stores where I could buy Christmas gifts and Wes knew a vintage gem. We went there after we'd been sledding.'

Jake frowned. 'I thought you were ice skating.'

'I was, we were,' Daisy explained. 'Then we hit the sledding slopes.'

Valerie blinked and glared at Wes. 'You went skating, sledding and shopping!'

Jake tried not to laugh. Daisy the mischief maker had caused trouble again.

'I inveigled Wes into going along with my adventures,' Daisy explained to Valerie. 'The time just flew in.'

'When you were having fun,' Valerie embellished for her.

Daisy smiled brightly. 'So, are the interviews all done?'

'We've just finished,' said Jake, hearing the hope in her voice that they could spend time together now. He didn't enjoy dashing it as he told her, 'Valerie has arranged for me to talk about my book on a radio show tonight.'

'Oh, wonderful.' Daisy tried to sound pleased.

'A guest cancelled,' Valerie told Daisy. 'They're snowed–in and can't make the slot, so Jake is filling in. It's a popular show and I didn't think he'd be on it. It's always fully booked for guest spots.'

Valerie named the show and Wes nodded excitedly. 'When is Jake on?'

'We've time for dinner, then we'll head to the studios,' said Valerie. She looked at Daisy. 'You might want to put all your shopping in your room and get ready to join us.'

'Will Daisy be on the radio show?' Jake said to Valerie.

'No, well, maybe. The presenter's personal assistant will brief us when we get to the studios.'

Daisy collected her bags from Wes. He had one bag of his own. 'Are those my vintage brooches in with your tie and hat?' she said, seeing that their purchases had become mixed.

'Yeah, here you go.' He handed them over having had no intention of waltzing off with them.

Valerie glimpsed the jewellery as Daisy checked it. 'Did you say...*vintage brooches*?'

'Yes, just a few little pieces I bought as Christmas gifts, and some I intend wearing.' Daisy saw the flicker of interest in Valerie's eyes. 'Here, have a look.' She held them up so Valerie could peer in the bag.

'They're exquisite, especially the floral brooches.'

Daisy followed Valerie's eyeline to the brooches she was peering at and picked up the floral bouquet and entwined roses. 'Try them on if you want.'

Valerie's hand lingered over them. 'I'll try the roses.' She pinned it on to the jacket lapel of her teal skirt suit and looked down to admire it. 'Vintage brooches are so classy.'

'Keep it,' Daisy told her, happy for her to have it.

'Oh, no, I couldn't,' Valerie said without making a move to take it off. 'You bought these as Christmas gifts.'

'I did, so consider it my gift to you,' said Daisy. 'It's just fashion jewellery.'

'If you're sure...' Valerie patted her lapel.

With the new gift now pinned permanently on Valerie, Daisy and Jake went up to their rooms to get ready for dinner.

'We'll meet you in the restaurant in twenty minutes,' Valerie called after them, and then whisked Wes off to do some actual work.

'The fun was unintentional,' Wes began to explain as he tagged along with Valerie.

'Save it,' she said with a wry smile, and then made a phone call to organise their excursion to the radio and television studios, while Wes booked their dinner reservation in the hotel's restaurant.

Jake took charge of Daisy's shopping bags as they headed to their rooms. He went to peek in one of the bags to see what she'd bought, apart from vintage brooches.

'No peeking!' she scolded him. 'There are a couple of pressies in there for you.'

'For me?' he sounded intrigued and succumbed to a quick look.

'I said no peeking!' She pulled the bag off him and smiled. By now they'd reached their rooms. Daisy fished her key out and unlocked the door.

'At least give me a hint at what you've bought for me,' he teased her.

She relented. His main gifts were in Cornwall and he looked like he could benefit from a boost after the hectic day he'd had.

'Two gorgeous ties. Designer vintage. Understated but sooo stylish.'

'It's a pity I have to wait until Christmas. I could've worn one for the radio interview.'

'No one will see you on the radio, Jake.'

He shrugged and feigned disappointment.

'Oh, okay.' She dug into one of the bags and handed him the ties. 'There, I hope you like them. You always wear such classy ties.'

Jake's expression showed he was more than pleased. 'These are perfect, just my style.'

'I don't think that one of them has ever been worn, and the other is in mint condition, maybe worn to a cocktail party decades ago. A little piece of the past in the present.' She sounded wistful.

Jake leaned down and kissed her. 'I'll wear one tonight. Thank you for buying them for me. You're always full of surprises.'

'Wait until you see my fifties wiggle dress. I'm wearing that for dinner this evening.'

Jake grinned. 'A wiggle dress. Do I even want to know what that is?'

'You'll find out in about fifteen minutes. I'm going to get changed.' Giving him a cheeky look, she went into her room and closed the door.

Smiling to himself, Jake headed to his room wondering which one of the ties he'd wear.

The wiggle dress lived up to its name. Daisy looked at herself in the wardrobe mirror. The deep, Christmas red fabric had a slight stretch to it, making it comfortable to wear and a figure–flattering fit. Too flattering? Was there such a thing?

The sweetheart neckline, long sleeves, knee–length hemline with a small split at the back, added to the subtle sexiness of the design. The fabric flattered her slender curves, gave her contours that she didn't know she had, and emphasised her slim waist while smoothing over her hips. Worn with heels, she felt herself wiggle slightly when she walked.

Selecting from the brooches, she pinned the diamante snowflake on to her dress for some festive sparkle.

Jake knocked on the door. 'Time to go.'

No time for second thoughts. The wiggle dress it was.

Picking up her bag that contained her sketch pad so she could work while she waited for Jake to finish his interview, she put her coat over her arm and opened the door.

Jake had worn the deep blue, aquamarine and other shades of blue and sea green tie with his suit. The colours brought out the blue of his eyes. Her heart leapt seeing him standing there smiling at her as he admired her dress.

'So this is the wiggle dress.'

'It is.'

'You look gorgeous, Daisy.'

'Your tie suits you.'

Jake smoothed his hand down the silk fabric. 'My new favourite.'

He carried her coat for her and escorted her downstairs to the restaurant.

Daisy paused at the entrance to the restaurant. Valerie and Wes were being seated at their table. She wiggled over to join them.

'Are you sure this dress looks okay?' Daisy whispered to Jake.

'It looks more than okay.'

She nudged him playfully and tried not to imagine that Valerie and Wes were staring at her.

'That dress is definitely you,' Wes complimented her.

'Did the vintage store have other dresses like that?' Valerie sounded interested.

'Yes, they had a few wiggle dresses,' Daisy told her. 'You should let Wes take you there to browse.'

Valerie considered this. 'Wiggle dresses? I might just do that.'

Ordering their meal without fussing and wasting time, they enjoyed their dinner while going over tips for the radio interview.

'Don't babble too much,' Valerie advised Jake. 'Don't fake laugh, especially on the radio. Keep your pitch steady. Not too loud, not too low. Don't mumble or mutter. Speak light, bright and full of interesting confidence without sounding like a bragger.'

Daisy couldn't resist making a quip as she tucked into her vegetable lasagne and salad. 'So Jake should just be himself.'

Wes snickered. Jake grinned.

Valerie was still wearing the brooch, along with a smirk.

The conversation moved on happily to making sure that Jake repeated the title of the book clearly.

'Listeners won't have any reference other than what you say,' Valerie told Jake. 'Slow your voice and tone it down when you say the title so people can hear it easily.'

Jake nodded, genuinely taking in Valerie's advice. She'd made a couple of remarks about things he wouldn't have thought of.

'And remember,' Valerie added. 'Silence isn't acceptable on the radio, so don't leave awkward gaps in the conversation. The radio presenter will have the savvy to fill in for you if you falter, but don't do that, keep sharp and talk about your new book and your cure for love.'

Primed and ready to go, they finished their meal and took a taxi to the studios.

Again, Daisy admired the Christmas lights throughout the city. 'Manhattan looks wonderful.' Sitting back in the seat, tucked beside Jake, she gazed out the window at the glittering splendour.

As they approached the studios, Valerie received a message.

'Great news,' Valerie announced. 'The Cure For Love hits the shelves tomorrow. Online pre–orders are now being posted out.'

Jake and Daisy exchanged an excited glance.

'Your book is out!' Daisy exclaimed.

'Congratulations, Jake,' said Wes.

'Thanks.' Jake smiled, taking this in. Was the whirlwind of publicity about to whip up into a storm? 'I thought the book was on sale in a couple of days.'

'At Christmastime schedules are flexible,' said Wes. 'Sometimes stores get copies earlier than planned and we have to just run with it. Yuletide schedules are always malleable when things get crazy busy.'

'Great timing for the radio interview,' Valerie told Jake. 'You can tell listeners the book is out in stores and available online.'

'I'll do that,' Jake agreed as the news started to filter through him.

'Message all our main media contacts,' Valerie told Wes. 'Tell them the book is out tomorrow. And that Jake is on the radio tonight. I'll message all the journalists who attended the interviews today.'

Splitting the task, Valerie and Wes erupted into action in the back of the taxi.

Amid the excited chatter and making publicity plans, the taxi pulled up outside the studios and they all went inside.

The radio host's personal assistant welcomed them and took charge of what Jake needed to do. Then she glanced at Daisy. 'And you are?'

Valerie stepped in to pitch for Daisy to be included in the interview. 'Daisy is the book's illustrator. She'd be happy to add to the conversation.'

Nodding and in a hurry to get them seated in the studio and ready for the start of the radio show, the personal assistant led Jake and Daisy along. They left

Valerie and Wes alone in a private reception area where they could listen to the show.

Daisy sensed the fast pace of the studio was usual. Even though they'd arrived on time, there was a buzz, a feeling of urgency to everything. She was even walking fast along the corridor and handling the wiggle with aplomb.

Jake and Daisy were shown into the studio where the sound proofing silenced the outside chatter. They were introduced to the radio presenter, seated opposite him at a desk, had headphones put on, and the microphones in front of them were adjusted to suit them.

'Say something,' a sound engineer's voice spoke into the studio.

Jake hesitated.

'I'm Daisy, the book's illustrator.'

Jake followed her lead. 'I'm Jake Wolfe. I wrote the book.'

A signal confirmed that the sound set–up was ready.

'Please don't touch the microphones,' the personal assistant told them. 'And don't lean forward towards the mics. We can hear you pitch perfect from where you're sitting.'

Jake nodded, and Daisy wondered if the waves of excitement, probably mainly nerves, were the same as Jake was feeling.

He gave her a thumbs up that no one else saw, sending a reassuring rush of confidence through her.

The presenter checked the run sheet. Everything was set for the running order of the show. The interview was interspersed with music and jingles.

The on–air sign lit up.

And the show began...

'The Cure For Love is a new book about a cure for lovesickness — to mend a broken heart,' the presenter announced. 'On the show this evening we have the author and herbalist of the book that's creating a romantic buzz this Christmas — Jake Wolfe. Hi, Jake.'

'Good evening,' Jake sounded composed.

'And with him is the book's botanical illustrator. We're pleased to have you here with us tonight, Daisy.'

'I'm delighted to be here.' She hoped she sounded upbeat.

The questions circled the same route as everything they'd been asked before. No surprises. So far.

Valerie and Wes sat listening to the show play over the area where they were ensconced.

'They both sound terrific,' said Valerie. 'Confident, calm and interesting.'

'Jake's had plenty of practice from the interviews all day,' Wes concluded. 'But Daisy is giving a savvy account of herself.'

Valerie agreed.

The personal assistant approached with two cups of coffee for Valerie and Wes. 'Nice brooch,' she observed, admiring Valerie's entwined marcasite roses.

Valerie gladly accepted the coffee and the compliment. 'It's vintage. A gift from Daisy.'

'Sweet,' the personal assistant said with a smile, and then left them to listen to the rest of the show.

'And when is the book coming out?' the presenter said, unaware of the latest news.

'The Cure For Love is out tomorrow,' Jake announced clearly. 'The book is available from stores and online.'

The presenter looked surprised. 'A great way to celebrate Christmas, Jake.'

'It is,' Jake replied.

'Daisy, you illustrated the book. Do you know the secret recipe that Jake has created for his cure for love remedy?'

'No, the only person who knows the recipe is Jake,' said Daisy.

'But when you were sketching the herbs in his garden in Cornwall, didn't you wonder exactly what the recipe was?' the presenter prompted her.

'I was curious, but watching Jake work in his study, taking notes, and seeing all the bottles of herbs and concoctions on the shelves...' Daisy laughed lightly. 'I realised that the only person who'd understand the recipe was Jake.'

'It's no secret that the two of you are now dating,' the presenter revealed. 'But were you dating Jake when you were hired to work on his illustrations?'

'No, we weren't a couple then.' Daisy felt a blush rise across her cheeks.

'I don't mean to make you blush, Daisy,' the presenter said. 'But would it be true to say that your romance blossomed while you were working on the cure for love book?'

Daisy's smile came across in her reply. 'Yes, that's true.'

Happy with the way the interview had gone, the presenter played some more music and then did the usual wind–up, encouraging listeners to tune–in again to the next show and wishing everyone a good night.

The on–air sign turned off.

Both Daisy and Jake breathed a sigh of relief.

The personal assistant took them back to join Valerie and Wes.

Jake thought they'd be able to relax now after the whirlwind events of the day, but Valerie sounded excited as she introduced them to the television presenter's assistant. It was going to be a long night.

CHAPTER SEVENTEEN

Dress to Dazzle

Jake was whisked off to hair and makeup by the television assistant and a stylist. Their take charge attitude had him in a double–pincer movement. There was nothing he could do.

Daisy joined Valerie and Wes, and waved to Jake as he was led away along the corridor.

'The television interview they've planned for Jake isn't going live,' Valerie told Daisy as they sat and had tea and coffee. 'They have a small studio that's set for short interviews. The presenter will chat to Jake about his book, and it'll be edited and shown as part of their entertainment news tomorrow.'

'Perfect for when the book comes out,' said Wes.

'They were listening to Jake on the radio show and decided to film an interview while he's here at the studios,' Valerie explained. 'In this business, you have to grab the opportunities when they're offered.'

'Yes, of course,' Daisy agreed.

'Don't feel slighted that you're not included in the television piece,' Wes said to Daisy. 'You were very impressive on the radio. But they want to focus on Jake and his book.'

'I'm fine with that.' This was true. Daisy was still buzzing from the radio show and was happy to relax while Jake was interviewed.

'I had an advance copy of the book in my bag. I gave it to them so Jake can show the book during the interview,' said Valerie.

'I'm looking forward to seeing it on the shelves tomorrow,' Daisy told them.

'I've updated the publicity schedule to include a couple of book signings tomorrow,' Valerie said to Daisy. 'Two bookshops are eager to have Jake stop by for an hour to sign copies in–store. They're putting the word out on their social media, but we really just need Jake to sign a few copies for a photo–op. I emailed the new schedule to you.'

Daisy went to check her phone and then remembered that it was turned off while she was in the studios. 'I'll check it later.'

Jake saw his reflection in the mirror as makeup was quickly and expertly applied to enhance him being under the bright studio lighting. A dusting of powder hid any hint of shine on his nose, cheeks and brow. His hair was brushed and styled to look smart but sexy. The latter was achieved with hair gel applied to the strands that fell across his forehead.

'Try not to mess with your hair during the interview,' the stylist advised.

Another dab of powder on his face and he was good to go.

'Jake Wolfe is ready for his interview,' the television assistant called to the presenter who was heading towards them.

The television presenter smiled at Jake. 'Pleased to meet you, Jake. I love the idea of a cure for lovesickness. Let's chat. Just relax and be yourself.

This isn't live so we can edit out anything that isn't a good fit for the show.'

Jake accompanied the television presenter into the small studio where he was seated opposite her. The book was propped up on the table between them, showing the cover to full advantage.

The interview began with a brief introduction about Jake and his new book, and then he answered more of the standard questions. By now, he was adept with his replies and came across as calm and confident.

'We'll give you copies of the radio and television interviews so you can have them on file,' Wes told Daisy while they waited for Jake.

'Here is he now,' said Daisy, seeing him being escorted by the television assistant.

'The interview was excellent,' the assistant said to Valerie. 'I'll contact you tomorrow to confirm the time slot.'

Valerie smiled. 'Thank you. We'll chat soon.'

After depositing Jake with them, the television assistant disappeared swiftly along the corridor.

'We can go now,' Valerie said, standing up and leading them out of the studio into the cold night. They'd picked up their coats and jackets from reception and had called a taxi.

While they stood for a moment waiting on the taxi pulling up, Jake confirmed that the interview did go well.

'The television presenter asked me the usual questions, but it was handy to have a copy of the book there to include in the interview. She says it'll air tomorrow on their entertainment updates.'

'It will and they'll tell me the time so we can watch it,' said Valerie.

The four of them got into the taxi and chatted about the early start they had again the following morning. It was approaching midnight when they dropped Daisy and Jake off at their hotel.

'See you bright and early at the hotel,' Wes called to them. Waving, he headed away with Valerie to their respective apartments in the city.

Snow fell gently around Daisy and Jake, and as she shivered in the icy cold, Jake took her inside and up to her room.

'I'm going to jump in the shower to wash this makeup and hair gel off,' he said as she stepped inside and kicked her heels off, feeling the soft carpet ease the tension.

'I'll see you downstairs for breakfast.' She stood up on her tip–toes and kissed him.

Feeling his heart fill with warmth, he gazed down at her. 'I'm glad you came with me to New York. I know how much you wanted to stay in Cornwall, so thanks for being here.'

'I never wanted to stay in Cornwall without you being there.'

He kissed her and then tore himself away to go shower and get some sleep.

Daisy peeled the wiggle dress off and hung it up in the wardrobe beside her red cocktail dress. It had been surprisingly comfortable to wear, and as it turned out, it was the ideal dress for her trip to the studios.

Two dresses down, she thought and then checked her messages. The one from Valerie had the updated schedule. Apart from the book signings which she didn't need to be part of, there was a party that night, another one like the previous media party. Valerie's message included a what to wear prompt.

Dress to dazzle, Daisy.

Dress three was due get its first outing. The new pink cocktail dress she'd bought shimmered and sparkled on a wardrobe hanger. Oh, yes. Number three was a winner in the dazzle stakes.

Bubbling with the embers of excitement from the events of the day, and the news that the book would be on sale in the shops in the morning, Daisy couldn't settle down to sleep.

Instead of flipping and fluffing her pillows, she got out of bed, flicked on a lamp and sat by the window with her sketch pad.

The city that never slept was awake to keep her company while she sketched.

She drew the design ideas that had been filtering through her mind since seeing the styles from bygone eras in the vintage clothes shop with Wes.

The view of New York rippled with energy, lights galore shining from the streets and stores, and Christmas decorations still twinkling way past midnight.

Jake stepped out of the shower, shook the droplets of water from his lean–muscled body and towel dried his hair.

Shrugging on one of the hotel's robes, he padded through to the bedroom, opened his laptop and dealt with the inevitable smattering of messages from Woolley about the shop's business and other matters.

Typing his replies, he found that he missed his shop more than he'd anticipated, despite the excitement of his book being out in the shops now. A longing for home kept washing over him.

The replies were easy, decisions dealing with orders and finance. He'd planned to keep on top of his emails and not let them pile up while he was away. Woolley and Karen, and to an extent, Mrs Lemon and Sharky, were all pulling together to keep things ticking over. Something he'd never take for granted or ever forget.

An early riser, Woolley would receive the messages in an hour or two, so Jake wanted to get them responded to before he went to bed.

Jake finally closed his laptop and got some rest. Unlike Daisy, he fell sound asleep moments after his head touched the pillow.

Daisy sent a copy of her new sketches to Franklin. He'd get them in the morning, which was fast approaching. She'd become lost in her artwork.

Sending them to Franklin, she noticed she'd missed a message from Mrs Lemon.

Photos, as promised, of the party night at the castle. Roman was happy to lay on Long Island iced tea cocktails for us. Even when you're on the other side of the world, Daisy, you're still a mischievous influence on us. But we had...FUN!

Daisy laughed as she scrolled through the photos of Mrs Lemon, Woolley, Karen and Sharky. They were standing in the main hall near the Christmas tree, holding up large glasses of iced tea, raised in a cheers. She felt the laughter from their smiles and wished she could've been part of the fun.

Another photo showed that Roman had joined them, along with Mr Greenie, in drinking the iced tea.

This made Daisy miss them all even more.

She typed a reply.

The party pictures look wonderful! I'm glad you enjoyed the iced tea.

Then she added the news.

Jake's book is on sale now in the shops! Or it will be when we get up in the morning. It's waaaay after midnight, and we're back from a radio interview where we both took part. Then Jake was filmed for a television interview that will air on their entertainment news tomorrow. I'll keep you posted.

After sending the messages, Daisy went to bed. Tucked up snug and cosy, she watched the snow flutter down outside the window, and fell asleep.

Daisy poured another cup of tea at the breakfast table as Jake finished eating his scrambled eggs and toast. She'd opted for cereal and fruit.

She showed him the pictures of the party at the castle.

'Is that iced tea cocktails they're drinking?' he said.

'Yes.' Daisy laughed. 'And I told Mrs Lemon that the book is out today. She sent a message back saying they're all going to buy copies.'

Valerie and Wes arrived and walked up to their table.

'Ready for the book signings?' Valerie said to Jake.

Jake stood up and put his jacket on. 'Yes.' He smiled at Daisy. 'I'll see you later.'

'You know you're welcome to join us,' Valerie told Daisy.

'No, it's fine. I'm going to explore the city, see some of the tourist landmarks that Wes said I should visit.'

'Okay,' said Valerie. 'We'll see you at the party tonight. Did you get my brief?'

Daisy nodded. 'Dress to dazzle.'

'A few of the journalists that were at the party the other night will be there, like Monica and Cole,' Wes added.

'Sounds like another fun night,' Daisy chirruped.

Jake left with Valerie and Wes, and Daisy headed out into the snowy city.

Wrapped up warm in her red coat, pink woolly hat and mitts, she set off, admiring the store windows all lit up in the pale winter light.

And there in a book store window was Jake's book. She stood there taking it in. The book looked beautiful. She remembered drawing the illustrations that were on the cover, each one inked or painted in watercolour. To see her artwork on the book cover sent a charge of elation through her. She went in and bought a copy, tucked it in her bag and then headed back out.

Two calls came through in quick succession. The first was from Franklin in London. She was so happy to hear his voice.

'Franklin! Did you get my latest sketches?'

'Yes, that's why I'm calling, to tell you to push on with more like these. I love them.'

'Hurrah! I'll do that.'

'What are you up to?'

'I've just seen Jake's book in a store window.'

'It's out in the shops in London now too. I've bought a few copies to give as Christmas gifts,' said Franklin. 'An excellent book. I think the cover art is beautiful.'

'Thank you.'

'And the content is fascinating. Tell Jake congratulations.'

'I'll tell him. He's doing book signings today. I opted to escape out into the city.'

'Enjoy yourself—' Franklin stopped abruptly.

Daisy heard a kerfuffle in the background and the shrill sound of Celeste's familiar voice.

'Daddy! Why does Sebastian get all the top editorial tasks?' Celeste demanded, marching into Franklin's office.

'You don't have the necessary experience, Celeste, to handle important book matters,' Sebastian said in that smooth, cold, calm voice of his.

Daisy jolted at the sound of it.

'We'll speak soon, Daisy.' Franklin ended the call and stepped into the fray.

'This book comes out at the beginning of January,' Franklin reminded his daughter as she glared dark daggers at him.

Celeste wore a fashionable skirt suit that flattered her slender figure and soigne styling. Her silky dark hair flicked in annoyance. 'I know that,' she snapped at her father.

Franklin calmly opened his desk drawer and pulled out an envelope containing a Christmas card and handed it to her.

'What's this?' She held it as if it was poison.

Franklin leaned back in his chair and steepled his fingers on the desk. 'Open it.'

Long, manicured nails ripped it open. 'A silly Christmas card!' Her nose turned up at the traditional festive scene.

Sebastian stood tall and stoically in the background, watching the chess moves play out.

'Read it,' Franklin told her with a smile.

Celeste skim–read it, and then re–read it as the message hit home. 'A skiing trip to Europe. A whole month. Leaving next week!' Each phrase pitched higher as her delight showed.

'Merry Christmas, Celeste,' said Franklin. 'An early gift from me.'

Completely icing Sebastian from the conversation, Celeste's face lit up picturing everything she had to do to get ready for her skiing trip.

'You said your friends were going, so I thought you'd enjoy going with them,' Franklin explained. 'As you'll be away for the book launch in the New Year, I thought that Sebastian should deal with the editorial work.'

No argument from Celeste. Her mind was already ticking over what to wear, and the calls she'd make to her friends.

'Thank you, Daddy,' she remembered to tell Franklin as she went to hurry out of his office.

'Remember, we have an important editorial meeting late this afternoon, Celeste,' Franklin called after her, genuinely expecting her to attend.

Celeste waved a dismissive hand in the air as she brushed past Sebastian. 'I won't have time for that now. I need to go shopping for new skiwear. I can't wear last season's colours. I'm now thinking ice blue. Sebastian can handle the editorial meeting.' With those swift words, she left Franklin's office, taking the turmoil with her.

'Checkmate,' Sebastian said with a wry smile and a shrewd look in his cold blue eyes.

Franklin frowned at him.

'Nothing, doesn't matter.' Sebastian headed out of the office. 'I'll go prepare the editorial notes for the meeting.'

Daisy's second call was from Cole.

'I heard you on the radio last night. You sounded great,' Cole complimented her. 'Valerie messaged me that Jake was being interviewed. It was a pleasant surprise to hear you too, chatting about your artwork for the book. That's why I'm calling. You said a couple of things and I'd like to quote you on those for the news feature I'm writing. It goes to press soon.'

'Yes, you can quote me on anything I said on the radio.'

'Great, I'll see you tonight at the party no doubt.'

'You will.'

'And I'll talk to you about my friends hiring Roman Penhaligan's castle for their wedding.'

Daisy jolted. 'They've gone ahead and hired it?'

'Yeah, they're getting married there in the spring. They've invited me to the wedding.' He let the news hang in the air.

Daisy blinked. 'You're going to Cornwall.'

'I sure am. I expect a tour of the local sights from you and Jake.'

Daisy laughed, still taken aback that Cole would be visiting Cornwall.

'I'll be staying at the castle. And although it's just a rumour at the moment, I won't be the only one from New York heading to the UK for the wedding. But I'll talk to you tonight at the party once I know for sure.'

After the call ended, Daisy put her phone in her pocket and tried not to speculate about Cole's rumoured guests at the castle wedding.

Roman looked in the window of Sharky's bakery, tempted by the crusty rolls. Sometimes, there was nothing nicer than a roll and butter with a cup of tea. And a sticky bun.

Sharky spotted him outside the window, gave him a cheery smile and bagged two sticky buns. He sat them on the counter as Roman walked in.

'You know me too well.' Roman joked.

'Anything else I can get for you?'

'Two crusty rolls.'

Sharky added them to the order.

Roman paid for his sticky buns and rolls, and then lowered his voice. 'A quick word with you.'

'What is it?'

'Cole, the journalist from New York,' Roman began, 'his friends have booked the castle for their wedding in the spring.'

Sharky looked concerned.

'Don't worry. The date of their wedding and your wedding date don't clash. And I've other dates earmarked for the two of you in case Karen wants to alter it when you surprise her at Christmas.'

'Phew!'

'I just wanted to tell you in private in case the gossip starts flying around, which it's bound to do.'

'New Yorkers coming here for their wedding. I'd be happy to bake their cake,' Sharky offered.

'I'm glad you said that, because I've told them you would.'

Sharky laughed.

'The thing is...they'll be flying over a number of guests from New York to attend their wedding. From what they've told me, a lot of them work in the media business. Cole is one of them.'

'Does Daisy know?'

'Not yet, but Cole says he's going to tell her.'

'New York comes to Cornwall, eh? Exciting times ahead.' Sharky smiled. 'For them, I mean. They won't know what's hit them.'

Roman agreed. 'That's sort of what I was thinking, especially as Daisy and Jake will be back by then.'

'Trouble and fun galore. I'd better bake an extra special cake for the media wedding.'

'They're all staying at the castle. They've booked out every room available.'

'That'll cost them a pretty penny.' Sharky knew how much he'd paid to hire the castle for his wedding with Karen in the main hall. But all their guests lived locally or in nearby towns. Roman had given him a large discount too.

A customer came in to buy a Christmas cake, so Roman headed out.

'Thanks for the tip–off,' Sharky called after him.

Roman raised his hand and waved as he left with his bags of sticky buns and rolls.

'What's your name?' Jake said to one of the customers at the first store's book signing. He sat at a table with a pile of books, but people were picking up copies from the shelves and bringing them over to him to be signed. It was reasonably busy considering it was an impromptu event.

'This is going well,' Wes whispered to Valerie as they oversaw the promo. 'Jake's handling the signings great.'

Valerie checked her phone. 'Word is getting around. Another two stores have invited us to stop by for book signings.' She showed Wes the locations. 'They're near our planned route so we'll drop by those too.'

Wandering around the city, with no sense of direction, only a sense of adventure, Daisy saw a couple of landmarks. Taking the escalator to the top of one, she stood admiring the view she'd seen so many times in movies, then having tick boxed that tourist trip, she headed to another, then had lunch in a shopping mall cafe, before circling back to the park near where she'd been skating and sledding — and ventured in.

The day was darkening to a picture perfect snowy late afternoon. People were sliding down gentle slopes on sleds. She was tempted to have another go, but instead hired a pair of skates and joined the fun of people circling around the frozen rink in the park.

She kept going around, loving the feeling of the cold air brush past her.

There were moments when she felt like she was in a real life Christmas card, part of the picture, a little figure in a red coat and pink bobble hat and mitts, skating outdoors under a darkening sky.

Snowflakes fluttered from the sky, creating a beautiful Christmas atmosphere. She would've skated another few laps if she hadn't needed to go back to the hotel to get ready for the party and dress to dazzle.

'Where's Jake going?' Valerie saw him walking away from the store in the shopping mall where they'd finished the last book signing of the day. She'd been talking to the store's owner, thanking them for going along with the impromptu event.

'He said he needs to do some special Christmas shopping,' Wes explained. 'I reminded him that there's the party tonight, but he assures me he'll be there with Daisy.'

Valerie nodded, watching Jake disappear into the crowd. He seemed to know where he was going and what he was aiming to buy. Something special for Daisy perhaps? Hmm.

Jake walked briskly along the busy street of shoppers heading to the one jewellers store he knew. It wasn't far from the mall, but he welcomed the walk in the cold, crisp air and a chance to stretch his legs after sitting for most of the day signing books. His hands ached, but he couldn't complain. The experience overall had been pleasant, meeting all the readers interested in his new book.

He buttoned up the dark jacket that he wore over his suit and stepped up the pace to reach the store before it closed for the day. A dark, early evening sky arched over the snow–covered streets, and he glanced around him at the bustling city. He'd barely had time to take in any of it. But he was here to promote his book, he reminded himself, not on a tourist's holiday. That didn't mean he couldn't mix a little of the two, especially as he'd been apart from Daisy for chunks of the time. He planned to make it up to her.

The jewellers store was where he remembered it from previous visits to the city. He went inside and knew exactly what he wanted to buy. He'd checked their selection online to save time and went up to the counter that sparkled with gold, silver and precious gems under the display spotlights.

'Can I help you?' an assistant said to Jake.

'Yes, I believe you can.'

CHAPTER EIGHTEEN

Snowy Night

Daisy put on the pink cocktail dress and glitter heels. She looked at herself in the wardrobe mirror. The dress shimmered and sparkled, and so did her shoes.

She wore her hair down around her shoulders, and her makeup emphasised her lovely features.

Picking up her evening bag, she heard Jake knock on her room door and hurried through, scooping up her coat and draping it over her arm.

'Wow! You look gorgeous.' Jake's reaction boosted her confidence.

She smiled at him. 'And you look handsome.' Her heart fluttered seeing him standing there dressed in a classic suit, shirt and tie. His expensive business–style coat was unbuttoned and complemented his tall, broad–shouldered look. His dark hair was brushed back, but a few of the rogue strands fell across his forehead.

He resisted the temptation to kiss those soft, deep pink lips of hers so as not to ruin her makeup. But later...no promises.

Jake helped her on with her coat downstairs in reception, and then they got into a taxi. The traffic was heavy. The party was in a hotel a few blocks away, so they settled in the back seat and admired the Christmas lights as they drove by.

Arriving at the hotel, they went inside, checked in their coats, and were met by Valerie and Wes. Valerie sparkled in a little black and silver number.

'Your television interview is due to air in the next few minutes,' Valerie announced to Jake, sweeping them through to a room just off reception where they could watch it.

'The word has gotten around,' Wes told them as they were joined by Cole, Monica and several other journalists and interested parties. Monica must've missed the dazzle memo because she didn't even shine, but her dark velvet dress suited her.

Cole wore a white dinner jacket, and with his blond hair sleeked back, he looked like he'd stepped off the set of a thirties era movie.

Jake and Daisy were introduced to a couple of magazine journalists keen to interview them about the book and their romance.

'I thought you could chat to them briefly before you head through to the party,' Valerie whispered to Jake and Daisy.

'There's a real buzz with your book hitting the shelves today,' Wes added.

'Sales are soaring,' said Valerie. 'Pre–sales gave your book a great springboard for the launch, but now it's starting to chart strongly.'

This news bolstered Jake and Daisy as they prepared to view Jake's interview.

Wes turned up the sound on the television and everyone stood watching the entertainment news that included Jake talking about his book.

Daisy squeezed Jake's arm. 'You look and sound great,' she whispered.

Jake couldn't judge himself squarely, but from the positive reaction of the journalists, he'd done well.

The interview was short but everything they needed for a prime opportunity to promote the book.

'Can we talk to both of you for a few minutes?' the first magazine journalist said to Jake and Daisy.

Cole moved over to have a quick word with Daisy. 'We'll chat later when you come through to the party.'

Daisy nodded, and then did her best to give interesting answers to the questions about her botanical artwork.

'It made such a difference having Daisy there in my garden to illustrate what I was writing about,' Jake told them. 'For my previous books, the artwork was good, but it was done after I'd finished writing it.'

'Did you anticipate falling in love with Jake Wolfe when you first started working on the illustrations?' the second journalist was keen to know.

'I didn't,' said Daisy. 'But I loved drawing them from real life in Jake's garden. He had photos too that I used as reference, though I preferred sitting in the garden sketching the herbs and flowers growing during the summer.'

Jake's television interview had given the magazine journalists answers to questions they'd planned to ask, so the interviews wrapped up with a magazine photographer taking pictures of Jake and Daisy standing together smiling.

Valerie and Wes then took Jake and Daisy away and led them through to the party that was being held in the hotel's function room.

Glitter and glamour was the order of the night. From the Christmas decorations to the guests — a mix of media, celebrity and business people, the room dazzled with the glitterati.

Jake and Daisy mingled and were introduced to various guests by Valerie and Wes.

While Jake was talking to Valerie and other guests, and Wes had disappeared into the crowd, Cole made a beeline for Daisy and swept her aside to chat.

Cole began by confirming that he was going to the wedding in Cornwall, and then addressed the rumour that he wouldn't be the only one from New York attending the wedding.

'Valerie has been invited,' said Cole.

Daisy looked surprised. 'Valerie is going to Cornwall too?'

'Yes, my friends have confirmed that she's accepted their invitation.'

'Is Wes going?'

'Yep.'

'Is this a secret? Can I tell Jake?'

Cole glanced over to where Jake and Valerie were standing. 'I think she's telling him right now.'

Jake looked as surprised as Daisy had felt, and then he glanced around to see where Daisy was and saw her standing with Cole.

'Want to dance?' Cole said to Daisy.

She nodded and walked with Cole on to the dance floor.

'You look beautiful this evening,' Cole told her.

Daisy felt a blush rise up.

'Don't worry, I'm not coming on to you. It's just a compliment.'

She smiled and continued to dance with him. 'Is your world always like this?'

'Pretty much, especially during the holiday season. But I'm looking forward to sampling a slice of your world in Cornwall in the spring. It'll be nice to relax and enjoy the slower pace.'

Daisy laughed. 'Don't bet on that.'

Cole smiled, but then Jake cut–in. 'Mind if I dance with Daisy?'

'No, we were just catching up on some news.' Cole stepped back and Jake clasped Daisy's hand.

'News about heading to Cornwall?' said Jake. 'Valerie told me she's going to the wedding. Wes is going too. And you.'

Cole nodded and then brought the conversation back to business. 'The feature I've written about you and your book, and Daisy's artwork, is due to be published in a couple of days,' Cole revealed. 'But can I get a picture of the two of you here at the party to include in the feature?'

Jake and Daisy agreed to pose together.

Cole snapped a couple of pictures with his phone and then held it up to show them. 'The feature lacked pictures of the two of you together.'

'Can I have a copy of those?' said Daisy. 'I don't have many photos of us together in New York.'

'Sure.' Cole sent them to her phone.

'Thanks, it's to show friends back home,' she said.

Cole beckoned Valerie and Wes over to join them. 'Let's get a group picture of us all together for Daisy.' They obliged, and Cole handed his phone to someone to take the photo.

For a moment, they stood together with Jake and Daisy in the middle, Valerie and Wes beside Jake, and Cole next to Daisy. There were smiles all round.

Cole checked the picture and sent it to Daisy. 'This will let your friends see who's coming to the castle wedding in Cornwall.'

'The bride is a friend of mine,' said Valerie. 'I've never been to Cornwall before. But a wedding in a real castle, I couldn't miss out on that. I'm thinking of it as a relaxing vacation.'

Cole laughed lightly. 'I'd check with Daisy about it being relaxing. She seems to think we're in for a whole different time there.'

Wes frowned. 'Isn't it a quaint little town? It's by the sea with lots of countryside and miles from the city.'

'It is,' said Daisy. 'But when I left London for a quiet time in Cornwall in the summer, it didn't exactly work out that way. Don't say you haven't been warned.'

'I'm liking the sound of that even more,' Wes confirmed.

'I guess we're going to be seeing a whole lot more of each other in the future,' Cole concluded.

'I suppose so,' Jake agreed.

Jake then swept Daisy into the dancing. Following his lead, Cole danced with Valerie. Wes ended up with Monica.

Later, Cole danced with Daisy while Jake partnered with Valerie.

'I bought a few copies of Jake's book to give as Christmas gifts,' Cole told her.

'You're the second person to tell me that today. Franklin said he's done that too.'

'He's the publisher you work with?'

'Yes, he phoned me earlier about the sketches I'd sent him. This is still sort of a working trip.'

'I'd be interested in meeting Franklin when I'm in Cornwall. He publishes some great books. I'm always keen to write features on new releases.'

'Franklin is based in London.'

'How far is London from where you are in Cornwall?'

'A few hours drive. I leave at the crack of dawn when I drive up to the publishing meetings, and spend the day there before driving back that night.'

'Maybe I could go with you, if you're heading to the city while I'm over there. You could introduce me to Franklin.'

Daisy nodded. 'Yes, I could do that. I'll tell Franklin.'

'Give him my number if he wants to talk to me before that.'

'I will.'

Jake partnered with Daisy again, and she always felt her heart flutter when he held her close.

Under the glittering lights they danced the night away, drinking champagne and cocktails and enjoyed the luxury buffet.

At the end of the evening, they all parted ways, with Jake and Daisy taking a taxi back to their hotel.

Daisy shivered as she stepped out of the taxi when it dropped them off outside their hotel around midnight. It was snowing, and Jake put his arm around Daisy's shoulders, shielding her from the cold as they hurried inside.

They said goodnight in Daisy's room as she turned the lamps on and stood in the warmth and cosy glow.

'I think I'm a little tipsy on that champagne,' Daisy admitted. 'I really never intended indulging in those extra glasses but...'

'It was a special night.' Jake felt the effects of it too.

'I haven't checked our schedule to see if it's been updated. What has Valerie lined up for us tomorrow?'

'Another early start unfortunately, so we'll need to get some sleep. The interviews start after breakfast, like the ones I did here before. One of the journalists wants to chat to you as well, but then you're free to escape to go shopping or whatever you want.'

'It's a pity you can't escape with me, but I know you're here for the publicity so...' she sighed. 'I'll just have to force myself to go exploring again.' She stepped close to him. 'But maybe we can find time to dine in New York. I pictured all the wonderful eateries where we could have dinner together.' She sighed again, and then a wave of emotion washed over her and she looked almost teary.

'What's wrong?' Jake said gently, gazing down at her.

'New York is exciting but...I really miss being home in Cornwall.' She shook herself and forced a smile. 'Blame the champagne for making me over emotional.'

Jake pulled her into his comforting arms and kissed her lovingly.

'Get some sleep. I'll see you in the morning. But call if you need me,' he told her.

She walked with him to the door and waved him off.

The effects of the busy day, the party and the champagne made Daisy fall asleep almost as soon as she got into bed. No sleepless night this time or drawing late into the evening.

Jake lay in bed wide awake, his mind whirring, thinking of the events of the day and the coming day. His book was doing really well and the publicity had worked as planned, but he missed spending time with Daisy.

The lights from New York glittered outside his window, and the snowflakes caught the glimmer as they fell, making it look like it was snowing starlight.

He was used to the quiet sounds of the sea lulling him to sleep, but the electric murmur of the city that never slept provided a background of ideas of how he could make this Christmas with Daisy truly special.

CHAPTER NINETEEN

Dashing Through the Snow

Daisy enjoyed the lavish topping of strawberries and blueberries on her breakfast cereal in the hotel restaurant. Jake joined her in having cereal and fruit and they shared a pot of tea.

'Valerie and Wes are setting up the interview room,' said Jake. 'The journalists should be arriving in the next five minutes.'

Daisy glanced out the restaurant window. 'It's been snowing overnight. The city is iced white.'

'Remember, one of the journalists wants to interview you, but when that's done, you can head out into the city rather than hang around the hotel.' Jake peered out the window. 'Unless the snow is too heavy and you'd prefer to stay cosy in your room.'

'Nope. I'm up for more adventures. I just wish you could go with me. Or at least meet up for lunch, even a cup of tea somewhere.'

'I'll try,' Jake promised.

Daisy retracted her request, seeing that she'd added to the pressure of Jake's hectic schedule. 'No, don't. It's fine.'

'I have a lot of things planned for today, but I will try to meet you for lunch,' he said.

She wished she hadn't mentioned it. He looked like he'd had a sleepless night, whereas she'd slept sound until her early morning alarm jolted her awake. Jumping in the shower, she'd washed her hair, and then dried and styled it smooth before getting dressed in her grey cords, boots and pink jumper. Running downstairs, she'd ordered breakfast in the restaurant. Then Jake arrived to join her, looking sharp in his suit as usual.

'We could have lunch here in the hotel,' Daisy offered. 'You get a break during the interviews, right?'

'Yes, but I'd prefer to escape and have lunch somewhere else with you today.'

'I know your schedule is tight, so don't stress about it,' she assured him.

Valerie waved from the restaurant doorway, a signal that the journalists had arrived in the interview room.

'Here we go,' Jake said, standing up.

Daisy gulped down the remainder of her tea and stood up too.

The interviews began with Jake and Daisy sitting on opposite sides of the room talking to two journalists about the book and their work.

'Do you plan to write a follow–up to your book?' one of the journalists said to Jake. 'You're still perfecting the cure, improving the remedy.'

Jake replied to the two–part question. 'There's been talk with my publisher that I might write a follow–up, but nothing is confirmed yet. When I get back to Cornwall, I intend to improve the recipe. The new book states quite clearly that the cure for lovesickness is a work in progress. I do have a remedy that seems to work quite effectively, but more improvements are planned. Then I'll have to test it on a number of people who are romantically broken–hearted.'

'What about the remedy being made available in your shop and other stores,' the journalist said to him.

'That's part of my future plans for the remedy,' said Jake.

Daisy tuned–out Jake's conversation to concentrate on her interview.

'Have you always been a botanical illustrator?' the other journalist said to her.

'Yes, floral art was my favourite when I was starting out in my career. I include bees and butterflies and other creatures in my illustrations, but flowers and herbs are the main focus of my artwork.'

'With the success of Jake Wolfe's book bringing attention to your art, do you have any plans to expand on it? Perhaps create prints and wall art, or greetings cards?'

'Nothing like that is planned, but I'm hoping to work on my botanical art when I get back home.' She was tempted to mention that Jake had promised to have a summerhouse built that she could use as an art studio, but she buttoned her lips. She thought about the painting she'd created for Jake's study and hoped he'd like it. And for a moment, her thoughts drifted home to Cornwall...

'This feature should be out in the next issue of the magazine,' the journalist told Daisy. 'I'll contact Valerie to confirm it.'

With her interview finished, Wes came over to chat to Daisy.

'Jake says you're escaping to enjoy another snow day,' Wes joked with her. 'I wish I could abscond with you, but we're going to be crazy busy today. Jake's even encouraged Valerie to pack in extra assignments that she'd scheduled for the next two days. What a trooper that guy is.'

'Jake has added to his workload today? On purpose?' Daisy gave up hope of them having lunch.

'Yep, he told Valerie to line up everything he needed to tick box on his schedule,' Wes told Daisy. 'Valerie has piled it on, so we're on hyper alert to squeeze it all in.'

'I'll leave you to it,' Daisy said, and then hurried upstairs to get her coat and hat on to tackle the snowy day.

Daisy waved to Jake as she headed out, feeling the winter air wrap around her as she walked to the shops.

The sound of the popular festive songs playing in the stores filled her with the joy of the season. She walked past a couple of eateries that she thought would've been nice for lunch with Jake, and not too far from the hotel. Keeping a mental note of them in case he somehow managed to find time for lunch with her, she headed towards one of the huge Christmas trees and stood there gazing up at the beautiful decorations.

A message came through on her phone, and she smiled when she saw it was Mrs Lemon replying to the photo she'd sent the previous night.

Your pink cocktail dress looked gorgeous at the party. That was a lovely photo of you and Jake. Hope you're not working too hard and finding time to explore New York with Jake. As you know, Roman has a lot of parties and events scheduled at the castle. Not trying to outshine you, especially as I couldn't when you're wearing a dazzling dress like that, but we're all getting ready for a festive dinner at the castle this evening. I'll send you photos.

Daisy replied.

The last time I was at the castle, I saw the Christmas schedule of parties and events. They looked great. Enjoy your festive dinner.

Daisy went to put her phone away when a reply came through from Mrs Lemon.

Hello, Daisy! Are you still there?

Yes, what are you up to?

I'm at home baking pies for the freezer. It's an old–fashioned recipe. And then I'm finishing the jumper I've knitted for Woolley's Christmas.

I'd love to improve my knitting skills, and home cooking with traditional recipes.

I would be happy to show you how to knit jumpers, hats, scarves and tea cosies — the cosies are easy and fun to knit.

Would you? That sounds lovely.

I have lots of patterns. And I'll teach you my recipes. They're economical, practical and taste delicious.

Count me in! I'm out shopping in New York. It's snowing. Jake is busy with press interviews. I did mine.

You sound as busy as ever.

Jake is even busier today.

Are you going to another glitzy party tonight?

Probably. I haven't checked the updated schedule. I wouldn't be surprised if it's two parties!

One is enough for me and Woolley.

As they ended their messages, a call came through for Daisy from Jake.

'Are you anywhere near the park?' he said in an urgent whisper.

'Fairly close.'

'Meet me at the entrance nearest the hotel.'

'I'm on my way.'

Putting on a spurt of speed, Daisy navigated the snowy sidewalks and headed to the park. She saw Jake striding towards her from the direction of the hotel. His dark coat was unbuttoned over his suit and flapping almost as much as Jake appeared to be.

Clasping her hand, he led her over to an open air, horse–drawn carriage that appeared to be waiting — for them.

Jake helped her in, threw the blankets from the back seat over their legs and instructed the driver to head off.

Daisy was breathless from the speed with which Jake had whisked her away.

'What's going on?' she said smiling.

'I didn't want you to miss out on a classic carriage ride during Christmastime in New York.'

'I didn't expect you to organise this.'

'I'm glad I surprised you, but it wasn't planned until this morning,' he told her.

Flakes of snow settled on his dark hair and he sat beside her while the carriage drove around the park and famous avenue landmarks.

Another movie moment tick boxed, Daisy thought.

'I still have to get back to the interviews this afternoon,' Jake explained. 'But I thought if I gave you the option of lunch together or this, you'd—'

'Take the carriage ride!' she cut–in.

He leaned close and kissed her warm lips and brushed against the tip of her nose.

'Your nose is cold,' he said lovingly.

Daisy pulled down the brim of her pink woolly hat until it covered her nose. 'Sorted.'

She couldn't see anything, but she could hear Jake laughing as he rolled it back up to her brow and straightened the brim.

'You always make me smile, Daisy.'

'And you always surprise me when I least expect it.'

His expression was both tempting and tender. 'You know I love you.'

Daisy smiled at him. 'I know. I love you too.'

His voice took on a confiding tone. 'I'm trying to arrange something special this evening for us, just you and me. But I've several things that I need to tie up with Valerie that I promised I'd do.'

'Go for it, Jake. If you get tied up with the promotion work, it's fine.' She pictured a candlelit dinner for two in a Manhattan restaurant overlooking the city. Something wonderful like this would be exactly Jake's style. 'I'll go along with whatever you've planned.'

'You will?'

She took off one of her mittens and held up a pinkie at him. 'Pinkie promise.'

'Oh, well then,' he said, going along with her playful mood, and held up his pinkie too. 'Pinkie promise it is.'

She knew in her heart that Jake would try to get time off for them to be together in the evening, but realistically, she didn't think the odds on him doing so were great. And she was fine with too, knowing he'd tried to wangle time off that night.

In the meantime, she snuggled into him and enjoyed the carriage ride that eventually took them back to where they'd started.

Jake helped her step down. She kissed him and walked away, heading to the shops, while he ran back across to the hotel to continue the promotion work with Valerie and Wes.

Disappearing into one of the shopping malls, the sky was light grey and dappled with snow when she went in.

Window shopping, chatting to a cheery Santa Claus, admiring the decorations and displays, plus buying a couple of little gifts, made the time whiz by.

An early twilight had descended by the time she emerged. The snow had stopped with only a few flakes fluttering down as she gazed around her at the bustling city.

She checked her phone. No messages from Jake. She pictured him working hard, using that organisational mind of his to work out a gap in his schedule for them to spend time together that evening. Santa had offered her a Christmas wish, and she'd taken it, wishing with all her heart for Jake's plan to succeed tonight.

The park beckoned again as she walked back to the hotel, and she gave in to temptation. No ice skating, just sledding, whizzing down the slopes on her own, yelling with glee because she found it so much fun.

Sliding into a drift of breathless giggles, her phone rang. It was Jake. Her heart soared with expectation.

'Where are you?' His voice had that urgent tone again.

'Sledding in the park.'

'I'm coming to get you. Head for the hotel.'

Daisy clicked her phone off, and dashed for the exit nearest the hotel.

The tall figure of Jake wearing his coat and suit hurried towards her.

She smiled when she saw him, but his expression was tense.

'Is something wrong?' she said tentatively.

'Yes, no and maybe.'

'Okay, all options covered. What is it?'

'I've something to ask you before I hope you'll keep that pinkie promise.' His voice was deep, filled with passion in the cold, twilight air.

The snow was starting to fall heavier, sprinkling them with icy starlight as he stood in front of her. They were alone is this part of the park. A moment of quiet descended as he said, 'Close your eyes and hold out your hand.'

She thought her heart would burst with anticipation. Not wanting to take anything for granted, she tried to be calm, but held out her left hand.

'Palm up,' said Jake.

Without opening her eyes, she did as he asked and felt papers being pressed into her palm.

'You can open your eyes now,' he told her.

Daisy blinked. 'Flight tickets?' She gasped and read the location. 'Back to London?'

'Yes. If you want to go, we can leave now, but we'll be cutting it close.'

Daisy's heart jolted with joy. 'We can go home to Cornwall for Christmas!'

Jake smiled at her and nodded.

'What about your promotion work?'

'There's no time to dawdle. I'll explain on the way to the airport.'

The urgency in Jake's voice made Daisy pick up her heels, clasp Jake's hand and dash with him through the snow back to the hotel.

'My bags are packed,' he told her, helping to pack hers at speed.

Daisy threw the contents of the wardrobe in one case while Jake scoured around for anything she'd left behind.

'I'll check you drawers,' he said, then noticed the sexy lingerie in one of them. 'Are these yours?' They weren't her style, not that he was complaining if she'd expanded her range of unmentionables.

Daisy grabbed them, blushing, and stuffed them in her bag. 'Those were for romantic emergencies. They were Karen's idea. But I didn't need them.'

'That's a pity.' Jake's response was edged with exaggerated disappointment and a sexy smirk.

'Jake!' Daisy scolded him playfully.

With no time to spare to discuss Daisy's underwear, he carried the bulk of their bags as they ran outside and hailed a taxi that took them to the airport.

Daisy gazed out the window of the plane. Jake had given her the window seat again.

'Are you okay?' he whispered to her. Her pink hat was slightly askew.

'I feel like I've been through a wind tunnel.' She pulled her hat off and shook her hair to ease the tension. 'Other than that I'm so excited to be going home for Christmas. Don't get me wrong, New York ended up being great, but...'

'There's no place like home for Christmas,' he said.

She nodded. 'How did you manage to pull this off? Weren't you due to attend other promo events with Valerie?'

'Nothing that had been on the original agreed schedule. I asked Valerie if I could finish the interviews that were necessary.'

'That's why you crammed everything into today's schedule.'

'Yes, it was hectic and I really didn't know if I could do it, but the interviews went ahead on time and...here we are.'

'So that's it, we're done with New York?'

'Nooo,' Jake emphasised. 'I've agreed with Valerie that we'll fly back to New York in the New Year for round two of the publicity tour.'

'We're coming back to New York in January?'

'No, probably nearer the spring.' He stifled a smile.

'There's something you're not telling me.'

'Valerie will schedule the promotion to tie–in with their trip to the wedding at the castle. Once we've finished the promo work, Valerie and Wes will fly back with us to London, then I'll drive us all down to Cornwall in time for their friends' wedding.'

Daisy laughed. 'Only you could pull something like this off.' She smiled at him, and then noticed him take a jewellery box from his jacket pocket.

'There was no time to give you this before we caught the flight.' He opened it to show her a scintillating diamond bracelet. 'I wanted you to have something special to remember our trip.' He fastened it on her wrist.

Daisy's eyes widened as she gazed at the expensive bracelet. 'This is beautiful.'

'You're beautiful,' he whispered and kissed her hand.

'You can put that box away. I'm keeping this sparkler on,' she joked, but deep down she appreciated the gesture. 'When did you find time to buy this? Or shouldn't I ask.'

'I made time. It might not seem like it at the moment, but I'll always make time for you, Daisy.'

'This calls for a celebratory toast,' she said.

'Champagne?'

'Tea. Not iced tea. A relaxing cuppa. I've no intention of falling asleep on the flight home.'

Jake agreed. 'Want to watch a film? We never finished that Christmas romance.'

Daisy sounded decisive. 'No, you've organised all this while I went shopping and sledding, so I'm prepared to watch a shark film.'

Jake tilted his head and looked impressed. 'Really?'

'Bring on the fins and the teeth. I'm just in the mood to be a little bit wild.'

'I must buy you diamonds more often,' he joked.

'Ah–ha! My planned worked perfectly.'

Tipping their teacups in a triumphant toast, they settled down to watch the shark movie...

And woke up as the plane arrived in London.

Jake nudged Daisy awake. 'We're here!'

'Where?' She blinked in quick succession as her mind processed various locations. Then she realised... 'We're in London!'

'Yes, come on,' he urged her.

'What time is it?'

'Early morning. Fancy breakfast in the city before we drive down to Cornwall?'

Daisy's heart leapt with excitement. 'We've never had a day together in London before.' Glancing out the window she smiled and squealed with delight. 'It's been snowing.'

'Perfect for Christmas in London,' said Jake.

'You can park your car at my flat,' Daisy told him, indicating the direction.

He pulled up outside the flat and drummed his fingers on the wheel. 'Do I get a peek inside your flat while we're here?'

'Yes, come on up. Leave the bags in the car.'

Daisy led Jake to her front door.

'Archie isn't a morning person. No doubt he's been partying in my flat last night, so it'll be spotless and Archie–less.'

Daisy unlocked the door, flicked a lamp on and Jake followed her inside.

Gazing around he nodded. 'Very nice. Oh, you have a coffee machine. I thought you only really liked tea.'

'The espresso machine belongs to Archie. He's letting me borrow it.'

'That's very neighbourly of him.'

Daisy smiled to herself and continued to show him around. 'There's not much to see except the view of the city—'

'And your artwork.' He stepped over to a couple of her paintings on the wall. A watercolour floral and an acrylic scene with figures. 'These are wonderful. Do you take commissions? I'd like something like this for my study.'

She was so tempted to tell him she'd created a painting for him. 'Maybe after Christmas.'

'Yes, of course. You'll have your work cut out for you illustrating the new vintage florals for Franklin.'

'Now that I'm home, I'll be able to push ahead with the illustrations, but I plan to have time off for Christmas fun.'

Jake moved close and took her in her arms. 'What kind of fun?'

Before Daisy could respond, Archie burst into the flat wielding a rolling pin and his phone, filming the culprits that he thought had broken into the flat.

'Phew!' Archie gasped with relief. 'I heard someone and thought it was an intruder.'

'Archie, this is Jake Wolfe,' she introduced him.

Lowering the rolling pin and his phone, Archie shook hands with Jake. 'Pleased to finally meet the elusive Jake Wolfe. I'm Daisy's nitpicking neighbour.'

Jake laughed lightly. 'Thank you for letting Daisy use your espresso machine.'

'She's welcome. We try to be good neighbours.' Then he noticed the bracelet sparkling on Daisy's wrist. 'Are those real diamonds?'

'Yes, Jake bought it for me as a memento of our trip to New York.'

'Gorgeous,' Archie summarised. 'So classy.'

Archie's girlfriend wandered in wearing her pyjamas and holding a hairdryer, and with her hair looking like she'd been through the same wind tunnel as Daisy. 'Where do I stick this plug in, Archie?' she murmured sleepily.

'Late night?' Daisy said to her.

'Yes, but a great party here.'

'Okay, I'll leave you two lovebirds to it,' Archie said, sweeping his girlfriend away. 'Nice to have finally met you, Jake.'

'Likewise,' Jake called after him.

Daisy and Jake looked at each other and laughed.

'Come on, I'll treat you to one of the tastiest breakfasts in London,' said Daisy.

'Lead the way. I'm hungry.'

They sat in the upmarket cafe eating a delicious breakfast and sharing a pot of tea as they had done that morning.

'I'm confused,' Daisy admitted. 'It seems like only this morning that we had breakfast in New York.'

'We've gone forward in time on the return flight.'

Daisy shrugged and didn't even want work it out. 'Two tasty breakfasts are fine by me.'

The remainder of the morning was a whirl of Daisy showing Jake her favourite shops and places to explore including a Christmas market.

London's Christmas decorations looked wonderful, and the shop windows were aglow with festive displays.

Later, they stopped for lunch at a restaurant she recommended — and then headed to the park.

Jake turned up the collar of his coat against the cold air. The park was covered in snow as if someone had iced it twice and sprinkled the bare branches of the trees with sugar crystals. 'So this is the infamous park where—'

'Let's not talk about Sebastian,' Daisy cut–in.

'I was going to say where you came during lunch breaks from Franklin's publishing company to sit and sketch flowers.'

'Nice save,' she said, knowing he had intended mentioning Sebastian, and that she came to the park to do her illustrations.

Jake smiled and looked around, trying to imagine what her life had been like in London. He could picture quite a bit of it, and she'd told him what she enjoyed.

'Franklin's company isn't far from here,' said Jake.

'It's close–by. Do you want to pop in and see him?'

'Yes, I haven't seen Franklin since his last weekend trip to the cottage.'

'He's been so kind to let me stay there,' Daisy added.

The snow started to whirl around them, and Daisy and Jake hurried along to the publishing company, shaking the snow from their coats in reception.

'Is Franklin in?' Daisy said to the receptionist.

'He's in his office, Daisy.' The receptionist smiled at them.

Daisy led the way to Franklin's office that as usual had the door wide open.

Franklin saw them approach and met them with a welcoming smile.

'Congratulations on your new book, Jake.'

'Thanks.' He shook hands with Franklin. They'd known each other for years.

Franklin gave Daisy a welcoming hug.

'I thought the two of you were in New York, tied up with the book promotion.'

'I managed to untie us so we could come home for Christmas,' Jake explained.

'Take a seat. Can I get you both a cup of tea? I was about to have a cuppa.'

Franklin's assistant brought a tray of tea and shortbread for three into the office and sat it down on the desk.

'That would be a yes,' said Daisy. And then she noticed the advent calendar on Franklin's desk showing how few days were left until Christmas Eve.

'We're just off the plane this morning,' Jake told Franklin.

'But we've never had a day together in London so...' Daisy shrugged and sipped her tea.

A firm but polite fist chapped on Franklin's office door. 'The printers are in a tizzy. Could you come and smooth things over?'

Daisy felt the hackles in her back rise up at the sound of the familiar voice. She glanced round and there was the suave and elegantly suited Sebastian standing there smiling at them. But behind his polite demeanour she sensed the vitriol boiling under the surface.

The calm veneer of Jake's expression hid his real feelings for Sebastian. None of which wished Sebastian a merry Christmas.

CHAPTER TWENTY

Festive Fun

Shame on her for taking a leaf out of Karen's playbook, but Daisy brushed non–existent strands of hair from her brow, making sure her diamond bracelet dazzled under the office lighting.

Sebastian didn't miss the sparkle, and she knew him well enough to see him suck up his reaction.

Daisy lowered her hand, but the diamonds were there in clear view. It wasn't an engagement ring, but it would suffice to thwart Sebastian's comments about Jake's feelings for her.

Jake stood up and smiled at Franklin. 'We won't keep you from your business. It was good to see you again.' Jake extended his hand to him.

Franklin shook hands with Jake. 'Have a merry Christmas, and I hope to see you both soon. Drop by whenever you're in London.'

Daisy quickly told Franklin about Cole. 'A journalist in New York, Cole, is keen to talk to you about your new book releases. He told me to give you his number if you'd like to chat.'

Franklin was keen to do this and put the number in his phone. 'It'll be morning in New York, won't it?'

'Yes,' Jake confirmed.

'I'll give him a call while you're here, Daisy.' Franklin waited for a moment and then spoke to Cole. He put his phone on speaker so that Daisy could hear and comment. He was in no hurry to deal with

Sebastian's issue, suspecting he'd used it as a ruse to interrupt his chat with Daisy and Jake.

'Hello, Cole, it's Franklin. Daisy tells me you'd like to chat. She's here with me right now in my office.'

'Daisy's in London?' Cole sounded surprised.

'Yes, she's here with Jake. My phone's on speaker so she can hear you,' Franklin explained.

'Hi, Daisy. Thanks for putting me in touch with Franklin. But what are you doing in London? I thought you and Jake were here in New York for Christmas.'

'A change of plan. But we're visiting Manhattan again early next year, and then Valerie and Wes are flying back with us for the castle wedding,' she summarised.

Cole laughed. 'You never cease to surprise me. And you too, Jake.'

'Let me wave Daisy and Jake off and we'll have a chat,' Franklin said to Cole.

'Yeah, sure,' Cole sounded keen. 'Have a wonderful Christmas, Daisy, and don't let that loser guy, Sebastian, spoil your fun.'

Sebastian took the insult on the chin and spoke up, letting Cole know he'd heard the barbed remark. 'Nice to meet you, Cole.' The icy tone in his confident voice sliced through the warm air.

A second's hesitation was followed by Cole's New York savvy counter remark. 'You'll be meeting me in person in the spring when I fly over to London and Cornwall.'

'I'll look forward to that,' Sebastian lied coldly.

'Okay,' Daisy chirruped, 'we're off.' She gave Franklin a hug and kiss on the cheek, and then left with Jake.

Outside the publishing company Jake shook his head. 'I don't think Sebastian and Cole are going to be buddies.'

'Shame,' Daisy said dryly, and then linked her arm through Jake's. 'Come on, there are other things I'd love you to see before we drive home to Cornwall.'

'I have to do some Christmas shopping while I'm here,' said Jake.

'I can recommend going to the shopping mall.' She gestured to the mall nearby.

'The thing is...I need half an hour or so to shop for special gifts.'

'Secret shopping?' She sounded pleased. 'I have something I'd like to pick up too.' She checked the time. 'Meet you back outside the mall.' They arranged a time.

'Perfect,' said Jake, and then hurried away into the crowd of Christmas shoppers.

There was an art and craft shop near where Jake was heading. She pictured him buying her paints and brushes and other items for her artwork. Walking in the opposite direction so he didn't think she was spying on him, she intended picking up a little extra for him from a menswear shop.

Jake went into the art and craft shop and didn't waste any time. He knew what he wanted to buy here for Daisy. He'd seen it in the window. Leaving the shop with an expensive wooden box, like a little chest of drawers where she could store her watercolour pencils and small tubes of paint, he ventured on to another shop...

They met back up as planned.

'Don't look at the name on the store's bag,' said Jake, trying to hide it from Daisy.

She recognised the art and craft shop logo, but pretended to be none the wiser. 'I saw and know nothing.'

She'd bought a canvas bag to pop her items in, and it hide the name of the shop where she'd bought the gifts for him.

Jake gazed up at the sky. 'The snow is becoming heavier. We should start heading home.'

Daisy agreed. They walked briskly to the car, and Jake drove them out of the city.

She phoned Woolley and Mrs Lemon to let them know they'd flown home and were driving back from London.

The snow eased as they left London, and Jake put on Christmas songs to cheer them along.

It was a cold, crisp, dark night by the time they got home. Jake pulled up outside Daisy's cottage. Although the cottage was in darkness, the feeling of being home lit up her heart.

He carried her bags into the cottage while she switched the lights on and felt the comfort of the cottage soothe her from the trip.

As Jake put the bags down in the hall, Woolley phoned him.

'Are you back yet?' Woolley said, sounding hopeful.

'Yes, we're unloading Daisy's luggage at the cottage. It could take a while,' he joked. 'Daisy has enjoyed shopping in New York.'

Woolley laughed. 'Come to the party at the castle. The night is still young. Roman says you're welcome to join us.'

'Oooh, I don't know...'

Daisy frowned. 'Something wrong?'

'Do you have enough energy to go to the party night at the castle?' said Jake.

'We slept all the way on the plane. It'll be like when we arrived for the party in New York, only in reverse,' she reasoned.

'I must be tired, but that made complete sense,' Jake told her, and then replied to Woolley. 'We're on our way.'

Daisy dashed through to her bedroom and tore through the dresses hanging in her wardrobe like she was tussling for a bargain in the January sales. The active social life she'd had in London with Sebastian had merited having a selection of little cocktail and party dresses. When she'd first arrived in Cornwall she didn't think she'd have the chance to wear them. However, she'd worn every dress locally at least once. She picked a cocktail dress from a hanger, giving the midnight blue number another outing.

Pinning on the aurora borealis star brooch, she hurried in her heels through to the lounge where Jake was sitting relaxing, waiting for her.

'What do you think?' Daisy stood smiling at him, smoothing her hands down the silky fabric of her dress.

'Gorgeous.'

Grabbing her cream coat, they hurried out to the car and drove to the castle.

Daisy admired the view of the sea as they headed along the coast road, feeling the calm wash over her.

'You're smiling,' Jake commented, glancing at her.

'I'm home,' she said wistfully.

'We are,' Jake agreed.

The short but scenic drive to the castle was just what she needed. They were back home for Christmas! The realisation kept hitting her in waves.

The windows and turrets of the castle glowed in welcoming as they drove along the driveway leading up to the front entrance.

Jake parked the car and then escorted Daisy inside, past reception where she left her coat, and into the main hall. Couples were up dancing, and others were seated at tables around the dance floor. A roaring fire added to the festive warmth, and the huge Christmas tree sparkled with traditional grandeur.

Mrs Lemon, Woolley, Karen and Sharky sat at one of the tables and smiled when they saw Jake and Daisy walk in.

Hugs all round welcomed them home from their trip.

Roman approached Daisy and Jake and offered them something to eat. The festive dinner had been served earlier in the evening. 'The kitchen can easily serve up dinner for the two of you. Have you eaten dinner?'

'No, we've had nothing since lunch in London,' Daisy explained.

'I'll organise a roast dinner for two,' said Roman. 'Welcome back. Have something to eat and then enjoy the dancing.'

Leaving them to chat to Woolley and the others, Roman sorted out their dinner order with the catering staff.

Mrs Lemon's eyes lit up as she admired Daisy's aurora borealis star brooch. 'Is that one of the vintage brooches you told me about?'

'Yes, this is the first time I've worn it.'

'It sparkles with so many beautiful colours,' Mrs Lemon enthused.

'That's a gorgeous diamond bracelet you're wearing,' Karen remarked.

'Jake gave it to me on the plane on our way back.' Daisy giggled. 'I haven't taken it off since.'

'It's a lovely gift,' said Mrs Lemon.

Daisy told them about shopping in New York, and that Jake had taken her on a horse drawn carriage ride around the park near their hotel.

'How romantic,' remarked Mrs Lemon. 'It sounds as if you had a wonderful time in New York.'

'We did,' said Daisy. 'But we're so happy to be home.'

'It was a hectic schedule,' Jake explained. 'Though I think the trip was worthwhile, I agree with Daisy that it's great to be home again.'

'We're all glad to have you home for Christmas,' said Woolley.

'What were the parties like?' Karen wanted to know. 'Was it all cocktails and glamour?'

Daisy and Jake glanced at each other and nodded. 'It sort of was like that,' said Daisy, then she admired the grandeur of the main hall. 'But I'm sure when Cole, Valerie, Wes and the others come to the castle for the spring wedding, they'll be impressed.'

'Are they really are all coming over?' said Sharky.

'Yes,' Jake confirmed. 'Valerie and Wes plan to fly back with us after our trip to New York.'

'What are they like?' Sharky was keen to know.

Daisy showed them the group photos on her phone. 'That's Valerie and Wes standing beside Jake. And that's Cole, the journalist, next to me.'

They peered at the photos, eager to see what they looked like.

'Let me have a peek,' Roman insisted, overhearing them. He studied the photos. 'I'm looking forward to having them as guests at the castle.'

'They've been warned that they're in for a lively time,' said Daisy.

Everyone laughed.

The music changed to a romantic waltz and more couples were getting up to dance.

Woolley held out his hand to Mrs Lemon. 'Would you like to dance?' She accepted and he escorted her on to the dance floor.

Sharky and Karen joined in the dancing, leaving Jake and Daisy to enjoy their roast dinner that was served to them at their table.

Daisy tucked into the roast potatoes. 'I didn't know I was so hungry. I think I'm all at sixes and sevens from the travelling.'

Their meal was served at their request with a pot of tea. Jake poured two cups and took a sip of his.

'Would you like to go to the Christmas Eve Ball here at the castle?' said Jake. 'It's part of the town's Yuletide celebrations.'

'I'd love to go to the ball.'

'Great,' he said and tucked into his roast dinner too.

Finishing their dinner, they joined in the dancing. Throughout the remainder of the evening, everyone danced with everyone else, and Daisy waltzed with Woolley, Sharky and even Mr Greenie.

Roman partnered up with Daisy and spoke to her as they danced near the end of the night. 'I want to thank you for recommending the castle as a wedding venue for Cole's friends. It's created a bit of a buzz already.'

'I'm glad to help. They wanted a special venue for the wedding, and the castle is perfect.'

They continued to dance, and then she ended the evening dancing with Jake.

After saying goodnight to everyone, Jake drove Daisy home to the cottage.

Daisy stood in the doorway, wrapped up in her coat, but feeling the chill of the late night reminded her that it was the heart of winter and only a few days until Christmas.

'I won't keep you standing in the cold,' Jake said, getting ready to drive to his house on the hill.

Daisy shivered. 'It's been quite a day. I'm going to try and get some sleep.'

'So am I. It's an early start for me at the shop, and there's other work to be done before Christmas.'

Jake kissed her tenderly and then walked down the garden path to his car. They waved to each other as he drove off.

She went through to the kitchen to get a drink of water before going to bed, and noticed that there was a fresh loaf of bread sitting on the table. She checked the fridge. Fresh milk, butter, eggs and cheese were in it. Smiling to herself, she made a mental note to thank Mrs Lemon.

On hearing from Woolley that Daisy and Jake were on their way home, Mrs Lemon had stocked the kitchen with the basics for Daisy before getting ready for the festive dinner at the castle.

Instead of having water, Daisy filled the kettle and made herself a cup of tea. While it boiled, she changed into her comfy pyjamas and slippers, reluctantly took off the diamond bracelet, and unpacked some of her things to make it less of a task in the morning.

Taking her tea through to the bedroom, she climbed under the covers and sat up in bed sipping it while gazing out the window at the starry sky. The view was so different from the lights of New York, or London, but the comforting feeling of the cosy cottage and the quietude was where she truly felt she belonged.

Jake walked into his study and flicked the desk lamp on. The calm, quiet atmosphere reassured him.

Nothing had changed. Everything was as he'd left it. Woolley had promised to check on the house while he was away, but there had been no need to do anything.

It felt like time had compressed, like the chapter of a book where a whole adventure could be lived, and then the pages turned to a new chapter in the present.

He looked out the window, down towards Daisy's cottage. It was in darkness, no lights shining from the Christmas tree. She'd be in bed, getting some much needed sleep, something he needed to do too.

He turned the lamp off, but glanced back into the study from the doorway. The glow of night shone through the window and streamed across his desk. The silvery silence reminded him of Christmases past. But there was something missing. A Christmas tree.

Walking out of the study and through to his bedroom, he left his bags unpacked in the hallway, and planned to add a Christmas tree on his busy to–do list.

The morning was bright, brisk and blustery.

The wind coming in from the sea blew Daisy along the road as she walked from the cottage to the main street. Wrapped up warm, she welcomed the fresh air, letting it blow away the cobwebs of sleep, and benefit from the new day.

The town was buzzing with activity. People were shopping for groceries, preparing for Christmas and buying gifts. The shop windows were lit up with twinkle lights and decorations, and the large Christmas tree was ablaze under the wintry sky.

Daisy walked the length of the main street down to the Christmas tree, and then back again, enjoying the festive atmosphere and the welcoming smiles of the local people. A few stopped to ask her about her trip to New York, and she was happy to chat to them.

Walking on, she went to the grocers to pick up fresh vegetables, fruit and other items to stock up her kitchen.

While she was in the grocers, she looked out the window and saw Jake talking animatedly to Mr Greenie. Whatever they were talking about, Mr Greenie nodded firmly, and then he continued loading the cake orders from Sharky's bakery into his delivery van while Jake went into his health food shop. Daisy assumed they were discussing the last minute orders for Christmas cakes and figgy puddings for Jake's shop. Jake seemed really busy, so she decided not to drop by and let him get on with his business.

Stocked up on groceries, Daisy headed to the craft shop to buy wrapping paper to take back with her to the cottage. The walk home was refreshing.

The breeze blowing up from the sea promised a dry but blustery day. Ideal for hunkering down by the fire and wrapping gifts for Jake and her friends.

After putting the groceries away in the kitchen, she lit the fire and started wrapping presents.

Carefully folding the waistcoat she'd bought for Jake from the menswear shop in London, she wrapped it in a piece of tissue paper so as not to wrinkle the fabric and then parcelled it up in Christmassy wrapping paper.

Other items she'd bought for him in the bargain vintage shop in New York were a pair of cufflinks and a tie pin, both with an art deco design. Jake owned some nice links and pins, but she'd never seen him wear anything like this, so she was pretty sure she'd bought him something original.

Hiding his gifts in the hall cupboard beside the painting and satchel briefcase, she sorted through the selection of vintage brooches to gift to Mrs Lemon and Karen. Mrs Lemon's reaction to the aurora borealis star brooch ensured that this one was going in the gold evening bag she'd bought for her. Daisy never liked giving anyone a bag or purse without putting something in it for luck.

The glittery gold and pink bags sat on the table and Daisy divided the marcasite brooches between the two. Lily of the valley was one of Mrs Lemon's favourite flowers, so Daisy put that brooch in the gold bag too. She thought the bouquet brooch suited Karen, so she added it to the pink bag, wrapping each brooch in pretty paper.

The daisy spray and diamante snowflake were her own favourites, so she kept them aside. Then she divided the hair accessories, allocating clips and a barrette to the bags. With the little extras tucked into the evening bags, she wrapped them up for Mrs Lemon and Karen.

Next for wrapping was a vintage tie for Woolley in colours to suit the muted tones he liked to wear. He kept a diary on him, and when she'd been in London, she'd bought items of stationery, including a large gardening diary for Woolley. She wrapped that too.

Other stationery gifts were a recipe journal for Sharky so he could note down his favourite recipes, new recipes he was working on, and there was a section where he could tuck written notes and pictures of his baking.

Daisy loved stationery and couldn't resist buying two wedding planner journals for Mrs Lemon and Karen that she wrapped separately from their evening bags.

The final stationery item was an organiser for Mr Greenie where his different jobs could be listed in categories and with plenty of diary space to organise the various tasks. The ideal minding for the man who wore so many different hats for work.

When she'd been in the grocers, they were selling little jam hampers filled with small jars of jam, marmalade and preserves. It included lemon curd, chutney and chocolate spread. She'd bought one for Archie and parcelled it up ready for posting in the afternoon so it would arrive in time for Christmas. Seeing all the tasty treats the hamper contained, she'd bought one to share with Jake. No plans had been made about where they'd have their Christmas dinner — at his house or the cottage, but she was sure they'd sort this out soon.

Meanwhile, she finished wrapping the gifts. Along with each of the stationery gifts she'd popped in a personalised bookmark. She made these from watercolour paper, cut to bookmark size. Each one was painted with a flower, bee, butterfly or dragonfly in watercolour. They were fast and easy to make but she thought they added a nice artistic touch to the gifts.

Likewise, she used watercolour paper to create her own Christmas cards, and painted each one with a watercolour Christmas tree, snowman, holly, poinsettia, Christmas cakes, winter jasmine, jingle bells clematis flowers, Christmas roses or a robin.

It was late afternoon by the time she'd finished. She put her coat on, tucked Mr Greenie's gift in her bag in case she saw him, and set off to post Archie's parcel.

The carol singers' voices drifted along the street, and the warm glow from the windows of the shops looked like a traditional Christmas scene. The glow transferred to her heart, reminding her how happy she was to be home.

After posting Archie's parcel, she meandered down towards the large Christmas tree — and there was Mr Greenie loading a Christmas tree into the back of his van along with a load of fairy lights and boxes of decorations.

'Mr Greenie!' Daisy called to him and hurried over.

He smiled broadly, closed the rear doors of his van, and gave her his full attention.

'Daisy, what can I do for you?'

'Nothing, I have something I'd like to give to you.' She dug the gift from her bag and handed it to him.

'A Christmas present!' He beamed with delight.

'As a thank you for always helping with things, like the photo you took of Jake and me for the newspaper.'

He gave her a sheepish grin. 'Sorry about the fiasco with Roman's fake wedding kerfuffle.'

'Ah, don't worry about that. I'm well–known for causing mischief myself.'

Mr Greenie eyed the parcel with glee. 'Can I open it now? Or do I have to wait until Christmas.'

'Open it now if you want to,' she encouraged him.

He unwrapped it, and smiled when he saw that it was the perfect gift for him. 'This is just what I need to keep all my jobs in order. Thank you, Daisy.'

'I'm pleased you like it.'

'Oh, yes, in fact, I've been jotting down the things that people have been booking me to do after Christmas.' He pulled a scrappy notebook from his jacket pocket to show her. 'Now I can use my organiser.'

Smiling and waving, Mr Greenie drove off in his van to deliver the tree, while Daisy wandered over for a look in the fashion shop window. Dresses for the castle's Christmas Eve Ball were on display, but Daisy didn't need to buy a new dress for the ball. Jake had bought her a fairytale blue evening dress months ago. She planned to wear that, even though she'd worn it before. The dress was perfect. The pale blue chiffon shirt was topped with a crystal encrusted bodice. The crystals and sequins had been sewn on by hand. It was a designer dress, expensive, that Jake had bought for her as a surprise for a party at the castle in the summer.

A Christmassy glow descended over the town, as Daisy saw Mrs Lemon in the health food shop chatting to Jake. Woolley and Karen were there too.

Mrs Lemon waved to Daisy, beckoning her to come in.

Daisy noticed that Jake's book was on sale in the window and that a *no more orders taken* notice was pinned near Sharky's Christmas cake and figgy pudding.

The warmth of the shop and delicious aroma wrapped itself around Daisy as she walked in. The atmosphere was cheery.

Mrs Lemon smiled and invited Daisy to have Christmas dinner at her cottage. 'The four of us were planning to have dinner together. There's room for two more if you and Jake would like to join us on Christmas Day. Unless you have something else planned.'

'No, we've nothing planned, have we, Jake?'

'Nothing at all. We'd love to join you.' Jake was happy to accept the invitation.

Daisy smiled. 'Thank you for inviting us.'

Mrs Lemon looked delighted. 'The more the merrier. The meal is around two o'clock, but come over before that and enjoy Christmas Day with us. I'm cooking a traditional dinner with all the trimmings. I make my own cranberry sauce and onion gravy.'

'That sounds delicious,' said Daisy.

'Are you busy tonight?' Mrs Lemon said to Daisy.

'No, why?'

'Would you like to come over and I'll show you how to improve your knitting.'

Daisy glanced at Jake. They hadn't made plans for the evening.

'I'm catching up with work,' said Jake. 'I'll be working late. I was going to tell you that I'd be busy tonight.'

'Yes, I'd like to practise knitting,' Daisy told Mrs Lemon.

'Pop over at teatime. We'll have something to eat and then knit the night away.'

'I'm not allowed to come over this evening,' Woolley explained. 'There's secret Christmas stuff going on.'

With her evening planned, Jake beckoned Daisy upstairs to the storeroom. 'There's something I want to show you.'

'Okay.' Daisy followed him upstairs.

Jake went over to the roll top dresser where he'd stashed the invitations that Roman had given him to attend the Christmas Eve Ball at the castle.

He showed her the two tickets. 'I don't know what made me keep these. I didn't think we'd be back here for Christmas.'

'I'm glad you kept them. Maybe it's a Christmas wish coming true.'

CHAPTER TWENTY ONE

Love at Christmas

Daisy walked across to Mrs Lemon's cottage. The night air's winter chill added to the festive atmosphere. She glanced up the hill to Jake's house, expecting to see the lights on in the study, but she hadn't expected to see a Christmas tree sparkling with fairy lights in the window.

Jake had put a Christmas tree up!

Hurrying on, pulling the collar of her coat up against the cold night, Daisy knocked on Mrs Lemon's door.

The cosiness of the cottage poured out when Mrs Lemon opened it to welcome Daisy in for an evening of knitting and chatter.

'Jake has a Christmas tree in his study.' Daisy gestured up the hill.

Mrs Lemon stepped out of the warmth into her front garden that was lit with decorations, and peered up at the mansion on the hill. The Christmas tree twinkled in the darkness and she was taken aback by it.

'It's big and bright,' Mrs Lemon exclaimed. 'I didn't think he was putting up a tree this year.'

'Neither did I. But we thought we were going to be away in New York,' Daisy reasoned.

Mrs Lemon admired the tree glowing like a beacon at the top of the hill. 'He's certainly gone to town with the lights and sparkle.'

Both of them shivered in the cold, and then hurried inside to get a heat by the fire.

'I've made a savoury pie topped with puff pastry and mashed potatoes to go with it.' Mrs Lemon scuttled through to the kitchen to serve up their dinner.

Daisy took her coat off and hung it up in the hall. 'What can I do to help?'

'Could you make the tea. The kettle's boiled.'

Daisy made two cups of tea and carried them through to the lounge where Mrs Lemon had set up a table in front of the fire with a comfy chair on either side.

Her Christmas tree was lit up and around it were prettily wrapped presents.

A craft bag filled with yarn and knitting needles was on the sofa ready for Daisy's tuition.

'What level of knitter are you?' said Mrs Lemon, bringing their dinner through to the lounge.

'Basic. I learned at school how to knit squares in plain rows. Garter stitch. I've knitted a scarf, attempting stripes, years ago, but the rows where I joined the different colours looked messy.'

'There's an easy technique to stop your stripes having that telltale dotted row of stitches where you've changed to a new colour. I can show you that.'

'Casting on and casting off are tricky for me too. I need reminding how to cast on properly. I don't do it enough to remember the method. Once I get started I can knit the rows, then I get stuck at casting off neatly.'

'I've almost finished knitting the jumper I'm making for Woolley. I'm about to cast off the last sleeve, so I'll show you how I do it.'

The jumper was tucked beside the craft bag. 'I like the colour of the yarn you've used.'

'It's a lovely double knit yarn in moss green with a slight fleck of sea green. The pattern knits up well in cable stitch and stocking stitch.'

'I can knit stocking stitch — one row plain knit and one row purl.'

'What would you like to knit to improve your skills?'

'I'd love to knit a jumper, but I'd prefer to start with something easy.'

'I have a great pattern for a tea cosy. It's a small enough project for you to complete, but it has a lot of the techniques that are handy to learn.'

'A tea cosy. Yes, I'd like to knit that.'

'I'll show you the pattern after we've finished our dinner.'

While they ate their meal, they chatted about Daisy's trip to New York and about the forthcoming ball at the castle.

'What are you going to wear to the ball?' said Mrs Lemon.

'The pale blue dress that Jake bought me. I wore it to the party at the castle during the summer. I feel like a fairytale princess when I wear it, so I'm going to wear it again.'

'It was a beautiful dress and really suited you. I'm wearing my fancy black and gold evening dress. I've worn it before too, but I like it. Karen is wearing a full–length pale yellow evening dress.'

'That sounds lovely.'

Clearing their dinner plates away, Mrs Lemon showed Daisy the tea cosy pattern.

'It's knitted in stocking stitch with three rows of garter stitch at the bottom to stop it curling up around the edges,' Mrs Lemon explained. 'I've plenty of double knit yarn you can use.' From the craft bag she brought out a large ball of red yarn that had a red sparkle fleck, pale blue and a pretty pink.

Daisy swithered, liking all of them. 'I'm in a festive mood, so I'll go with the Christmassy red yarn.'

Mrs Lemon handed her the large ball of red yarn and a pair of knitting needles.

Daisy felt the soft yarn beneath her fingers and was eager to be reminded how to cast on the stitches to begin the pattern.

'Before we start, I'll show you how I cast off.' Mrs Lemon lifted the knitted sleeve she'd been working on and demonstrated slowly. She knitted the first two stitches and then used one of the needles to lift the first stitch over the second one.

Daisy watched and nodded enthusiastically. 'That's right. I remember now.'

'Keep the tension even and not too tight,' Mrs Lemon advised as she continued to work her way along the row, casting off. Finishing, she put it aside and got ready to show Daisy how to cast on.

Daisy followed Mrs Lemon's example and then started to cast on the stitches herself, smiling as she got the hang of it.

'It just takes practise, Daisy.'

'This yarn feels lovely to knit with.'

'It knits up great. You'll have one side of the tea cosy knitted in no time.'

While Daisy started working the rows of the pattern, Mrs Lemon pressed the pieces of the jumper ready for stitching together with yarn and a large eye needle.

Enjoying sitting by the fire knitting and stitching, they chatted about the forthcoming ball and plans for Christmas Day.

Jake worked in his study by the glow of the Christmas tree lights. He wondered if he'd overdone the lights, but he remembered Daisy telling him that you can never have too much sparkle.

Mr Greenie had delivered the tree and helped set it up on a stand at the study window, and advised on the lights and decorations.

Jake had been extra busy with all the business offers that were coming in due to his book being released. Some of them were quite lucrative and he was keen to reply to them, while not getting bogged down in work. It was a difficult balance, especially as he wanted to spend more time with Daisy. But at least they were home for Christmas.

At twenty minutes to ten o'clock at night, the cuckoo made an appearance, popping out to remind him it was getting late.

He smiled when he saw that Mr Greenie had tied a piece of silver tinsel around the little bird's neck.

Chirping three and a half times, the cuckoo disappeared back into the clock and the doors closed again.

Maybe it was jet lag, or perhaps love lag, if there was such a thing, but the tiredness Jake felt jarred against his longing to be with Daisy. But there would be plenty of time for romance soon he assured himself. Christmas was always a hectic melee of merriment and chaos.

Daisy waved to Mrs Lemon as she headed back home after an enjoyable night knitting and chatting.

Approaching her cottage, she saw that Jake's tree was still all lit up, and took out her phone to message him.

I love your Christmas tree!

He replied almost instantly, before she'd fished her keys from her bag to open the front door.

Thank you, Daisy. It's feeling a lot more like Christmas here in my house.

She unlocked the door and stood gazing up at the glow from his window as she continued messaging him.

Not long now until Christmas Eve. Today whizzed by.

I've been snowed under with business offers due to my book being out. A few lucrative deals that I'm interested in. New product lines for the shop. Giving talks about my work. But I'd rather be spending time with you.

Take the offers while they're on the table. I'm happy for your hard work to be recognised. We'll have Christmas Eve and Christmas Day together, that's what matters.

Are you sure?

Yes, and I've promised to send more illustrations to Franklin. I'll be busy sketching those and getting my outfit ready for the castle ball.

I'm looking forward to enjoying the Christmas Eve ball with you.

I plan to wear the blue dress you bought me.

You looked beautiful in that dress.

His comment warmed her heart.

And I have a gorgeous diamond bracelet to wear with it this time. Be prepared to be dazzled.

You'll always outshine everything in my eyes, Daisy.

Jake's words tugged at her heartstrings, and for a moment she resisted the urge to run up that hill to be with him. But instead she bid him goodnight, and he did the same.

Don't work too late, Jake.

I won't. I'm heading to bed now to catch up on some sleep.

Daisy saw the lights go out in his study. His house was now a dark silhouette against the night sky.

She went inside her cottage, locked the door against the world, and went to bed too.

The next two days compressed into a Christmas concertina of festive fun in the town. People were shopping for last minute gifts and groceries to tide them over the holidays. All the shops were aglow from morning until closing, and Daisy popped into the health food shop to see Jake a couple of times in passing, so it wasn't a complete Jake–free time.

She succumbed to the temptation of another figgy pudding, curtesy of Sharky. It was a meal in itself accompanied with custard.

Franklin liked the next set of illustrations, and it let him organise the new book's content before he finished work on Christmas Eve.

As for her tea cosy...she was becoming accustomed to knitting in any spare moments, and it was so relaxing in the evenings sitting by the fire and adding a few rows. One side was complete and the other side three–quarters finished. Not bad she thought, considering she'd been working on it in snatched moments.

A second tea cosy was definitely in her future. The pink one next. There was an old–fashioned pink floral teapot on one of the shelves in the kitchen that it would fit well.

Her dress for the ball hung on the outside of her wardrobe ready for wearing the following night. Christmas Eve was a few hours away. The time had flown in yet again, but there was a buzz of anticipation throughout the town as everyone looked forward to the celebrations.

Climbing into bed, Daisy flicked the lamp off and lay there looking out the window at the wintry night. Moonlight streamed through like beams of silvery stardust and made the crystals and sequins on the bodice of her dress scintillate as it hung on the hanger.

Tomorrow night she was going to the ball with Jake.

A glance at the time showed that Christmas Eve was fast approaching. A wave of excitement charged through her.

In her mind she went over everything she needed to do the following day. All the gifts she'd bought were wrapped, cards made and written. Now all she had to do was relax during the day, snuggle up warm in the cottage in the cold afternoon, so she'd have plenty of energy for the ball.

Jake had agreed to pick her up at the cottage and drive them to the castle.

He arrived on time, dressed to impress in an evening suit, hair sleeked back, the most tamed she'd seen it. He looked like he'd made an extra attempt to look his best, and she appreciated his effort. His handsomeness and well–dressed style made her heart squeeze when he arrived at the cottage and stood in the hall, filling it with his tall stature as always.

Daisy felt like a fairytale princess as she walked out of the bedroom wearing the pale blue dress and the diamond bracelet. She wore her hair down in soft waves, and her makeup was suitably glamorous.

Jake's intake of breath was noticeable in the quiet cottage. 'You look so beautiful.'

Daisy smiled at him, and then he helped her on with her coat, and escorted her outside to his car.

They drove off towards the castle, both anticipating a wonderful night ahead.

The castle glowed with lights and activity as they headed along the driveway and parked the car.

Jake assisted Daisy to step out. 'Do you want me to help you off with your coat?' he offered.

'Yes, I'll leave it in the car.' She clasped his hand and felt the cold, crisp air brush against her bare arms and shoulders as she walked beside him. The sequins on the bodice of her dress glistened in the glow of the lights shining out from the castle.

Music wafted out of the front entrance, and the chatter of cheery voices as people went inside added to the party atmosphere.

Once inside the castle, it was obvious that the festivities were more than a party. The main hall glowed with Christmas lights, chandeliers and the flickering fire in the ornate hearth.

Tables around the dance floor were set with white linen and silver with touches of festive sparkle.

Daisy had checked the menu online and they were in for a treat. Roman's chefs had created a menu fit for the glamorous ball.

Jake handed in their invitations.

A member of staff showed Daisy and Jake to a table where they were seated along with Mrs Lemon, Woolley, Karen and Sharky. It was next to the large Christmas tree. Daisy couldn't imagine anything more like a fairytale Christmas Eve Ball than one like this.

Complimenting each other on their evening attire, they chatted and perused the menu.

'We're spoiled for choice this evening,' Woolley commented, eyeing the dishes available.

'Roman said he's trying new dishes that he'll add to the wedding menus if they're popular,' Daisy explained. 'I sampled some of them recently and they were all delicious.'

After their dinner orders were taken, Sharky proposed a toast. 'To a memorable night and a happy Christmas.'

The others raised their glasses of champagne and soft drinks in celebration.

And then Sharky made an announcement. He cleared his throat. 'I, eh...I was going to give you a special gift on Christmas morning,' he said to Karen. 'But I feel you'll enjoy it all the more if I give it to you tonight at the ball.'

Karen frowned, and the intrigued glances circled the table as Sharky continued.

He took an envelope from the inside pocket of his jacket. He'd worn a sharp suit, had tidied his hair and was a fine looking man with eyes filled with love for Karen.

'I thought you'd like to share this moment with us all here,' Sharky explained. 'I feel we've all become like family.' He handed Karen the envelope. 'Open it.'

Karen opened it and pulled out an embossed card that presented the date of her wedding to Sharky in the spring.

She smiled as she read it and realised what Sharky had done. 'You've booked the castle for our wedding!'

'If the date suits you,' said Sharky. 'Roman has other dates if you prefer, but this would be in the heart of the spring and it's your favourite number. I thought you might like that.'

Karen jumped up from her seat and threw her arms around Sharky, giving him her response to his surprise gift. 'It's the perfect date.'

The others cheered and shared in the joy.

Karen couldn't stop looking at the card and showed all of them. 'I'm getting married in the castle!' And then she gazed at Sharky. 'This is sooo expensive.'

'I want it to be special for you,' Sharky said to her.

It was only as their dinner was served that they managed to peel Karen off of giving Sharky hugs of delight.

Mrs Lemon beamed at the news, and Woolley squeezed her hand, looking forward to the day when they would be getting married too. But this was Karen and Sharky's moment, and Woolley made no mention that a second wedding at the castle was in his mind.

Daisy smiled, genuinely happy for them, but when she glanced at Jake, she wasn't sure what his expression was telling her...or hiding...

Jake looked nervous, but in a good way, wasn't it? Daisy hadn't seen this look before so it was difficult to know what he was thinking.

She couldn't ask him in front of the others if he was okay, so she tucked her question to the back of her thoughts and began to eat her dinner. She'd opted for the roast vegetable medley with cranberry mousse and minted potatoes.

Jake ate his Christmas casserole with duchess potatoes and herb sauce.

Variations of these choices were selected by the others at the table, with Sharky and Karen enjoying

Sharky's figgy pudding with whipped cream and brandy sauce.

For her pudding Daisy ordered the strawberry, double cream and meringue confection served in a tall glass with a long silver spoon.

Jake preferred the Christmas crumble made with apple and berry fruits.

Mrs Lemon and Woolley both had the traditional trifle and thoroughly enjoyed it.

The nervous look on Jake's face was now gone, replaced with a confident smile, so after their meal when Daisy was dancing with Jake, she didn't mention it.

'You look wonderful this evening,' Jake said to her as they waltzed around the room.

She smiled at him and blushed. 'I'm having a great time.'

And then, in that moment, there was that look again.

Before she could ask him if something was troubling him, he spoke up. 'I need to ask you a favour.'

'What is it?'

'I'm reluctant to bring up work, but with it being Christmas Day in a few hours time, I wondered if you'd come up with me to my house after the ball. I'd like your input on the reply to a press feature about my book. I said I'd email a reply today.'

'Yes, I'd be happy to help you,' she agreed, sensing it was important to him.

'Great,' he said, fiddling with his forelock. 'It'll mean that I've sorted out every bit of business before Christmas Day.'

Daisy put the telltale gesture down to him feeling awkward and nervous.

They didn't cut short their evening at the ball, and enjoyed the whole event, dancing to popular songs, a mix of festive and favourites.

Twirling around the floor under the glistening chandeliers in a dress that made her feel like she was dancing in a romantic fantasy at times, Daisy felt wonderful and enjoyed being with Jake and the others.

Roman came over to wish them merry Christmas as they were leaving at the end of the night, and waved them off.

'We'll see you for Christmas dinner,' Daisy called to Mrs Lemon, Woolley, Karen and Sharky as they got into the bakery van. Sharky and Jake had kept to soft drinks so they could drive home.

Daisy gazed out the car window at the sea glistening far into the distance as they drove along the coast road.

'The sea looks like it's celebrating Christmas too,' Daisy remarked. 'Look at the shimmer on the surface and the lights twinkling way off in the distance.'

Jake glanced at the view and was surprised to see the water sparkle under the silvery moonlight. 'You're right. The wintertime is beautiful here.'

He drove them along the coast and then up the hill to his house and parked the car out front.

Helping her from the car, she walked with him to the front door. He led the way inside, taking her through to the study and switched the Christmas tree lights on.

'Your tree is lovely.' She went over to admire it, and then smiled at him, taking off her coat and getting ready to help him with his work. 'Where's the feature you want me to read?'

'I, eh...' Jake looked hesitant, and there was that expression she'd seen earlier in the evening. 'It's on my laptop. I left it in the kitchen. Wait here, I'll go and bring it through.'

Wondering if he was maybe overtired or overexcited about it being Christmas, she shrugged off her doubts that there was something wrong and admired the tree again.

Jake hurried back into the study moments later, but he wasn't carrying the laptop.

Her immediate reaction was to look at his desk to see if he'd left it there.

'I'm sorry, Daisy. I've finished all the work.'

Daisy frowned. 'But I thought you wanted me to—'

He stepped forward and clasped her hand. His blue eyes held her gaze. 'There's something I'd like to show you. I wanted it to be a surprise.'

Leading her through to the kitchen, she saw that the back garden was all lit up.

They stepped outside into a fairytale Christmas setting. Twinkle lights were draped across the garden like a canopy of stars, and entwined through the winter plants, hedging and branches of the trees.

Daisy gasped when she saw it. 'Wow! This is magical.'

'Mr Greenie helped me when he delivered the Christmas tree.'

The air was crisp, but she didn't feel the cold, only the warmth of Jake's hand in hers as he led her into the heart of the garden under the canopy of lights.

He took a velvet ring box from his jacket pocket.

Daisy's heart fluttered as he opened it to reveal a diamond daisy flower cluster engagement ring set in yellow gold. The brilliant cut diamonds sparkled under the lights.

Jake looked at her. 'Daisy, will you marry me?'

Her heart was filled with joy as she said, 'Yes, I will marry you.'

He slipped the scintillating ring on her finger, pulled her close and kissed her.

'I love you, Daisy.'

'I love you too.'

He kissed her again, and they stood for a few moments under the fairy lights.

Then he took an envelope containing a Christmas card from his pocket and handed it to her. 'Merry Christmas.'

She opened the card and saw that there were architectural sketches on a folded piece of paper tucked inside it.

'I've been planning the summerhouse. Woolley made the sketches. He's not an illustrator like you, but I think you'll see what I have in mind.' He pointed to an area of the garden. 'We're going to start building it over there, as I discussed with you.'

'This looks even more like an artist's studio than I imagined.'

'I thought it would be better for you.'

'It is. It's wonderful.'

He squeezed her tight. 'You're wonderful. And we're starting work on it soon. A summerhouse for late winter. It'll be cosy for wintry days, and in the summer it'll open up to let plenty of air in. Your own studio where you can ink your illustrations and paint.'

'Thank you, I love it.' Her heart hadn't yet settled from his proposal, and she doubted she would sleep from the sheer excitement.

'Come on, you're getting cold.' He went to lead her inside, but she hesitated.

'Take a few pictures of this, of us,' she said.

Jake put his arm around her and captured them together on their special night.

Daisy headed inside, glancing back at the garden with all the lights.

The busy day, the Christmas Eve Ball and the excitement of Jake's proposal, made Daisy feel waves of tiredness wash over her.

Jake helped her on with her coat in the study. 'You should get some sleep. I'll come down to your cottage in the morning with presents for you and the others.'

'We'll have breakfast together and you can open your gifts.'

Jake smiled at her, then escorted her to the car, and drove her down to the cottage.

He walked her to the front door and kissed her goodnight. 'I'll see you in the morning.'

'Woolley, Mrs Lemon and the others are going to be so surprised when we tell them we're engaged,' said Daisy. 'Or does Woolley know that you were planning this tonight?'

'No, the only one was Mr Greenie, and he promised not to tell anyone until we'd announced it to the others when we go over for Christmas dinner to Mrs Lemon's cottage. So get some sleep. It's going to be an exciting day.'

Kissing her again, Jake got into his car and drove home, feeling that everything in his life was changing for the better. Daisy had agreed to marry him. He'd been planning to ask her for a while, but he wanted it to be special. He'd bought the ring in London that day they'd flown home. He'd known her ring size for weeks, but didn't want to propose in the melee of work and book publicity. Christmas seemed like the perfect time now that they were home.

Daisy sipped a mug of hot milk, hoping it would soothe her senses from the overload of excitement from the ball, to the proposal, the diamond ring that sparkled like her bracelet — and that it was Christmas!

Sitting at the window in the lounge wearing her cosy pyjamas, she gazed up at Jake's house and saw the Christmas tree lights turn off. Jake had gone to bed, and she should too. Finishing her milk, she climbed into bed and admired her ring that sparkled in the moonlight streaming in, and fell asleep thinking about the wonderful night she'd had.

Daisy bounced out of bed early, eager to get everything ready for Christmas morning.

She wore a deep, red velvet dress and cardigan, the diamond bracelet, and every now and then she looked at her engagement ring, happy that Jake's fairytale Christmas proposal wasn't just a dream.

The Christmas tree lights were on, and she'd set up a table for breakfast in front of the cosy fire ready for Jake's arrival.

The picture she'd painted for him, along with the other gifts, were beside the tree at the window, and her heart leaped when she saw his car drive down the hill and park outside.

Jake got out, smartly dressed and laden with gifts.

Daisy hurried to the door to welcome him in. He put all the gifts down in the hall and then wrapped his arms around Daisy, almost lifting her off her feet with a hug and kiss.

Her giggles filled the hallway as they wished each other a merry Christmas, and then she went through to the kitchen to make the tea for breakfast.

'Let me do that,' he said, eager to help while she poured the milk on their cereal topped with fruit.

Jake then carried the breakfast tray through to the lounge where they tipped their teacups together in a triumphant toast.

'We did it!' she said. 'We went to New York and then made it back home for Christmas.'

'And you agreed to marry me.' His smile lit up her heart.

They ate breakfast and planned their day.

'When we go over to Mrs Lemon's cottage, I don't want Christmas Day to be all about us and our engagement,' said Daisy. 'I thought that when we arrive we'll join in the festive fun and then tell them.'

'Yes, I know they'll be happy for us.'

Daisy held up her ring hand and showed Jake how the diamonds caught the light. 'It's a gorgeous ring. Look how it sparkles!'

He smiled broadly at her. 'I recognise that mischievous twinkle in your eyes.'

'Huh! Be prepared for a lot of ring sparkle moments in your future, Jake,' she teased him.

Clearing the breakfast tray away to the kitchen, they both went back through to the lounge.

'Gift time,' Daisy announced, handing him the well–wrapped painting.

He started to smile in anticipation as he took the wrapping off.

'I was going to put it in a box so you wouldn't guess what it was, but...' she shrugged.

By now Jake's expression had turned to awe. 'It's my house and garden.' He blinked and peered at the artwork. 'Is that...me?'

'You happened to be in the frame that summer's day when I was taking photos, so I put you in it too.'

'I thought you didn't paint people,' he said, impressed that the figure really did look like him working in his garden.

'I'm expanding my botanical artwork repertoire, especially for you.'

He held the painting up and admired it. 'This will look great on the wall of my study.'

'I painted it with that in mind.'

He propped it up on a chest of drawers in the lounge and stepped back. 'I love your artwork.' He glanced at her. 'And you.'

Delighted that he liked the painting, they exchanged the other gifts they had for each other. Every present was appreciated, from the artist paints, easel and fashion items he'd bought for her, to the waistcoat, vintage tie, links and pin, and the satchel briefcase for him.

The morning flew in until it was time to head over to Mrs Lemon's cottage, both carrying lots of presents.

Everything sparkled under a bright wintry sky and the air was so crisp and clear that Daisy felt it invigorate her senses as they walked across to the cottage and Jake knocked on the door.

Mrs Lemon and Woolley welcomed them in, and the aroma of the dinner cooking wafted through from the kitchen.

'Merry Christmas!' Jake announced, and was duly smothered with welcoming hugs.

Woolley's eyes lit up as he grinned at Jake. 'I'm so glad you're home for Christmas.' He glanced at Daisy too. 'Both of you.'

'Come on through to the lounge,' Mrs Lemon beckoned them.

They were all well–dressed, and the smiling faces and cheery atmosphere pulled them in. The Christmas tree lights were on and the fire was lit, and a table was set up for six with fancy dinner plates, decorations and crackers to pull.

'Dinner is almost ready,' said Mrs Lemon. 'We thought we'd open a present each before the meal, and then open the rest after.'

Sharky smiled and hurried through to the kitchen. 'I'll just check the oven.'

Mrs Lemon whispered to Daisy. 'It's great having Sharky help. Woolley is helping too, but Sharky is a whiz in the kitchen.'

Sharky had brought cakes and pastries galore. One of his Christmas cakes sat on a side table along with his popular rich chocolate and buttercream cake, and other festive nibbles. Jake added boxes of luxury chocolates to the table, and Mrs Lemon had to scold Woolley for eating the chocolates before his dinner.

Mrs Lemon had made her cranberry sauce, onion gravy and a traditional sherry trifle, but Sharky insisted on cooking the roast dinner, including his special roast potatoes and parsnips.

Jake glanced at Daisy. In all the excitement none of them had noticed Daisy's ring yet. She gave him a reassuring smile that she was waiting on the right moment.

Woolley stood next to the gift wrapped box containing the hoover. 'What present would you like to open before dinner?' he said to Mrs Lemon. She'd been eyeing the box with intrigue ever since he'd arrived with it that morning and placed it down beside the Christmas tree.

'That large box there. I've no idea what you've bought me.' Mrs Lemon's tone assured him that she hadn't guessed what it was.

Woolley gestured for her to come over and open it.

Peeling back the wrapping, her face lit up with glee. 'My hoover! This is the one I've been wanting for ages.' She hugged the breath from him. 'This is wonderful. It's got all the attachments.'

Jake opened a present from Sharky — a large bottle of champagne and chocolate liqueurs. 'Thank you,' Jake told Sharky. 'This is ideal, especially for today.'

Sharky assumed it was to celebrate Christmas, but Jake exchanged a secret knowing look with Daisy.

Karen hoped Sharky would open a personal gift she'd had framed for him at the craft shop. Seeing her eye the parcel, he selected to open it and found a large photograph of the two of them in a heart–shaped frame.

'This is going up in my shop behind the counter,' Sharky announced with glee.

Karen laughed. 'I thought you'd put it up in your house.'

'Nope, I'm sharing this with the world,' Sharky insisted.

Mrs Lemon hoped that Daisy would like the three sets of knitting needles and a selection of yarn she'd bought for her from the craft shop. A row counter, yarn needles, a measuring tape, pom pom maker, other little accessories, and patterns were in a pretty knitting bag. The patterns included a tea cosy, woolly hat, egg cosies and wrist warmers. There was even a pattern to knit a cute softie snowman. All great practise for brushing up Daisy's range of knitting skills.

But before Daisy picked a present, Woolley opened a gift from Daisy.

'A gardening diary,' Woolley exclaimed, and began to look through the large, book–size diary that was filled with lots of handy information and photographs. 'I didn't know I could easily prune my hollyhocks.'

Everyone laughed, but Woolley became engrossed in the handy hints.

And they all admired Daisy's handmade bookmark and watercolour card, included with Woolley's gift, not knowing that she'd included them in some of the other presents too.

Karen lifted up one of the gifts from Daisy. From the size of it and structure she assumed it was a book. Her face lit up when she saw that it was a wedding planner journal. A bookmark and card were included.

'A wedding planner journal is just what I need,' said Karen. 'I've been planning lots of things and scribbling them down on scraps of paper. Ideas for my wedding dress, flowers...and now that I have a date for the wedding at the castle, this planner is perfect.' She saw that it had checklists, pockets for storing notes, and hints and tips on all things bridal. 'I'll be able to write down when I need my engagement ring cleaned at the jewellers.' Karen held her ring finger up to Daisy as she said this, once again flashing her diamond and ruby ring.

Mrs Lemon held up her ring too. 'Well, let me know when you're doing that, and I'll get mine done too.'

Daisy felt this was her moment. She held up her hand to show the diamond ring sparkling on her finger.

There was a moment's pause, and then a burst of squeals and joyous cheers.

'When did this happen?' said Mrs Lemon, admiring the ring.

'Jake proposed last night after the ball at the castle.' Daisy revealed the details, and let them see the pictures they'd taken in the garden with the lights twinkling.

There were hugs, handshakes and congratulations all round.

Woolley couldn't stop smiling at Jake. 'I'm delighted for you.'

'Thank you, Woolley,' said Jake.

'You'll make a wonderful couple,' Sharky told them.

Mrs Lemon and Karen admired Daisy's ring, and she let them try it on and make wishes.

Karen gasped. 'Your ring looks like a daisy made of diamonds.'

'It's perfect for you,' Mrs Lemon agreed.

The whole happy atmosphere of Christmas Day was lifted even further by the engagement announcement.

'I should've known that Jake was making up an excuse about needing my help with his work to get me to go to his house after the ball,' Daisy told Mrs Lemon and Karen. 'He fiddled with his forelock.'

The women gave a knowing nod.

Jake overheard and frowned. *Fiddled with his forelock?*

The women laughed and giggled, and didn't explain.

The timer pinged on the oven.

'Oops! I'd better check on the dinner.' Sharky dashed through to the kitchen.

Mrs Lemon, Sharky and Woolley served up the delicious roast dinner with all the trimmings.

Jake squeezed Daisy's hand and gazed at her. 'I love you,' he whispered amid the cheery chatter.

Daisy smiled. 'I love you too, Jake.'

Sitting around the table, everyone raised their glasses in a festive toast.

'Merry Christmas!' they cheered.

End

About the Author:

De-ann Black is a bestselling author, scriptwriter and former newspaper journalist. She has over 100 books published. Romance, thrillers, espionage novels, action adventure. And children's books (non-fiction rocket science books and children's fiction). She became an Amazon All-Star author in 2014 and 2015.

She previously worked as a full-time newspaper journalist for several years. She had her own weekly columns in the press. This included being a motoring correspondent where she got to test drive cars every week for the press for three years.

Before being asked to work for the press, De-ann worked in magazine editorial writing everything from fashion features to social news. She was the marketing editor of a glossy magazine.

She is also a professional artist and illustrator. Embroidery design, fabric design, dressmaking, sewing, knitting and fashion are part of her work.

Additionally, De-ann has always been interested in fitness, and was a fitness and bodybuilding champion, 100 metre runner and mountaineer. As a former N.A.B.B.A. Miss Scotland, she had a weekly fitness show on the radio that ran for over three years.

De-ann trained in Shukokai karate, boxing, kickboxing, Dayan Qigong and Jiu Jitsu. She is currently based in Scotland.

Her 16 colouring books are available in paperback, including her latest Summer Nature Colouring Book and Flower Nature Colouring Book.

Her latest embroidery pattern books include: Floral Garden Embroidery Patterns, Christmas & Winter Embroidery Patterns, Floral Spring Embroidery Patterns and Sea Theme Embroidery Patterns.

Website: Find out more at: www.de-annblack.com

Fabric, Wallpaper & Home Decor Collections:
De-ann's fabric designs and wallpaper collections, and home decor items, including her popular Scottish Garden Thistles patterns, are available from Spoonflower.
www.de-annblack.com/spoonflower

Also by De-ann Black (Romance, Action/Thrillers & Children's books). See her Amazon Author page or website for further details about her books, screenplays, illustrations, art, fabric designs and embroidery patterns.

Amazon Author page:
www.De-annBlack.com/Amazon

Romance books:

The Cure for Love Romance series:
1. The Cure for Love
2. The Cure for Love at Christmas

Scottish Highlands & Island Romance series:
1. Scottish Island Knitting Bee
2. Scottish Island Fairytale Castle
3. Vintage Dress Shop on the Island
4. Fairytale Christmas on the Island

Scottish Loch Romance series:
1. Sewing & Mending Cottage
2. Scottish Loch Summer Romance

Quilting Bee & Tea Shop series:
1. The Quilting Bee
2. The Tea Shop by the Sea
3. Embroidery Cottage
4. Knitting Shop by the Sea

Sewing, Crafts & Quilting series:
1. The Sewing Bee
2. The Sewing Shop
3. Knitting Cottage (Scottish Highland romance)
4. Scottish Highlands Christmas Wedding
(Embroidery, Knitting, Dressmaking & Textile Art)

Cottages, Cakes & Crafts series:
1. The Flower Hunter's Cottage
2. The Sewing Bee by the Sea
3. The Beemaster's Cottage
4. The Chocolatier's Cottage
5. The Bookshop by the Seaside
6. The Dressmaker's Cottage

Scottish Chateau, Colouring & Crafts series:
1. Christmas Cake Chateau
2. Colouring Book Cottage

Snow Bells Haven series:
1. Snow Bells Christmas
2. Snow Bells Wedding

Summer Sewing Bee

Sewing, Knitting & Baking series:
1. The Tea Shop
2. The Sewing Bee & Afternoon Tea
3. The Christmas Knitting Bee
4. Champagne Chic Lemonade Money
5. The Vintage Sewing & Knitting Bee

The Tea Shop & Tearoom series:
1. The Christmas Tea Shop & Bakery
2. The Christmas Chocolatier
3. The Chocolate Cake Shop in New York at Christmas
4. The Bakery by the Seaside
5. Shed in the City

Tea Dress Shop series:
1. The Tea Dress Shop At Christmas
2. The Fairytale Tea Dress Shop In Edinburgh
3. The Vintage Tea Dress Shop In Summer

Christmas Romance series:
1. Christmas Romance in Paris
2. Christmas Romance in Scotland

Oops! I'm the Paparazzi series:
1. Oops! I'm the Paparazzi
2. Oops! I'm Up To Mischief
3. Oops! I'm the Paparazzi, Again

The Bitch-Proof Suit series:
1. The Bitch-Proof Suit
2. The Bitch-Proof Romance
3. The Bitch-Proof Bride
4. The Bitch-Proof Wedding

Heather Park: Regency Romance
Dublin Girl
Why Are All The Good Guys Total Monsters?
I'm Holding Out For A Vampire Boyfriend

Action/Thriller books:

Knight in Miami
Agency Agenda
Love Him Forever
Someone Worse
Electric Shadows
The Strife Of Riley
Shadows Of Murder
Cast a Dark Shadow

Children's books:

Faeriefied
Secondhand Spooks
Poison-Wynd
Wormhole Wynd
Science Fashion
School For Aliens

Colouring books:

Summer Nature
Flower Nature
Summer Garden
Spring Garden
Autumn Garden
Sea Dream
Festive Christmas
Christmas Garden
Christmas Theme
Flower Bee
Wild Garden
Faerie Garden Spring
Flower Hunter
Stargazer Space
Bee Garden
Scottish Garden
Seasons

Embroidery Design books:

Sea Theme Embroidery Patterns
Floral Garden Embroidery Patterns
Christmas & Winter Embroidery Patterns
Floral Spring Embroidery Patterns
Floral Nature Embroidery Designs
Scottish Garden Embroidery Designs

Printed in Great Britain
by Amazon